Prai... v

Mandy Baggot

"Once again, Mandy Baggot has created a cast of characters that you can not only imagine but feel as though you know personally. Her writing style is here to withstand the test of time."
-Lindsay Gentles, Turning The Pages ~ Taking Charge

"One thing that we can always count on from Mandy Baggot and that is to provide us with a mouth wateringly handsome man, but she goes one step further in this book and provides us with a whole team of them! This is definitely one to look out for and Mandy Baggot is becoming an author to watch out for. A down to earth day to day storyline with dreamy romance and testosterone dripping from every page!"
-Rea Sinfield, Rea's Book Review ~ Taking Charge

"Robyn Matthers might be the most courageous and confident romantic heroine I have ever come across. For women readers who prefer their female heroines with a bit of get up and go, then this book is for you!"
-Rose McClelland, Judging Covers ~ Taking Charge

"I've just read your book and thought it was excellent! It had a real 'feel good' factor about it."
-L. Lev ~ Excess All Areas

"I was entertained by the book from beginning to end and when I finished reading it, I felt the same satisfied feeling I have after watching a good film."
—M. Leese ~ Breaking the Ice

"The book takes a thorough look at relationships, love, commitment and honesty and all the complicated baggage that comes with the territory. It is chick-lit to its fingertips!"
-Cyprus Well ~ Knowing Me Knowing You

Taking Charge

To katrina cheepie
Best wishes!
Happy 50th Birthday!

MANDY BAGGOT

Sapphire Star Publishing
www.sapphirestarpublishing.com
First Sapphire Star Publishing ebook edition, May 2012
First Sapphire Star Publishing trade paperback edition, May 2012

ISBN-13: 978-1-938404-02-3

Cover Design by Jane Dixon-Smith
www.jd-smith-design.co.uk

www.sapphirestarpublishing.com/mandybaggot

About the Author

Mandy lives in leafy Wiltshire and has Sting as a neighbor. She lives with her husband, two daughters and two cats (Kravitz and Springsteen). When she isn't writing she loves to sing and do Lady Gaga impressions (check out YouTube). She will soon be working on her sixth novel—if she can stay off Twitter for long enough.

Dedication

To Dad, for introducing me to Portage, Michigan and for passing me your firm values, your worldly wisdom and not forgetting the bad ass attitude!

Acknowledgements

First of all, I have to say a big thank you to all my family and friends in Portage, Michigan. Dad, Mum, Cindy, Iain, Taylor, Tessa, Bob, Mary, Beth, Gerry, and Bradley. You all made us feel so welcome when we stayed for twenty-one nights instead of ten! Thank you Icelandic volcano, too! This family reunion/holiday turned into research, and I want to thank you for providing help and inspiration for the novel without even realising it!

Thank you to the Kalamazoo Wings who are the inspiration behind the Portage Panthers in this book. Go Slappy! Go Wings!

Thank you to Special Guest, who is a real band. Mr. Big and I saw them at Logan's Roadhouse in Portage. You rock guys and I hope to see you again someday!

Thank you to the amazing country music artist Sean Patrick McGraw who has spent time Tweeting with me and provided me with a backing track for Git Yer Cowboy On so Hard Drive can perform this at a launch celebration!

Thank you to my Loveahappyending.com associate readers and authors, especially Team Baggot. You are all amazing, and I really appreciate all your hard work on my behalf xx.

Thank you to the rest of my friends and family for their support, patience, emails, love, and childcare!

But thank you most of all to the team at Sapphire Star Publishing who have taken me on and given me this incredible opportunity. They fell in love with Robyn's story from the beginning, and I hope all my readers will too!

Playlist

Set the mood for Taking Charge with this suggested playlist!

Keep Your Hands To Yourself – The Georgia Satellites
Old Time Rock 'n Roll – Bob Seger
Johnny B Goode – Chuck Berry
Jump – Van Halen
Tush – ZZ Top
Rockin' In The Free World – Neil Young
Red House – Jimi Hendrix
Summer Of '69 – Bryan Adams
All Summer Long – Kid Rock
Sweet Home Alabama – Lynyrd Skynrd
Light The Fuse Up – Raintown
Need You Now – Lady Antebellum
Guitar Man – Bread
Coward Of The County – Kenny Rogers
Too Rock For Country Too Country For Rock 'n Roll – Lonnie Mack
I'm Gonna Love You Through It – Martina McBride
Long Hot Summer – Keith Urban
Girly Girl – Courtenay Conway
Just A Kiss – Lady Antebellum
Still Under The Weather – Shania Twain
Play Something Country – Brooks and Dunn
Honky Tonk Stomp – Brooks and Dunn
Git Yer Cowboy On – Sean Patrick McGraw
Good One – Blackberry Smoke
A Quarter To Three – Shy Blakeman
Wonderful Tonight – Eric Clapton
One Night – Martina McBride
Beer Drinkin' Girl – Sean Patrick McGraw

Explanatory Terms

Roadhouse - local inn or restaurant the "roadhouse" or "road house" commonly serves meals, especially in the evenings, has a bar serving beer or hard liquor, and features music and dancing for entertainment.

Hooking - in ice hockey the act of impeding or obstructing an opponent's progress by placing the shaft or blade of the stick on the midsection of the opposing player and pulling him or her back. Hooking is illegal and normally results in a minor penalty being assessed to the offending player.

Roughing - an offense and penalty in ice hockey when two players are in a minor altercation. The incident would have to be minor for either player to be categorized as such an offense such as:

A player striking another opponent

A goalie using their equipment to punch an opponent

NHL - National Hockey League (ice hockey)

Yankees - New York Yankees (baseball team)

Red Wings - Detroit Red Wings are an ice hockey team in the NHL

Power play - in ice hockey a team is said to be on a "power play" when at least one opposing player is serving a penalty, and the team has a numerical advantage on the ice.

Enforcer - is an unofficial role in ice hockey. The term is sometimes used synonymously with "fighter," "tough guy," or "goon."

Chapter One

Robyn could feel the sweat trickling down her back. It was pooling at the waistband of her jeans, and she also had underarm issues that no amount of Mitchum roll-on was going to cure. She heaved her backpack further up her shoulder and hurried on. There wasn't time to stop and worry about how rank she felt. The backpack was digging into her shoulder bone and, if she didn't keep up the pace, she would miss her connecting flight to Kalamazoo, Michigan and be stranded in Chicago for the night.

She'd already spent eight hours on a plane from London and hadn't slept a wink. The guy on her left, who was in a business suit, but obviously not wealthy enough for a seat in business class, had spent the whole flight on his laptop, loudly tapping at the keys and saying "hmm" every twentieth tap — she'd counted. The guy on her right, balding, yet bearded, had the flu, probably swine or avian or maybe a lethal mixture of the two. He'd gone through a box of tissues in the time it took to cross the Atlantic, and now she could feel the beginnings of a sore throat. Illness was inevitable when you were trapped in the equivalent of a tin can with so many people.

She checked her watch again and, seeing time was slipping away, she quickened her step. The small jet that would take her back would begin boarding in little more than five minutes.

As she broke into a jog and maneuvered past other passengers, the strap on her bag gave way, and the backpack fell to the floor, almost pulling her over with it.

"Shit!" Robyn cursed as some of her things fell onto the airport floor.

That was all she needed.

"Stupid, pathetic bag!" she screamed out loud, giving it a kick and letting out an exasperated hiss.

"Hey, need some help?" a male voice asked.

Robyn looked up at the man who had appeared at her side, ready to tell him where to get off. She opened her mouth and then paused, taking in the dark hair, inky eyes and broad shoulders.

"I could tie a knot in it," he suggested, picking up her backpack and inspecting the damage.

"No thanks. I haven't got far to go. It'll be fine," Robyn answered, rescuing her baseball cap and a Haynes motor manual.

"This is a heavy carry-on. Where you headed?" the man asked, helping put her things back into the bag.

"Terminal three," Robyn said, observing him again.

He was as tall as he was broad and she gauged he was probably in his early twenties. She couldn't remember seeing anyone looking so good for quite some time. It was also unusual that she'd noticed.

"I'm terminal three bound too. Let me carry it for you," he offered, effortlessly throwing the sack over his shoulder.

"No, that's okay, I can do it. I mean, it isn't that far now," Robyn started, taking hold of the corner of her bag.

"Hey, I promise I'm not a stalker or an axe murderer, and I don't have my mother embalmed in the basement," the man told her with a smile.

"But you're at an airport, heading out of town, and that's exactly what an obsessed son with a mother in the basement would do, and he would definitely make a joke about it. Don't you watch The Mentalist?" Robyn asked.

She stared at him, as if hoping to find the truth in his eyes. They were nice eyes, she decided, but whether they were honest eyes she wasn't sure. You needed to share at least ten minutes with someone before you knew that.

The man let out a laugh and nodded.

"Listen, I'm headed to Portage. Apparently, it's something close to Hicksville. Let me help you with your bag and I promise you'll never see me again."

"I wouldn't count on it. I'm heading there too. And if I was you, I wouldn't let the locals hear you call it Hicksville. They sacrifice visitors they take a dislike to," Robyn said, applying a poker face.

"You're kidding right?"

"Do I look like I'm kidding?" Robyn asked him.

"Shit."

"You can carry the bag, but any more cheap shots about my town and I'll ask the pilot to drop you off in the lake. The water can be pretty unpredictable this time of year," she told him as she started to walk in the direction of the other terminal.

"Sure, no problem. I'm Cole, by the way. Cole Ryan," he said, hurrying after her.

"Robyn Matthers."

"So, I guess you're not on vacation," Cole spoke, catching up to her.

"Nope. I'm heading home," Robyn informed him.

"Been away long?"

"Just about nine years," Robyn said with a heavy sigh.

It always surprised her when she said those words. It felt like a lifetime and, in a lot of respects, it was. She was nine years

3

older on the outside, an adult with a life in a different country, but inside nothing had changed.

"So why now?" Cole asked her.

"My dad's sick."

"Oh, I'm sorry."

"Yeah, I think I am too. Not quite sure yet. I might want to give him a hug; I might want to rip his drip out," Robyn said with half a smile.

Her relationship with her father had never been straightforward. She loved him, but she found it quite hard to like him. He made most people feel that way with his strong opinions and megaphone-styled voice.

Cole looked at her, seeming uncertain whether she was serious. Robyn laughed out loud at his bewildered look.

"We have a complicated relationship. Gum?" she offered, taking the packet from the pocket of her jeans.

"No thanks," Cole replied.

"So, you know why *I'm* here...why are *you* going to Hicksville?" Robyn asked in a whisper.

"I got a job there," Cole informed.

"Really? So you must be able to repair boats."

"No."

"Cars?"

"No."

"You're not a cop, are you?"

"No."

"Then you must be a realtor or a bartender, because that's all that's left," Robyn answered with a confident nod.

"Not exactly," Cole answered.

"Can you work a bar?"

"Sure."

"Then I might need your mobile number."

"What?" Cole asked, confused.

"Sorry, I mean cell phone number. Nine years in England and all my terminology is up the shoot," Robyn told him.

"I thought you had kind of a weird accent thing going on," Cole admitted.

"Yeah, this is what half English half American sounds like. I need to practice getting my pronunciation of 'water' sounding right or no one is going to understand a word I say," Robyn said.

"So, why would you need a bartender?"

"My dad owns a roadhouse, and things aren't going so well. Pam...she's my auntie...says there's three regulars and a goat in there most nights at the moment. I can't see three people drinking enough to pay the bills, and I don't know enough about the drinking habits of goats to comment on him...or her. I guess it could be a her." Robyn shrugged.

"So, what are you gonna do?" Cole inquired.

"I'm going to take charge, of course. Just need to get a team together I can trust and get rid of the deadwood. Apparently she goes by the name of Nancy, and has a tattoo on her navel...hi there, here's my ID and my ticket," Robyn said as they approached the American Airlines desk.

"Thank you, Ma'am...here's your boarding pass, you're all set."

"Thanks."

Robyn turned her attention back to Cole. "Here, let me take that. I'll save you a seat," she said, as she hauled her backpack from Cole's shoulder and headed off toward the boarding gate.

"It's over three hours by car, you know. Three long hours. A thirty-minute plane hop like this is so much more civilized, don't you think?" Robyn said, sipping from her can of Coke.

She was so close to home now, it was both unnerving and exciting. Half of her couldn't wait to see Portage and all the places she had missed. The other half of her was concerned being there again would bring back memories of the past, and not all of them were good.

"I don't know. I like seeing new places. You know, little towns along the way you would never normally see," Cole replied.

"Three hours on I-94 and you'd change your mind. And there aren't any little towns on that route, just gas stations and branches of Bob Evans' diners," Robyn answered.

"You've done it before?"

"Yeah, when we left," Robyn replied as her mind traveled back.

Her dad had driven her and her mother to Chicago O'Hare airport. Her parents had yelled at each other most of the way, and the rest of the time Country Drive FM was on at full volume.

"He shouted a lot and sang Kenny Rogers," Robyn said, thinking out loud.

"He sounds like quite a character," Cole answered.

"Sorry, I'm rabbiting on, aren't I? You don't want to hear all about my messed up family."

"Rabbiting?" Cole queried.

"Going on, talking too much, hind leg, donkey," Robyn replied.

"Maybe you're nervous," Cole suggested to her.

"Nervous? Me! What do I have to be nervous about?" Robyn exclaimed, taken aback by his suggestion.

Scared to death was probably closer to the truth, but she didn't want a stranger getting perceptive. Even a good-looking stranger.

"Seeing your dad again? Taking control of the roadhouse?" Cole prodded.

"No, piece of cake! Now the ice hockey team, that might be more of a challenge," Robyn answered, finishing her drink.

"Hockey?"

"Yeah, my dad manages the local team, the Portage Panthers. My dad's friend, Grant, has been looking after things while Dad's been ill and results have taken a real nosedive. I haven't been able to do that much checking up in England, but Pam taped a couple of games and sent them to me. They were dire," Robyn informed.

Dire was actually verging on the optimistic side. It was so awful, she'd sat in her flat at home, viewing the game through her hands. The team seemed to have forgotten how to play. They lost the puck constantly, couldn't seem to stand up to the slightest challenge, and as for actually netting anything—well it seemed beyond them.

"So what are you gonna do?" Cole inquired.

"I'm going to take charge, obviously. Aren't you getting the whole theme of my visit yet?" Robyn asked.

"I should have guessed. But do you know anything about managing an ice hockey team?" Cole asked.

"About managing? No, absolutely nothing. Apart from what my dad does. That's basically scream a lot and bang his fists against the Perspex. I play though...well I used to play," Robyn said.

"Really?"

"You didn't try very hard to keep the patronizingly surprised tone out of your voice. I think you need some practice with that," Robyn said.

"Whoa! Are you trying to say I'm sexist?" Cole asked.

"Aren't you?" Robyn asked, raising an eyebrow at him.

"No," Cole insisted.

"Not convincing me," Robyn said.

She looked out of the window and saw Lake Michigan slip out of view and Kalamazoo County come into sight. Familiarity tugged at her. She was nearly home.

"So where are you staying?" Cole asked.

"With Pam and my Uncle Bob. Nancy, with the decorated navel, lives with Dad now, apparently. She's probably turned the house into a piercing parlor or a dope den or something," Robyn answered.

"You don't have a very high opinion of her," Cole stated.

"I've never met her, but in the last nine years, my dad's had a succession of unsuitable women. I can't imagine someone called Nancy with tattoos and piercings is going to be any different," Robyn said.

"You need a ride anywhere? I'm picking up a car," Cole told her.

"No thanks, I'm good. Anyway, here's you knowing all about me and my character of a father…I still want to speak to your mother. I need reassurance that she isn't decomposing in a cellar," Robyn reminded him.

"She was very much alive when she was bear-hugging me at the airport and ordering me to vacuum at least twice a week," Cole assured her.

"Twice a week, huh? She has high expectations."

"And what did your mom say to you before you left?" Cole wanted to know.

Her mom. It sounded strange someone referring to her mother. She hadn't thought about her for years, hadn't seen her for longer. She was like someone who had been there in name only. Then, when Robyn hit eighteen, she considered her role had come to an end and she terminated the part like an employment contract.

"We're not in contact. She married husband number three and they moved. Wales, I think, but who knows? She could be in Vegas or somewhere. That would be right up her alley."

"Oh man, sorry, I just assumed…" Cole began to apologize.

"It's fine. I don't need anyone to tell me how many times to hoover," Robyn replied with a smile.

He smiled back at her.

"You're cute. Are you married?" Robyn asked bluntly, looking at Cole and noticing again the dark eyes and wide mouth.

"Married? No!" Cole said, laughing.

"What's so funny?" Robyn wanted to know.

"Well, because I'm only twenty-five and...well, I've never really thought about it," Cole answered.

"Everyone thinks about it."

"Girls maybe, not guys."

"My friend, Sarah, she talked about it all the time in high school. She even had a folder with magazine cuttings of potential dresses and some silver tuxedo gross out thing she wanted her groom dressed in. Ugh!"

"So that must mean *you* think about it."

"Yeah, I think about it. I think how glad I am I'm never going to go down that road. What a ridiculous situation to be in...tying yourself to someone else forever. Besides, it never works." Robyn scoffed.

Cole smiled at her.

"Girlfriend, then? I mean, you can't look like you do and not have a girlfriend," Robyn said, still absorbing the firm jaw and well-built shoulders.

"No. Not at the moment."

"Ah, so you've just broken up with someone."

"No," Cole denied.

Robyn raised her eyebrow at him unconvinced. She could read him already, and the eyes were honest, she was sure of that now.

"It was a few months ago," Cole admitted.

"Was it serious?" Robyn asked.

There was something in his tone that made her curious. There was definitely more to his story.

"No, not really."

"Did you live together?" Robyn probed.

"No. Look...I'm not really comfortable talking about it," Cole said.

He looked flustered and the easy manner and smile had almost evaporated. The girlfriend had hurt him bad.

"Listen, who would you rather? Me or Oprah?"

9

A hint of a smile played on his lips.

"Anyways, I've been good enough to tell you half my life story, why can't you tell me about your girlfriend? I mean, you carried my bag about a mile. In my town, that makes us almost related."

"It just wasn't the best break up," Cole admitted as the plane came in to land.

"Who dumped who?" Robyn continued, turning to him almost enthusiastically.

"It wasn't that clear cut."

"Well, what *was* it like?"

"She was seeing someone else," Cole admitted. A sad expression and a heaviness to his words told her everything.

"That's low. Was it someone you knew? Work colleague? I bet it was a work colleague, wasn't it? Their eyes met over the boardroom table and they just couldn't help themselves."

"My brother," Cole answered, his eyes meeting hers and locking there.

Not even Robyn could find the words to respond straight away to that. She concentrated on looking out the window and watched as the ground came closer and the wheels of the jet touched down.

She talked too much, that she knew, particularly when she was scared to death. It was easy to focus on something else, in this case *someone* else. Taking the lead in conversation meant she could boss the flow, leaving little space for anyone to direct the questioning at her. She'd give a little but never everything. If she was honest, she wouldn't know where to start with *everything*.

"You know, I don't know your brother, but I can't imagine he's got more going for him than you. I mean, you're cute and you're funny and you carried a damsel's bag. It doesn't get any better than that in my opinion," Robyn finally spoke up as the plane taxied to a gate.

"Thanks," Cole replied, his smile returning.

"Did you fight?" Robyn inquired suddenly.

"What?"

"You and your brother. Did you have a scrap? You know, fisticuffs, slugging it out? Bit of roughing?" Robyn asked, punching her arms forward to demonstrate. She made the noises of someone sparring in a boxing ring and got a few concerned looks from other passengers.

"Not really."

"Oh my God. You *so* did. Who won? You did, didn't you! He begged for mercy and he cried! Oh God, he so cried, didn't he?" Robyn rambled on with a little too much excitement.

"They're going to open the doors," Cole said as a clear distraction as people stood up to remove their bags from the overhead bins.

"Don't feel guilty about it. Sometimes people need a bit of rough justice, even family. What am I talking about? *Especially* family! They're the worst. Think they can treat you like crap whenever they feel like it, walk all over you, and then ask for help when they need it. I'm not a fan of that way of thinking myself. Tell it like it is and say what you think, I say. There's no time to fanny about around people," Robyn said with a nod.

"Fanny about?"

"Shit, I do need to find the American in me, don't I? I need to remember I want fries with my steak, not chips. Chips over here are crisps in the UK and a swede, well a swede is a rutabaga!" Robyn spoke as she almost buckled under the weight of her bag.

"Are you sure you don't need a ride?" Cole offered, steadying her backpack for her.

"No, I'm good. Pam should be waiting for me," she said.

"Well, I guess I'll see you around, Robyn Matthers," Cole said as they prepared to leave the plane.

"Sure. Hey, Eddie's Roadhouse, it's on Shaver Road if you fancy beer...or if you want to ditch your job and work a bar," Robyn told him.

"I might just drop by," Cole replied.

"Good. Then you can tell me the full story about you and your brother," Robyn answered.

"See you," Cole said and he headed up the tunnel toward the exit.

She was nice. Really nice — but kind of crazy. She'd hardly stopped to take a breath between sentences on the plane, but he'd enjoyed it. It had made him forget about his own issues — until she'd made him talk about them. He couldn't believe he had told her about it. And he'd sounded so hung up on it still. He wasn't. He was over it. It had been a couple of months now; he was moving on. Not just because he was leaving Chicago — he was moving on inside. The proof of that was a wrecked car, bleach stains on one of his t-shirts, and a small scar on the knuckles of his right hand.

She watched him go. The easy, yet confident way he moved, how his jeans hung on his hips and the way his t-shirt enhanced the shape of his back. She bit her lip, but her mouth had other ideas.

"Hey! Cole! Wait!" she called.

Cole stopped walking and turned around to face her.

She jogged awkwardly toward him and, as she reached him, she dropped her broken backpack to the ground.

She didn't think, she just acted. She pulled him by the arms, closed her eyes tight, and kissed him full on the lips. She drew his dark head to hers with her hand and urged his mouth to part.

She felt his momentary hesitation and surprise, but then he relaxed and kissed her back, tentatively at first and then with more purpose. It felt as good as she knew it would.

Then, she ended it and stepped back, quickly heaving her bag off the floor.

"I just wanted to thank you...you know...for carrying my bag," she said, smiling.

"Well, I'm liking the Michigan thank you," Cole answered with a laugh.

She smiled, adjusting the band in her hair and standing on the outside edge of her tennis shoes.

"So, I guess I'll see you around?" Cole asked, studying her expression.

"Sure, see you around," Robyn replied, nodding.

He picked up his duffle bag and, with one last smile at her, he walked away.

She watched him all the way up the tunnel before the smile fell from her face. The distraction was gone, and it was time to come to terms with being home.

Chapter Two

The wind almost knocked her sideways as she came out of the airport. It was mid-October and today the sky was clear, but the Michigan wind was biting. Autumn in the county of Kalamazoo meant weather for all seasons. Tomorrow could be a bikini day, the next you might need your snow clothes. It was predictable in its unpredictability.

"Robyn? Robyn, is that you? Oh, honey, you're all grown up! Look at her, Bob! She's all grown up! Look at your hair, it's so different!"

"It's not different, it's exactly the same. I'm the same, completely the same, nothing changed at all," Robyn said, pulling a section of hair and observing it closely.

"Come here, honey, let Bob take your bags. Take her bags, Bob. Is this all the luggage you have?" Pam questioned as she enveloped Robyn in a hug and began peeling her backpack and case from her.

Robyn was pleased to see her aunt. She was just as she remembered her. She was rounded and buxom, with the same kind eyes and wide smile. They spoke on the phone about once a month, but time had passed, and it was good to know that Auntie Pam still looked every inch the mother figure she always had been. It was familiar and comforting, and Robyn hadn't realized until now how much she had missed that familiarity and comfort.

"I traveled light. Thought we could always go shopping for new stuff. Aren't you always telling me how many sales they have on?" Robyn said, smiling at her.

"Hi Robyn," Bob greeted.

Uncle Bob looked the same too. Perhaps slightly more gray and a little more weathered, but there were the same doe eyes and the hunched shoulders from years of huddling over a fishing pole. Pam wore the pants in their relationship, but Bob wouldn't have it any other way. He was a man who lived for ice hockey and fishing and, as long as he had those simple pleasures, he was more than content with his lot.

"Shopping, as you know, is one of my favorite words! Oh, honey, it's so good to see you. Bob, put Robyn's luggage in the trunk. Robyn, let me introduce you! This is Sierra and Sienna. Girls, this is your cousin, Robyn," Pam spoke proudly.

Robyn looked through the open window of the car at two identical girls, both with dark brown hair, tied in braids. Both had sullen looks on their faces and glared at her with attitude. They looked a million miles away from the angelic cousins Pam had described in their phone conversations. Robyn had imagined them with ringlets, white gloves, and fans. These two looked like they'd been styled by the Twilight team.

"Say hello, girls," Pam ordered.

"Hello girls," they replied together.

Then they cackled to themselves, looking at Robyn out of the corners of their beady eyes.

"Hello. How old are they now?' Robyn questioned as the twins stuck their tongues out at her.

"Almost nine. I was pregnant when you left, remember? Size of a large family home! Doesn't time fly by? Bob, are you okay, honey? Do you need some help?" Pam offered, turning her attention to her husband who was putting Robyn's backpack in the trunk.

"I'm just fine," Bob answered.

"So, shall we go and see your dad?" Pam suggested, clapping her hands together.

"Oh, well, it's probably too late for visiting right now right?" Robyn began.

The question had fazed her. Sure, she knew seeing her dad was the whole purpose of her trip, but presented with the immediate possibility of being face-to-face with him in minutes, frankly, it freaked her out.

It was too soon. She knew she'd had the plane journey to prepare herself, but she still wasn't ready. She didn't know what he looked like now. He was ill; he was going to look different—maybe thin or old or frail. She couldn't imagine her dad looking frail. It just wasn't in his nature. But then, maybe that had changed too. Maybe he was less John Goodman and more Tony Shalhoub in Monk now. No, that didn't bear thinking about.

"The nurses said we could go any time."

"Oh, well, I guess…" Robyn began.

She knew when Pam had an idea about something it was pretty hard to oppose it. Though usually it involved shopping malls and large lunches, not hospitals.

"Pam, Robyn's flown nine hours to get here, don't you think she might want to wash up and have something to eat?" Bob interjected.

"Oh, honey, I'm sorry, of course you must be starving. Let's go eat," Pam said, opening the car door and leaping in.

"Thanks, Uncle Bob," Robyn said quietly as he prepared to get back into the driver's seat.

"Eddie is sick, Robyn, but he isn't going anywhere today," Bob assured her.

"Bob, come on! Old Country Buffet, I think. Robyn can have a bit of everything there," Pam called, rolling down the window.

"Is it still seven dollars all you can eat?" Robyn asked her uncle.

"Yepper," he answered with a smile.

"Have you tried the mashed potatoes? They still do great mashed potatoes here don't they, Bob? And you must try the fried chicken, the fried chicken's still good isn't it, Bob?" Pam gabbled as they ate.

"She still gets indigestion because she talks too much while she's eating," Bob informed Robyn quietly.

Robyn laughed into her napkin, and Sierra and Sienna looked up at her with their eerie dark eyes, like the raisins on the Gingerbread Boy's face. They had streaks of spaghetti sauce around their mouths that could have doubled for blood.

"The girls must keep you on your toes," Robyn whispered back to her uncle.

"You know what? We wanted children for so long, now I'd actually pay someone to take them away," Bob answered, pasting a smile on his face when his daughters looked in his direction.

"You don't mean that," Robyn replied.

"You've spent twenty minutes in a car with them, give it a few days and you'll be begging for ear plugs," Bob told her.

"What are you two talking about? I can't hear you. Girls, use your knives and forks properly," Pam ordered her children.

"Is she here because Uncle Eddie's going to die?" Sienna questioned, looking straight at Robyn with an emotionless face.

"Sienna! Why would you say something like that? That's very rude and disrespectful," Pam exclaimed in horror.

"Well? Is he?" Sierra asked defiantly.

"We're all going to die one day. Some of us get longer than others. At nine you have quite a good chance of surviving longer than me but, you know, you never can account for those freak accidents. Car pileup, snake bite, someone sneaking into your room at night and strangling you with your braids," Robyn told them a serious expression on her face.

"Mommy! She's being rude!" Sienna shouted in a whimpering voice.

"Girls, you need to mind your manners. Now if you've finished making a mess with that food, I suggest you go visit the bathroom," Bob said.

"But we haven't had dessert yet," Sienna moaned, rolling her eyes.

"Bathroom. Now," Bob ordered.

Both girls let out a disgruntled sigh, but got off their seats and headed toward the restrooms.

"Is it really serious? I mean, you can tell me the truth. I'm twenty-five now, not the sixteen-year-old who left all those years ago. I can handle it," Robyn told Pam and Bob, looking at them both.

"It's serious," Bob informed her bluntly.

"But the surgeon says once he's had the operation, he'll feel like a new man. Well, if he loses a bit of weight and lowers his blood pressure," Pam chipped in, an optimistic expression on her face.

"When's the bypass scheduled?" Robyn asked.

"We don't know yet," Bob told her.

"Why not? You said it was serious. If it's serious, he needs the operation as soon as possible, doesn't he? Is this a money thing? Because if it's a money thing, I can get money."

"It isn't the money, he has insurance. He's just not in a very good state, Robyn. His blood pressure's through the roof, he's got other patients and their visitors bringing him junk food, and he doesn't do as he's told. They're worried he might not survive the operation," Bob said. The doe eyes showed real concern and Robyn knew then things were serious.

"Take me there," Robyn said, standing up and rocking on the outside edge of her tennis shoes.

"Let's not panic. I mean, I saw him yesterday and he'd eaten his greens and his blood pressure was okay..." Pam started.

"I want to go there, now. He won't have eaten the greens. Did you check under his sheets?"

"Well no, but..."

"I haven't flown all this way to fanny about around him...I mean tiptoe...whatever. He needs the truth and I'm going to give it to him. Take me there. I'm ready," Robyn ordered again.

"He knows what he should be doing, he just doesn't do it," Pam admitted with a sigh.

"Yes, well, he will. Or I'm going to ask the surgeon to wire his jaw shut before he starts with his heart," Robyn said with determination in her tone.

"We've tried shock tactics, Robyn. Nothing seems to sink in," Bob said.

"Are you going to take me there or am I getting a cab?"

Chapter Three

"Now, honey, don't be put off by the monitors and things in his room. It's just to assess his condition and keep a track of everything," Pam explained, trying to keep up with Robyn as she strode through the front doors of the hospital.

Robyn was trying not to breathe. She hated the smell of hospitals almost as much as she hated the smell of the inside of airplanes. Both seemed to have a combination of cleaning solution and body odors. It wasn't a good mix.

"Does he know I'm coming?" Robyn asked, striding on purposefully.

"Well, I didn't know whether to say anything or not. I mean, it could have gone either way. You haven't spoken for a while and…" Pam began, getting out of breath as she chased Robyn.

"Does he know I'm coming or not?" Robyn asked.

"No," Pam admitted, flushing.

"Which way is it? What floor is he on?" Robyn questioned as she looked for any signs indicating cardiology.

"I'll show you, just slow down a little, honey. Your aunt's not as young as she used to be," Pam said, taking a deep breath, her cheeks reddening more every second.

"Does she come and see him much?" Robyn asked as she finally relented and let Pam take the lead.

"Nancy?"

"Yeah, Nancy."

She couldn't help but grit her teeth.

"Most days, I think. Eddie talks about her a lot. I think she spends most of her time at the roadhouse, though," Pam told her.

"That's my next port of call, then the ice hockey team," Robyn stated, ticking things off a mental list.

She wouldn't feel in control unless she had been everywhere she needed to go, scared or otherwise.

"Oh, I don't think you should do any of that tonight, honey. I mean, you must be exhausted," Pam said quickly.

"It needs to be done. Someone needs to oversee things. Brad still plays for the team, right?" Robyn asked, looking at Pam.

"Yes."

Robyn nodded.

Brad Willis was her ex-boyfriend. The last time she had seen him, he had already been six feet tall with blond shoulder-length hair. He was good-looking, he'd liked sports back then, and he had been her first boyfriend. Their first kiss had been at the drive-in in front of Planet of the Apes, and they had dated in a rather innocent high school way for almost a year. After that, Robyn had left. Her mother had given up on Eddie and was glad Fate had given her a reason to leave. At that time, Robyn had been more than happy to go with her.

"Brad's an officer in the police department now," Pam said.

"I know. In fact, you remind me every time I call," Robyn answered.

"He was dating Michelle Diamond for a long time..." Pam started.

21

"Yeah, I know. Aren't they still together?" Robyn asked.

"No, didn't I tell you? She went off with Randy Dennis," Pam said.

"No way!"

She remembered Randy Dennis. He had been the ugliest kid in school. He'd had ears the size of plates, glasses with lenses two inches thick, and a body odor issue.

"He had plastic surgery on his ears and laser eye surgery," Pam informed as if reading her mind.

"When did that happen?" Robyn asked.

"The ears?"

"No, when did Michelle leave Brad?"

"About six months ago now. He took it really badly, almost got kicked off the force. He drank a lot, tried to start fights, and the whole town got pretty pissed at him," Pam explained.

"Why didn't you tell me any of this?"

"Well, you always spend longer talking to Bob about the hockey than you do to me. And you haven't called for three months. I left messages, but you never called back...until the one I left about your dad," Pam said.

"It hasn't been that long," Robyn insisted. She hid her eyes from her aunt.

Three months was nothing. She hadn't spoken to her friend Sarah for almost a year. She was ashamed about that, but she would call her now that she was home. There were a lot of reasons she hadn't returned her friend's calls, but the main one was she didn't want to hear what was going on in Portage because it made her ache not to be there. Sarah would describe the weather and the lake and places they used to go and, despite the mixed feelings she had for the town, the feeling that overrode all the others was longing. Her dad getting ill had somehow given her the courage to return. It was a reason she had long been looking for.

"Well, anyway, you're here now aren't you?' Pam said hastily.

"So what happened? With Brad?" Robyn asked, desperate to take the spotlight off her lack of communication.

"Your dad happened. He gave him a focus, made him captain of the Panthers, and it turned him around," Pam said, turning down another corridor.

"Well, Dad always did want a son," Robyn answered.

"Brad visits too, at least once a week, and he's been holding the Panthers together. Results haven't been great, but they're hanging in there," Pam said, coming to a halt outside one of the doors.

Robyn suddenly felt the urge to vomit. It was either the sudden smell of antibacterial gel and urine or the realization that she was about to see the father she hadn't set eyes on in nine years. She gagged and put her hand to her mouth, trying to stifle the feeling.

"Are you okay, honey? If this is too much, we can just turn around and go back to the car. We don't have to do this now," Pam reassured her.

"I'm okay. This it?" Robyn said, indicating the door in front of them.

"Yes. Should I go in first? Let him know you're here? It will be a shock and…" Pam suggested.

"No." Robyn shook her head. "Listen, why don't you go and wait with Bob and the girls? I think I'd like to do this on my own," Robyn said.

"Are you sure, honey?"

"Yes, I'm sure," Robyn said a bit more forcefully than she had meant to.

Her aunt looked like a wounded puppy. She opened her mouth to apologize, but before she could, the door of Eddie's room opened, and a nurse came bustling out with a tray. On it were the remains of a McDonald's meal.

"Excuse me, are you here to visit?" the nurse inquired.

"Yes, Eddie Matthers," Robyn replied.

"Good luck. He has a bad attitude right now because I confiscated this," the nurse said, indicating the leftover takeaway.

"Can I have it?" Robyn asked, putting her hands on the tray.

"You hungry? Because I'm pretty sure he's bitten into everything," the nurse responded.

"I'm starving," Robyn insisted, taking a firm grip and pulling the tray away from the nurse.

She gave Robyn a funny look and raised her eyes at Pam. She finally relinquished the tray and carried on down the corridor.

"He's in the bed by the window. A guy named Max is in there with him. He has bad lungs and coughs all the time," Pam informed her.

Robyn didn't listen to anything else. She pushed open the door and entered.

In the first bed, a man was sitting up in bed reading. He had wild tufts of gray hair on his head and thick glasses that sat halfway down his nose. He put his newspaper down and looked at Robyn with suspicion.

"You a nurse?" he barked in a thick Brooklyn accent.

"No," Robyn answered.

"What you want?"

"World peace. You?" Robyn retorted.

"Very funny. Hey Eddie, we got ourselves a comedian here," the patient called out before succumbing to a fit of coughing.

Robyn moved forward to the bed nearest the window. It was then she saw him.

Eddie only vaguely looked like the dad she remembered saying goodbye to. With less hair on his head and more hair on his face, he looked older. His beard was shabby and flecked with gray, and his pallor didn't look right at all. Eyes that were ringed and heavy bulged from his face and he was fatter than ever. He looked like someone who could advertise the long term damage of a high cholesterol diet. Propped up in bed, Red Wings ice hockey shirt on over his hospital gown, remote control for the TV in one hand, the other vigorously picking from a bag of peanuts...there he was, her dad.

Robyn just stared at him from the end of his bed, trying to take it all in. This was what nine years had done to him. It looked like nine years of neglect, and she was suddenly pricked with a feeling of guilt. Perhaps she shouldn't have left. Maybe if she had stayed he wouldn't be in this situation. Had leaving him been selfish? She could have stayed, she could have confronted things — she might have found the strength from somewhere.

Eddie looked away from the television and noticed Robyn for the first time.

"What the Hell?" he exclaimed, clutching at his chest and knocking the bag of peanuts onto the floor.

"Hello, Dad," Robyn greeted, putting the tray of food down.

'Hello dad?! Hello dad?! You can't just come waltzing in here and say 'hello dad' after ten years," Eddie exclaimed, sitting up and wiping his peanut sullied hands on his sheets.

"Nine years, actually. What do you want me to say?" Robyn asked him.

"I don't want you to say anything. What are you doing here? What d'you want? You need money? If you need money, ask your mother," Eddie continued, adjusting the tube under his nose.

"I don't need money," Robyn answered, staring at him.

"Then what d'you want?"

"I brought this back for you. That Hitler of a nurse said she took it from you. Well, I know what the food's like around here. Here, it's all yours," Robyn said, pushing the McDonald's food nearer to him.

Eddie eyed her suspiciously, then his gaze fell to the paper bags on the table in front of him.

"Go on, it's your favorite, isn't it? Big Mac with extra cheese?" Robyn guessed.

"Why don't you talk right any more? I thought it was just the telephone, but here you are, talking like that right in front of me. You didn't speak like that when you left. You don't sound right," Eddie said as he grabbed the bag and his hand ferreted inside for the burger.

"England's ruined me. I'm actually halfway to becoming the Queen," Robyn replied, watching him.

"Where's your mother? She ain't here, is she?" Eddie asked, sinking his teeth into the food.

"Dunno. Wales? Blackpool? Vegas? Got married to a magician called Des. I've told you all this before. He can saw her in half," Robyn answered.

"I wouldn't mind a go at that myself," Eddie replied.

"So, how are things with you? The house in such a state you needed to move in here?" Robyn questioned.

"Very funny," Eddie responded, concentrating on eating.

"Auntie Pam says you need a bypass," Robyn continued.

"So they say. You know the clever guys with the funny white coats and the glasses. They all wear glasses round here. I don't know if they need them, I think they just wear them to look smart," Eddie answered, spitting pieces of meat into his beard.

"They say you can't have the operation unless you lose some weight and start eating properly," Robyn carried on.

"Yeah, they say that too. Don't know what their problem is. McDonald's has been the staple diet of Americans for years and we're all—" Eddie began.

"Dying of heart disease caused by obesity. Enjoying the food?" Robyn interjected.

"Yeah, beats the green pasta stuff they tried to force-feed me at lunchtime. It had bits in it. I don't like bits," Eddie said, shaking his head and breathing in through his nose as he devoured the burger.

"That's a shame because I spit all over that Big Mac, pretty sure there'll be bits," Robyn informed him matter of factly.

Eddie clutched at his throat, turned bright red, and began to regurgitate what he had just eaten, doubling over and retching.

Robyn took the paper bags from the table, screwed them into a ball and, in one quick move, threw them in the hazardous waste bin.

"Jeez! You're sick! What's wrong with you? You trying to kill me?! Get me a nurse! Nurse!" Eddie yelled as he began to splutter and gasp for breath.

"I don't need to try and kill you; you're doing that all by yourself, eating this crap and not getting up and about. If you don't do as the doctors say, they're not going to give you the operation because they don't think you'll survive it," Robyn blasted, looking at her father with fury in her eyes.

"Who cares? I don't want an operation! They're the ones who want me to have an operation. Do you think I want to be in here? Get me some water! I want this taste off my tongue!" Eddie ordered, wiping his mouth with a napkin.

"So you're just going to lie here, eating shit and watching TV? What about the roadhouse? What about the Panthers?" Robyn questioned.

"Oh, what about them? Roadhouse has been going downhill for years, the same with the Panthers. No one cares any more, why should I?"

"Oh, I see, you want sympathy for the sorry ass state you're in, do you? Well too bad, because you're getting none of that from me," Robyn told him.

"No one asked you to come."

"Actually, they did. Auntie Pam begged me to come."

"She always was an interfering…" Eddie began, wiping his tongue with the tissue.

"You think I want to be here? You think I wanted to leave England and travel nine hours across the Atlantic? I have a great job and a place and a life back there. Here I've got Auntie Pam and twin cousins who look like they belong in a remake of The Omen. And

27

then there's you. A fat, ungrateful, angry old man who wants to fester in a hospital bed when he has what could be a profitable business and what could be a successful ice hockey team sitting in his lap. Stop behaving like an idiot. You have no idea what it's like for me to come back here!" Robyn yelled at him.

"How dare you speak to your father like that? You always were stubborn, you get that from your..." Eddie began.

"From you, Dad. I get it from you. Now listen to me, if I hear that any more fat-loaded meals have passed your lips, I will come in here and see to it that the doctor with the best glasses wires your jaw shut," Robyn threatened.

Eddie glared at her.

"I'm going to get the roadhouse back on track, I'm going to manage the Panthers, and I'm going to get the house ready for you for when you come home," Robyn told him.

"You can't..."

"I can, Dad. Don't underestimate me," Robyn said. Her eyes flashed.

Eddie just continued to glare at her, still wiping at his mouth.

"So, did you want that water?" Robyn asked, putting a smile on her face and picking up the pitcher.

Chapter Four

It was good to arrive at Pam and Bob's ranch-style home. It hadn't changed a bit. The American flag still hung from a pole by the porch, Bob's fishing boots stood on the step, and the tubs of flowers bordering the front of the house were still in bloom, just like they had been when she'd left.

Once inside, there was the familiar scent of home-cooking and the chintz decor practically enveloped you in old-fashioned charm.

"I made brownies. Girls, can you get changed for bed, it's late," Pam ordered as everyone entered the house.

"Oh Mom, you have to be kidding! It's like not even ten," Sierra complained straight away.

"It's like only nine thirty! Taylor's mom lets her stay up 'til eleven," Sienna joined in, stamping her foot and glaring at Pam.

"Not on a school night. Shoo!" Pam said.

"This is not fair! This is because she's here!" Sierra shouted, fixing Robyn with a stare.

"Hey, leave me out of this," Robyn begged.

"She doesn't have to go to bed," Sierra continued.

"I'm twenty-five," Robyn answered.

"So?" Sierra replied, looking at her cousin with defiance in her eyes like the Gingerbread Boy.

"Remember what I said at the restaurant about life expectancy? If I were you, I'd take those braids out before you close your eyes tonight," Robyn said, slight threat to her tone.

"Girls, I can hear everything you're saying. Now you apologize for being rude to Robyn and do as your mom tells you," Bob spoke sternly as he came out of the garage with Robyn's case.

Sierra let out an agitated sigh and folded her arms across her chest.

"Sierra, I'm warning you," Bob threatened.

"Oh whatever! Sor-ry!" Sierra yelled in Robyn's face.

Then the girl turned and ran up the hallway toward the bedrooms.

"Sienna, go and change and maybe you can have a brownie before bed," Pam suggested, smiling at her other daughter.

"More sugar just before bed?" Bob raised an eyebrow.

"Oh, it won't hurt this once. Now Robyn, is there anything I can get you? Some coffee? A brownie?" Pam asked.

"No, honestly, I'm fine. I mean, I'm good. I think I'll just go to bed if that's okay," Robyn said.

"Of course, honey. You're in the guest room. You remember where it is, don't you?" Pam asked.

"Yeah, thanks. Well, goodnight and thanks for the meal and for picking me up and everything. I guess I'll see you in the morning," Robyn said, gathering up her luggage and heading down the hallway.

"Goodnight, honey. Let me know if you need anything. There's a clean towel on your bed and there's a new toothbrush and toothpaste in the en-suite," Pam called after her.

Robyn entered the room, dumped her bags in the corner, and leapt onto the big double bed. It was covered in a thick quilt with huge floral cushions. She kicked off her tennis shoes and lay back. There was something to be said for Pam's whimsical taste in decoration; it was both comforting and comfortable. She had always felt more at home at Pam and Bob's house than she had in her own. Pam and Bob had spats, usually when Pam objected to the amount of ice hockey on the television or to Bob spending both days of the weekend fishing, but their "discussions" had nothing on the arguments her parents used to have. They had always started small and escalated into full scale war. Glasses were smashed, her mother would cry, Eddie would holler until he almost turned blue, and Robyn had hidden in the basement until it was over.

She closed her eyes and turned onto her side. Childhood wasn't something she looked back on or wished she could repeat. Childhood was something belonging to other people that she had missed out on and envied.

Her stomach was so full she felt as if she might burst. She had eaten her own body weight at the Old Country Buffet, and seeing her dad had been testing to say the least. She should feel tired, but the truth was, she didn't feel settled enough for sleep. There were far too many thoughts running through her head.

She pulled her cell phone from her pocket and looked through the list of contacts. She picked one and set it to dial.

"Hello," the female voice answered.

"Sarah Gorski, what are you doing in a nightclub? Haven't you got work tomorrow?" Robyn greeted.

"What? I'm not at a nightclub. Who is this?"

"Oh, I like that. It hasn't been that long since I called you. Have you forgotten me already? I thought we were friends."

"Robyn? Is that you? Where are you?" Sarah questioned.

"Aunt Pam's."

"No way! I don't believe it! How long have you been here?"

"Flew in today. Listen, are you busy? Wanna meet up?"

"When?"

"Now."

"Crap, Robyn. I'm at the garage picking Mickey up from work."

"Well bring him with you."

"But I promised him pizza tonight. We've got coupons that need to be used up and everything," Sarah responded.

"Bring the pizzas."

"Well, where were you thinking of meeting?"

"Eddie's."

"You are kidding?"

"No, why? Don't tell me even you and Mickey don't go there any more."

"Robyn, it's turned into a dive! The only people that go in there now are the motorbike gang and anyone with an armful of tattoos," Sarah explained.

"Have you seen this Nancy lately?" Robyn asked.

"Not lately, not since Eddie got ill."

"What's she like?"

"Well, she's very blond and she smiles a lot, mainly at men."

"Not ideal stepmom material then. Not going to be teaching me needlework any time soon."

"The whole place smells, and it doesn't even do food any more."

"What?! Why hasn't anyone told me about any of this? I may be on the other side of the world, but it's just a telephone call away."

"You don't return my calls," Sarah replied.

"Have you called? There must be a problem with my voicemail," Robyn said quickly.

"It's really changed, Robyn."

"Right, well, I need to see it for myself. You and Mickey meet me there."

"Robyn, I..."

Robyn ended the call and got off the bed. She caught sight of herself in the mirror and let out a sigh. She was back and not everything was the same.

There was another phone call she should make, but she couldn't face that just yet. She was here now, back in her old life. There wasn't room to think about anything in England. Her dad needed her, whether he wanted to need her or not, and she had to focus on that.

She rubbed her eyes, swept her hair back behind her ears, and unclasped her baseball cap from the handle of her backpack. She put it on, stuffed her feet back into her tennis shoes, and headed over to the window.

She pulled up the blinds, quietly opened the window, and hoisted herself up onto the ledge. If she told Pam she was going out she would only worry. Having two children, each with an unrivalled death stare, was enough worry for anyone. The wind chilled her as she slipped out and she reached back in for her sweater before closing up the window.

It was time to meet Nancy.

Chapter Five

It was a fifteen minute walk to Eddie's Roadhouse on Shaver Road and, when Robyn arrived outside, she hardly recognized it as the buzzing diner it had once been. Lined up near the front entrance were half a dozen Harley Davidson motorcycles, and in the parking lot were two very run-down RVs that looked like they had people living in them.

From inside, Robyn could hear the sound of ZZ Top blaring out and the barking of what sounded like half a dozen dogs.

She pushed open the doors and stepped inside, only to be overwhelmed by the rather obvious scent of marijuana.

The place looked like something that had been blown up and then haphazardly put back together. Through the gloom of smoke, everything looked filthy, tired, and tattered. Some of the chairs were broken, the seat covers in the booths were ripped, and the wallpaper was peeling away everywhere you looked.

There were a group of men in one corner, clad in leather jackets. They wore bandanas on their heads and each had a denim-skirted woman on their knee. They seemed to be playing cards.

A group of teenagers were huddled around the pool table, and a middle-aged couple were dancing by the jukebox, almost undressing each other. There were four dogs in the middle of the bar, barking and running in circles, slobbering on everything they came into contact with.

Behind the bar was a guy who barely looked old enough to drink himself. He had blond hair that curled tight to his head, and he was wearing a black t-shirt that had seen better days. Robyn sat up on one of the bar stools and beckoned him over.

"What can I get you?" he asked, giving her a creepy smile.

"What's your name?" Robyn asked, raising her voice over the music.

"Milo."

"I'll have a Bud Light please, Milo," Robyn ordered, taking in the grime on the bar top before deciding against leaning her arm on it.

The bartender popped the cap on the bottle and set it in front of her.

"Thanks," she said, looking at the lip of the bottle before taking a swig from it.

"You're welcome. So, you on vacation?" Milo asked, leaning on the bar and gazing at her.

"Nope."

"Oh, I thought, because of your accent and all..." Milo began.

"Where's Nancy?" Robyn asked, looking over at the teenagers as they began to tussle with each other, using the pool cues as swords.

"She's out back," Milo answered.

"So who's in charge out here?" Robyn asked him.

"Why that would be me," Milo announced proudly, sticking out his chest in a desperate show of authority.

"Ah, I see. So, you let customers smoke pot, bring dogs in, and fight with the pool cues, do you?" Robyn questioned.

35

"Well, I...you ain't a cop are you?" Milo asked, suddenly looking concerned.

"No. I'm from a much higher authority than that, and I want you to tell them to leave. All of them," Robyn ordered him.

"Me? You want me to ask them to leave? I...I can't do that," Milo said, shifting from one foot to the other and looking highly uncomfortable.

"Well, I thought you said you were in charge here," Robyn responded, fixing the bartender with a stare Judge Judy might use toward a time-wasting plaintiff.

"Yeah I know, but I meant serving drinks and...and...fixing the jukebox and stuff," Milo replied.

"Oh, just serving drinks and doing maintenance, huh? Well then, you'd better go get Nancy. Tell her Eddie's daughter's here to see her," Robyn said, waiting for the shock to hit his expression.

Milo's jaw very nearly hit the countertop, and she was sure it was all he could do to stop drool from dripping out of his mouth.

He stumbled from the bar, knocking into a crate of empty bottles on the way. When he'd regained his balance and trotted off, Robyn turned to survey the rest of the cliental. It wasn't pretty.

The youths by the pool table now had one of the girls dancing on top of it, and the bikers had been joined by the middle-aged dancing couple. In the furthest corner, near the door to what had been the kitchen, was a disheveled, bearded man in a dirty coat and woolen hat, slumped over the table, seemingly asleep.

Within a minute or so, Milo returned to the bar. Following close behind was a peroxide blonde, tottering on too high heels, wearing a denim mini-skirt and crop top that were at least thirty years too young for her. Hideous large hooped earrings hung from her ears and on her arms were an assortment of cheap bangles and bracelets. Her blond hair was piled high on her head and some curly tendrils snaked down at the side of a face that was thickly plastered in make-up.

"This is Nancy," Milo introduced quickly.

The woman stepped forward, chewing gum and toying with the ugly gold necklace she had around her neck.

"This ain't Eddie's daughter! You shitting me, Milo? Who is this? Some girl of yours? You trying to give me a freaking heart attack?" She turned her attention to Robyn. "Nice try, sweetheart. Want a drink on me?" Nancy offered, cackling loudly and leaning close to Robyn.

"Don't you mean on Eddie? If you're handing out free drinks so readily, maybe that's why business isn't so good," Robyn replied, trying to avoid looking at Nancy's cleavage as it bounced up and down in her face.

"Listen, missy, what business goes on here is my business," Nancy informed her, narrowing her eyes.

"Is that so? I thought Eddie Matthers was the owner," Robyn retorted.

"Yeah? So? Eddie's my guy and when he's not around, I'm in charge. You got a problem with that?" Nancy questioned, staring at Robyn.

"Yeah, actually I do. This is supposed to be a roadhouse and it used to serve food. Where's the food?" Robyn asked.

"We've had problems. Anyhow, who do you think you are? Coming into my roadhouse trying to throw your weight around," Nancy demanded to know.

"He told you who I was. I'm Eddie's daughter, Robyn. And your presence here is no longer required," Robyn said.

"Look, lady, I don't know who you are, but you ain't Eddie's daughter. She lives in England," Nancy answered, her mouth furiously working the gum up and down.

"I got a flight," Robyn responded.

"I don't believe you."

"You should really leave, because until this place has had a thorough revamp, we're going to be closing," Robyn told her.

"Okay, enough's enough. Come on, out of my bar," Nancy said, teetering forward and approaching Robyn.

"I think you'll find it's more mine than yours. What, with me being Eddie's next of kin," Robyn replied.

"Yeah? Well, we'll see about that. Where's your proof?" Nancy hissed, moving up close to Robyn.

"I went to see him today, room two zero nine. That enough for you? Thanks for keeping things ticking along, well...kind of...but I'll be taking over now," Robyn said. Her voice was steady and controlled.

"Look, sugar, I've been running this place for the last year and I don't answer to nobody...least of all someone I ain't met before," Nancy spat.

"Well, I told you, I'm Robyn Matthers. There, now we're introduced. So, are you going to kick their asses out of here and close the door on your way out? Or are you going to let things get ugly?"

She slipped down off her stool and squared herself up to the woman. It wasn't such an easy task when she was in sneakers and Nancy was in platforms that could rival a stilt walker.

"Milo, call the cops," Nancy ordered the bartender, her eyes not leaving Robyn's.

"No need, Milo, already done. They'll take one step through the door and arrest the biker group for drug possession. And, you know, the gang might just hold a grudge if you don't forewarn them about the imminent arrival of the police. Although I don't really know them, they don't look like the type of people to get on the wrong side of," Robyn told her.

"Those cigarettes are medicinal," Nancy said, holding Robyn's gaze.

Robyn let out a laugh.

"You're not serious!"

"You're really Eddie's daughter?" Nancy asked again.

"Yes I really am, and I'm taking over the roadhouse...ooo, is that a siren I hear?" Robyn asked, cupping her hand over her ear and leaning toward the door.

Nancy hurried over to the table of bikers, whispered something into the ear of the most bearded man and, within seconds, the cards were dropped to the table, chairs were being pushed back, and the owners began rounding up their dogs.

"Turn the jukebox off and start cleaning up. I'll get rid of the school kids and the hobo," Robyn ordered Milo.

"Are the cops really coming because…" Milo began, looking uncomfortable.

"Milo, do you want to keep your job?" Robyn questioned.

"Yes, ma'am."

"Then get cleaning up!"

The door opened almost cautiously, and then Robyn caught sight of Sarah for the first time in nine years.

Her friend seemed taller, but she had the same familiar dark, wavy hair that sat around her shoulders. She wore a gray business suit, and black designer glasses rested on her face. She was an adult. Robyn should have expected it, but hadn't. Part of her thought Sarah would still resemble the picture she had in her head — a sixteen year old student wearing a spaghetti-strapped sundress and Converse sneakers.

"Hey! About time! I thought I was going to get a beating from the Hells Angels," Robyn joked as she smiled at her friend.

"Robyn! It's so good to see you!" Sarah said. She rushed to the bar and put her arms around her friend, hugging her tightly.

"You too," Robyn replied, patting her on the back.

"There were motorcycles roaring up the road. What's happened?"

"That was the biker gang. I've taken over. You're looking at the new manager of Eddie's Roadhouse!"

"Mickey! Jeez! What have you been feeding him? You're so…wide!" Robyn exclaimed as Sarah's stocky, tawny-haired boyfriend entered the building.

"Can I take that as a compliment?" Mickey asked her.

"Of course. Oh, it's so good to see you!" Robyn said, smiling at her friends.

"Listen, we ran into..." Sarah began as the entrance door opened again.

Before Sarah could finish her sentence, Brad walked into the bar. Robyn felt her stomach tighten as she looked at a taller, more muscular version of the boy she had left behind. He was still athletic in build, but had filled out a lot since high school. He was broader, and his blond hair was shaved close to his head. His eyes were still as blue as the ocean, though, and he smiled the second he saw her.

"...Brad," Sarah finished as he walked up to the bar to join them.

"Hey," Brad greeted, looking at Robyn with something close to admiration in his expression.

"Hey, wow, everyone must eat a lot of greens around here, you've all gotten massive," Robyn stated, her cheeks flushing.

"Whereas you don't look any different," Brad said, smiling bashfully.

"That's because I'm not different, at all. Just the same old Robyn! God, well, this is so weird," Robyn said.

"Where's Nancy? Is she here?" Sarah asked, setting the pizzas down on the countertop.

"She left with the biker gang, temporarily, I expect. She didn't seem like the type of woman to take things lying down. Well, perhaps some things, if you know what I mean, but I don't want to think about that. Anyway, now all I need to do is get rid of the sleeping tramp and the teenagers. Who wants to help? There's a Bud in it for you," Robyn offered.

"Just one?" Mickey asked.

"Okay, a pitcher then. This is my dad's profits we're talking about."

"Leave it to us," Brad assured her, and he headed off toward the group of teenagers who were now sitting down playing Spin the Bottle.

Robyn let out a heavy sigh and took a long swig from her bottle of beer.

"It's so good to see you, but we could have met somewhere nicer. This place smells really bad," Sarah remarked, opening up a pizza box and taking out a slice.

"I know," Robyn answered.

"And it's really dirty. I mean, I don't know if I really want to even have a drink here," Sarah continued.

"I know."

"Sorry."

"No, it's okay, you're right. The place is wrecked," Robyn admitted.

"What are you going to do?"

"I'm going to clean it, decorate it, and re-launch it," Robyn informed her.

"That's going to be a hell of a job," Sarah replied.

"I know, but hey, I've got nothing else to do," Robyn answered with a half-hearted smile.

Chapter Six

"I can't tell you how good this pizza is. I mean, in England they have loads of pizza restaurants, but they just don't taste like this," Robyn said as she ate her third slice of pepperoni thick crust.

Milo had cleaned up the empties from the floor and started the dishwasher, before Robyn had dismissed him until the following day. He was still shaking when he left, but seemed grateful he still had a job. She didn't think a little fear of your boss was a bad thing.

Now the three friends were eating pizza and sharing a pitcher of beer. It was just like old times and Robyn couldn't stop smiling. It was her gang, back together again.

"So you still love food, that's obvious," Brad said, watching Robyn eat.

"Oh God yeah! Pam and Bob took me to the Old Country Buffet after they picked me up from the airport. Oh man, that place has just got better, if that's possible," Robyn remarked.

"Her accent's coming back, have you noticed that? Three beers and half a pizza and it's back," Mickey said with a laugh.

"It's so good to see you," Robyn said.

"You've said that five times now," Sarah told her.

"So? Come on, tell me what I've missed. Who's doing what? Who's dating who? Who's feuding? I want to know everything," Robyn said energetically.

"We're still dating," Mickey announced with a laugh, snaking an arm around Sarah.

"We're hardly dating. We live together," Sarah reminded with a tut.

"But you still go on dates. Look at you! Pizza at Eddie's Roadhouse," Robyn said.

"Yeah, it's pizza vouchers and a burger at the Texas Ranch House if we're lucky," Sarah announced with a sigh.

"There ain't nothing wrong with pizza and burgers, and you gotta love the discounted ones," Mickey said.

"Things aren't so good here right now, Robyn. You know, economically," Brad informed her.

"Yeah, well, I know. It's like that the whole world over."

"People aren't going out as much as before or buying houses…especially buying houses," Sarah said with another sigh.

"Come on, how many you sold this week?" Robyn asked, wanting to know.

"This week? None! This whole month only four. Things are quiet."

"Well, what about hockey? How many spectators on average per game?" Robyn asked.

"Approximately one hundred and thirty-four last game," Mickey told her.

"There was no approximately about it. We counted them," Brad added.

"No!" Robyn couldn't believe it. "We used to have a crowd of at least a thousand every week!"

"Not for a long time. To be honest, we're not sure how long the town's going to have a hockey team," Brad told her.

"You're kidding me? Things are that bad?"

"We've only got a squad of ten," Mickey added.

"Guys, what's been going on?! A squad of ten! How did this happen? And why hasn't Bob told me this?" Robyn said in horror.

"We lost a lot and missed out on promotion. Some of the guys went to play for other teams, and when Eddie got sick we..." Brad began.

"That's it, I've heard enough. Can you tell everyone to meet at the arena tomorrow night? We need to strategize and get things back on track," Robyn said. She tugged hard at her ponytail and nodded her head.

"Well, Grant's been kind of managing the team since Eddie went into hospital and..." Mickey started.

"I know he has and he barely knows the difference between hooking and roughing," Robyn announced.

"He's done his best and he's a good guy," Mickey replied.

"Yeah, course he is," Robyn answered in an unconvincing manner.

"I don't think he has much contact with Jason anymore," Sarah spoke up.

Robyn felt her stomach contract, and a shiver ran over her whole body. She fought the urge to show any emotion and tightened her grip on her beer glass. She'd been here a good few hours but it was inevitable his name would come up sooner or later.

"We don't need to talk about him tonight. Robyn's just come home for Christ's sake!" Brad blasted. He slammed his beer glass down onto the bar top.

"Sorry, I just...you can't blame Grant for what Jason did and..." Sarah began.

"I don't blame Grant," Robyn piped up.

She let out a breath to try and compose herself. She'd said the words, but she didn't know if they were true. She wanted them to be, but perhaps she was fooling herself.

"I just don't think he's the best person to manage the team, that's all," she finished.

"Well, I think you're exhausted and jetlagged. I don't think you should be worrying about the hockey team right now. You should concentrate on spending some time with Eddie," Brad said, changing the subject.

"Did that already, right after the Old Country Buffet. He's still the same arrogant, pigheaded, stubborn ass he always was. No, I need something else to focus on—the roadhouse and the hockey team. Tomorrow night, at seven, can you do that? Can you get everyone there?" Robyn asked Brad and Mickey.

"Sure," Mickey agreed with a nod.

"Good. So, who's the best person to get in to redecorate this place? Does Old Man Harrison still do painting and stuff?" Robyn asked.

"Oh Robyn, Old Man Harrison died," Sarah informed her.

"He did?"

"Yes, it was about what? Five years ago?" Sarah asked the two men.

"Something like that," Mickey agreed.

"But who has the annual town barn dance now? Pam always made pumpkin pie, and I could never remember the steps to any of the dances and...why didn't she tell me? I always rode his pony and..." Robyn started, her eyes welling up with tears.

"Okay, I think it's time you went home. The veil of jetlag is finally descending," Brad said, taking the beer glass from her hand and helping her down from the stool.

"Why didn't anyone tell me about Old Man Harrison? I mean, I was only in England, we have phones there and the internet and...what happened to Bessie the tractor?" Robyn questioned.

"She's still going. Come on, I'll give you a ride," Brad said, coaxing her toward the door.

"But I need to lock up. Shit, I don't have keys! I don't have keys to my own roadhouse!" Robyn screeched.

"Don't worry about it. We can get the locks changed in the morning. Night guys," Brad called as he pushed open the door.

"I'm not tired. Sarah, I'll call you tomorrow and we'll maybe go for lunch or go and see if we can find a decorating firm. Or maybe I could do it myself. Do they still do paint in Wal-Mart?" Robyn called as Brad hurried her out of the roadhouse.

"Night Robyn," Sarah called with a giggle.

"She hasn't changed," Mickey remarked with a smile.

"Nice ride," Robyn said as Brad drove his expensive-looking station wagon up the street toward Pam and Bob's home.

"Thank you."

"So, you've gone all lawman on us," Robyn continued.

"Yep. It's been six years next month."

"Well good for you. Never would have thought it, but…"

"What did you think I'd be doing?" Brad asked, glancing at her as he drove.

"I don't know, captaining an NHL team or playing for the Yankees or something."

"I wish."

"Do you?"

"Maybe, I don't know. Your expectations change when you grow up, don't they?" Brad replied.

"Yep, didn't think I'd be back here helping out Dad. Didn't think I'd ever be back here to be honest," Robyn said.

"So, what's England like? What do you do there?" Brad asked her.

"This and that," she replied.

"That's evasive."

"It's different. It isn't like here. I'm an office manager for a motor company," Robyn informed him.

"You're shitting me! A manager!" Brad exclaimed with a laugh.

"Why are you laughing? I've always been good at organizing and I've always been good with cars. It's the perfect job for me."

"There is no way you would prefer sitting in an office to having your head underneath a hood," Brad answered.

"Well, given the tough economic climate, I had to opt for the job that was going to pay the most," Robyn told him.

It was as close to the truth as she was going to give. She answered the phone, she made appointments, and she did the filing. But all the while, she gazed into the workshop, envying the mechanics covered in grease, their hands in the engine of the latest job. It was all she could do not to roll up the sleeves of the blouse Clive had bought her from Saks and climb under the hood of a car on her lunch hour. But she knew Clive would hate that.

"My, my, Robyn Matthers the office girl," Brad teased.

"Brad Willis the cop sounds more ridiculous to be honest," Robyn replied with a scowl.

"I'm not so sure."

"Sorry to hear about you and Michelle. I mean, I never really liked her much, she always called me Bobby and said she would rather die than wear jeans, but Pam says you were dating a long time before she ran off with…" Robyn began.

"Randy Dennis. Yeah, Randy Dennis, the ugliest kid in school," Brad interrupted.

"That surgery he had must have been pretty extensive."

"Yeah, right," Brad agreed with a sigh.

"Plenty more fish in the sea, right? No point looking back when forward's the only way you can go," Robyn said.

"So they say. So, are you dating?" Brad asked.

"Nope, too busy being an office girl."

"I don't believe that."

"Believe it!"

"I can't imagine you're short of male admirers working in a garage, though. All that testosterone and having to look at a pretty manager all day."

"Most of them are over forty and married."

"Bet they've thought about it."

"Eww! Brad, don't! That's creepy!"

He laughed and pulled the car up outside Pam and Bob's.

"They don't know you're out, do they?" Brad said.

"Well, Pam worries and she wouldn't understand that I had to go to the bar tonight. She thinks I need sleep and…"

"You do need sleep. Did you sneak out the window?"

"Kind of," Robyn admitted.

"You'll be okay getting back in?"

"Of course. It isn't like I haven't done it before, right?"

"It's great to see you, Robyn," Brad said as she opened the car door.

"You too, and you won't forget about tomorrow night. Seven at the arena, the whole squad of ten."

"I won't forget," Brad promised.

Robyn shut the car door and hurried up the driveway, hugging her sweater to herself.

Once at the house, she eased open the window and climbed up onto the sill. She looked back to Brad who was still watching her from the car and she waved, before disappearing inside. One mission was accomplished.

Chapter Seven

She tried to open her eyes, but it wasn't working. They felt so heavy and sticky, like they were glued together. She grabbed hold of the pillow and hauled herself up into a sitting position, rubbing at her eyes with a fist. Her head ached, her mouth was dry, and she smelled bad. Sunlight streamed through the blinds, and that hurt her eyes, too. She looked at her watch. Her vision blurred and she blinked to focus on the dial.

"Shit!"

It was almost midday.

She stumbled out of bed, caught her foot in the bedding, and fell flat on her face. God, she felt terrible! And she so desperately needed coffee.

When she had managed to stagger into the kitchen, there was a note on the table and a set of keys beside it.

Keys for you! Help yourself to everything! Dinner at six – meatball stew! Pam

The thought of meatball stew made her stomach rumble. She was starving and she needed breakfast.

She dialed Sarah.

"Hi, it's me. Wanna meet for breakfast? Yeah, I know it's almost lunchtime, but I slept in. Theo and Stacey's in an hour? I really stink and need to shower. Hey Sarah, do you know anyone who could lend me a car?"

Robyn was on her third mug of coffee when Sarah joined her at the table in the diner.

"You made it! Did you manage to get me a car?" Robyn asked, signaling to the waitress that they were ready to order.

"Are you crazy? Where did you think I was going to get a car from in an hour? You're lucky I'm here! Someone called wanting to see a property on Romence Avenue, and I had to give it to Sheryl. I should be hoping they buy, but I'm not."

"I really need a car. It doesn't have to be anything fancy, but I need something to get me from A to B, plus I need to go to Meijer's after here and get ten tons of cleaning equipment to make a start on the roadhouse. Meijer's is still the best supermarket, isn't it?" Robyn asked, taking another look at the menu.

"Why didn't you rent a car?" Sarah asked.

"Because Pam and Bob insisted on picking me up, and I didn't really think about it. I'd forgotten how spread out everything is over here. It isn't like that in England where there's Park and Ride," Robyn reminded her.

"Well, I'll give Mickey a call. Steinberg Motors might have something, I guess," Sarah said with a sigh.

"You sigh a lot. When did you start sighing so much? You never used to do that. Is something wrong?" Robyn asked.

"No. Shall we order? Can I have a Greek salad with everything?" Sarah asked the waitress.

"Sure. And what can I get you ma'am?"

"I'll have sausage patties, er no, I want links, links are the long ones right? And bacon, two eggs over easy, hash browns, and wheat toast, thank you," Robyn reeled off.

"You're welcome, I'll bring it right out," the waitress said, writing everything down.

"Did you want some coffee?" Robyn asked Sarah.

"No, it's okay. I'll just have water," Sarah said, picking up the glass of iced water on the table and sipping from it.

"What's wrong with you? You're not on another bizarre diet are you? Because don't think I didn't notice you ordered salad. You remember I think it's the Devil's food, right?"

"I'm not on a diet," Sarah said, sighing again.

"Then have some more to eat."

"I don't want more to eat."

"You're not pregnant, are you?"

"There's nothing wrong with me!" Sarah shouted loud enough to turn heads.

Robyn's eyes met with a middle-aged woman seated at the adjacent table, and she mouthed an apology.

"Okay, so that outburst's really convinced me," Robyn said, lowering her voice.

"I'm just not in a good place right now, that's all," Sarah spoke quietly.

"Theo & Stacey's?"

"No Robyn, in life! I'm not in a good place in life!" Sarah yelled.

"The housing market will pick up," Robyn assured her.

"It isn't realty, it's reality. It's Mickey...me and Mickey," Sarah blurted out.

"I don't understand."

"We're treading water, we're not going anywhere," Sarah continued.

"Well, where do you want to go? Tell him."

"I'm not talking about going to the movies or out on the lake, I'm talking about life. We're not going anywhere in life," Sarah said to her.

"But you're happy together, you've always been happy together. You've been happy with Mickey since you were thirteen. You were the couple everyone said would get married and have hundreds of babies. Okay, maybe not hundreds, but at least half a dozen," Robyn said.

"Yeah, I know," Sarah sighed.

"So what's changed?"

"Nothing."

"Then I'm not seeing the issue here."

"Nothing's changed, that's the whole point. Everything's just like it was when we were thirteen. We're not married and we haven't got half a dozen babies," Sarah said in frustration.

"Ah! Now I get it," Robyn said, taking a sip of her coffee.

"Do you know how much gentle persuasion it took me to get him to even consider moving in together? I mean, to just consider it? To get him to actually do anything about it was torture. Do you know he wouldn't move into anywhere that didn't have a view of a lake," Sarah said, opening up.

"Sounds expensive."

"Yeah, too expensive! Out of our price range completely. So, I had to wait until the most run-down pit you can imagine came on the market. I think Mickey thought it would never happen, but it did."

"So you got a crap house with a great outlook."

"It isn't crap now, it's really nice. But it took a lot of hard work and, even when it was finished, he didn't seem to want to move in," Sarah said, taking a drink of her water.

"You think he's a commitment phobe?"

"I don't know, but to be honest, if things don't move on from how they were in the beginning, I don't see the point of carrying on," Sarah admitted.

"Shit, you'd leave Mickey?" Robyn exclaimed.

This was like suggesting the Queen and Prince Philip were going to go their separate ways and fight acrimoniously over the Crown Jewels and Corgi dogs.

"Well, we've been together forever, but he's still in first gear. I want more than that, I want marriage and a family."

"So tell him."

"Oh Rob, you know it isn't that easy. This is Mickey we're talking about," Sarah said with yet another sigh.

"I don't see the problem. Tell him you want to get hitched and you want kids. Job done."

"But what if he says that isn't what he wants?"

"Then you'll know you're wasting your time with him. Ah, great!" Robyn announced as the waitress arrived with their food.

"So, what about you? Do you have someone in England?" Sarah inquired, picking a bit of lettuce up with her fingers and nibbling on it.

"Someone?" Robyn asked.

"Yeah, a guy, you know…a boyfriend."

"No, too busy."

"Well, who was the last guy you dated? Did he have commitment issues?" Sarah wanted to know.

"Do you want to try some of this? I mean, that salad looks nice and everything, but it's missing some meat in my opinion," Robyn told her.

"No thanks," Sarah declined.

"Are you sure? 'Cause I'm going to be as fat as a house if I eat all of this and…Well, well, well, doesn't he clean up nicely?" Robyn remarked as the door to the diner opened.

"Who? Who are you looking at?" Sarah asked, turning around.

"That guy who just walked in. The one in the suit," Robyn replied.

"Wow, the really hot one?" Sarah said, noticing him.

"Yeah, give me a second and I'll ask him to join us," Robyn said, standing up.

"What?! Robyn! What are you doing?" Sarah exclaimed.

He was starving. He missed the hot dog stand outside the front doors of the Gen-All offices in Chicago already. Maggie, one of his new assistants, had suggested this diner and recommended the soup. The state his stomach was in right now, he was thinking about ordering two bowls.

Meeting the team had been hard. The people he'd worked with in Chicago had been friends, people who'd understood what he'd been through and what drove him to do the work he did. They got his determination and drive and no explanation was necessary. The inquisitive faces today had looked at him like a specimen on a Petri dish. He knew what they were thinking. Here he was, Cole Ryan, the person they had heard so much about. He was barely out of college, how could he be the leading expert in his field? He knew he would have to earn their belief and trust, but it was so hard having to prove himself all the time. Especially when his mind wasn't fully on the job. He needed to focus more. If he didn't focus, he might not be able to control what happened next. He might be forced to think about something other than work. He wouldn't be able to handle that. Work was his priority now. It had to be.

The suit suited him. His dark head was down, studying a newspaper and, for a second, Robyn didn't know what to say. Robyn Matthers — lost for words — it was unimaginable.

He looked up all of a sudden, and Robyn stood on the outside edge of her tennis shoes and opened her mouth to speak.

"Now how did you know this was the best diner in town?"

"Hey, Robyn Matthers," Cole greeted, smiling back at her.

"I have the best table in the place over there and a salad-nibbling friend. If you're going to join me in eating real food, you can come and sit with us," she invited.

"I've been told the soup is good here. Does that count?" he asked.

"Just this once. Come on," Robyn said, encouraging him out of the seat.

Sarah was flushing with obvious embarrassment when they joined her.

"Sorry about my friend. She's from England and I can only guess inviting strangers to eat with them is a quaint old custom," Sarah began awkwardly.

"Oh, relax, we know each other. Sarah, this is Cole Ryan. Cole, this is my friend Sarah Gorski," Robyn introduced.

"Oh, hello," Sarah greeted, holding her hand out to him.

"Hi, nice to meet you," Cole greeted, shaking Sarah's hand.

"Excuse me...could we have some soup? And some more coffee? You want coffee right?" Robyn asked as the waitress came over.

"Sure," he replied.

"So, how do you two know each other?" Sarah asked.

"We met before the flight to Kalamazoo, and he carried my bag," Robyn informed her.

"And she talked a lot," Cole added.

"And I kind of kissed him," Robyn blurted out.

"What?!"

"Oh, you know, it was just one of those moments," Robyn responded, putting more food into her mouth but checking for Cole's reaction.

"Have I slipped into a vortex?" Sarah asked, looking open-mouthed at both of them.

"So what's with the suit anyways? You looked like a strictly jeans and sneakers guy on the plane," Robyn told him.

"Oh, I am. This is only for today. I've had a meeting at work. You know, getting to know everyone, meeting the team," Cole explained.

"What do you do?" Sarah asked.

"I work for Gen-All Pharmaceutical."

"You and half the town. I don't know why I didn't guess that. So, do you play hockey?" Robyn asked.

"A little."

"Good, you can come along tonight. The Panthers are meeting at seven at the arena. Apparently we only have a squad of ten. Want to try out?" Robyn asked him.

"Sure," Cole agreed.

"So what are you? Forward? Defense?"

"I played center."

"Oh yeah? Who for?"

"Chicago Wolves," Cole answered.

Robyn's jaw almost dropped to the table, and she had to stop herself from spitting out the coffee she had in her mouth. The Chicago Wolves were a team doing well in the American Hockey League and they were a division above the Portage Panthers.

"Is that good?" Sarah asked.

"Yeah, it's good. Good, wow, you're full of surprises," Robyn said when she had regained her ability to speak.

"Right back atcha," he replied, his dark eyes meeting hers.

Robyn smiled and then took to concentrating on her brunch. There was something very Freddie Prinze Jr. about him. Maybe it was the dark eyes, or perhaps the black, glossy hair. Or it could be the chiseled jaw and friendly smile. It was a memory from her youth, a poster on her wall, a pin-up to be admired. A crush! She felt immediately better at this realization. A crush was fine because a crush was far removed from reality. She'd had a long flight and fantasizing went hand-in-hand with jetlag. This wasn't real attraction.

But would she really know? What markers did she have for that?

"Shall I go? I'm feeling like a spare part in this double act," Sarah spoke up.

"Eat your nutritious Devil's food," Robyn ordered, smiling at Cole.

"So, how's the roadhouse? As bad as you thought?" Cole asked, changing the subject.

"Worse. Are you any good with wallpaper?" Robyn asked him.

"Never tried it before."

"Do you want to? I remember you saying you like new experiences."

"Don't feel obliged, she does this. She's been asking everyone about their decorating skills," Sarah said, pushing her salad around the plate.

"Well, I wouldn't be if Old Man Harrison hadn't gone and died," Robyn said, pouting.

"Someone died?" Cole queried.

"It was a few years ago," Sarah informed him.

"I'm off to the roadhouse next, wanna come?" Robyn invited.

"Sure," Cole replied.

"Can I drive your car?" Robyn asked with a grin.

Chapter Eight

It wasn't far to Shaver Road, and soon Robyn was pulling into the parking lot of Eddie's Roadhouse. A large security van was parked outside, and a man in overalls looked to be installing new locks on the front door.

"New locks, huh?" Cole remarked as Robyn pulled up by the entrance.

"Looks that way. Hey there!" Robyn called, opening the window and greeting the man.

"Afternoon ma'am," he replied.

"What are you doing?"

"Fitting new locks, ma'am. You work here?"

"Yeah, I'm the manager."

"Ah, you must be Miss Matthers. Officer Willis said you might be by. I've fitted new locks, front and back, and I've installed a new alarm system. Shall I run you through it?" he asked.

"Oh man, is it expensive? I have money, but it's kind of tied up at the moment," Robyn began, pulling on the handbrake and getting out of the car.

"No need to worry, ma'am. It's all been paid for, Officer Willis settled everything up already," the locksmith informed her.

"Brad paid for it?" Robyn said, looking at the man for clarification.

"Yep. You're all square with me. Wanna see what I've done?" he queried.

"I think I'd like that. Come on Cole, come and see the place," Robyn called to him.

"So? What do you think?" Robyn asked, bringing Cole a bottle of beer and brushing dirt off of one of the chairs.

The locksmith had given her new keys and run her through the intricate workings of the new security system. She had no doubt she was going to fail hopelessly at working it. She never remembered her PIN number and had it written on a piece of paper under the insole of her left shoe.

"I think you definitely need to find a decorating firm," Cole answered, accepting the drink.

"Yeah? You don't fancy helping me strip? Wallpaper. Strip wallpaper," Robyn said, her cheeks glowing.

What the Hell was wrong with her? She was acting like a teenager around him. Any second now she might ask him who his favorite member of The A-Team was. She'd done that a lot in the nineties. Boys had been keen to tell her, girls had looked at her pitifully.

"I think you need professional help," Cole said.

"I know that, but what about the decorating?" Robyn replied with a nervous laugh.

"Are you sure you want to take this on? I mean, it's going to take a lot of work to get it straight," Cole told her.

"I have to take it on. This and the hockey team, they're what Dad lives for. He may say he isn't interested, but he doesn't mean it. When I was young, this place was buzzing. It had a great reputation for food and we had bands here and everything. I need to get that back," Robyn explained.

She didn't just want it back for Eddie; she wanted it back that way for her. The roadhouse was where she had some of her best memories; she didn't want to lose those. The good memories were what she clung to.

"It might take some time," Cole said.

"I've got a couple of weeks," Robyn informed him.

"Man, you've got your work cut out."

"Well, I need to make a list, don't I? I need to find someone to decorate, I need to hire a chef and some more bar staff, and I need to organize some posters telling people we're back in business. What else?" Robyn asked.

"You need to call suppliers, hammer them down on the price of beer, and talk to the people at the diner…ask them the best place to get produce. You're going to need a menu, too," Cole said.

"I'll find a pen and paper, there must be some here somewhere, amongst all the dirt and grime and years of neglect," Robyn said, getting up and going behind the bar.

"So who's this Officer Willis who's kindly paid for your new security? He your guy?" Cole asked.

"My guy? No! I don't have a guy. Listen, about the kiss yesterday. It was just a thing, you know, just because you were really nice, and I just wanted to see what it would be like. I mean, it wasn't a prologue to anything," Robyn explained, shifting awkwardly from one foot to the other.

"Sure, I get it," Cole responded, watching her.

"Cool. I mean, not that it wasn't great or anything, because it was…"

What had it been? She didn't know. Her big mouth had called him to a halt, and then she'd just kissed him, without warning. She'd done some pretty out there things before but never that.

"It was..." Cole prodded, waiting for her to finish her sentence.

She was blushing now. A whole, full-on body blush like someone had caught her in her underwear, dancing to Madonna.

"To be honest, I get girls on planes kissing me all the time. I think it's customary, actually," Cole said, easing the tension.

"It is! You're right, I read it somewhere," Robyn replied gratefully.

"So, Officer Willis..."

"Yes, Brad. He's an old friend, you'll see him tonight at the arena. He plays for the Panthers. I'll pay him back for the alarm. I have money. I just need to get to the bank. Anyway, soon I'll be making a profit here, won't I?" Robyn said as she carefully peeled the label from her beer bottle so she had something to write on.

"I like your optimism," Cole replied.

"You being funny?" Robyn asked, returning to her seat.

"No, I wasn't. I meant it. It's good to have a project," Cole answered.

"Yeah? And what's yours?"

"At the moment, I'm trying to find a cure for cancer," Cole said straight-faced.

Robyn looked up at him, waiting for the smile and the laughter as he admitted to the joke. It wasn't forthcoming. In fact, she had never seen him look more serious. It was like a thought or a memory had come into his head and taken over.

"That's what I do...at Gen-All Pharmaceutical," he added.

She watched him nod, and then he cleared his throat, almost nervously.

"But hey, running a roadhouse sounds much more fun. Bands. You need to book some bands," Cole said quickly, pointing to the list Robyn was compiling.

"You're really clever, aren't you? No wonder girls are kissing you any chance they get," Robyn said, locking eyes with him.

"You'll need furniture," Cole added, gazing back at her.

"Yep, furniture. I'm going to need new tables and chairs," Robyn said, writing it down.

"And a TV, there's no TV in here. You need to show sports."

"Mr. Ryan, may I officially make you the first member of Team Matthers?" Robyn asked him.

"Definitely, count me in," he answered with a smile.

He'd told her what he did. Actually told someone what he really wanted to achieve. She obviously thought he was crazy, but she hadn't laughed out loud. In fact, she had looked at him as if she could see right inside him. She was so different. She always spoke before she thought about what she was going to say. She was honest too and, if he was honest, he was disappointed the kiss wasn't a prologue to anything. Not that he was looking for anything serious. A few months had gone by but, well, it was too soon to think about anything else, wasn't it? Besides, he had work to do. He didn't have the time or the headspace to get involved in anything else. Look at what had happened the last time he had let someone in.

She was cute though.

Chapter Nine

"So, honey how was your day?" Pam asked.

It was six p.m., and Pam, Bob, Robyn, and the twins were all seated around the dining room table behind mountainous portions of meatball stew. Robyn wasn't sure whether to try and eat it or climb it. The twins sat opposite her, swinging their legs and catching her shin any chance they got.

"Good. I've got two decorating firms coming to look at the roadhouse tomorrow and give me quotes. I've shaved five percent off the beer prices, and I'm advertising for staff in the paper," Robyn informed her aunt.

"My, you have been busy! She's been busy, hasn't she, Bob? Girls, stop swinging your legs like that and eat your food," Pam ordered.

"We never eat at the table normally, it's because she's here, isn't it? Why does everything have to change because she's here?" Sierra moaned, glaring at Robyn.

"Sierra!" Pam exclaimed in horror.

"Pam, if it's too much having me stay, I understand. I mean, you have your routines and things and…" Robyn began.

"It's not too much having you stay, Robyn. You're always welcome in this house, you know that, you're family. I didn't realize how rude my daughters had gotten. Frankly, I'm embarrassed," Bob said sternly, looking at Sienna and Sierra.

"So am I. What's gotten into you two?" Pam wanted to know.

Sierra and Sienna just looked sullenly back at their parents and offered no response.

"It's fine. Kids are kids," Robyn insisted.

"No, it's not fine. Come on you two, out with it!" Pam ordered in a voice usually reserved for price checking at Meijer's.

"People at school say she's a witch. They said someone took her into the woods and hurt her. They say, because she's our cousin, they're going to come and take us to the woods, too," Sierra blurted out, her eyes wide.

"Sierra, you're not supposed to tell!" Sienna exclaimed in fear.

Robyn looked at her plate of food and swallowed. A familiar feeling of fear washed over her, and she adjusted her position in the seat to disguise the visible shiver. There she was again, transported back to another time when she was lost, alone, and vulnerable.

"That is enough! Now, I don't know who told you this, but it's not true. Come on girls, you're nine, you know witches aren't real! Who are these people? I'll speak to the teacher and we'll put a stop to this," Pam said, flustered.

"Listen, thanks for the dinner, Pam, but I'd better go. I've got to be at the arena at seven," Robyn said to her as she stood up from the table, her meal untouched.

"Want a ride?" Bob offered.

"Oh no, don't worry, I can walk," Robyn said.

"You will not walk that road, Robyn," Pam ordered, her tone severe.

"I'll be fine," Robyn answered, ignoring the loaded response.

"No, let Bob take you. He wants to come anyway, don't you, Bob?" Pam urged him.

"If that's okay with the new manager," Bob said, looking at Robyn and smiling.

"Sure," Robyn accepted gratefully.

"Come on then, let's go see what these Panthers are made of," Bob said, standing up.

Her mobile rang again on the drive. It had been ringing all afternoon and she had switched it to silent. It still vibrated though, reminding her she had to answer some time or make a call. She didn't want to talk, though, not even a polite "checking in" conversation. It felt wrong now that she was back here. All the justification she had accumulated over the years was fading fast since her return.

"I can't apologize enough for the girls, Robyn," Bob said.

"It's okay. I have kind of invaded, and they've never met me before."

"That's no excuse for it and what they said about Jason..." Bob began.

"That all happened a very long time ago, eons ago, almost a decade...it's forgotten," Robyn interrupted quickly.

"But still, it wasn't nice to bring up bad memories and..."

"So do you go and watch the Panthers every game?" Robyn asked, cutting him off.

"Sure, I'm not one of those supporters who only watch a team when they're doing well. I've been to every game since 1987," Bob reminded her.

"Are they really awful?" Robyn asked, putting some chewing gum in her mouth.

"No, not awful...well, you know..." Bob began.

"No, Bob, I don't know, and that's half the problem."

"Well, they lost the main sponsor, and then money was short for wages and players, so people went elsewhere. We have a great new guy, though, Henrik. He's Swedish, I think."

"And how is the actual play on the ice? What sort of a job has Grant been doing?" she asked.

"The best he could with what he had to work with. Eddie's better, because he's more vocal and he lives and breathes the Panthers, but Grant's done okay," Bob told her.

"Okay isn't good enough, though, is it?" Robyn remarked, looking out the window as the arena came into view.

Driving into the parking lot of the arena was like going back in time. She had seen her last Panthers match the night before she left. She had stuffed herself full of hotdogs and pickles, thinking she might never taste either again. They had lost, her dad had almost burst a blood vessel shouting at the players and, when they got home, her mother had finished packing.

"So, has the old place changed?" Bob asked as they got out of the car.

"It's been painted," Robyn remarked, looking up at the building and putting her baseball cap on her head.

"A few years ago now," Bob said.

"The sign's the same, but where's the 'Home of the Portage Panthers' banner?" Robyn asked him.

"Ah, went missing a while ago, probably kids," Bob admitted.

"Well, it needs to be replaced. I'll get it replaced," Robyn told him firmly.

"Come on, let's go and get you reacquainted with that ice. You been on it in England?" Bob asked.

She shook her head.

It was weird being back. Just seeing the building she had spent so many of her high school days in was making her heart pump faster.

"You know people still talk about the night you knocked out that girl from the Grand Rapids team. Best punch I ever saw," Bob told her with a laugh.

"I got sent off, they had a five minute power play, and we lost," Robyn reminded him.

"But it was worth it and she deserved it. Took out Lindsay Jacobs and didn't even get a warning," Bob recalled.

"I never really liked Lindsay Jacobs. Before the Grand Rapids girl wiped her out, I was thinking about doing it myself," Robyn admitted.

Getting his hockey things together had felt weird. He hadn't even thought about the game since he quit the Chicago Wolves. He'd just got back on track before he found out about Bryn and Veronica, and then he'd thrown in the towel again. But it had seemed natural to say yes to Robyn. When he said he could play, she'd assumed he would help her out, and it seemed natural for her to assume. Perhaps that was what he needed right now.

He parked the car and fondly rubbed the steering wheel. The Mustang had been parked in the next bay when he'd got back from the diner at lunchtime. That had to be something like Fate.

Now it was time to meet another team. Even though he knew they'd look him up and down, meeting new people was a good thing, he could start over. He grabbed his kit bag from the passenger seat and noticed Robyn up ahead. She was wearing a baseball cap, a Red Wings t-shirt, and jeans. He smiled and locked the car.

"Hey!" he called out.

Robyn turned around and was met with the sight of Cole running across the parking lot toward them.

Why did he always look so hot? He was wearing jeans, Converse tennis shoes, and a gray Chicago Wolves t-shirt. Robyn felt something inside her lurch. It was obviously the huge breakfast she'd eaten repeating on her. It couldn't be anything else. She didn't know anything else. Apart from the crush thing. It was just that Freddie Prinze Jr. in I Know What You Did Last Summer thing.

"Hey! Bob, this is Cole. Cole, this is my Uncle Bob. Cole's going to join the team. He played center for the Chicago Wolves," Robyn informed her uncle, quick to recover her senses.

"Pleased to meet you, sir," Cole greeted, holding his hand out to him.

"Hey there."

"You got skates?" Robyn asked him.

"Yep and a full set of armor and pads," Cole answered, lifting up the duffle bag he was carrying.

"Good. Well, locker rooms are to the right, go and get changed," Robyn urged.

"Yes, ma'am," Cole replied with a smile.

When Robyn and Bob got ice side, Grant was already putting the team through their paces in a warm up.

"Wes! Put more effort into the skating and stop talking," Grant called to him, turning when he noticed Robyn and Bob approach.

"Yeah, yeah...why don't you get out here?" Wes yelled back.

"Hey, Bob, hey, Robyn, good to see you," Grant greeted, holding out his hand.

Robyn swallowed as she met his gaze. She was shocked by how much he and Jason looked alike. She hadn't realized the similarities before, but they were there by the bucket load. It was the smile and the pale, blue eyes, the freckled features, and even the stature.

Bob quickly took hold of Grant's hand and shook it, smiling at him, while Robyn took a moment to compose herself. Grant wasn't responsible for what his son had done all those years ago. He was a good man, her dad's friend, she needed to remember that.

"Is this really it?" Robyn asked, looking out at the ten men.

They were all kitted up in full gear, passing pucks to each other on the ice.

"Ten isn't good, I know, but…"

"Eleven. I've got someone getting changed. We need to get some more team members, hold try outs," Robyn told him.

"We did try that at the start of the season but…" Grant began.

"Well? What happened? I mean, even the worst of the bunch would be better than no one at all," Robyn said.

"No one turned up," Grant responded despondently.

"Oh my God! What has happened to this place? The hockey team should be the life blood of the community! Jeez! Right, okay, I want a match now, no holding back. Do we really only have one goaltender?" Robyn asked, fueled by the humiliation.

"Yeah, well, Adam left us last year for…" Grant started.

"I'm not interested in who isn't here. I'm interested in who is here. You! What's your name?" Robyn asked, pointing at a tall player with brown hair.

"Wade," he drawled.

"Well, Wade, go and get a full face mask on and some keeper's pads…" Robyn glanced to the side when she saw movement. "Oh good, you're ready. Everyone, Brad, Mickey, Wade, Wes, the others I don't know…this is Cole Ryan. He's going to be your new center," Robyn informed them.

"Robyn, maybe we ought to discuss this before we make any decisions," Grant suggested quickly.

The team looked less than excited by the new arrival and started to mutter amongst themselves.

"We aren't making any decisions, I am. Get into two teams."

"Come on, Grant, man, you can't let..." one of the players began.

"I'm sorry? I thought I just asked you to get into teams. Why are you looking at him? I'm the manager now. Is anyone unclear about that?" Robyn questioned, narrowing her eyes at them all.

No one answered.

"Good. Grant, can you get some skates on and referee," Robyn said as more of an order than a request.

The team stood like statues on the ice, all looking to Grant and wondering what was going on.

"Come on! Move! Jeez! If it takes you this long to get going, no wonder you're not doing well in the league," Robyn exclaimed.

"Come on guys, let's go," Brad told his team before slipping in his mouth guard.

"Why was that so difficult?" Robyn asked Bob as they went to sit down.

"Grant's approach is different, that's all. They weren't ready for a full-on replica of Eddie," Bob said with a grin.

"God, don't say that! Next you'll be telling me I'm growing a beard," Robyn said, touching her chin.

"No, just starting to inherit the bad ass attitude."

"You can't say that, you're my uncle!"

"And you've never had anything but the truth from me," Bob replied.

"Come on, guys! You starting this game or do you need an air horn?" Robyn screamed at the players on the ice.

Play began, and Robyn watched intently as the two sides battled against each other. It didn't take long for her to work out the best players and the members of the team that were the weak links.

"What's happened to Mickey? He's all over the place," Robyn commented as she watched Sarah's boyfriend get bundled off the puck by Wes.

"He got injured in the last match, took a nasty fall," Bob replied.

"Henrik's good."

"He scored three last game."

"And Cole is…" Robyn started.

"The best player I've seen for a long time," Bob finished for her.

She was finding it hard to concentrate on Cole's speed and athleticism. She was distracted by the way he wiped at his lip with the sleeve of his shirt when play halted. It was cute the way he did that.

"Yeah, he's real good. He's a cut above the rest of them out there," Robyn said, watching Cole hone in on the goal and shoot the puck past the goaltender.

"What you gonna do?" Bob wanted to know.

"When's the next game?" Robyn asked.

"Saturday, at home — against Reading," Bob informed her.

"Shit, aren't they…"

"Top of the league, yepper," Bob answered with a nod.

With practice over, all that was left for Robyn to do was talk to her team.

"Listen, you all did well tonight, but we can do better. We need to find that camaraderie, you know, the team spirit. We may not be the best team in the league, but we're going to be the best unit. We're going to get to know each other inside and out. And we're going to practice more than you've ever practiced before," Robyn informed them.

There were audible grumbles.

"So, this is your new morale officer, Bob. He's going to be in charge of the tab when we go to Taboo on Friday night," Robyn announced.

This news was met with collective excitement, surprise, and happy faces.

"What is Taboo?" Henrik asked.

"Girls, Henrik, girls and poles," Mickey informed him.

"We're all going to bond over beer and burgers and..." Robyn began.

"Boobies!" Henrik announced with a high-pitched laugh.

"We?" Brad asked.

"Yes, Brad, we."

"You're coming to a strip club?" he clarified.

"I'm the manager, of course I'm coming. Now go and get changed and get out of here," Robyn ordered.

Most of the team skated off the ice and headed toward the locker rooms, glad the vigorous session was over.

"They worked hard tonight," Grant said to Robyn.

"I know, I told them."

"I'm just saying, don't be too hard on them."

"Are you trying to tell me how to manage the team, Grant?" Robyn asked. She set her expression to suggest it would be unwise to challenge her.

"I'm sure he wasn't trying to do that," Brad spoke quickly.

"No, of course not, I just..." Grant began.

"Grant, why don't we go get a drink, huh? Robyn, I'll meet you at the car," Bob said, putting his arm around the man and leading him off.

"You were a bit harsh with him. He hasn't had much luck himself these last few years," Brad said to Robyn, hopping off the ice and joining her.

"I'm not sure I want to know."

"After Jason went away, Francine died. Then a couple of years later, he lost his job at the factory, had to start over again, retrain. All he's got is the hockey team. Don't take it from him."

"Some people say you make your own luck," Robyn answered stiffly.

"He's a good guy," Brad reminded her.

"People used to say that about Jason," Robyn replied.

"Let's not talk about him,"

"Has he ever been back here...you know...since I left?" Robyn asked, swallowing the knot of emotion that had risen up.

"No," Brad answered. His words couldn't have been more definite.

Happy with the response, Robyn let out a breath of relief she hadn't realized she was holding in.

"You okay?" Brad appeared concerned.

"Yeah, I'm fine. Listen, thank you for arranging the new locks and the alarm for the roadhouse, I'll pay you back."

"It was no big deal. Was it all okay?" Brad asked.

"Yes, as long as I remember the code number. If I don't, it's going to set off some alarm at the Portage Marshals' office," Robyn replied with a grin.

"So, where did you find Cole?" Brad wanted to know.

"He kind of found me, halfway to terminal three in O' Hare. Isn't he great? He's so quick over the ice, and some of those goals he netted were unbelievable," Robyn said with a touch of pride.

"Yeah, he's good," Brad admitted reluctantly.

"We're so lucky to have a player of his caliber, I mean..." Robyn began.

"So, are you seeing him?" Brad asked briskly.

"Seeing him?" Robyn asked.

"Yeah, you know...dating him or whatever."

"No! I mean, I've only known him a couple of days. Why is everyone around here so concerned about my status?"

"I just wanted to know, that's all."

"You know I can't date anyone from the team. It would be highly unethical—I'm the manager now."

"Yeah, but we dated before."

"I wasn't the manager of the ice hockey team then, and anyway, we were just kids," Robyn said.

"We weren't kids."

"Well okay, young adults, teens, whatever the watchword is these days. It was just high school stuff," Robyn said, bending her feet outward and balancing on the edge of her sneakers.

"I wanted to ask you the other night, but you were tired, it was late, and you'd just got back and everything...I was just thinking maybe we could..." Brad began tentatively.

"God, is that the time? I'd better catch up with Bob," Robyn said, looking at her watch and backing away from him.

"I thought maybe we could have some dinner together some time," Brad suggested.

"No. I mean, no thanks. I'm not really into dinner these days. I'll see you," Robyn called.

She turned her back on him and rushed down the tunnel like she was trying to outrun a grizzly bear.

Chapter Ten

"Can we go? Like now," Robyn said, tugging at Bob's arm.

He and Grant were having a beer in the corridor, courtesy of one of the refreshment stands they'd taken the liberty of opening.

"Why the hurry? Grant and I were just reminiscing about the old days when we all used to play. Your dad was the best goaltender in the state," Bob reminded her.

"Yeah, I know. Heard all the stories at least a zillion times— can we go?" Robyn begged.

"Listen, Robyn, I hope you didn't think I was out of line earlier..." Grant started.

"No, of course not, and I really need you to carry on being my assistant. There are going to be training sessions I can't make if the roadhouse does as well as I'm hoping. Bob, I need to go," Robyn repeated.

"You need to find that Portage pace of life. Quit rushing around like you do in England," Bob insisted, taking a slow sip of his beer.

"No rush, I just want to get back and tell Auntie Pam all about it," Robyn said, looking down the corridor, concerned Brad was going to try and catch her up.

"Like she's ever had an interest in hockey," Bob replied.

"She has, she offered to make shirts once."

"Yeah, with rosettes on them," Bob reminded her.

"Gimme the car keys, then. I'll drive home and Grant can give you a lift," Robyn said, anxious to get going.

"What's got into you?" Bob wanted to know.

"Nothing. Oh, here comes Cole. Cole, can you give me a lift home? Uncle Bob seems to want to stay here drinking all night, reminiscing about the good old days," Robyn said as Cole came along the corridor.

"No one said anything about staying here all night," Bob retorted.

"Yeah, but I know how you talk. A good story takes like half a day to tell. Can you give me a ride?" Robyn asked Cole bluntly.

"I can do a bit better than that. I've got something for you," Cole replied.

"What?" Robyn asked.

"Come on, it's outside," he informed her with a smile.

"This better be good," Robyn said as they arrived in the parking lot.

"I think it's good. Here," Cole announced, gesturing to an old car in front of them.

"Oh my God! This is a Mustang, circa 1984," Robyn said, approaching it with excitement in every step.

"1985, actually," Cole answered.

He watched as Robyn went around the red car, fondly rubbing the rusty fender and looking inside the windows.

"This is a classic. I mean, some people hate the look of this compared to the first editions, but to me, it totally sums up the eighties," Robyn told him.

"I'm glad you think like that because…it's yours," Cole informed her. He'd said the last two words in a whisper she had barely heard.

"What?" Robyn questioned, turning around to look at him.

"I saw it in the Gen-All car park, for sale notice stuck on it. I knew you were looking for a car so…" Cole trailed off.

"You bought me a car," Robyn remarked, eyeing him with suspicion.

"Yeah, I know how that sounds. But it was a great price and it isn't a prologue to anything. If you don't want it, I'll…"

"I didn't say I didn't want it," Robyn said quickly.

"Try her out," Cole suggested and he threw Robyn the keys.

"Her?" Robyn asked, holding the keys and still admiring the car.

"I'm afraid so. One previous owner, a guy named Gerry who works in maintenance. She's called Leonora. First love, first wife — she died," Cole explained.

"God, you're kidding me, that's tragic. I don't know if I want a tragic car."

"Think of the history. I bet Gerry and Leonora had a whole pile of fun in her."

"I'm not sure I want to think about that, either," Robyn admitted.

"Are you going to get in?"

Robyn eagerly wrenched open the door and jumped into the driver's seat. She put the keys into the ignition and the engine roared to life.

"Will you listen to that!" she screamed excitedly.

The hum and rattle of the engine was like music to her ears. She revved it up, enjoying the sounds of 1980s manufacturing.

"She might need some TLC, especially on those rust patches, but..." Cole shouted over the engine.

"It'll be fun, and it will give me a chance to get Uncle Bob's welder out. I'm always looking for an excuse to get the welder out!" Robyn yelled back.

"So you think you might keep her?" Cole asked.

"We're going to be inseparable, me and you, aren't we?" Robyn said, patting the steering wheel affectionately.

Cole smiled as Robyn put her foot to the floor again. The other players arrived, appearing eager to find out what all the noise was about.

"Hey, a Mustang!" Mickey exclaimed, touching the curves and looking at it in appreciation.

"Actually, she's my Mustang," Robyn answered, taking her foot off the accelerator.

"What is Mustang?" Henrik asked, looking puzzled.

"Henrik, you have to be kidding me! It's an American classic. They must have American classics in your town in Austria," Brad replied, opening the door and jumping into the passenger seat.

"It's actually my American classic," Robyn said, wearing a smile from ear to ear.

"Where d'you get it?" Wes asked.

"Cole got it," Robyn announced.

"Yeah? What you trying to do? Buy your way into the team?" Brad questioned accusingly.

"Brad!" Robyn exclaimed.

"No, of course not. It was a steal of a price and I..." Cole began.

"You barely know her and you're buying her a car, that's weird man," Brad said, getting out of the car and squaring up to Cole.

"It was a good deal, Robyn needed a car..." Cole responded.

"You've known her what? A day?" Brad exploded.

"What has that got to do with anything?" Cole asked.

"What has it got to do with anything? I'll tell you, shall I? You don't know Robyn yet and we don't know jack shit about you. Who are you anyway?" Brad yelled. He was pointing at Cole, his finger shaking, his face contorted with anger.

"Brad! Have you gone crazy? Leave him alone," Robyn screamed, jumping out of the car and attempting to diffuse the situation.

"Hey, listen, this is just about finding a ride for someone. If that's out of line in this town, then I apologize," Cole replied, standing his ground.

"I don't trust him," Brad announced to everyone.

"What did you say?" Robyn asked, narrowing her eyes at Brad.

"I said I don't trust him. What do you know about him, Robyn? Nothing. And he's buying you a car!" Brad exclaimed, his eyes fixed on Cole.

"I know enough to know that I trust him," Robyn responded angrily.

Brad just continued to stare at Cole, his blue eyes cold and full of anger.

"And, just so we're clear, not that it's anybody's business, but I will be paying him back for the car. Just like I'll pay you back for the alarm system," Robyn retorted.

"Hey, everyone, come on, she is beautiful, isn't she?" Mickey interjected, trying to change the mood.

"Want to help me weld her up?" Robyn asked him.

"Sure, if Sarah lets me out. She's taken to dragging me past bridal boutiques on weekends lately," Mickey informed her with a sigh.

"Oh man, have you not given in yet? Give the poor girl a ring," Wade said with a laugh.

"She want to get married?" Henrik queried.

"I think so, Henrik. She talks about nothing else. Like, did I know that American Woman magazine states that any woman not married before thirty is considered one of life's rejects? Or did I know that all wedding gowns at Pollards are sixty percent off and, if she bought one now, did I think it would go out of fashion before we set a date."

"I am not listening," Robyn announced, clamping her hands down over her ears.

"Women aren't worth the bother man; no woman is worth the bother," Brad said, staring at Robyn and throwing his bag over his shoulder.

"Maybe that's why Michelle left you for the ugliest kid in school," Robyn blurted out before she could stop herself.

She bit down hard on her lips, instantly regretting the statement, but it was too late. She stood on the outside edge of her tennis shoes and tried not to meet his eyes.

She didn't need to look up to imagine his expression. He would look wounded and she had caused that by not keeping her mouth in check. Pam had told her he was still working through his troubles, and she'd said something stupid to hurt him just because she didn't want to go on a date with him.

She raised her head and met his eyes. It was like a light had gone out somewhere inside him.

"I'm out of here," he said, turning his back on the group and heading off across the parking lot.

Chapter Eleven

"Listen, I'm sorry if the car thing has caused a problem. I didn't mean anything by it. I just saw it, and I thought of your whole no car issue and…" Cole began.

Robyn was at the wheel of Leonora, driving Cole back to his house. She was enjoying every moment of the classic car's ride but was trying not to show too much delight in case he thought she was weird. She loved cars—all cars. Small, large, monster trucks, anything with four wheels and an engine she could tinker with. She had been helping her dad with cars since she was old enough to balance on the toolbox and get a wrench in the engine.

"There's nothing wrong with the car. I love her and I'm going to pay you back for her, every cent, no matter how much she cost. How much did she cost?" Robyn asked, glancing over at him.

"Five hundred dollars," Cole informed her.

"Wow! You officially got the deal of the century," Robyn squeaked.

"I know," Cole replied.

"It wasn't you buying the car that made Brad flip out, not really. He asked me out to dinner and I said no. Well, I said something stupid like I don't really do dinners and then ran away from him. I think that pissed him off, seeing as he bought me an expensive alarm system. What is it with guy's buying me stuff today? Not that I'm complaining," Robyn informed him quickly.

"I can understand it in a way. I mean, I've only just come onto the team, it could have looked like I was trying to buy my place," Cole admitted.

"Or trying to hit on me," Robyn spoke without thinking.

He glanced over at her and she met his eyes. She had to turn away because her chest was tightening.

"I wasn't trying to hit on you," he said.

"I know. You're so not over the whole brother stealing your girlfriend thing," Robyn replied.

"Believe me, I am."

"I don't believe you. If you were, you'd be trying to hit on me," Robyn said, stealing another look at him.

"So, why no dinner with Brad? I mean, he seemed cool, before the whole going all redneck on me," Cole said, changing the subject.

"I've only just got here, I've barely had time to indulge myself in dill pickles and monster trucks, let alone think about dating. It didn't seem right. So, do I take a right here?" Robyn asked.

"No, keep going. What didn't seem right? Going on a date? Or going on a date with Brad?" Cole inquired.

"You never asked this many questions on the plane."

"I couldn't get a word in. And you haven't answered me."

Robyn let out a sigh. He was making her feel vulnerable. She needed to speak, but she didn't know what to say. If she actually thought long enough, she would do her usual nervous trick of reciting notable events from the Portage Panthers' history books. She didn't want to do that.

"There's something in my life I'm not quite over yet. I don't do dating in the normal sense right now," Robyn said quickly as if forcing the words out as fast as she could would make it sound better.

She closed her eyes and took a breath.

"In the normal sense?" Cole asked.

"Yeah, you know, hand-holding, going to the movies, sharing a sofa in front of re-runs of The Gilmore Girls," Robyn told him stiffly.

"Okay, got it," Cole answered with a nod.

Robyn swallowed and chanced a glance at him. His hair was still wet from the shower and he smelt of something fresh and oriental. He glanced over at her and she jerked her head back.

"So, how did you find the team? I mean, I know they're not exactly the Wolves but..."

"I enjoyed tonight and Henrik's awesome. He could play at a much higher level."

"Please don't tell him that. I don't want you both getting poached before I've even had one game in charge," Robyn said.

"I wouldn't do that—here it is, just on the left," Cole said, indicating to a house.

"This house? You live on this street?" Robyn said, sounding shocked as she pulled over to the side of the road.

"You can pull into the drive, if you like," Cole offered.

"You mean the drive that's almost as big as the road," Robyn commented.

"That's the one."

"I can't believe you live here. This house is huge, and you must back right up to the lake," Robyn exclaimed, staring up at the beautiful white wood house in front of them.

"I've also got a Jacuzzi, a boat, and a refrigerator that talks to me," Cole informed her.

"The rent on this must be extortionate. I know how much these places cost to buy, Sarah sold one for a million once. She rang me up twice to tell me."

"Do you want to come in? Have a conversation with my kitchen appliances?" Cole offered.

"No, thanks. I'd better get back; I've got an eight a.m. delivery at the roadhouse. How many bedrooms?" Robyn asked, still looking at the property in awe.

"Four."

"Wow! They must think highly of you at Gen-All."

"I guess they must," Cole agreed.

"Right, well, I'd better go. Thank you so much for Leonora. I'll pay you back and I'm gonna take the best care of her," Robyn said as Cole got out of the car.

"I know you are."

"So, shall I see you for lunch tomorrow? About one? Theo & Stacey's?" Robyn suggested.

"Yeah, sure, why not," he agreed with a smile.

"Not that it's a date or anything, because you know, I don't do dates," Robyn clarified.

"Sure."

"Okay then, I'll see you...go talk to your fridge," Robyn called.

"Goodnight," Cole said, waving a hand.

"Hello!" Robyn called as she entered the house, jingling the car keys in the air.

She was excited to tell Pam about Leonora. The car was her own piece of American automobile history, and she loved it. She couldn't wait to buy a motor manual on her and read it cover to cover.

"Oh, hi, honey, how was the training?" Pam asked, fidgeting and not meeting her eyes.

Something wasn't right. Pam looked flustered and she was wearing rubber gloves. She did love to clean but not usually at night.

"Not too bad, they're a bit rough around the edges, but I can iron them out. Is Bob back yet? Did he tell you about my car?" Robyn asked, shaking the keys even harder.

"Yes, he did. Wow, that's great," Pam said unenthusiastically.

"It's so cool, come and see it."

"I will, honey, in a while. I'm just in the middle of something," Pam said, pausing at the sink and wringing out a cloth.

"What are you doing?" Robyn asked.

"Just cleaning up."

"Cleaning up what? Where's Bob?" Robyn wanted to know.

"He's, er, in the garage," Pam said quickly.

"No he's not, I parked Leonora in there. Why can I hear scrubbing?" Robyn asked her.

"Oh, it's nothing, honey. Why don't you make us all a pot of coffee?" Pam suggested.

"It's coming from my room," Robyn said, moving toward the sound.

"Robyn, don't go in there. Bob's fixing it. Robyn..." Pam began, hurrying down the hallway after her.

Robyn entered her bedroom to find Bob fiercely rubbing at the wall of the room with a hard-bristled brush. On one wall, the words "Jason loves Robyn" were daubed in three foot high red letters.

"Robyn, I don't know what's gotten into them. This isn't like them at all. I am so sorry. Bob is going to get this off the wall even if we have to buy every product Meijer has to offer, or even redecorate. We could do with redecorating anyway and wallpaper is twenty percent off right now," Pam babbled.

"It's okay," Robyn replied, swallowing a lump in her throat.

"No, it isn't okay, Robyn. Their privileges have been taken away for a month; it's no TV in their room, no candy, and no weekend trips. And they are going to apologize to you," Bob told her as he continued to scrub.

"And we're going to go to the school and see the principal. We're going to get to the bottom of who's been filling their head with all this stuff," Pam added.

"I'm just going to go. It's too much having me here. I should have realized that when you offered," Robyn said, picking up her backpack and scanning the room for her things.

"No, honey! Don't do that! We want you to stay," Pam insisted.

"I know you do, but I'll be fine. It can't be easy for the twins having someone else sharing their space, especially a strange cousin from England who everyone still thinks is a witch," Robyn added with half a smile.

"Robyn, this is as much your home as theirs, I hope you know that," Bob told her.

"Thank you for saying that, but it isn't, not really, not now. I'm going to go, it's just easier for everyone," Robyn replied, putting her baseball cap into her bag.

"Robyn, please don't. Tell her Bob, tell her she can't go," Pam blubbered, tears forming in her eyes.

"Robyn, we don't want you to go. I'm going to speak to those two monsters I've raised and…" Bob began.

"You don't have to do that. Honestly, it's fine," Robyn insisted.

The situation was just too awkward and she needed to get out of it. She was used to standing on her own two feet…well, to a certain extent. How hard could it be?

"But where will you go?" Pam asked, wiping at her eyes.

"I'll stay with Sarah," Robyn said confidently.

"But her place is really small, and the last time I went, there was a motorcycle in the spare room," Pam informed her.

"It'll be fine, I'll be fine," Robyn assured her, hoisting her backpack onto her back and picking up her case.

"I don't want you to go, this isn't right. Bob, this isn't right. Make her stay, at least until the morning. Stay until the morning, honey," Pam said, shaking her head and dabbing at her eyes.

"I'll give you a call tomorrow, and Bob, I'll speak to you about arrangements for our night out on Friday," Robyn said, backing out of the room.

"Er, yeah, sure, Friday," Bob replied, not daring to look at Pam.

"See you!" Robyn called as cheerily as she could as she headed out toward the garage.

She closed the door behind her, threw her luggage into Leonora, and let out a heavy sigh. Who was she trying to kid? She couldn't stay with Sarah and Mickey, not after her friend had poured her heart out over lunch and what she had heard Mickey say at training. It would be like living in a melting pot of tension the whole time and that was the last thing she needed at the moment.

She could go to her dad's, but that would mean confronting Nancy, and she wasn't sure the woman would welcome her with open arms after what had gone on at the roadhouse. In fact, she would probably get the door slammed in her face while being subjected to quite a few well-chosen words, most of them beginning with the letter "F".

Brad's was out of the question because of his whole asking her on a date moment and the fuss he had made about Leonora. Apart from a hotel, there was only one other place she could go.

She started the car.

The photo album had been on the top of his case. His mother must have slipped it in because he sure as Hell wouldn't have packed it. Everything was still too raw. But he'd taken it out, he didn't know why, and now it was on the coffee table. He put the bottle of beer to his mouth and took a swig of the liquid inside. Why was life so difficult? Or was it? Maybe it was just his life, or maybe not his life, maybe it was just him. The hockey team had made a judgment. Like his team at Gen-All, they had all stared and looked him up and down and made a decision about him. First impressions, taking things at face value, that's what people did. And they all had such high expectations—impossibly high expectations. Well, he had to be good enough or else what was the point? If he didn't matter, if he couldn't achieve what he wanted to achieve, he may as well drink himself stupid and find a wall to drive into. He opened the drawer of the sideboard and threw the album inside.

"Look, I know this is really weird and you probably think I'm a crazy stalker or something, but I can't stay at my aunt's any more. The Devil children did something really crazy and it freaked me out. And if I have to look at them across the dining table one more time, I'll want to grab them by the pigtails and string them up from the ceiling fan. See, you can tell I've really thought about it. And I can't go to Sarah's, her and Mickey are having a silent domestic. He's a commitment phobe and her biological clock is ticking. And if I turn up at my dad's, I think Nancy might just punch me out. I've phoned the two hotels in town, the posh one that's apparently full because of a Jehovah's Witnesses conference and the seedy one run by Psycho Mike-o and he only has his basic room left. I've seen those rooms and, believe me, if he calls his last available room basic, it means it probably doesn't have its own bathroom and I'd be sharing with a family of cockroaches. So, I'm asking—no—I'm begging you to let me stay in one of those four bedrooms. Not the one with the best view or anything, well a lake view would be nice, but it isn't a deal breaker. I just really need somewhere to stay. Please?" Robyn gabbled when Cole had opened the front door.

He looked at her in amusement, a smile on his lips.

"Why are you looking at me like that? I've begged haven't I? My next plan of action is to ask for a duvet so I can get some sleep in Leonora," Robyn said.

"Come in," Cole invited, taking her case from her hands.

"I can stay? You don't think I'm a stalker?" Robyn asked in relief.

"I don't think you're a stalker, you can stay. I got you the car to drive, not to live in," Cole told her.

"I'll pay rent or do the housework or something. I have money. Vacuuming. I can vacuum at least twice a week like your mom wanted," Robyn suggested.

"We'll work something out. Do you want a coffee?" Cole offered.

Robyn dropped her bag on the floor and pulled him toward her, kissing him hungrily on the mouth. She felt him kiss her back, more intently than he had at the airport. She backed him up against the wall. Her mouth didn't leave his for a second. She didn't want to stop. She wanted to hold on to this feeling, this indescribable urge she had to get intimate with him every time they were together.

His lips were so smooth, yet the way he used them to kiss her was firm and suggestive. His hands touched her skin at the waistband of her jeans and it was like she'd been scorched. A warm, unrecognizable sensation shot up her spine, and she shivered.

Then he ended it. He pulled his mouth away from hers to take a breath. He looked at her, his dark eyes questioning. He didn't know what was going on between them and neither did she.

"This isn't a date," Robyn said quickly, enjoying the way his arms felt circled around her waist.

"I know...you don't do dates," he answered, still looking deep into her eyes.

"Have you got any beer?" she asked.

Chapter Twelve

He ran his finger over his lips as he lay in bed. She'd kissed him again last night and he'd kissed her back. He'd held her close to him and he'd felt her quake. She was holding on to something, he could tell. She put on this brave front, talked her way out of situations, but inside she was vulnerable. Just like him. The job and his project was the only thing holding him together sometimes. What was holding Robyn together?

He'd given her the best room. She had a panoramic view of West Lake and all its natural Michigan beauty. When she'd woken up the next morning and drawn back the curtains, the scenery had stunned her. The sun was already up and the lake was still and calm. Like a mirror, it reflected every tree standing along the banks. The sky was a cornflower blue and there wasn't a cloud in sight.

She was still suffering from the time difference, but this morning, opening her eyes to the fantastic garden, the boats moored around the edge of the water and the lake itself, everything seemed a little bit better. Today was a good weather day. The sun was shining and there was little wind, and in Portage, that meant getting intimate with the barbecue.

She was already outside on the deck, a pair of tongs in her hand, and the lid of the grill open, when Cole appeared.

"Morning! Bratwurst?" she greeted, waving a sausage in the air.

"Man, it's not even seven yet. How long have you been up?" Cole asked, joining her at the barbecue.

"I don't know, about five-thirty. The sun was up, I went for a walk around the lake, came back, put a load of washing on — it's in the dryer now, by the way, if you're looking for something — then I thought I'd cook breakfast. Well, I was going to do eggs, but you're all out," Robyn informed him, turning the sausages over.

"I'll pick some up today," he answered.

"Oh no, don't worry, there's some other stuff we need. I'll go to Meijer's later, use Pam's discount. No point having family working at a store if you don't take advantage of their discount card," Robyn said.

"Listen, Robyn, you don't have to do this. Doing my laundry and cooking me breakfast. I said you can stay, I don't expect anything in return. And I mean anything in return," Cole assured her.

"You're talking about the kiss, aren't you? That wasn't a down payment on the room. What sort of girl do you think I am?" Robyn asked, trying to avoid looking at him.

Last night's kiss had been even better than the kiss at the airport. She'd wanted more, she'd wanted him more. She'd wanted something to stop her thinking, just for a few moments. Something to wipe away the sick graffiti the twins had painted and what it meant. What better distraction than getting a little intimate with her crush?

"That wasn't what I meant. I just..." Cole began.

"You need help with your grocery choices, that's all. You don't even have any crisps in the cupboard. I mean chips, you know, deep-fried sliced potatoes with salt. They come in large bags that are never quite big enough to share. Every house should always have chips in the cupboard, if only for emergencies. They're a comfort food, a basic necessity. And there were no gherkins, you know, dill pickles," Robyn told him.

"I've only been here two days and I didn't know I was going to be having a house guest. I just bought the essentials...you know, bread and milk, pasta and fruit," Cole said.

"That's a staple diet for someone who always does what their mother tells them. You want two or three?" Robyn asked as she began putting sausages on a plate.

"No more than two! I can't believe you're barbecuing for breakfast," Cole remarked.

"You need to get into the Michigan ways. It's always time for a barbecue around here," Robyn told him as she brought the plates over to the table.

"So it seems. So what are your plans for today? Still want to meet for lunch?" Cole asked.

"Delivery at eight at the roadhouse, visiting Dad, overseeing the decorating. Don't you want to meet for lunch? I mean, I guess it might get too much seeing each other all the time if we're living together...I mean, sharing a house. And people might get the wrong idea," Robyn remarked, trying not to focus on his lips.

"We wouldn't want them to think we were dating," Cole said, looking up at her.

"No, we wouldn't," she agreed with a stiff nod.

"We could always skip lunch and go to the supermarket — do the shopping together," Cole suggested.

"You really want to shop with me, don't you! You're worried I'm going to stock your ridiculously large, talking refrigerator with goodies," Robyn said, laughing.

"Maybe a little," Cole admitted, smiling back at her.

"Well, I promise it's only my Aunt Pam who has a whole drawer dedicated to ice cream. But then again, she has taught me quite a lot. I can use a slow cooker, don't you know."

"Now you really are scaring me."

Robyn picked a sausage up with her fingers and headed toward the backdoor.

"I've got to go. I told Milo he had to be in by seven-thirty to let the decorators in," Robyn said, waving her hand at him.

"Hey! What time at the supermarket?" Cole called after her.

"I can tell you're getting excited about this."

"Just want to know what a girl like you likes to eat."

"Anything and everything, with everything on it—usually with a dozen sides," Robyn replied.

"Okay. Got that."

"One, outside Meijer's on Westnedge," Robyn said, turning her back on him and retreating into the house.

"Fine."

"But it's not a date," Robyn called back as she disappeared.

"Morning, Milo, you're late. I'll overlook it this once. Okay, here's your uniform. Let's put it on, see what it looks like," Robyn said, throwing him a plastic wrapped parcel.

"What...now...here?" Milo exclaimed, looking like a terrified little boy.

"Are you kidding me? No, definitely not here! Out the back! Come and show me when you have it on and not before," Robyn ordered.

"Sure thing," Milo replied, taking the package and heading behind the bar.

There was a sudden banging and thumping on the door, and Robyn hurried to open it, excited about the start of the decorating. She had chosen cream for the top half of the walls and a deep plum for the bottom half with a chair rail separating the two. She wanted traditional, comfortable, and classic, something that wouldn't date too much.

She opened the door expecting to see Martin from Decor with his painting equipment. Instead, she was face-to-face with Nancy.

Nancy was wearing a fluorescent pink, velour tracksuit. Her hair was piled high on her head and she had thick gold hooped earrings hanging from her ears. She was trailer trash personified.

"Oh," Robyn stated, unable to hide her disappointment.

"An early riser, I see. What you doing?" Nancy asked, trying to look past Robyn into the bar.

"Nothing you need to concern yourself with. What d'you want?"

"This is for you," Nancy said, thrusting a large box at her.

"What is it?"

"Old stuff of yours from the house. Haynes motor manuals for about a dozen cars your dad tells me he's never owned, vintage boy's toys, little dinky cars, a prom dress that's seen better days and, surprisingly, no dolls. I need the space. I've got someone moving in to help with the bills. There's invoices in there for this place—they need paying," Nancy informed her.

"Who's moving in?" Robyn wanted to know.

"That's no concern of yours. Your dad knows all about it."

"Does he?" Robyn asked, unconvinced.

"Yes, he does, ask him. Listen, you've taken this place, I'm not going to let you muscle your way into the house, too," Nancy snarled.

"It's Dad's house, not yours," Robyn stated.

"I'm his fiancée," Nancy snapped back.

"We'll see about that," Robyn said, fixing Nancy with a stare.

"Whatever, sugar. Me and your dad, we have history," Nancy answered.

"Funny enough, so do we—like twenty-five years."

"Couple of flowery letters in there too, from Brad. Amused me all morning," Nancy replied.

"Are we done?" Robyn asked.

"We're done."

Robyn dropped the box on the floor and slammed the door closed. She leaned against it and closed her eyes. Nancy was a hassle she could do without. She'd been away too long. She should have been around to make sure her dad didn't do stupid things like hitch himself to a gold-digger.

When she opened her eyes, Milo stood in the middle of the room dressed in his black trousers and new burgundy t-shirt that read "Eddie's Roadhouse" on the front.

"Ooo, you look cute! In a very masculine and cool way…that goes without saying. Turn around, turn around," Robyn encouraged excitedly.

Milo turned his back to her, and Robyn clapped her hands together as she read "Eddie's Roadhouse, Shaver Road, Portage, MI—Come here for beer and cheer."

"I love it! Don't you love it, Milo? It's great!" Robyn said.

"I'm not sure about the color," Milo replied stiffly.

"The color's perfect. It's the same color as the bottom half of the walls are going to be and the new sign," Robyn told him.

"When are you planning to re-open?" Milo asked.

"Next Friday," Robyn informed him.

"Next Friday!"

"Is that panic in your voice, Milo? I hope it isn't panic, because I need all the help I can get, and what I don't need is panic. In fact, panic is not even a word I want mentioned at all in this bar. I have a chef coming today, someone I'm trying to poach from another roadhouse. I have old Ada making new covers for the seats, interviews for staff, and I'll have menus and flyers printed by the end of the week," Robyn stated, writing things down on her list.

"What about plates and knives and forks and stuff?" Milo asked.

"Shit! Good, Milo, you're right. We need something for people to eat with. See, this is why you're my head bartender. Right, I need to source some plates and things. I wonder if we should have them personalized. What do you think?" Robyn asked him.

"I think I'm not sure burgundy's really my color," Milo replied, staring down at his t-shirt.

Chapter Thirteen

"Okay, don't get up. I'm here with grapes. Hands up, who wants some?" Robyn announced as she entered Eddie's hospital room and waved a bag of fruit in the air.

"Are they the ones dipped in chocolate?" Max asked, propping himself up and looking eager.

"What do you think?" Robyn asked, staring back at the wrinkled old man.

"Eddie! This can't be your daughter. She's bringing in healthy stuff," Max called across the room.

Then he gasped and started having a bout of coughing. His whole body contorted, and it sounded as if he was about to heave up all of his internal organs.

"Morning, Dad," Robyn greeted, grabbing a chair and pulling it up alongside Eddie's bed.

He was wearing glasses and seemed to be studying the local paper. He didn't move the paper or respond to her, he just carried on reading as if she wasn't there. She poked him hard in the leg with her forefinger, and he didn't even flinch.

"Nurse says you had oatmeal for breakfast," Robyn commented.

Still no reply was forthcoming.

"Hey! Hello! I'm here! Come to see you! Brought grapes, which I think are the closest thing to sweets you can get. Put the paper down!" Robyn ordered, taking it from him.

"I hear you drive a Mustang these days and have a boyfriend already. Someone called Cole," Eddie remarked, taking off his glasses and fixing her with a disapproving stare.

"You've seen Brad this morning. How was he? Has he stopped behaving like a complete jerk?" Robyn asked, stuffing a handful of grapes into her mouth.

"Who is this guy you're with? Brad thinks he's shifty," Eddie continued.

"Christ, Dad! I don't have a guy. He's a friend, that's all. And Brad behaved like an ass last night, squaring up to people. Cole played for the Wolves, Dad, the Wolves! I have an ex-Wolves player playing for the Panthers. Isn't that the best thing you've ever heard?" Robyn asked, hoping the namedropping would earn her some favor.

"Brad's been with us a long time and he's been good to me," Eddie said gruffly.

"What's that supposed to mean? I have to put up with him being an idiot?"

"He's had things tough."

"He's not the only one," Robyn stated under her breath.

"Why didn't you want to go to dinner with him?" Eddie questioned.

"Jeez! Did he come in here and pour his heart out or something? What have you turned into, Dad? Some sort of agony aunt?" Robyn exclaimed, poking in more grapes.

"He likes you, Robyn, he's always liked you. He's a good guy," Eddie stated.

"I am going to speak to the doctor about your medication. It's changing you, turning you into someone else. We are not having a conversation like this. Next you'll be wanting to talk about your feelings," Robyn said.

"Nancy tells me you've taken over the roadhouse," Eddie continued.

"Yes."

"Good. She isn't the most organized of women, but her heart's in the right place. She's got someone moving in to the house to help pay the bills."

"What is it you see in that woman? I've seen more meat on a kebab and the attitude—well!"

"I thought you didn't want to talk about feelings. Tell me about the team. How do they look?"

"A lot better now Cole's playing. Henrik's pretty amazing too," Robyn said excitedly.

"That boy can move like no one I've ever seen before," Eddie replied a smile crossing his face.

"They play Reading this weekend," she reminded him.

"It's going to be a hard game. They're a good team, very tactical," Eddie told her.

"Have you seen them play this year?"

"Yeah, it wasn't pretty. What's your line up going to be?" Eddie wanted to know.

"I haven't finalized anything yet."

"Well, maybe we could look at it together," he said with a sniff.

"You're supposed to be resting, not getting excited over ice hockey. I can manage," Robyn insisted.

"Listen, I had oatmeal for breakfast and some awful shit with asparagus last night. I need something to focus on," Eddie informed her.

"Not one gram of trans-fatty acids has passed his lips," Max piped up loudly.

"I don't believe that for a second. You're obviously just getting better at stashing it," Robyn answered.

"Robyn, that hurts me," Eddie said.

"Hmm, well, we'll see. Robyn made a beeline for the closet next to Max's bed.

"Did you know I can sniff out trans-fatty acids from fifty yards?" Robyn asked Max.

"Yeah? So what?" Max said, screwing up his face and crossing his arms in front of his chest.

"So I think you and Dad might just be storing up some goodies nearby, like—in here!" Robyn announced as she pulled open the door.

Out fell family-sized pack after family-sized pack of chips, followed by enough Hershey's chocolate bars to restock a large store.

"None of that has anything to do with me," Eddie spluttered immediately.

"This is unbelievable! Oatmeal and something disgusting with asparagus and, all the while, you're topping it with chips and chocolate! I knew it was too good to be true!" Robyn blasted, pulling out the contraband and piling it on Max's bed.

"Stop it! If the nurse comes in, she'll take it all away! You have to let a dying man have a few simple pleasures," Max croaked, leaning forward and trying to get his hands on the treats.

"You're not dying," Robyn announced crossly.

"We're all dying, gal," Max answered with a throaty cough.

"But not all from cholesterol overload. These are coming with me, and if you get more, I'll tell the first nurse I see that you both want a sponge bath," Robyn informed them.

"She's evil, your daughter, Eddie, pure evil," Max yelled.

Chapter Fourteen

He'd spent all morning looking forward to a shopping trip. He liked his food as much as the next guy but shopping for it? He knew the anticipation wasn't the idea of cruising down a few aisles, it was Robyn. What was her story? He really wanted to know. He wanted to get to know her. So, she didn't do dates. Neither did he right now. He'd slept with three women in two months just to prove he could, just to take away the humiliation of the whole damn episode. It hadn't been good, it wasn't his style, and he didn't want to do it again. But Robyn was different. He'd only known her a few days, but there was something almost familiar about her.

His phone bleeped and he took off his eye protectors. He looked at the screen and his face began to heat up. Veronica. What the Hell could she have to say to him?

"What flavor chips? And we have to have some dips? Which dips? Ranch? Cheese and chive?" Robyn asked as she stopped the cart opposite a shelf at Meijer's that afternoon.

"You choose," Cole suggested, looking at his mobile phone and starting to type.

"Well, ranch is my favorite, so we'll have ranch. Oh, let's take one of each of these because, to be honest, I can probably get through a bag a day on my own. But then again, I have just confiscated at least ten bags from Max and my dad, so maybe we don't need more. You should have seen their faces!" Robyn exclaimed with a laugh as she remembered the frosty looks and the arms folded across their chests.

"Yep," Cole replied, not looking up.

"What you doing? You thought shopping was going to be the highlight of your week this morning, now you're barely showing any interest. Who you texting?" Robyn asked, attempting to look at the screen of his phone.

"Veronica," Cole replied.

"Veronica?"

"Yeah."

"And Veronica is? Your sister? A friend? A cool girl from back home?" Robyn asked.

"My ex."

"Your ex."

"Yeah, the one who went off with my brother," Cole informed her.

"And you're texting her, why?" Robyn asked, intrigued.

"She texted me, I'm texting her back."

"Okay, are we going to start talking in riddles to each other because I'm good with that. My first is in RAT but not in CAT," Robyn answered.

"She wanted to meet up, to talk," Cole said.

"To explain why she was doing the dirty with your brother? That would have been good to hear. Cole, I thought it was you, you look so similar...we weren't really kissing...I just slipped and his tongue just fell into my mouth, it could have happened to anyone."

"Okay, we're done. Let's finish shopping," Cole replied, putting his phone back in the pocket of his jeans.

"Finish shopping? We've barely started!"

"The cart's full of junk food," Cole remarked.

"Shame on you! Dill pickles are not junk food. They are one of the staple ingredients of the all-American diet, and blueberry muffins have blueberries in them, that's fruit. And they really sort out your insides," Robyn replied.

Cole laughed.

"So, what did you say?" Robyn asked, setting off again with the cart.

"What?"

"To Veronica."

"I told her I didn't want to talk and I didn't want her contacting me again," Cole replied.

"Nice work—oh dear, doesn't sound like that idea worked for her," Robyn said as Cole's phone announced the arrival of a new text.

"Pasta," Cole said, grabbing a package from the shelf and putting it in the cart.

"You have pasta at home. Do you go through a bag a week or something? Well?"

"Well what?"

"Aren't you going to see what it says?" Robyn asked.

"No."

"No?"

"I don't care what it says. There's nothing she can say that would make me want to speak to her again, okay?" Cole snapped.

"Man, she hurt you bad," Robyn remarked.

"Can we just shop?"

"Sure, of course, it's none of my business," Robyn said, pushing on with the cart.

"Listen, I wasn't being an ass, it's just..." Cole began, hurrying after her.

"It's fine, I shouldn't have asked. I know I talk too much and, seeing as we're sharing a house, you have my permission to tell me to shut up when it gets to be too much."

"Robyn, I didn't mean…"

"Now, onto my favorite aisle—ice cream," she announced, a look of delight crossing her face.

"You told me it was only your aunt who had a drawer dedicated to ice cream."

"I did, didn't I? But you have a fridge that talks to you! In fact, it suggested to me only this morning that it was severely lacking in the whole ice cream department and begged to be restocked," Robyn said, opening a freezer door.

"Did it really?"

"Didn't you hear it? Didn't it wake you up with its constant muttering, I need chocolate toffee and mint chocolate chip."

"No, someone cooking on the barbecue, singing 'Sweet Home Alabama' woke me up," Cole informed her.

"I don't sing."

"Pinocchio, your nose will grow!"

"Was it really bad and out of tune?"

"The birds had their wings over their ears."

"That is so mean! And birds don't have ears, do they?" Robyn asked, piling more tubs into the cart.

"Stop! You're crazy!" Cole exclaimed as he attempted to halt her.

Robyn hoofed another half dozen tubs into the cart and set off down the aisle as quickly as she could. This was more fun than she remembered. She jumped onto the cart and let it glide down the aisle toward the cereal section. She jumped off and was about to turn down into the next row, when the sight of something stopped her in her tracks.

Just up ahead was a man, six foot tall, wearing a green baseball cap, a gray t-shirt, and faded blue jeans. Just peeking out under the cap was a shock of ginger hair.

Robyn felt the breath catch in her throat as she watched him put a packet of Cheerios into the basket on his arm. The way he moved, his gangly, awkward appearance and the red hair—she knew instinctively who it was. She felt the realization wash over her.

Her heart was hammering so hard in her chest it hurt. She backed away, frantically dragging the cart with her. She didn't want to see his face. She couldn't bear to see his face.

She pulled the cart hard, didn't see Cole, and collided with him.

"Whoa! You okay?" he asked, steadying her as she threatened to fall into the display of half-price liquid hand soap.

"I have to go," Robyn stated, perspiring and wringing her hands together.

"Go? Go where?" Cole asked, his head tilted as he took in her anxious expression.

"I just have to go. I'm sorry," Robyn said, backing away from him and abandoning the cart.

"Robyn? What's happened? Come on, look, don't go, I'll pay more attention. Hey, I love ice cream, I could eat it for every meal, talk to me," Cole urged, taking hold of her arm.

"No, let go," Robyn ordered, and she wrenched her arm free and began sprinting down the aisle toward the exit.

Tears were welling up in her eyes, and she needed to get out of the store before she came face-to-face with him.

What was he doing here? People said he wasn't around. He shouldn't be here, not now—not ever.

Chapter Fifteen

Robyn ditched Leonora outside the front of Gold Realty and rushed into the office, still sweating and breathing like she was about to have a heart attack.

"Good morning, ma'am. How can I help you today?" a middle-aged woman with gold-rimmed glasses questioned, beaming at Robyn with a pearly white smile.

"I need to see Sarah Gorski please," Robyn announced nervously.

She felt sick and faint and she couldn't catch her breath. She could see his face in her mind's eye. The freckled complexion and the crooked smile.

"Are you looking to buy or to sell?" the woman asked, picking up a pen and preparing to write on a clipboard.

"What?" Robyn asked, looking at the woman and trying to concentrate on what she was saying.

"What sort of property are you looking for?"

"I'm not looking for a property. Could you tell her Robyn Matthers needs to see her?"

She was feeling really sick now. It was like seeing him had turned her insides out. Her stomach felt heavy and twisted. She could smell him; the memory of it was almost forcing her to retch.

"Take a seat. Would you like some coffee?" the woman offered.

"No, no thanks," Robyn replied, thankful to have the opportunity to sit down before she fell down.

It was all so long ago, but sometimes it felt like it had happened yesterday. The fear hadn't lessened, the memories hadn't dulled, and the pain still felt raw. Whatever she told people about it being forgotten was a lie. She hadn't forgotten a thing. Everything was etched on her like an internal tattoo.

"Robyn? Is everything okay?" Sarah asked as she appeared in the reception area.

Her glasses were perched on her nose, her portfolio was in her hand, and she was looking like the efficient professional she obviously was. Robyn, for some reason, felt worse. She was the girl who liked to get covered in oil, the childish one, the girl whose parents should never have got together in the first place. Sarah was an adult, and Robyn knew she was one tug away from unraveling again.

"Have you got like ten minutes?" Robyn asked awkwardly, still wringing her hands together.

"Sure. What is it? You don't look too good. Are you okay?"

"Sit in Leonora?" Robyn suggested.

"Leonora?" Sarah asked.

"Come on," Robyn urged, pulling her friend by the arm.

She led her outside and opened up the door of the Mustang. Sarah got in and Robyn joined her, instinctively locking the door.

"What's happened? Is it your dad? Oh Robyn, has he had another heart attack?" Sarah asked, concerned.

"I saw Jason," Robyn blurted out, looking at her friend with wide, tear-filled eyes.

"What?" Sarah exclaimed in horror.

"He was right there, in Meijer's, right in front of me," Robyn said, her voice cracking and tears spilling from her eyes.

"No, Robyn, he couldn't have been. He hasn't been back here, not since...not since everything happened," Sarah assured her.

"I know it was him," Robyn stated, wiping at her eyes with her fingers and trying to stabilize her breathing.

"Are you sure? I mean, you haven't seen him for years. I haven't seen him for years. No one I know has seen him for years, except Grant. Anyway, Grant flies to Mississippi to see him, that's where he lives now," Sarah explained.

"It may be where he lives, but it isn't where he is! He's on Westnedge, in the freaking supermarket!" Robyn announced hysterically.

"Okay, well let's think about this logically. Why would he be here now? I mean, he's been gone nine years, why would he come back now? I mean, there's nothing here for him, no job, no friends. Okay, there's his dad, but their relationship is as up and down as the housing market. And nobody in this town wants him here. What's he got to come back for?" Sarah asked her.

"Do I have to spell it out for you? He's back because I'm back! Grant probably told him I was back, and he's come here to make me live the whole thing all over again!" Robyn shrieked.

"But what has he got to gain from doing that?"

"What's he got to lose? I can't be here with him here. I can't be in the same town as him, the same state as him. I don't even want to be in the same country as him—that was the whole point of leaving," Robyn began, struggling to maintain control of her emotions.

"Listen to me, Rob, it won't have been Jason. It can't have been Jason. You saw Grant last night at hockey practice, didn't you? If he was here, he would have told you, you know he would. He wouldn't be stupid enough not to tell you," Sarah reassured her, taking hold of her friend's hands.

"You think I'm crazy, don't you? You think I'm seeing things because of what the twins did," Robyn said with a shake of her head.

"The twins? What have they got to do with anything?"

"They're ghoulish little freaks I can't believe are related to me! Painting things on walls and whispering to each other, looking at me with those black, soulless eyes. They wrote Jason loves Robyn on my bedroom wall and it made me feel sick. I couldn't stay a second longer, I couldn't bear to see them sniggering across the breakfast table. Pam and Bob couldn't have been sorrier, but those brats rule that house and they're out of control."

"You left?"

"Yep, ran away to a million dollar house on the lake."

"What?"

"Brad hates Cole, Cole probably hates Brad, and they're supposed to be gelling as a team. At least they both seem to like Henrik, although none of us know what nationality he is. Dad's started a Hershey's chocolate diet, and he's in cahoots with Max who must have a porter in his employ to be able to smuggle that amount of crap in without detection. Milo hates the new uniform and I'm scared he's going to grow a beard, and I haven't managed to order any plates for my customers to eat off of when I reopen the roadhouse next week. I should phone Clive, but I can't bring myself to because I know, deep down, that how I've been living my life isn't right. And Cole, well he doesn't like ice cream quite as much as I do, although he lied and said he did to make me feel better, and I left him, at the supermarket, with a cart full of food," Robyn blurted out.

"I think you're going to have to explain because I didn't understand any of that," Sarah admitted, looking at her friend with concern.

"I don't know what to do," Robyn said, sighing heavily.

"Maybe you should go back and see the counselor," Sarah suggested.

"You still don't believe me. You don't believe I saw him," Robyn stated, staring at her friend.

"I'm not saying that. I just think it's unlikely, that's all. You're tired, you're probably still jetlagged, and…" Sarah answered.

"Get out!" Robyn ordered, leaning over Sarah and opening her door for her.

"Robyn, don't be stupid. I just don't think it was Jason. It's too much of a coincidence."

"Get out!" Robyn screamed.

"Robyn, I…"

"By the way, Mickey doesn't want to get married, so you really need to stop dragging him past wedding dress stores. They could be giving the frocks away for free and he still wouldn't set a date!" Robyn blurted out.

She clamped her lips shut and bit down on her tongue. Why had she said that?

Sarah just stared back at her friend, tears immediately pricking her eyes. She didn't say anything else. She got out of the car and shut the door behind her, hurrying back into the office, clutching her folder to her like a shield.

Robyn let out a frustrated sigh and punched the steering wheel with her fist. Why was this happening?

The shopping was all put away and he didn't know what to do next. Where was she? He was worried. Hell, he was more concerned for Robyn now than he had been when Veronica had pulled an unannounced all-nighter — probably with his brother.

He shouldn't have let her go. He should have gone after her, caught up with her. They could have left the store and gone for a drink and he might have found out the reason for her panic. He was a tool. This was how he let people down. He shouldn't want to be involved. Being involved just got your heart stomped on. Anyway, he didn't need someone to make his life worthwhile—he had his career for that. Didn't he?

He looked at his watch and then heard a tentative knock on the front door.

Cole opened the door and Robyn pushed him inside. She grabbed hold of his hands and put them on her hips. She kissed him, pushing him down onto the floor of the hallway. She wanted to get as close to him as she could. She pulled his t-shirt over his head and looked appreciatively at the firm, muscular chest underneath. She ran her fingers down, across his sternum to the waistband of his jeans.

Cole stopped her, taking hold of her hand and squeezing it in his.

She looked into his eyes, those deep, dark eyes. She kissed his lips again, closing her eyes and savoring every second of how it felt to lose herself in someone, without any questions or recriminations. Without anyone having to get up and go home.

Cole brought her fingers to his mouth and softly kissed each knuckle in turn. His gentleness was too much to bear, and she drew herself away, let him go and got to her feet, sweeping her hair back out of her face.

"Sorry about the whole leaving you in the supermarket thing. How much do I owe you for the food?" Robyn asked.

"Nothing, it's fine. They had a special offer on the ice cream," Cole answered, getting to his feet.

"So, can I help put it away? I mean, I like things ordered a certain way and, although you might think that's a bit freaky, you really need to just let me do it because…" Robyn began, heading into the kitchen.

"It's done. Look, do you want coffee, or a beer or something?" Cole offered.

"Don't you have to get back to work? Don't you have some deadly diseases to cure this afternoon?" Robyn asked, opening the fridge and looking at the groceries.

"I have assistants for that if I can't make it," Cole answered, his eyes not leaving her.

"Oh," Robyn said not knowing what else to say.

"What happened back there, Robyn? You took off like you were doing the hundred meters in the Olympics," Cole said as Robyn closed the fridge and leaned against the countertop, trying to avoid his gaze.

"I saw someone I didn't want to see," she admitted, biting her lip.

"Who? An ex or something?"

"No, nothing like that."

"Then who?"

"You don't want to know. The last thing you want to hear about is my messed up past. I mean, you know about my useless mother and my ill dad and my love of ancient old cars. I think that's about enough for anyone," Robyn said with an unconvincing laugh of nerves.

"I also know you kiss me when you want to lose yourself in something...when you need to escape your life for a second," Cole told her.

He hadn't put his t-shirt back on yet, and his body was just there, he was just there, looking like he did, attracting her with all his Freddie Prinze Jr. similarities.

"Robyn, at the moment you know more about me than anyone round here. We're friends already and we're living together. I'm exactly the person who needs to know, and Robyn, I want to know," Cole spoke.

"I saw Jason, Grant's son," Robyn blurted out, putting her fingers to her mouth and chewing her nails.

"Okay, and you're upset because..."

"Because...before I left for England...he raped me," Robyn admitted, swallowing a knot of tears as her stomach contracted in remembrance.

Cole let out a long, slow, almost inaudible breath, but his expression gave all of his feelings away. Robyn saw a flicker of anger and then something like pain in his eyes as he looked at her. He put his t-shirt back on and pulled it straight, as if being topless was inappropriate.

He crossed the room and wrapped his arms around her, pulling her protectively into his embrace. He began stroking her hair so softly.

She shut her eyes for a second and enjoyed the feeling of being held.

She could just relax into him, she could let out a breath and all the tension might slip away. He would probably hold her for as long as she needed him to, maybe even forever. She just had to let him in.

She pulled away suddenly, like she'd been jarred by something, and she shook her head vigorously.

"No, don't. I don't want you to do that. Don't be nice to me like that. I couldn't stand it," Robyn said, wrapping her arms around herself.

"Did he go to jail?" Cole asked, watching her.

"Yeah, four years."

"Is that all?!"

"Yeah. That's all you get for raping someone and reminding the whole town about how in olden times apparently that's what they used to do to the witches round here. And now he's back, just when I'm back," Robyn said, her hands trembling as she held them together.

"Well, he can't be allowed near you, can he?" Cole asked.

"I don't know. I saw him, it freaked me out, you saw me, you said it yourself—I did a world record breaking sprint out of the shop," Robyn said.

"And is that why you give Grant a hard time?"

"Do I give him a hard time?"

"A little. But now that I know, it's understandable. I mean, his son did that to you. Man, where was he when that was all going on?"

"I know it isn't his fault, but when I look at him, all I can see is Jason. I'm messed up right?"

"No, you're not. It's horrific what he did. Seeing him again, I can't imagine..." Cole began.

"Everyone around here knew, you know, and they all looked at me with pity in their eyes. They treated me like someone who had had their insides scooped out and should now be left alone and put in a secure room lined with cotton wool. Well, most of them thought that, some thought I should be ducked in the lake because I was obviously a descendant from the last witch brought to justice in the town in 1898. I could never be Robyn again, and that's all I ever wanted to be, just Robyn. Now, I was Robyn who'd been violated, not the same person at all. That's why I left. That, and the fact my own mother couldn't even look at me. I think she thought moving to England would kind of cleanse me, or maybe cleanse her. She was a great one for making herself the victim. Anyway, she wanted someone cleansed, it didn't really matter who. She said the word a lot. She said it so much, I almost felt like I was clean from hearing it—almost," Robyn carried on, tears running down her cheeks.

"What this Jason did to you is the worst thing anyone can do to another human being. You know that, right?" Cole told her, taking hold of her shaking hand.

"No, that's murder."

"You'll never forget it. You're going to carry it around for the rest of your life."

"Thanks, like I didn't know."

"I didn't mean it that way. I just meant stuff like that does change you, it's no use pretending otherwise."

"But I should be moving on, it should have dulled by now. That's what everyone thinks and that's definitely what Sarah thinks," Robyn said, holding his hand.

"To Hell with what everyone thinks. It's how you feel that's important," Cole assured her.

"Sarah didn't get it."

"I do. I get it," Cole told her.

Robyn looked up at him and let herself have a moment in his ebony eyes. He was so genuine, so comforting, so different from anything she'd had in the past.

"Well, so, there we go," Robyn said, breaking the tension. "Which camp are you in? Want to wrap me in cotton wool or duck me in the lake?"

She wiped her eyes with her fingers and side-stepped away from him.

"Both sound kind of fun," Cole admitted with a smile.

"Listen, all you've done since we met is listen to me prattle on about my baggage. Tell me about your issues, I don't know nearly enough about you, and you still haven't let me talk to your mother. I'm concerned by that," Robyn said.

"Veronica's having my brother's baby," Cole informed her, his lips tight as he formed the words.

"Whoa!"

"And you wanted to know about the fight we had. Well, I put him in hospital, broke his nose, his collarbone, and four ribs," Cole continued.

"I knew it."

"Then I smashed up his Porsche and poured bleach all over his apartment."

"Way to go."

"My mother, the one I will let you talk to the next time she calls, cried for days when I said I was leaving. Half of her wants to cut Bryn off because of what he did to me, but she doesn't want to

115

miss out on a grandchild. I can understand that, but it still hurts, you know."

"Could the baby be yours?"

"No."

"Are you sure?"

"I'm a scientist, Robyn. I deal with diseases every day. I know better. You get what I'm saying?"

"Loud and clear. So where the Hell does Veronica get off texting you after all that?" Robyn wanted to know.

"She wants me to make up with Bryn, for the baby's sake."

"The audacity!"

"Yeah, I know."

"So what did you say?"

"Nothing. I've nothing to say to either of them anymore," Cole informed her.

"Did you love her?"

"You know, I don't know. I don't know whether I was mad because she'd broken our trust or just mad because it was Bryn she broke it with."

"Well, I'd move on, it's the only way. Besides, you have an ice hockey team to focus on, and I'm going to need your help with the roadhouse and — shit! The interviews! I've got to get back to the roadhouse, I'm interviewing staff," Robyn exclaimed, looking at her watch and rushing toward the door.

"Hey, Robyn, wait! Here, I got you these," Cole called to her, waving something in the air.

"Keys?"

"To the house. Next time you storm out of a store, at least you can come home,"

"Thanks. And thanks for listening and…well, you know," Robyn replied, smiling at him.

"Anytime."

"You might regret saying that, I'm a woman with many projects."

"And a woman with a whole freezer drawer dedicated to ice cream," Cole reminded her.

He sat down at the kitchen table and put his knuckles to his mouth. Someone had raped her. Someone had had sex with her against her will. Someone had forced themselves on her, when she would have been scared and screaming for help. They had violated her and left her with an indelible memory that would always try to shape her future. No wonder she had run from the store if her attacker had been right in front of her. Hell, he wished he had seen him. He thumped his fist on the table and tried to quell the bubble of anger burning in his gut. People like that took things that weren't theirs to have, and they didn't care. They knew what they were doing was wrong, but they did it anyway, regardless of the consequences. They took advantage—just like Bryn had.

Chapter Sixteen

"So, Grimalda, let me just check that I've got all your details correct. You haven't worked a bar before, but you used to make coffee in the office and you went to the store for doughnuts, so you're used to dealing with money," Robyn said, trying not to look too hard at the young girl with dreadlocks who sat opposite her.

She had three studs in her nose and a variety of gold earrings in a line up each ear. She was also wearing a t-shirt stating the slogan "You Suck" and her tattered jeans were being held together with safety pins.

"Uh, huh," Grimalda replied, chewing gum and smiling at Milo.

"Okay, well, I think that's all I need for now. I've got your number, so I'll be in touch," Robyn said, standing up and offering her hand to the girl.

"So have I got the job? I could start right now, but I'd have to leave about eight—band practice," she informed them, shaking Robyn's hand and then taking her gum out and putting it behind her ear.

"We've got a few more people to see. I'll call you," Robyn said, leading the way to the exit.

"Awesome. Catch you later," Grimalda responded, directing another smile at Milo.

Robyn waited for her to leave and then let out a shriek of despair.

"Shit, Milo! What's happened to this town? Why are there no decent bar workers within a fifty mile radius? She was grimy! Larry was so old he would've needed to sit behind the bar to serve, Julie wanted to bring her kids to work, Sapphire had ideas above her station and thought this was a cocktail lounge, and as for Teresa...well, if she's twenty-one, the Panthers are going to beat Reading six zero on Saturday," Robyn exclaimed.

"Sapphire wasn't so bad," Milo replied, looking at his notes.

"And what did you make notes on? Nice hair? Slim and pretty? You would..." Robyn glared at him.

"She *had* worked a bar before," Milo reminded her.

"I think you'll find she said she was a 'drinks coordinator.' She couldn't even bring herself to say bartender. No, she wouldn't last in a roadhouse. It's going to be busy, Milo, full of families pre-nine and then full of people wanting a beer and some good music after that. *And* she wanted to make cocktails. We are *not* doing cocktails. My dad would have another heart attack if he came back here and found me serving margaritas," Robyn informed.

The front door swung open and Nancy strutted in, dressed in a short, gold sequined skirt and a barely there strappy vest in the same shade.

"Afternoon," she greeted with a smile, approaching Robyn and Milo.

"What are you doing here?" Robyn questioned.

"I hear you're holding interviews," Nancy replied, sitting down in the interviewee's chair.

"Yes. And?"

119

"Fire away. Interview me. There's nothing about this place I don't know," Nancy replied confidently.

"You want to work here—for me," Robyn said, staring at the woman.

"I saw your dad today, he thinks you need help," Nancy answered.

"Well, I don't."

"Robyn, you've hated everyone we've seen," Milo reminded her.

"Not everyone. Larry was okay; we could get him a stool," Robyn suggested.

"Listen, kiddo, whether you like it or not, me and Eddie are for keeps. I'm gonna be your step-mom and, I figured we should be getting to know each other better," Nancy told her.

"Really. That's what you think, is it?"

"That's what Eddie thinks and it's what he wants. Okay, so I didn't do such a great job of running this place, perhaps I took on more than I was capable of, and maybe Eddie deciding not to do food any more was a mistake. None of that means I don't know my way around a bar," Nancy continued.

"She's good, Robyn, fast too, and the guys like her," Milo chipped in.

"What about the kids? Can you serve them chicken and fries without scaring them half to death or suffocating them with your perfume?" Robyn wanted to know.

"Give me a trial. I don't come up to scratch, you can let me go," Nancy replied unfazed.

"Why are you doing this?" Robyn asked, looking at her suspiciously.

"I love Eddie and you're his blood. What can I say? I'm a sucker for a heart-warming reunion story. That and the fact I watched him eat a whole plate of salad at lunchtime. I've no doubt that was your doing," Nancy told her.

"He's never eaten salad on its own! You must have missed the fries. He hid them. Did you blink, like, at all? Did you check under Max's sheets?" Robyn asked.

"So do I get the job?" Nancy wanted to know.

Robyn looked at Milo, who was vigorously moving his head up and down like a rocking horse.

"We have a uniform now. Let me know your chest and waist measurements. I want no biker gangs, no drugs, no funny business at all. And you answer to me and, when I'm not around, you answer to Milo. Can you handle that?" Robyn asked her firmly.

"Yes, ma'am," Nancy replied.

"And no sarcasm, at all—none," Robyn retorted.

"Who was being sarcastic? So, shall I call you Boss Lady?"

That afternoon he'd received a report from Chicago, results he'd been waiting on for weeks. He'd been so sure of this trial, so convinced this was a breakthrough. When he read the findings, he'd wanted to weep. Maggie and Aaron had both watched him read the email, although she had made a good effort at pretending to clean her workstation. He'd wanted to cry and smash everything on the counter. But he'd chewed the inside of his mouth, shut the email down, and retreated to the bathroom with his dignity intact. Once alone, he'd lost it. He'd punched the mirror, leaving a fist sized crack in it, and then taken the rest of his anger out on the hand dryer. He needed this to work. He needed to know that he was worth something. But it wasn't just that. It was what Robyn had told him, too. The mirror and the hand dryer weren't just the unoptimistic results, they were Jason, this man who had hurt her. The man he would gladly pulverize.

Now he was home and he could hear Robyn in the kitchen. She was singing something country. She had a God-awful voice but he liked it. He couldn't face her yet. His hand was still bleeding and he needed to take a breath and recollect himself. He sat down on the stairs.

"Listen! I'm opening beer. This is because I have something very awkward to tell you. Well, a couple of things, really, but one is definitely worse than the other, but I'll let you decide which is which…to be honest, I'm not quite sure myself. And I'm making dinner, although it's been a while since I had pasta, so I'm probably burning it. Can you burn pasta?" Robyn called from the kitchen.

There was no reply.

"Cole Ryan! Don't you dare leave because you know I'm cooking! If it goes really wrong, I'll send for takeout or I'll barbecue!" Robyn shouted.

There was still no response.

"Cole! Is that you? Or did you give someone else a set of keys?" Robyn called as she went toward the hallway to investigate.

When she got there, Cole was sat on the stairs, his head in his hands.

"Look, I know I'm not Michelin standard, but there's no need to have a breakdown over it. I'll get Chinese," Robyn said, looking at him with concern.

He stood up, took hold of her hands tightly in his, and kissed her. She returned the kiss with as much passion as he gave and backed him up against the stairs. She sat astride him, dropping the wooden spoon she was holding to the carpet.

"The random kissing is supposed to be my thing," she said, laying another kiss on his lips and slipping her hands underneath his t-shirt.

"Have you patented the idea? Am I infringing on copyright?" he asked, taking her face in his hands and drawing it to his.

"Do you care?"

"Not right now."

He kissed her again, this time for a long time, until she had to pull away to breathe.

"This isn't a date," she clarified, trying to get her breath back and ignore her racing heart.

"I know," Cole answered with a smile.

"So, what's up?" Robyn asked, getting off him and standing up.

"Just a bad day at work, when it was so close to being the best day ever," Cole replied with a heavy sigh, sitting up on the bottom step.

"How does that happen? Man! Look at your hand! Did you hit someone?"

"No."

"So what happened?"

"We created a new vaccine. We thought this was it, the closest thing we could get to a cure for something we've been working on for over a year. But it hasn't worked as well as it should have. It's only shown regression in fifty-two percent of the cases," Cole explained.

"Fifty-two percent is impressive, though, yeah?"

"Not impressive enough for anyone to do anything about it," Cole replied.

"So what do you do next?"

"Go back and look again. Try and work out why it didn't perform better. And, if we can't find the answer, we start all over again," Cole said, shaking his head in frustration.

"How did you get so smart? I mean, I barely know the difference between penicillin and Prozac," Robyn told him.

"I'm not that smart, just determined," Cole answered.

Robyn looked at him, sensing there was more to come.

"I lost my dad to cancer. Before that, I had no idea what I wanted to be. If he hadn't have died, I probably would have tried my luck as a pro ice hockey player. But losing him to something like that, it blew my mind. I had to try and make it better somehow. Does that sound really lame?" Cole asked her.

"No, it sounds very noble and grown up and sensible."

"You mean boring."

"I didn't say that."

"You thought it, though."

"I would not be living with you if you were boring, believe me."

"You didn't have anywhere else to go apart from the basic room at Psycho Mike-o's," Cole reminded her.

"And there was that, too. So what did you hit? Nothing containing anything viral, I hope," Robyn said, smiling.

"Bathroom mirror," Cole admitted.

"The janitor's going to be pissed at you."

"I'll pay for it."

"So, Cole Ryan beats up on things and then settles up for the damage. I like that," Robyn told him.

She leaned forward and softly kissed his lips, taking hold of his injured hand and gently running her fingers over the wound.

"I'll get some ice," she whispered.

"So, about those things I wanted to tell you. Well, all the bartenders who came for interviews were useless, except Nancy, and she gave a rousing speech about togetherness and blood and family, so I gave her a job. Then Aunt Pam came in and she wants to meet you, so I kind of had to accept an offer of dinner tomorrow night at six before we all hang out at Taboo," Robyn spoke quickly.

"Okay," Cole answered, unfazed.

She watched him drain the pasta. His t-shirt rode up a little, giving her the slightest glimpse of his flesh. She swallowed. She had to stop this fantasizing or things were going to get complicated.

She cleared her throat.

"Okay? Did you hear everything I said? I gave my trampy future step-mom a job at the roadhouse I kicked her out of, and we have to go to dinner at Aunt Pam and Uncle Bob's and sit opposite the satanic twins," Robyn repeated.

"I heard, it's all good," Cole answered, putting the pasta onto plates.

"Really?"

"Sure. Free dinner, what's not to like?"

"Trampy step-mom?"

"I'm sure you'll keep her in line."

"Hopefully."

"So who else did you hire?"

"Hmm, yeah, well, she was it. I'm going to have to contact agencies next, and that'll cost more."

"How about me?" Cole asked.

"How about you, what?"

"I could work the bar," Cole offered, stirring a pan of gray looking sauce.

"You already have a job."

"Not in the evenings."

"Yeah, but you have hockey."

"Not every night. We agreed practicing every night was over the top, remember?"

"You haven't ever worked a bar."

"Sure, I have. I worked a bar in Chicago to help pay tuition fees. Do you need references?"

"Is there no end to your talents?"

"I'm pretty hot, right?" Cole replied with a laugh.

Robyn's cheeks flushed as she looked back at him. She wanted to see more than what was under his t-shirt. She was dangerously close to thinking about what lay beneath his jeans. He looked at her again and she felt her whole body flush. He had the darkest eyes, like pools of oil. It would be all too easy to give in. But if she gave in, what happened next? She had no idea.

Suddenly her mobile rang. It jolted her out of the daydream and back to reality. She took her phone out of her pocket and looked at the display.

Clive — again.

She should have called him by now. She'd promised to call him as soon as she'd arrived, and it was days now.

"Who is it?" Cole asked, watching Robyn just staring at the ringing phone in her hand.

"Oh…it's my work…back in England," she answered, hiding her eyes from him in case her expression gave her feelings away.

She was saved from having to say anything else when the doorbell rang.

"I'll get it. It's probably one of your neighbors with chicken and rice. That would save you from the pasta!" Robyn called as she ran up the hallway.

She opened the door to Brad.

"Hey," he greeted sheepishly.

"Hey."

"Look, um, I wanted to apologize for the other night, being a jerk and sounding off," Brad began, looking down at his feet.

"How did you know I was here? And what's so good about your shoes?"

"I called over to Bob and Pam's. She said you were here on Woodhams. I saw the Mustang," Brad admitted, raising his head.

"D'you wanna come in?" Robyn invited.

"No, I can't really. I'm about to go on duty and…" Brad began.

"Come in. Come and eat some pasta with us. I made it, it looks terrible, but Cole's trying to fix it," Robyn said, ushering him in.

"I don't want to put anyone to any trouble," he said, reluctantly stepping in.

"Cole! Get another plate out, Brad's here! And don't worry, he basically had an olive branch between his teeth," Robyn called as they made their way into the dining room.

"Look, about the way I reacted last night. I care about you, Robyn, I always have and I just..." Brad began, taking off his hat.

"I overreacted, too. Of course I eat dinners—you surprised me, that's all. We'll have dinner, I promise, just as soon as I have the roadhouse up and running."

"Hey," Cole greeted, entering the dining room with the food.

"Hey, Cole. Listen, I apologize for last night. I acted like a tool. Can we put it behind us?" Brad asked, offering him his hand.

Cole looked at the offering but made no move.

"Cole, come on. I promise, he's not usually a fruitcake like he was last night," Robyn said.

"I mean it, man, sincere apology. I was out of line," Brad told him.

Cole took his hand and shook it.

"She looks like a great car, by the way. Does she run good?" Brad asked as they all sat down at the table.

"Don't ask *him*, I haven't let him drive it! She runs just fine. She needs a tune up, but I intend to sort that out this weekend," Robyn informed him.

"Wow, pasta looks...interesting," Brad remarked, observing the gray colored sauce.

"Yeah, what is in the sauce?" Cole asked Robyn, preparing to take a mouthful.

"Not telling. It's a secret recipe," Robyn said, spooning some into her mouth.

Brad looked at Cole and Cole looked back at Brad. Both waited to see who was going to sample the food first.

Cole opened his mouth and put in a large forkful. Not to be outdone, Brad followed his lead.

"It's anchovy, pepper, mushroom, dill pickle, and Bud Light," Robyn informed them.

"I think I'm going to be sick," Brad announced, leaping up from the table and hurrying to the kitchen.

"What's his problem?" Robyn asked with a shrug.

"Damned if I know," Cole replied, piling up his fork.

Chapter Seventeen

"Good morning, Max, raisins for you. They're full of goodness and taste like sweets, remember," Robyn announced the next day, depositing a large packet on the old man's bed.

"Huh! You said that about the grapes and I've been on the bedpan all night long," Max grunted, picking up the packet and putting it on his locker.

"Cinnamon doughnut, Dad? Or a nice bag of low sugar popcorn? I'll let you choose. Doughnut or popcorn? Popcorn or doughnut?" Robyn asked, swinging both items in front of Eddie's face.

"Take the doughnut, Eddie, we can share it," Max called gruffly.

"I promised Nancy a wedding when I get out of here, gimme the popcorn," Eddie said, grabbing the bag from his daughter.

"Ah ha! I knew there was a reason she's being nice to me. You're really going to marry her. You've set a date?" Robyn asked.

"Three months' time. Did you give her a job?" Eddie wanted to know, pouring popcorn into his mouth.

"Did I have a choice?" Robyn replied, sinking her teeth into the doughnut.

"She's not like you think, Buttercup," Eddie insisted, popcorn tumbling out of his mouth as he spoke.

"You called me Buttercup," Robyn remarked, stopping chewing.

"Yeah, so? What of it?"

"I forgot you used to call me that."

"Don't go getting all sentimental. I thought we weren't talking about feelings. How are the Panthers going? You talked tactics with them yet?"

"Tonight. We're going out to Taboo," Robyn informed them.

"Jeez! Taboo! That takes me back! Haven't been there for years. I can't believe it's still going."

"Thought it would be a good distraction from tomorrow's game. Give them some bonding time, let them kick back a bit," Robyn told him.

"What's Taboo?" Max questioned, leaning forward in his bed and peering over at them.

"What's Taboo? Max! Shame on you, old man! You never been?" Eddie called.

"What the Hell is it? A bar or something?"

"A strip club. You want to see the girls they got there, Max!" Eddie remarked excitedly.

"Apparently, they have a room for ladies now, with men on stage," Robyn informed him.

"Hell no! That's all wrong!" Eddie exclaimed.

"Why?"

"It just ain't natural."

"Women like men appreciating them," Max added.

"Leering at them more like," Robyn commented.

"They earn good money, we like looking at them, everyone's a winner," Eddie told them both.

"So when we going?" Max asked with a chuckle as he opened the bag of raisins and sprayed them across the bed.

"Never, unless you get your blood pressure down. I'll give you a blow by blow account when I come in next," Robyn said.

"Not of the men's room though...we don't wanna hear nothing about that," Eddie answered.

"Roadhouse opens next week. It's almost decorated and I have plates coming today," Robyn informed her dad, finishing the doughnut.

"Plates? We had plates. Why do we need new plates?" Eddie questioned.

"Dad, it doesn't look like you've served food for years. I've had to get a company in to steam clean everything. New plates have a motif on them," Robyn told him.

"What sort of motif?"

"It matches the sign. 'Eddie's Roadhouse' written on a huge burgundy baseball cap," Robyn informed him.

"Sounds great," Max replied, chewing up raisins.

"Sounds expensive," Eddie said grumpily.

"I've paid. I've paid for everything," Robyn assured him.

"On a mechanic's wage? You're still a mechanic, right?"

"Sometimes. I work in the office mainly."

"In the office! Did you hear that, Max? My daughter works in an office!" Eddie exclaimed proudly.

"Punches holes in things and does filing, I bet," Max muttered.

"Must pay well, though," Eddie said.

"Something like that. Listen, I've spoken to the doctor, and he's really pleased with your latest tests. He reckons you might be able to have the operation next week," Robyn told him.

"And that's a good thing?" Eddie moaned.

"Dad, do you want to be stuck in this bed with him next to you forever?" Robyn asked.

Max was now doubled up having another coughing fit.

"Hey, what d'you mean? I'm good company. Tell her, Eddie," Max spoke through the coughing.

"I guess you have a point, Buttercup," Eddie agreed.

"So, what's on the menu today?" Robyn asked, picking up a menu card.

"Dunno. Some God-awful shit, I expect."

"Baked fish with tomato and basil, new potatoes, and green beans. That sounds nice," Robyn said, smacking her lips together.

"You were never a good liar, you hate that shit," Eddie reminded her.

"It's good for you," Robyn retorted.

"Yeah, unlike chips and dips, which is probably what you got on your menu," Eddie replied.

"Actually, I had pasta last night," Robyn informed him.

"Ugh! Like worms, that is, Italian worms. Gives me the heebie-jeebies," Max announced, shivering.

"How do you put up with this all day? I only come for an hour, and I want to smother him with his pillow by the end of it," Robyn said.

"If I could get out of this bed, I would do it for you," Eddie remarked.

She had a dirt mark on her cheek. Her sleeves were rolled up and half of her hair was hanging out of its ponytail. He had to put his hands into the pockets of his jeans to stop himself from trying to rub the mark away. Since she had told him about the rape, he found himself wanting to try and look after her. She'd obviously been through it, her mother was gone, her father was in the hospital, and her aunt and uncle had spawned the offspring of Beelzebub. Who did she have? But then again, it was none of his business. He didn't do involvement any more. Did he?

"See! What do you think of the décor?" Robyn asked.

It was lunchtime, and she had invited Cole to the roadhouse to see how work was progressing. So far Nancy had proved invaluable. She had completed a stock check, ordered tablecloths and napkins, and phoned back all the beer suppliers, knocking them further down on price.

"It's great. Wow, this looks like something out of a Western film," Cole said, admiring the surroundings.

"God, does it?! Don't say that! I wanted traditional but not old fashioned. Is it old fashioned? Milo! Cole thinks it's old fashioned. Do you think it's old fashioned?" Robyn called out to her bartender.

"Robyn, I didn't mean it like that. It's homey, you want it to be homey right? It isn't old fashioned, it's retro," Cole told her quickly.

"I want you to be honest with me. Don't save my feelings, tell me how it is," Robyn ordered him.

"It's great. It's homey, it's smart, it's comfortable, and it's traditional. It's everything a good roadhouse should be. It's...unpretentious," Cole said positively.

"Unpretentious. I like that. Yes, it is unpretentious, isn't it? Milo, do you think it's unpretentious?" Robyn called.

"Absolutely, ma'am," Milo shouted back.

"He keeps calling me ma'am lately. I've told him to call me Robyn, but he can't get his head round it. So, come on then, get behind the bar," Robyn ordered Cole, ushering him forward.

"I knew it!"

"You knew what?"

"I knew this wasn't an invitation for lunch and a look at the décor. This is a test," Cole responded.

"I don't know what you mean,"

"You want to see if I can work a bar before you give me a job here," Cole remarked.

"Absolutely not. I just fancy a nice pitcher of Bud Light with the sandwiches Nancy's making, and Milo hurt his thumb in the stock room this morning. He needs to rest it," Robyn insisted, making big eyes at Milo.

"Bad thumb, huh?" Cole said, eyeing the bartender with suspicion.

"Yeah, I, er, dropped a barrel on it," Milo replied.

"Let me see," Cole said, trying to get a good look at his hands.

"That's not necessary. I've assessed the injury and rest is all that's required. Milo, go and see what Nancy's doing with the sandwiches," Robyn ordered him.

"Yes, ma'am," Milo replied, hurrying out toward the kitchen.

"Don't you think I've worked a bar before?"

"You said you worked somewhere that sounded campier than Graham Norton. I'm not sure it's a real place," Robyn answered.

"Who's Graham Norton?"

"Actually, I Googled it. Your old bar does not exist."

"No, not now. It got shut down and they made it into a Chuck E Cheese," Cole replied.

"Oh," Robyn said.

"But if you want me to show you what I can do, fine, bring it on," Cole said, rolling up the sleeves of his shirt.

"I'll have a pitcher of Bud Light, please, a Jack and Coke, and a glass of red wine," Robyn ordered, jumping up onto a bar stool.

"Yes, ma'am. Would you like ice in the Jack and Coke?"

"Please."

"And a large wine?"

"Regular, actually, but liking your style."

Cole began to pour the beer, turned around and grabbed a bottle of whiskey, added ice, a dash of Coke, and a squeeze of lemon. He found the red wine and poured a glass before the pitcher had reached the top.

"There, ma'am, and that will be...I would tell you, but I don't really work here and I don't have a card for the cash register," Cole said, lining up the drinks in front of Robyn.

"Hmm," Robyn said, eyeing the pitcher and the glasses.

"What does 'hmm' mean?"

"I don't think there should be more than half an inch of foam at the top of the pitcher."

"There isn't!"

"That's almost an inch, Cole."

"I don't think you know what an inch is."

"Excuse me. Who is the boss around here?"

"The boss you may be—just didn't realize you were shaping yourself on Stalin."

"That's insubordination."

"So fire me."

"You don't have a job yet."

"I might decide I don't want one, given the décor is so old fashioned."

"Whoa! That's below the belt and you said it wasn't! Is it? Tell me honestly," Robyn urged.

"I'll tell you that there's not more than half an inch of froth on that pitcher, the red wine's good, and the Jack and Coke will be the best you've ever tasted."

"You put lemon in it, for Christ's sake. What if I'd had a lemon allergy?"

"I'd expect you to be wearing a big sign round your neck. Taste it," Cole urged her.

Robyn picked up the glass and took a swig.

"It's disgusting," she said, downing the rest of the drink in one go.

"You're a liar."

"You're full of yourself."

"Back atcha."

"Can you make another one?" Robyn asked, holding the glass out to him.

"That depends. Do I get the job?"

"I suppose I could make an allowance for the extra foam just this once—but don't let it happen again," Robyn said, shaking a finger at him.

"Cheese and dill pickle and sliced pork and apple sauce, just like you asked," Nancy announced as she arrived from the kitchen with a tray full of sandwiches.

"These look great. Did you make these?"

"No, sugar, I got a biker gang out the back with a liking for sandwich-making. Of course I made 'em. Hey! Who are you, honey? You're cute," Nancy remarked, looking admiringly at Cole.

"Cole."

"Yeah, yeah, he's cute. Cole, this is Nancy, Nancy, this is Cole. Apparently, Nancy's going to be my step-mom in three months' time. I haven't had my bridesmaid invitation yet, but we're trying to bond," Robyn informed him.

"Nice to meet you. So, you married?" Nancy asked, getting close to Cole.

"No, he's not, but you nearly are. Back off," Robyn warned her.

"So, meeting him's fast work for someone who's only been in town this week."

"We're not dating. I've got someone in England."

"Have you?" Cole asked.

"Oh my! Looks like this beautiful relationship is about to hit the skids," Nancy remarked.

"You told me you didn't have a guy," Cole repeated.

"I don't, not really," Robyn said awkwardly.

"You said you didn't do dating."

"I don't. I..." Robyn started.

"So what is it then?" Cole wanted to know.

"God, what is this! Now who's behaving like Stalin?"

"You said you weren't seeing anyone, now you say you are. Which is it?" Cole asked.

"Why do you care so much?"

"I'm just intrigued why you'd hide it."

"Well, go and be intrigued by something else. Find a cure for herpes or something. That's what you do all day, isn't it? Or are you toying with the idea of taking a diploma in being an ass?" Robyn asked.

"Touchy," Nancy remarked.

"And no one asked your opinion on it, either," Robyn snapped.

"Fine. I'm going to help Milo with the delivery. Enjoy your food," Nancy said before disappearing out the back.

"So, who is he?" Cole pressed.

"Jeez! There is nobody. I just said that to shut her up. Man! What's with you?" Robyn exclaimed.

"You're lying to me," Cole said, watching her.

"I'm not! I do not have a boyfriend," Robyn insisted, sinking her teeth into a pork roll.

"Then what do you have?"

"I have a guy I sleep with now and then, okay?" Robyn blurted out.

"I think that's called a boyfriend."

"It isn't like that. I don't care about him."

"You don't care about him?"

"No."

"So you sleep with him, but you don't care about him."

"That's right," Robyn admitted.

"That doesn't sound right at all."

"He's my boss—at the garage. He likes me and, well, he looks after me," Robyn stated.

"Jeez, Robyn! He pays you for sex? Man!"

"Don't say that. He doesn't do that."

"Well, that's what it sounds like to me."

"I don't want to have this conversation. It's none of your business. Perhaps this house sharing wasn't such a good idea if it means we have to tell each other everything."

"So you like this 'having sex for money' arrangement, do you?" Cole questioned.

He looked angry. His eyes bored into her. They didn't look so attractive now, they looked accusing. Robyn swallowed and looked down at her plate.

"Listen, sometimes people have to do things to get on in life. I needed Clive to get on in life," she tried to explain.

How did she explain what she'd done for the last nine years? It wasn't normal, she knew that. It wasn't how ordinary people led their lives, but that was all she knew, and it was better than the loneliness and the complete emotional isolation.

"And now? Do you still need him to get on in life?"

"He's paid for all the improvements to the roadhouse. What do you think?"

She raised her eyes to meet his, and he shook his head in disgust. Suddenly she felt very small and very sad. She put down her roll and pulled self-consciously at her hair.

"You're judging me, and that's not fair because you don't know the whole story."

"So tell me the whole story," Cole said, his tone calmer.

"You wouldn't understand," Robyn answered, her voice wobbling.

How could he understand? She didn't even understand.

"Try me," he urged.

She shook her head and pulled her stomach in, trying to suppress the ball of emotion inside. How could she tell Cole she had been sleeping with her boss for as long as she could remember? She hated it, yet she needed it. And he did pay her. Okay, he didn't leave a pile of cash on the bedside table, but he may as well have. He had bought her the flat, he paid all her bills, and she earned far more than any office manager for a garage should earn. But suddenly, now that she was home in Portage, she couldn't even bring herself to call him. She didn't want to be that person any more, and she didn't want Cole to know that Robyn. Back here, she wanted things to be different. Or more accurately, she wanted things to be the same.

"You know too much about me already, now you think I'm a prostitute. Leave it at that and eat your roll," she ordered him.

"Robyn, if you need this guy to be financially secure, I can help you out. Don't go back there, cut him loose," Cole told her seriously.

"So you can pay my way for me? No."

"I wouldn't ask you to sleep with me," Cole said firmly.

Robyn ignored the comment and took her wallet from her back pocket. She got out a wad of bills and held them out to him.

"For Leonora, like I promised," she said.

"Is this his money?" Cole inquired, looking at the money as if it was dirty.

Robyn shrugged.

"I don't want it," Cole told her.

He picked up a roll from the tray and turned away from her.

He knocked another clipboard of papers on the floor. That was the second one of the afternoon. He couldn't concentrate. He kept thinking about Robyn and some middle-aged garage owner, in bed together. The visual made him feel sick. He thought he knew her, but now — why would she do that? She was so beautiful, so smart and funny. Why would she want to give all that to some guy she admitted to not caring about?

"Cole, do you have the info on the Barracol trial?" Maggie called.

Maybe he had some hold over her. But what? She hadn't seemed as afraid to talk about him as she had when she'd spoken about Jason and the rape. There had to be something, though. People just didn't do that sort of thing if they had a choice. But then, who was he to talk about choices? He'd almost thrown his whole life down the drain. He wasn't saintly enough to talk about rights and wrongs.

"Cole, sorry to interrupt but…"

"Do you want a coffee, Maggie? I could really do with a coffee," Cole announced, raising his head to look at her.

"Sure, I'll go and get it," she offered.

"No, it's okay. I'll go."

He needed the walk.

Chapter Eighteen

"So, this is nice, isn't it?" Pam remarked that evening.

Cole and Robyn were barely speaking after their lunch at the roadhouse, and now they were sat opposite the Omen twins, trying to eat their way through two tons of chicken and rice.

"It's lovely food, ma'am," Cole said, forking some more in his mouth.

"Cole, please call me Pam. Can't remember the last time anyone called me ma'am, can you Bob?" Pam asked her husband.

"Nope," Bob replied, drinking from his bottle of beer.

"Are you her new boyfriend?" Sienna asked, giggling into her glass of water.

"No," Cole replied sharply.

"They're just friends, honey," Pam added quickly.

"Why aren't you her boyfriend? You're a boy, aren't you?" Sierra continued.

"Last time I checked," Cole remarked.

"He's not my type," Robyn answered bluntly.

"Robyn actually already has a boyfriend," Cole snapped back.

"Oh, honey, do you? What, in England? You never said. What's his name? What does he do? How long have you been together?" Pam gabbled, putting her knife and fork down and giving her niece her full attention.

"Ages. He owns a chain of garages. He's very successful and rich. His name's Clive," Robyn said quickly.

Cole let out a snort of annoyance.

"Ignore him," Robyn ordered.

"He's married," Cole informed the table.

"What?" Pam exclaimed in horror.

"I never told you he was married," Robyn said.

"But he is, isn't he?" Cole continued, looking at her defiantly.

"Oh, Robyn, that isn't right at all. I mean, what are you thinking? Does he have children? What about his poor wife?" Pam began.

"I don't know why we're even having this conversation, especially in front of the children," Robyn said, indicating to Sienna and Sierra who were both looking at Robyn with wide eyes.

"How old is he? Fifty? Fifty-five?" Cole carried on.

"Robyn, he isn't that old, is he?! Honey, this isn't right. It isn't right, Bob, is it? Tell her," Pam urged, her mouth opening in horror.

"It isn't right, Robyn. There, I said it. Now I think we ought to change the subject and carry on eating this delicious meal," Bob suggested to everyone.

"Rhett, at school, his mom had an affair with the mailman. He was married, too. His mom had to move to Nevada, but Rhett and his dad kept the dog," Sierra informed the group.

"Well, Cole's ex-girlfriend is having his brother's baby," Robyn announced loudly.

Cole put down his silverware and sent a glare across the table to Robyn.

"Oh my!" Pam said, dropping her fork with a clatter.

"This is like an episode of Jerry Springer!" Sienna said delightedly, clapping her hands together.

"That was unnecessary," Cole said to Robyn, wiping his mouth with his napkin.

"And your comments weren't?" Robyn retaliated.

"Listen, I think you two ought to take this outside, don't you?" Bob suggested firmly.

"We're fine," Robyn snapped.

"Outside, both of you. Sort yourselves out and then come back and get along," Bob ordered them.

Robyn rose from her chair and stormed toward the door. She pulled it open and stepped out onto the deck.

"Why did you say that stuff in front of Pam and Bob?" Robyn questioned, squaring up to Cole as soon as he joined her in the backyard.

"Why did you tell them about Veronica?"

"I asked first."

"I don't like your arrangement with your married boss."

"I don't like you not tightening the lid on the milk."

"That's a pathetic come back."

"I don't want to sleep with my boss!"

"Then why do it? For the money?"

"It isn't about the money."

"Then what is it about?"

"It's none of your business."

"I'm making it my business."

"How macho. You want some dumbbells?"

"Not really."

"I told you about Jason, I told you everything. After it happened, I couldn't move on, you know, with a guy. I still can't. Not in the normal sense. I told you that. I don't date, I don't do anything like that, I can't."

"I don't get it."

"Jeez, Cole do I have to spell it out for you? I couldn't get close to anyone. I wanted a new memory, something to wipe out the bad one, but I couldn't do it. Clive was nice to me; he seemed to genuinely care about me."

"Yeah, well there's only one problem with that...you kissed me just after we met," Cole reminded her.

"I know," Robyn answered, swallowing.

"So what's that about?"

"I don't know."

Cole let out an exasperated sigh and put his hands to his head. He looked at her, his eyes wide and full of concern.

"If you don't feel anything for him, how can it be right?" he asked.

"I sleep with him to forget the rape, to push it away. It's not romantic, it's not good, but it's better than not being able to even go through the motions. And that's all I can do with him, it's just mechanical—I don't feel it. But, it's one step up from nothing," Robyn tried to explain.

Tears welled up in her eyes and she fought to control the urge to sob. She hated the way he made her feel vulnerable. There was something about him that made her want to let it all go.

He took hold of her hand and squeezed it firmly. It felt so good, the reassurance, the genuine affection without an ulterior motive. She wasn't used to it. She didn't know how to deal with it.

"I know I'm damaged, Cole, but you can't fix me. And I don't want you to try," Robyn interrupted quickly.

"That isn't your decision to make," Cole answered, looking at her.

She swallowed, looking into his ebony colored eyes.

She felt his body move, just slightly, and it unnerved her. She dropped his hand like it was a scorching hot cup of tea.

"So, how about you apologize for telling my family I sleep with a married man and I'll apologize for telling them about your incestuous family issues. Sorry," Robyn spoke quickly.

"I'm sorry, too," Cole added.

"Great, so let's go and see if we can kick the twins shins without them telling on us," Robyn suggested and she opened the door.

"Robyn..." Cole started.

"I'll give you first shot at Sienna," she replied.

The conversation was finished.

"So, is he going to leave his wife?" Sienna asked as Cole poured Robyn some more water.

"Sienna, we are changing the conversation. Now, tell me about this go-karting night. Is the whole team going?" Pam asked, smiling at Cole.

"I only asked if he was going to leave his wife. Rhett said that his mom went with the mailman because he was better in bed and he had a pool in his yard," Sienna continued.

"Well, for the record, he won't be leaving his wife, and I'm going to be here for a good few weeks yet. He'll probably find someone else to sleep with," Robyn said matter of factly.

"So, the go-karting," Pam said again.

"Yes, go-karting. I'm really looking forward to it, aren't you, Bob?" Robyn asked, grinning at her uncle.

"Yepper."

"Is the married guy really fifty-five? Because that's gross," Sienna piped up.

"Sienna. We're not talking about the married guy any more," Bob ordered his daughter.

"Does he have really gray hair?" Sierra added.

"Yeah and false teeth and sometimes he has to use a walking stick," Robyn said as she kicked her cousin hard on the leg.

"Ow! Mommy!"

"Brad came to dinner last night," Robyn said, changing the subject.

"He came to our school last week and let me wear his hat," Sienna announced.

"Yes, he goes to a lot of the local schools and talks to them about stranger danger and road safety," Pam informed them.

"He didn't tell us that! Wait 'til I tease him about that one! Stranger danger!" Robyn said, laughing.

"Teaching the children is very admirable," Pam insisted.

"Yeah, but it isn't exactly catching the bad guys and throwing them in the lock up, is it?" Robyn answered.

"She's been watching too much CSI, you'll have to excuse her," Cole said.

"He uses hair products, did you know that?" Robyn informed the table.

"She eats with her fingers and has an obsession with tightening the lid on the milk," Cole retorted.

"Will you two stop sparring with each other? You sound like a married couple," Bob remarked.

"She doesn't believe in marriage. She didn't even have a scrapbook," Cole said.

"He did, but he won't admit it," Robyn replied.

"Is your girlfriend really having your brother's baby?" Sierra inquired, batting her eyelids innocently.

Chapter Nineteen

The pink neon sign of Taboo throbbed in front of them. Mickey and the rest of the team had been at another bar before arriving at the club, and they were already well lubricated.

"Now, listen up. Bob has the kitty—strictly beer, no ridiculously, expensive, potent cocktails, no shots, and absolutely no tequila. I want you all to enjoy yourselves, but we do have an important game tomorrow, so let's remember that," Robyn said.

Henrik repositioned a bright yellow cowboy hat on his head and loosely strung a red feather boa around Mickey's neck. Robyn had no idea where he had got them from.

"What about the kitty for the girls? You get special treatment if you throw money at them," Art piped up.

"If you want to throw money at them, Art, you knock yourself out, but you won't be throwing my money at them," Robyn informed him.

"Let's get in there, boys!" Wes shouted, pumping his fist in the air.

"Yeah, let us go. I cannot wait to see American girls do jiggy jiggy," Henrik said, swaying his hips.

"OK, let's go. Bob, get the beers," Robyn ordered, leading the way through the doors.

"No Grant tonight?" Cole remarked to Brad as they entered the club.

"No, he had to work. Plus, I think he finds it difficult being around Robyn, you know," Brad replied.

"So he should after what his son did," Cole said firmly.

"Yeah, well, it wasn't his fault."

"He might have taught his son right from wrong," Cole suggested.

"We all make mistakes, though, huh? Come on, let's get a drink," Brad urged, patting Cole on the back.

Taboo had been modernized since Robyn had last been in it. She and Sarah had sneaked in via the back entrance once and dressed up in some of the dancers' outfits. It had been fun until the owner had turned up and offered them jobs. That had been scary. Then, the club had been a seedy, run-down place for sleaze. Now it was a funky, chrome, and neon entertainment center with almost as many female customers as men.

"Brad, give Bob a hand with the pitchers," Robyn said as she pulled up a seat.

"Look at girl with legs up over head. How she do that?" Henrik wanted to know, sitting down and craning his neck to see.

"Where did you tell Sarah you were going tonight?" Wes asked Mickey.

"Go-karting," he replied.

"That's so funny! That's what we said!" Robyn remarked, taking another handful of nuts as a blond-haired dancer came close to the edge of the stage.

"Couldn't exactly tell her the truth, could I? She's been in a weird mood all day, anyway. Started throwing out a load of women's magazines and brochures, crying and sniffing. I asked her what was wrong but she wouldn't answer me," Mickey continued.

Robyn swallowed and took some more nuts. She knew she was responsible for that. She shouldn't have told Sarah what Mickey had said about marriage. It had been cruel and unnecessary. She'd been upset and thinking of herself, and now she had upset her best friend. She would call her. She would try and make things right. She didn't want to be responsible for a relationship breakdown.

"Oh, I wouldn't worry about it, that's what women do, isn't it? Cry and moan and make our lives that much harder," Wes commented over the music.

"You single, Wes?" Robyn questioned, looking at him.

"Currently."

"I'm shocked."

"Whoa, boss is getting testy, look out," Jon called as Bob and Brad arrived with the pitchers of beer.

"It's foreplay, obviously. She can't keep her eyes off me," Wes replied, standing up and making a grab for the beer.

"Dream on! And I'll have pick of the first pitcher. Bob, man, what are these glasses for? We don't need glasses, get some straws," Robyn said, and she proceeded to drink the beer from the pitcher.

"She is crazy, yes?" Henrik said, watching in astonishment as Robyn downed half the pitcher in one go.

"Yeah, that's Robyn," Brad remarked, watching her.

"I want this girl; excuse me, what is name?" Henrik shouted to a dancer with long, red hair.

"Henrik, they don't talk to you, they just dance for you. Stick ten bucks in her panties," Wade told him.

"Ten bucks?" Henrik said, looking at his team mates quizzically.

"A ten dollar bill, here, give it to me," Mickey ordered, snapping his fingers at him.

Henrik passed a ten along and Mickey approached the stage, put the bill in the girl's panties, and pointed out Henrik.

"Come on, man, she wants you!" Mickey said, beckoning him closer to the stage.

"I feel, how do you say? Embashed?" Henrik admitted, blushing.

"Bashful? Look, come on, don't be a tool, man! Get up to the stage!" Wes ordered, giving him a shove in the right direction.

"If you won't have the dance, I damn well will," Wade said, pushing past Henrik to get to the front.

"Well, that should keep them entertained for five minutes. Pass me Wes' pitcher," Robyn said to Cole.

"You're going to steal their beer? Shame on you," Cole remarked as he passed the pitcher to Robyn.

"Well, I figured it's okay if I drink more than them because I'm not playing tomorrow."

"Good plan," he agreed.

"Bob! More beer!" Robyn called, banging her fourth pitcher on the table.

"Yeah, more beer!" Mickey agreed, putting his arm around Henrik and swaying back and forth.

"So, aren't you going into the room for the ladies?" Wes asked Robyn.

"All the boys I need are right here," she informed him.

"Hey, hey, hey! I knew she had it bad for me!" Wes yelled above the music.

"Before you get any ideas, I prefer you all with your clothes on. Preferably in pads, with sticks in your hands," Robyn said.

"You're welcome in the locker room any time," Wade remarked with a laugh.

"Don't say that! She'll come in and give us a hard time about the game," Brad told them.

"She won't come in. Is private, for men only," Henrik said, spilling beer down his shirt.

"Oh dear," Brad said with a shake of his head.

"I won't come into the locker room? I'm the manager, I can go where I like," Robyn reminded him.

"Yes, but locker room is, how you say? Like church—is safe," Henrik said again.

"Hen, just quit while you're not ahead, or she's going to be waiting for you when you come out of the shower tomorrow," Brad warned.

"It's a sanctuary? Why? You don't want me looking at your scrawny white butts?" Robyn asked.

"Hey, I won Butt of the Year at the garage," Mickey commented proudly.

"Did anyone else enter?" Robyn asked.

Brad let out a snort of laughter.

"You're my team! You're all asexual as far as I'm concerned."

She couldn't help but look to Cole. This speech was to deter unwanted attention and to highlight the professional sporting boundaries. But she had the feeling she had said the words more for her own benefit. She had to stop wondering what it would be like to…

"I'm not sure I like being called asexual," Mickey said.

"Live with it, she doesn't think you're hot," Wade said.

"Brad has the best chance with Robyn anyway, they've dated before," Wes reminded them.

"Yes, well, that's all in the past," Robyn said hurriedly.

"I like childish romance," Henrik said.

"Childhood romance," Wade corrected.

Brad smiled over at Robyn and she hid her face in the nearest pitcher of beer. This was awkward and not how she'd wanted the conversation to turn.

"Aww, he's still got it bad!" Mickey teased, jabbing Brad in the ribs with his elbow.

"Anyway…who's next for a dance? Wade! Which girl do you like?" Robyn wanted to know, turning away from Brad and focusing on the other player.

"Can't say I'm that particular, they're all good," he responded, licking his mouth in anticipation.

"Here, this one's on me," Robyn said, passing out some dollars.

The majority of the team whooped and hurried off to the stage with Wade.

"We should definitely take photos," Robyn said, laughing as she watched the team.

She picked up a pitcher of beer, and that was when she noticed him on the other side of the room.

Suddenly, there was no air, the music seemed to lower, the lights brightened, and she came to eye-to-eye with Jason. He was older and taller, but it was him. There was no case of mistaken identity this time. He sat at a table alone, holding a bottle of beer and looking directly at her.

The dancer on stage had Wade backed up against a pole and was cavorting around him, while the other players cheered her on. But Robyn didn't see it. She was practically having to force herself to breathe.

"Cole," she said in barely more than a whisper.

Cole was laughing with Bob at Wade who was trying to look like he was enjoying the performance but actually looked terrified. He hadn't heard her.

"Cole," Robyn attempted again, keeping her eyes on Jason.

She thought if she looked away he might vanish into thin air and no one would believe he was ever there.

Jason got up from his chair and began moving toward their table.

"Cole!" Robyn screamed at the top of her voice.

She leapt up from her chair and grabbed him by the sleeves of his t-shirt. She was shaking now and had closed her eyes tight. She couldn't look at Jason. She clung to Cole.

"What is it?" Cole asked, putting an arm around her and holding her trembling frame.

She carefully turned her head away from his chest, but when she did, she came face-to-face with Jason. He was now standing right by their table.

"Robyn, listen. Don't freak out or anything. I..." Jason began, reaching out to her.

"Don't touch me! Cole, don't let him touch me! Get him away from me!" Robyn shrieked, clinging to him.

"Jason?" Bob questioned as if not sure.

"Listen, I just wanted to talk to you. I mean, it's been such a long time now, I thought..." Jason began again.

"This is Jason?" Cole asked Robyn.

She nodded as tears began to spill from her eyes. She had to hold herself together. She couldn't let him see that she was still the terrified wreck she'd been back then.

"Robyn, I didn't do it. I said that at my trial and I'm still saying it now. I didn't do it," Jason said, looking straight at her.

In one rapid movement, Cole sat Robyn down and punched Jason hard on the jaw. He crumpled and fell back into an adjacent table.

Robyn was practically hyperventilating. She couldn't bear to look at him. She couldn't bear to be anywhere near him.

"Leave him, Cole! Cole! I said leave him! I'll go and get security," Bob said, pulling Cole away from Jason and signaling to the bouncers on the door.

"What the Hell is he doing here?" Brad questioned as the team hurried back to the table.

"He's freaking Robyn out, he tried to touch her," Cole replied, shaking his aching fist.

"I didn't do what you all think I did," Jason said as he attempted to get to his feet.

He was winded, and his nose was bloodied and misshapen. He clung to a chair to aid him.

"No? Well, that isn't what the jury said, was it? Out! Now!" Brad ordered, roughly grabbing Jason's arm and hauling him up off the floor.

"I no understand. Who is this Jason?" Henrik queried, his cowboy hat falling over his eyes.

"I want to go," Robyn said, scanning the room for the nearest exit she could make it to.

"No, he's leaving, right now," Brad informed them, and he wrenched Jason's arm behind his back.

"Robyn, please, just listen to me…" Jason begged as the security team moved toward them.

"No one wants to listen to what you've got to say, it's all lies," Brad hissed.

"I'm launching an appeal. They've got new information. I want the conviction quashed. I want my good name back, and I want Robyn to realize that I didn't hurt her," Jason informed him.

"I don't want to hear this," Robyn said, biting her fingernails and balancing on the outside edge of her tennis shoes.

"You had photos of her all over your bedroom wall," Brad reminded Jason.

"Yeah, I had a crush on her, I admitted that. She was the only girl in school that spoke to me, and I was the class dweeb," Jason said.

"Cole, please, make him go away!"

"You drag all this history up again, and I'll make sure you spend the rest of your life in a rehabilitation center," Brad threatened.

"I'm only going to say this once more. I did not rape Robyn, and you're all going to find that out soon enough," Jason informed them.

"Get out of here!" Brad ordered, pushing him toward the doormen.

His fist was aching but he didn't care. When she'd said that he was her rapist, the blind fury had taken over. It was how he had felt when his father had died, how he had felt when he found out about Veronica and Bryn. But it wasn't quite the same, because tonight the feeling hadn't been about him, it had been about her. All he'd wanted to do was protect her. How could he feel like that about someone he had only just met? He'd promised himself never again. Caring was just too painful and it had no place in his life any more.

Chapter Twenty

"Ow!" Cole exclaimed as Robyn put a tea-towel containing ice on his knuckles once they got home.

"Come on, if it's that bad, it might be broken. Do you want to go to the emergency room?" Robyn asked, sitting next to him on the sofa.

"No."

"Then quit with the dramatics."

"It isn't just the hand. I got worse from our friendly hockey match the other night and Henrik jabbed me right there when he was dancing with the chair," Cole informed her. He stood and pulled up his t-shirt, revealing a bruise on his back the size of North America she hadn't noticed earlier.

The washboard midriff was there again, just a few inches away. She bit her lip.

"Who did that?" Robyn asked.

"Brad doesn't like getting beaten to the puck, does he?" Cole said, sitting down again.

"No," she agreed.

He looked at her, his black eyes studying her face as if it was important. Like she was important. Her heart quickened and she had to moisten her lips.

"I wanna kiss you," she said, putting the ice down on the coffee table.

"You're asking now?"

"I do have some manners."

"What if I say no?"

"Are you going to? Because that would be really embarrassing."

"I don't know, Robyn, I think things have changed. I don't want to do the whole random thing anymore," Cole told her with a heavy sigh.

"Oh, I get it. You've found out I'm not the easy going girl you thought I was. You found out, not only have I been raped by the town freak, but I also sleep with my boss because that's all the relationship I'm capable of."

"No, it isn't that," Cole told her, his eyes meeting hers.

"Don't give me the eyes, please don't give me that look. I don't want your sympathy. I know I'm screwed up. I've told you I don't want you to try and make me feel better, it isn't your job."

She felt uncomfortable. She felt hot and she couldn't look at him. He was sitting so close to her, and it was making her prickle with something like excitement or maybe anticipation. Whatever it was, it was indescribable.

"Well, whose job is it? Clive's? Because you told me when he makes love to you, you don't feel a thing."

"Stop it! Don't say that!"

"Why, because it's so close to the truth?"

"I'm not some sort of project."

"I think you feel it when we kiss. I think you try to pass this off as something random, something unimportant, but that isn't true, is it?" Cole continued.

She could feel his breath on her face and, suddenly, she couldn't focus on anything but his full, fleshy lips.

"That sounds like psychobabble to me," she responded, pulling at her ponytail and averting her gaze for a second.

"Is it? Believe me, I really don't want to feel this way, but no matter what I do, I can't get away from the fact that we fit, Robyn. I don't know why or how, but we fit."

"You're so obviously drunk. Shame on you."

"I think you feel it, too, but you won't admit it, because Clive and whatever 'make-do' life you have back in England is familiar—no matter how shit it is."

"Oh my God, Cole! Where is all this coming from? I have a bit of a thing with the rapist turning up and you go all caveman on me and want to be my protector? I appreciate you having my back with Jason, but…" Robyn began.

"Close your eyes," Cole told her.

"Why?"

"I'm going to kiss you. And although I know I shouldn't, I want it to be a prologue to something," he whispered.

Her eyes closed of their own accord, like a magnetic clasp had drawn them shut, and she felt the soft, smooth lips on hers, tempting her mouth to open. She wanted to let the feeling he gave her fill her whole body and take away every horrible memory. She reached for him, drawing his head closer to hers, her lips demanding more from his, until tears were seeping from the corners of her eyes.

She broke away, out of breath, her cheeks damp, and her heart hammering in her chest. Cole took hold of her hand and gripped it tightly in his.

"You felt that, right?" he asked.

Robyn watched the rise and fall of his chest and nodded her head. She had felt more from every kiss they'd shared than she had felt for the last nine years. Her heart was racing, her palms were itchy, and she couldn't stop looking at him.

"Marry me," he said, his eyes not leaving her for a second.

"What?"

"You heard me," Cole said steadily.

His expression was serious. The inky eyes were focused on her and the intensity made her shiver.

"Is this a dare? Have one of the team put you up to this?"

"Marry me," Cole repeated.

"I heard you, but one more time, and I'll think you actually mean it. I'll hold you to it," Robyn said with a swallow.

"Marry me."

"We've known each other three days."

"You haven't given me an answer."

"We have a game tomorrow, the biggest game of the season. I have to focus on that."

"You're changing the subject."

"Of course I am. You're being crazy!"

"Yeah, maybe I am. I mean, I've never thought about marriage before, you know that. And I really didn't ever have a scrapbook of potential outfits. Hell, after the year I've had, I was never having any sort of relationship ever again. But then I met you and you're messing things up, messing me up."

"We should rewind. We can forget I said I wanted to kiss you, we can forget you kissing me, and we can go and ask the refrigerator what it suggests we snack on at this time of night."

"Are you saying no?" Cole asked.

"Yes."

"Yes? You're saying yes?"

"No! I'm not saying yes. This is insane."

"Do you want me to ask your dad first? Because I'm serious about this. I don't know why, I can't explain it, just call it a chemical reaction I can't analyze yet."

"Jeez! Are you for real?"

"I'm going to ask one more time. Robyn Matthers, will you marry me?"

She pulled at a section of hair in her ponytail while biting the inside of her cheek. She raised her eyes to meet his.

"Yes," she answered.

Chapter Twenty-one

"Did you say yes?" Cole asked.

"I...I don't know. Did I?"

"I think so."

"This is weird."

"Yeah. I wasn't sure you'd say yes."

"Why did you ask me?"

"Because you make me feel...I don't know...better. When I'm with you it's like finally something else matters. D'you know, since you've been living here, I haven't thought about work once when I've come home. Not even when you made me sit through every replay of the Red Wings game twice last night. I can switch off, I can be twenty-five, playing hockey, being who I am without the white coat and the safety glasses."

"I'm not like other girls. I don't do emotion and Meg Ryan films or the color pink."

"I know that. I live with you," Cole reminded her.

"I'm screwed up, and I've been sleeping with someone who pays my bills and keeps me in crisps and beer."

"I know that, too. And I hated it. I hated it so much, I almost had another crack at the mirror in the Gen-All bathroom."

"You're smart, Cole, and really clever…and whenever you walk into anywhere, every woman checks you out."

"Now you're making things up."

"They look you up and down and mouth *wow* as nudge their friends."

"They do not!"

"You've played for the Wolves, and you've had a nice, normal relationship with someone called Veronica. She sounds very sensible and attractive and probably had a really high-powered job wearing expensive suits and make-up. I don't do make-up, by the way, just lip-gloss," Robyn continued.

"Come on! Normal? She had an affair with my brother."

"But I bet she was normal once. She hadn't been raped and she hadn't slept with her married boss. She liked Meg Ryan, too, didn't she?"

"Listen to me. Make that fresh start and make it with me. We can both start again. Just be Robyn. That's who I met at the airport and on the plane. That Robyn had a mouth full of opinions and she said I was cute," Cole told her, taking hold of her hands.

"I did, didn't I?"

"Yes, you did."

"Must have been the altitude."

"Or maybe the jetlag."

"Or maybe the hostesses nudging each other and going *wow*."

"Maybe that did it," Cole replied with a smile.

"This is weird," Robyn said.

She didn't know what to do. She didn't know how she should behave. She didn't know if she was thinking straight. It had come so out of the blue. But she had reacted with her gut and her gut had said yes. Her instincts had told her that saying yes was the right thing to do. Her instincts were rarely wrong. They were about the only thing she still trusted. But wasn't it madness agreeing to marry someone after only knowing them three days?

"Cole, this is crazy. This is a sympathy proposal. The psycho turned up, you feel sorry for me, you want to protect me, and this is your way of doing it. You don't need to. It isn't your place."

"I'd like it to be."

"This isn't how things usually go. There's usually a prologue."

"I think ours started at the airport."

"You're on the rebound."

"No, been there, done that. Sally, Avril, and a real crazy chick called Cleo."

"I'm not right for you. I'm not educated and I've been stealing from your t-shirt collection," Robyn admitted bashfully.

"I know all that. I also know you drink way too much, and I know how bad you look before your first coffee in the morning. We're just right together, Robyn, don't ask me to explain it. When we first met, you bowled me over, just because you were you. Robyn Matthers, straight talking, unpretentious, bossy, opinionated, determined…" Cole began.

"You can stop now."

"I like you, you like me. You can't deny that. It doesn't matter whether we've known each other three days or three decades."

"Is being attracted to each other enough, though?"

"How does everyone else start off?"

"On a date."

"And you don't do dates, so why don't we start off with a proposal," Cole suggested.

Robyn let out a laugh and shook her head. She took a deep breath and looked at him. He was perfect. In every way he was perfect—and he was asking her to marry him. Despite the anxiety she felt, the overriding emotion was excitement and the promise of a life with someone who knew everything about her and only cared about her all the more for it.

"What?" Cole asked, looking at her intently.

"I don't need looking after."

"Neither do I."

"Good."

"Good."

She threw her arms around him and pushed him down onto the sofa, savoring the way his mouth tasted entwined with hers. She ran her fingers through his thick, black hair and felt him hold her to him so tightly. She wanted so much for it to be real. She wanted the way she felt for him to be what she had been too scared to look for. She wanted to be free from everything she'd been before. She wanted a new start and she wanted to share that with him.

She stopped kissing him and held him away from her, drinking in his masculine beauty.

"Your mother's going to hate me. I'm no good with the vacuum," she spoke, touching his lips with a finger.

"And she does love the color pink."

"Stop it!"

He'd just proposed. In the middle of the den of a house he had only spent a few days living in, in a state he had just moved to, to a girl he had met at the airport. It was crazy, one of those stories you read in magazines. A hurried proposal, a short-lived romance, and a messy divorce. But he didn't feel that way about it. He felt invigorated. He felt alive. So much for choosing the single life! So much for focusing on his work, giving the project his full and undivided attention, and steering clear of potential heartache. She'd somehow got inside him. He felt more for her than he had ever felt for anyone. They shared an undeniable connection. She needed stability in her life and he could give her that. He could be the person to show her that life was full of ruts in the road, but the damaged tires made you stronger, you just had to put on a new tread and keep going. That's what he'd done and he was hanging on despite himself. Maybe they needed each other.

He smiled. She was singing in the bathroom. Tammy Wynette.

The weather was terrible. The Panthers had lost three-zero and her dad was staying behind lecturing them, making them train for an hour before he let them leave the arena. They had been awful, Brad had got injured just before half time, they had lacked pace, and their mistakes in defense had given away the goals.

Robyn was walking home and the wind was threatening a bad storm. It started to rain and she quickened her pace, breaking into a jog. She was wearing jeans, her Panthers shirt, and her mom's bright yellow rain coat. It started to stick to her as she sweated and it rained. She was concentrating so much on getting out of the weather, she didn't see, hear, or feel anything before it was happening.

Suddenly everything went dark, someone grabbed her. Her head was covered, she couldn't see and she couldn't breathe. Hands were pulling at her, dragging her off the roadside. She screamed, but the wind was too loud, the rain too heavy. His gloved fingers dug into her arms as he wrenched her out of sight. She gasped for air, she couldn't see, the Panthers had lost, and she was going to die.

Robyn bolted upright in bed, her breathing rapid, sweat forming on her brow. It was the dream again. She hadn't had the dream since she had arrived back in Portage, but here it was, same as always. She usually could never get through a week without having the nightmare. It never changed; it was just a re-run of events leading up to what happened that night.

She looked at her watch. It was almost 3:00 a.m. The wind blew a gale outside and the rain battered the windows. She was never going to get back to sleep.

She got out of bed, went to the door, and opened it. Just across the landing was Cole's bedroom. He was probably asleep. Her head ached. She had drank too much at Taboo—everyone had. She only hoped they recovered before the game that evening. They had to win, or at least draw. She couldn't have the humiliation of defeat on her hands.

She crept across the landing and knocked on the door. She didn't wait for a reply but opened it. Cole raised his head from the pillow and looked over at her, his eyes half open.

"Are you awake?" Robyn asked, self-consciously pulling her t-shirt down over her thighs.

"I am now. You okay?" Cole asked, propping himself up, straightening the covers, and flicking on the lamp.

"Look, being as how we're engaged and everything—or did I imagine that? Because I can tell I drank a lot tonight and I'm not so good at recalling everything perfectly when I've had a few drinks— but if I'm right and we are engaged, can I sleep with you? And even if we're not engaged, could I still sleep with you? You know, have a pillow or two, share the duvet," Robyn said, her cheeks flushing as she spoke.

"You don't like the wind? I would have thought you would love the Michigan elements," Cole remarked with a smile.

"Not all of them," Robyn admitted.

"Come here," Cole said, opening up the covers for her.

"You do have some sort of clothing on under there, don't you?"

The thought of lying next to him naked gave her a dual emotion. One half of her felt a jolt of excitement and the other half was stricken with fear, like a nervous virgin in a room full of dildos.

"No. Generally don't sleep in my clothes."

"Oh," Robyn said, pausing by the bed and wondering what to do.

"Relax, Calvin Klein's covering me up, get in," Cole urged her.

Robyn got into the bed and he put his arms around her, pulling her into him.

"Listen, about this getting married stuff," Robyn said, turning over and facing him.

"Yes?"

"Can we keep it to ourselves for a while?"

"Sure," Cole agreed.

"I'm not having second thoughts, but in the morning that might be different. You know after about three pints of water and some Advil. It's just my dad hasn't had his bypass yet and..." Robyn started.

"You think the news might make him have another coronary," Cole said with a smile.

"I don't know, maybe, I mean, it's almost making me have one," Robyn admitted.

"I'm not perfect, Robyn," Cole whispered, looking at her.

"You're not?"

"No. But I think we might be pretty perfect for each other," he said, linking his hand with hers.

"I'm really not very good with the vacuum, is it going to be a deal breaker with your mom?"

"How about I do the vacuuming and you fix Leonora."

"And you'll cook, right? And fold sheets."

"Right, that's it. I'm turning off the light."

Chapter Twenty-two

The doorbell rang.

Robyn opened her eyes and closed her mouth. For a second she couldn't remember where she was, and then she felt Cole's arm around her and suddenly memories of the previous night came flooding back, along with a banging headache.

"Cole, there's someone at the door. What time is it?" Robyn asked, nudging him awake.

He opened his eyes and looked at his watch.

"It's not even nine," he replied with a groan.

The doorbell rang again.

"It might be important. Go and see who it is," Robyn urged, tugging at his arm.

"Man, if I'm vacuuming in this relationship, can't you be the one who opens the door when people call too early?" Cole asked, reluctantly getting up and throwing a t-shirt over his head.

"Is this our first row?" Robyn asked innocently.

He hurried down the stairs as the doorbell rang again, this time incessantly. He opened the door.

"Hey Sarah. Robyn, Sarah's here!" Cole called up the stairs.

She couldn't hear what Sarah was saying to him, but it sounded probing. Poor Cole, having to endure a hundred questions from her inquisitive friend who could very easily have got a job with the FBI. She grabbed the closest thing and made her way down the stairs.

"...it just made sense," Robyn heard Cole say.

"What made sense?" Robyn asked as she entered the kitchen, wrapping Cole's robe around her.

"Cole was just telling me about you moving in here."

"Oh yeah, old news," Robyn replied stiffly.

"Oh Robyn, I am so sorry about everything I said about Jason. Mickey told me about last night, said he turned up at the go-kart center," Sarah said, tears pricking her eyes.

"Yeah," Robyn answered.

"Are you okay? I mean, Mickey said he basically attacked you, insisted he speak with you," Sarah carried on.

"I'm okay," Robyn replied, knowing she didn't sound very convincing.

"I'm going to call Grant; I'm going to tell him what I think of him. He should have told you he was back, he should have told us he was coming back," Sarah exclaimed.

"No. Don't do that. I'll be seeing Grant later at the arena. I don't want anyone to do anything on my behalf. I can deal with it," Robyn insisted.

"Can you?"

"Yes."

"It might be worth speaking to the cops. I mean, it is harassment," Cole told her.

"Haven't you made coffee yet?" Robyn asked, tightening the robe around her.

"Shall I remind you where the vacuum lives?" he retorted.

"God, you two sound like a couple," Sarah remarked, looking at Robyn with wide eyes.

"Don't be ridiculous, we've…" Robyn began.

"Only known each other four days," Cole added.

"Do you want to listen to the fridge? If I open the door, it'll say something really cool," Robyn said, heading for the door.

"Robyn, you should have called the police. He can't be hassling you like that," Sarah said.

"I don't want the police, I just want to – I don't know – make a fresh start, move on," Robyn said, looking up at Cole.

"And you can do that now?"

"I don't know, I hope so. We'll have to see, won't we," Robyn answered.

She wasn't sure of anything. She only had to hear his name and bile rose in her throat. She didn't know whether she could move on yet, especially now that he was back in town. But what else could she do? She was so tired of being a victim.

"I'll look after her," Cole stated, looking at Sarah.

"You will not! I don't need looking after, I told you that! Why does everyone want to look after me all of a sudden?" Robyn exclaimed, letting out a frustrated breath.

"Okay, okay, no looking after. How about shopping? I finish work at lunchtime. We could hit the mall. We haven't done that since the time we set the fire alarm off in that snooty handbag shop," Sarah reminded her.

"I don't know, I don't think I'm going to have time. I'm going to see my dad this morning, then I've got to get to the roadhouse, and then it's the game tonight. Anyway, I'm surprised you want to go anywhere with me after what I said about Mickey not wanting to get married," Robyn said, taking the milk out of the fridge and tightening the lid.

"It isn't like I didn't know that already, is it? You just told me the truth," Sarah said with a swallow.

"I said it to hurt you, though," Robyn admitted.

"I know."

"But you're my best friend. I don't want to hurt you."

"I know that, too," Sarah said, looking up at Robyn and offering her a faint smile.

"What d'you need to do at the roadhouse?" Cole asked.

"I need to oversee. We're supposed to be opening next Friday, and half the new stuff hasn't arrived yet and the place still isn't how I want it. Does Mickey have some car parts I can have?"

"Car parts?"

"Yeah like a fender or some hub caps. I was going to hang some stuff on the walls."

"I'll ask him."

"I can oversee whatever needs overseeing if you want to go to the mall."

"You think you can keep an eye on Milo and Nancy? Alone?" Robyn commented.

"What's the worst that could happen?" Cole asked her.

"Er, let me think. Nancy invites all her low life friends over, they ruin the new décor, fill the place full of marijuana plants, and start bare knuckle fighting," Robyn suggested.

"That's the worst you got? I might even join in," Cole joked.

"That's settled then. I'll meet you outside the entrance to the mall about one," Sarah said, heading toward the door to the hall.

"Coffee's nearly ready," Cole announced.

"Oh thanks, but I'd better not. Got a nine thirty appointment out at Vicksburg," Sarah informed him.

"He needs to make it quicker. I'm still training him," Robyn said as she walked Sarah to the door.

"I heard that!" Cole called.

"So, are you and Cole…"

"Are me and Cole what?"

"You know, like together?"

"No! God, no! Of course not, I mean we've only known each other four days!" Robyn exclaimed dramatically, clutching her throat for effect.

171

"I know. You said. It's just, you seem very comfortable with each other."

"Wouldn't you be comfortable in a million dollar house? Look at it! Plasma TVs in every room and a talking Smeg!" Robyn said quickly.

"Does it have a movie theatre?"

"No, but the basement is huge! We're going to set up goals and practice hockey," Robyn informed her with a grin.

"That's so you."

"Actually, it was Cole's idea."

"God, Robyn, he's so cute. You should make a move on him," Sarah told her.

"Yeah, well, he's not all that when it comes to personal hygiene. He leaves his toenail clippings on the arm of the sofa and he doesn't shower much," Robyn said.

"No! But he looks so…" Sarah began.

"Groomed, I know. Well, they say you never really know someone until you live with them. Okay, so I'll see you at the mall at one," Robyn said, opening the door.

"Great, it's been ages since I went shopping, we'll have ice cream too," Sarah continued.

"Great! Now go, will you? I have a sick dad to get to this morning."

"Bye," Sarah said, hurrying down the driveway to her car.

Robyn closed the door and walked into the kitchen where Cole was pouring two cups of coffee.

She took the pot from him, put it on the counter, and kissed him.

"Sarah thinks we look comfortable together," she said between kisses, running her hands through his hair.

"And that's bad because?"

"Because it's too soon for us to look comfortable together. We have to make everything seem normal," Robyn suggested.

Cole kissed her lips and shook his head at her.

"What?"

"Everything is normal."

"No, it isn't. Sarah says we look comfortable, you asked me to marry you, and I said yes."

"No one knows that yet. No one has to know that yet. We're friends, that's all we're going to look like...unless you can't keep your hands off me, of course."

"It's so the other way around, I mean, you practically undress me with your eyes whenever I walk into a room."

"You've noticed."

Robyn smiled at him.

"Here, want to tighten up the lid?" Cole asked, passing her the milk carton.

"Can we go on a date?"

Cole looked at her, unsure.

"Can we go on a date?" Robyn repeated.

"But you don't do dates," Cole reminded her.

"I'm changing my mind."

Chapter Twenty-three

"Good morning! Wakey wakey! Half the day is gone! Max, is that the form guide you're studying! Do you have someone who comes and puts in bets for you?" Robyn exclaimed in horror as the old man shoved the papers under his covers.

"None of your business. Who's this?" Max questioned, narrowing his eyes and staring at Cole.

"This is Cole. Cole this is my dad's roommate, Max," Robyn introduced.

"Pleased to meet you, sir," Cole greeted.

"What's this? Manners? He can't be with you, gal, if he has manners. Eddie! Someone with manners! Got any Twinkies?" Max questioned, grabbing Cole's arm as he passed the bed.

"Don't answer that. Whatever you say, he'll want to strip search you. Hi Dad, brought you some more juice," Robyn said, putting a bottle of apple squash on top of his locker.

"It tastes like gnat's pee," Eddie grumbled, trying to sit up in bed.

"Shall I prop up your pillows?" Robyn offered.

"No! Get off! I'm not helpless, I can do it," Eddie insisted, swaying left and right and trying to get comfortable.

"He can't. He had the nurse in three times yesterday to do it, gave her Hell, he did," Max informed them.

"They don't know how I like to sit. So, this is Cole, is it?" Eddie said, looking him up and down.

"Yes. Cole, this is my dad, Eddie," Robyn introduced.

"It's nice to meet you, sir," Cole said, holding out his hand. Eddie shook it.

"So, you played for the Wolves, huh?" Eddie asked.

"Yes, for three seasons."

"Robyn says you're a center."

"That's right."

"What's your strike rate?"

"I average two goals a game."

"Why aren't you playing pro?"

"I had other priorities."

"Like what?"

"Dad! Why are you interrogating him?" Robyn exclaimed.

"If he has talent, he should be playing in the NHL. I want to know why he isn't in the NHL," Eddie replied.

"It's none of your business. You should just be grateful he's playing for the Panthers," Robyn answered.

"It's okay, Robyn. My father died. I decided to study and now I work for Gen-All," Cole explained.

Eddie didn't respond.

"I had a trial for the Red Wings once, though," Cole informed him quickly.

"The Wings!" Eddie said, his face lighting up.

"Yeah, I actually played alongside Zetterberg for about five minutes."

"Man! How about that! Did you hear that, Robyn, played alongside Zetterberg," Eddie said, obviously impressed.

"I heard. I'm totally jealous. What I'd give to share some ice with him," Robyn said with a sigh.

"It's a big game today. Max and I have been studying Reading's form. They're unbeaten," Eddie informed them.

"I know that. That just means they're due a loss."

"It means they're good, and you're only going to beat them if you're better," Max piped up.

"Ignore him, he doesn't know too much about hockey," Eddie said.

"I know about averages, though, and my money isn't going on the Panthers tonight," Max answered with a throaty chuckle.

"You're not helping," Robyn told him.

"You're going to have to play hard. I mean, really hard. It's no use putting out your best, most skilled players. These suckers are sluggers. You want your biggest, strongest players. I'm not sure Henrik's going to be your best option," Eddie told her seriously.

"If we play Henrik, I could cover him," Cole suggested.

"That would never work. You can't be two places at the same time. Who's going to cover you?" Eddie wanted to know.

"I just think we need strength and skill," Cole said.

"What you need is a miracle," Max announced, laughing so hard he started to cough.

"Shut up, Max!" Eddie bellowed.

"Dad, don't get worked up over it. It's going to be fine; I have a good feeling about tonight," Robyn assured him.

"Yeah? You said that the night you punched out that girl from Grand Rapids," Eddie said.

"She did what?" Cole exclaimed.

"Best punch I ever saw."

"I need to hear more," Cole replied.

"No, you don't. Listen, I'll talk to Grant, see what he thinks about the line up," Robyn said, picking up Eddie's chart from the bottom of the bed and looking at it.

"Don't ask him! Waste of time. He might be a pal and everything, but he was never as good a tactician as me," Eddie boasted.

"Hark at him! Anyone would think he was trying to plan the Iraq invasion," Max remarked.

"Dad, don't worry, we're going to win. I promise you," Robyn said. She was determined to.

"You're going to win? You're going to be lucky to keep the score down to single figures," Max told her.

"We'd better go; I don't like leaving Nancy unsupervised at the roadhouse," Robyn said, checking her watch.

"You can't go yet!" Max exclaimed.

"Why not?"

"Because you haven't told us about Taboo," Max said, practically foaming at the mouth.

"Nothing much to tell. We went, we drank too much, we saw lots of girls with very little on, and then we went home," Robyn stated quickly.

"Lordy! Bet you had a close look, didn't you, son?" Max remarked to Cole.

"Closer than I anticipated at times," Cole admitted with a smile.

"Right. Are we done? Beef stew on the menu today with fruit salad for dessert. Make sure you eat it. And you, Max, you dare to bet against the Panthers winning tonight, and I'm going to force-feed you tomorrow's lunch—I hear it's chickpeas," Robyn warned, pointing at him.

"Eddie, you have to do something about your daughter, she's unhinged," Max exclaimed.

Chapter Twenty-four

"Welcome to the Portage Arena, home of the Portage Panthers! Tonight, in charge for the game of the season, Robyn Matthers! Let's hear it for Robyn, everyone! For anyone who doesn't know Robyn, she is none other than Eddie Matthers' daughter and also the only player to net three in one game and get sent off for misconduct. Now, time for the team news," the PA announcer said, his voice echoing around the arena.

Robyn had been at the arena since 5:30 making sure everything was ready for her first game in charge. Before that, she had spent two hours at the mall with Sarah hearing all about Mickey's failings as a boyfriend. She had also caught Sienna and Sierra trying to shoplift half the make-up counter in the department store, devoured two toffee chocolate ice creams, and bought half a dozen t-shirts she didn't need. Now it was time to turn herself into an ice hockey manager.

"I feel sick," Robyn told Cole as he skated up to her.

It was less than ten minutes until the game started and seats were rapidly filling up. It was good news for ticket sales but bad because Robyn didn't want the entire county scrutinizing her team choice if it all went wrong. She had chewed every nail down to the quick and she was seriously concerned about the size of Reading's enforcer.

Cole looked completely hot in full hockey uniform too, and that wasn't helping her temperature. She was already sweating. She'd argued with him over not paying attention to her team-talk to throw the players off the scent of their coupling, but what she really wanted to do was take off his pads, strip him of his underwear, and see how far she could get before the fear kicked in.

Now she sat on the bench, watching the team warming up. The Reading team was doing some complicated drills. They looked so professional.

"Hey, it's going to be fine," Cole assured her.

"Dad's going to be listening on the radio, you know. They're just giving out the team news and he's going to be shouting and cussing and going crazy. He might even go so nuts that he ends up down here chastising me in his hospital gown," Robyn said, putting her fingers in her mouth to chew her nails again.

"You did the right thing picking Henrik. The team relies on him. We don't have someone who goes insane and hits people and we have to stick to what the team knows," Cole replied.

"Cole, I'm expecting you to enforce where you have to. I've seen you can throw a punch. Don't let me down and go all namby pamby on me," Robyn ordered.

"Namby pamby?" Cole questioned with a smile.

"See the big guy? He's slow, but he looks like he could crush Wes with one arm and probably snap Mickey in two at the same time. Don't let that happen," Robyn told him.

"I've got it covered. Relax, have an energy drink," Cole suggested, putting his mouth guard back in and joining the team.

"Yeah, like I need any more energy! I'm still wired from that extra strong coffee this morning," Robyn yelled after him.

"Hey," Grant greeted as he sat down on the bench next to her.

"Nice of you to join us," Robyn remarked, not looking at him.

"I'm sorry I'm late. Listen, Robyn, Jason…" Grant began.

"Stop. Stop right now. This is an important game, I need to focus," Robyn said, dismissing him at the mention of his son's name.

"Just…let me say this," Grant begged.

He stood in front of her so she couldn't avoid him.

Robyn met his eyes and tried to remember he wasn't Jason. It was almost impossible when they looked so similar.

"I didn't know he was coming back here. He's been staying with a friend. He told me he tried to speak to you last night and I apologize for that. He shouldn't be bothering you after everything that's happened," Grant told her.

"Cole hit him," Robyn stated.

"I know. I don't blame him for that, but I really think Jason's telling the truth," Grant stated.

"What?" Robyn said coldly, looking straight at him.

"He's always said he didn't do it, right from the start. I know he didn't have anyone to substantiate his alibi, but I believe he was at home," Grant continued.

"I was raped, Grant," Robyn said, standing up and facing him.

Her body prickled with rage. His words acted like a thousand pinpricks being jabbed incessantly all over her skin.

"I know. It was horrible and we all feel so…" Grant began.

"It was his DNA," Robyn accused, scrunching her fingers up into a ball.

"So they say," Grant said.

"So they say? What's that supposed to mean?" Robyn snapped.

"Well, mistakes are made, aren't they? And I believe Jason; I've always believed Jason, deep down," Grant told her.

"Well I don't. He had photographs of me all over his bedroom; he had a sweatshirt of mine…" Robyn began.

"He had a crush on you, Robyn, he was fifteen. He was a shy, nervy boy, and he liked you, that's all," Grant insisted.

"I don't want to talk about this. We're about to play Reading! Reading who are unbeaten and have an enforcer who looks like he should be in the WWF," Robyn announced, moving past Grant and going to stand beside the ice.

"He's hired a solicitor to try and get the case reopened," Grant informed.

"Come on Panthers!" Robyn yelled at her team.

She had to blank him out. She didn't want to hear it. If she couldn't hear it, it wasn't really happening.

Grant let out a sigh and picked up the tray of water bottles. For now the conversation was over.

"They're holding their own," Grant commented, watching play.

"There's only ten minutes gone," Robyn reminded him.

"Yeah, but still…"

"Hold him up, Cole! Don't let him get past you! Bam! In the boards, that's what I'm talking about!" Robyn hollered, clapping her hands together as Cole crushed a Reading player against the advertising hoardings.

"Wes looks like he's taken a knock," Grant remarked, watching as the player held the side of his body.

"He got swiped by the number eleven; it's probably just bruised ribs. Come on Brad! Pass it to Henrik. Yes! That's it! Shoot God damn it! Argh…Oh my God! It's! He's scored!" Robyn shrieked hysterically, raising her hands in the air and leaping off her seat.

The crowd went wild, Robyn screamed at the top of her lungs, and the team bundled on Henrik. They all skated toward the bench where Grant was dancing excitedly along the edge of the ice.

Victory horns and organ music filled the air and the lights flashed up on the scoreboard.

"Get in!" Brad exclaimed as the team high-fived Robyn and jostled with Grant.

"Henrik, I am now in love with you!" Robyn squealed, hugging the player.

"We're gonna win!" Mickey said with a smile a mile wide and jubilation in every step.

"I want focus; don't let this lead go. Back out there, one hundred percent," Robyn ordered, trying to calm herself down.

She couldn't believe they were winning. She couldn't believe they had scored against the best team in the league. Her heart was pounding so hard in her chest it hurt. It was the best feeling.

"It was an amazing goal," Grant remarked as the referee recommenced play.

"Yes, it was. Are they filming the game for the website?" Robyn inquired.

"I believe so."

"I want that DVD; I want to relive that goal twenty times over. Oh, what's happening? Where's the defense? Shit! Cole! Get back! Oh man! No! No! This can't be happening!" Robyn yelled as Reading scored at the other end of the rink and their fans began celebrating the equalizer.

"Stupid error from Wes caused that. He needs to come off, he's hurt," Grant told her as the heads of the Panthers team went down in recognition of their lost lead.

"There's only five minutes until the end of the period," Robyn said, looking at the clock counting down.

"Yeah, but that player just skipped past him. He does that again, we're losing," Grant told her, stating the obvious.

"Who would you put on?"

"Art."

"He's defense."

"I know."

"We can't do that. We can't start defending a draw, we need to win," Robyn told him.

"A draw against this team would be a great result," Grant told her.

"That wouldn't be good enough for me. Jon, you're going on for Wes. Wes!" Robyn shouted, beckoning him over as play was stopped.

"You're doing really well," Grant said to the team at the end of the second period.

The score was still one all, but the Panthers were looking tired. Their squad was smaller than Reading's, and they didn't have the option to change players around so much.

"We need another goal," Robyn told them seriously.

"I'm done," Mickey announced, drinking water like it was going out of fashion.

"Me too. My ribs are on fire," Wade said, supporting his side with his hands.

"I have ankle that feel like large rock hit it," Henrik announced, holding up his skate as if everyone could see.

"Anyone else got any complaints? Because I thought you were an ice hockey team and not a ladies club," Robyn shouted at them.

No one dared answer back.

"Now, what we need to do is hold up their attackers and at every opportunity get the puck to Henrik. He's your main front man. Everyone else…I want you to consolidate their attack. That's all," Robyn instructed them.

"Their number fourteen's carrying an injury," Brad informed everyone.

"Then take him out. It isn't rocket science, guys, is it? We can beat them, they're nothing special. I have no idea how they're top of the league if they play like this every week. We're better than them," Robyn told her team.

"She's got a hundred dollars on us to win," Cole spoke up.

"A hundred dollars! You're kidding me! Are you crazy?" Mickey exclaimed as the players all turned to stare at Robyn.

"You promised you wouldn't tell them!"

"What were the odds?" Brad inquired.

"Fifty to one."

"Oh man! You get five thousand dollars if we win?" Mickey said excitedly.

"What is odds?" Henrik wanted to know.

"I put that bet on because I have faith in you. Don't prove me to be as stupid as the bet sounds," Robyn said as the team huddled close together.

"A hundred dollars," Brad said shaking his head at her.

"Oh, easy come, easy go," Robyn replied with a smile.

"You know, if Reading get another goal, we're done for, don't you?" Grant remarked as Robyn gnawed at her fingers.

"Thanks for that Grant, what d'you want me to do? Sub myself on?" Robyn asked.

"I'm just saying; don't be disheartened if we leak a goal now. We're under constant attack."

"I am well aware of that."

"You've done a good job picking their chins up off the floor, you know. They all really want to play for this team now, the camaraderie is returning—that's because of you," Grant told her.

"That's all they needed. Success is eighty percent belief, don't you know," Robyn replied.

On the ice, Brad picked up the puck, dodged past one player, and laid the ball off to Henrik. Henrik picked it up but was immediately slammed into the boards by the Reading enforcer. The puck slipped free and Cole caught it with his stick and turned. He looked up, shrugged off a tackle from a Reading defender, drew back his stick, and hit the puck toward goal.

The goaltender went down on his knees, the puck flew past him into the top of the net, and the light lit up — Goal!

Robyn let out an ear splitting scream, throwing her hands in the air and punching it in delight. Cole was mobbed by his team and Grant was almost on the ice, jigging up and down and yelling while the referee was surrounded by Reading players demanding the goal be disallowed.

Two minutes later, time was up and the Panthers had won. It was unbelievable, no one had thought victory was achievable but they had done it.

The Portage crowd seemed more satisfied than they had been in months and excited about the games to come.

"I can't believe we won, I mean, Hell!" Mickey exclaimed loudly.

He then threw his head back and howled like a wolf.

"Jeez man! You have to stop doing that, it freaks me out!" Wes said as they all began to strip off their kit and get into the showers.

"He's done it since we were kids," Robyn informed them from the corner of the room where she was sorting out the water bottles.

"Is that traditional celebration noise?" Henrik asked, pulling down his jockstrap and getting under the water.

"Absolutely not," Wade said, wetting his hair.

"So Cole, I guess getting on the score sheet makes you an official Panther," Mickey said, splashing him with water.

"I can't believe it went in. I caught it all wrong," Cole said with a laugh.

"Speaks the pro! Who cares? We won! We beat Reading. Did you see their faces, man? They were freaked," Mickey said.

"What the Hell is this?" Brad asked, picking up Cole's shower gel and holding it up for all to see.

"Oh man, come on, it isn't mine. I picked up the wrong one, it's Robyn's," Cole tried to explain.

"It's purple and it's called Exfoliation. Is that even a proper word? And it's got grapefruit and guava in it. Interesting," Brad teased.

"It is very purple," Wes commented.

"Give it here," Cole said and he made a lunge for it, knocking it out of Brad's hands.

The bottle fell out of the shower and onto the floor. Cole got out of the shower and bent down to pick it up just as Robyn walked passed on her way out.

She looked straight at him. There was no hiding his nakedness, and she found herself immediately reddening and not knowing what to do. She couldn't turn away; she couldn't stop looking at him. If ever there was an advertisement for the perfect man the image before her would be what they would use. He was toned and molded in all the right places and he was hot and wet from the combination of the game and the shower. She chewed on her thumb and closed her eyes as soon as she remembered she should.

"Sorry," Cole said hurriedly, turning his back to her and returning to the shower.

"Hey, Boss! Get your kit off and get in the shower! We freaking won!" Mickey yelled, and he leaned back and howled the loudest howl he could manage.

"Jesus! Man!" Wes exclaimed, holding his hands over his ears.

"Woman in locker room is not right," Henrik said, covering his private parts with a lather of soap.

"Listen up! I just wanted to say something before you all disappear to the bar and start celebrating. First off, training tomorrow at twelve, don't be late. We may have won today, but we need to keep up the momentum. And second—well—I am so God damn proud of you!" Robyn exclaimed, clenching her fist and gesturing it at them.

The team let out a group cheer and started singing the Portage Panther's team song as they linked arms and swayed in time under the showers like a group of kids.

"Where's Grant?" Brad questioned when the singing had finished.

"Grant and Bob are in charge of the kitty for the celebration drinks. They're getting them as we speak. But listen, before we get all excited about more freebies, club funds are all but gone and I have a limit on my finances. I won't be doing this every time you win, which I expect every game now," Robyn explained.

She still couldn't keep her eyes off Cole. He was showering, rinsing off the shower gel, water running through his hair and down his face, along his chest, and over his buttocks...

"Okay, so, one other thing. Barbecue tomorrow at Cole's place. 3540 Woodhams Avenue. From after training 'til the last person passes out. My treat for you doing so awesome today. They're predicting record October temperatures so bring your trunks," Robyn informed them.

"3540 Woodhams? Isn't that one of the million dollar houses? Man, are you loaded or something?" Mickey asked of him.

"I'm renting," Cole replied.

"I love party!" Henrik said, slapping Cole on the back and grinning widely.

"Great, right, so, I'll just go and give my commiserations to the poor, dejected, rather useless Reading manager and let you all get decent," Robyn said, backing toward the door.

"I want to smile right in the face of Gillies. The tool," Wade said, speaking of the Reading enforcer.

"Just let Mickey do the wolf howl in the bar, that will be enough to piss off everybody," Brad told them.

"Okay, so, I'll see you in the bar," Robyn said, still looking at Cole as he grabbed a towel and began to dry himself off.

"Tradition that the boss gets in the shower after a win," Brad called to her.

"Since when?"

"We had Eddie in here last season," Mickey informed her.

Robyn bolted from the room. She slammed the door shut and leaned against it, trying to get the image of Cole's nude body out of her mind. They were all supposed to be asexual to her here, even her fiancé.

Chapter Twenty-five

"Dad? Can you hear me? Dad?"

"I'm here! Jeez, Max, quit with the barking for Christ's sake! Robyn's on the phone. He's coughing his guts up again. That's what you get for smoking sixty Marlboro a day since time began," Eddie replied.

"We won, Dad, we beat Reading," Robyn said, holding the phone closer to her ear.

She was smiling as she looked at her team sitting together drinking pitchers of beer and filling the jukebox up with tunes of glory.

"I know, Buttercup, I heard every God damn second on the radio. I wish I could have been there. What was it like? Was it a big crowd?" Eddie asked.

"The biggest all season, so Grant said. It was almost like the old days. There were families there and two of the local school football teams came. There was probably almost three thousand," Robyn told him.

"And how did it feel when Cole hit the back of the net? The commentator went crazy, said he'd never seen a goal like it. Did he look every inch Wolves material?"

"He was awesome, Dad. The goal was awesome but so was the whole team. They really played as a unit. They supported each other after the equalizer and they never gave up—not once," Robyn continued.

"That's because of you, Buttercup."

"They're your team, Dad, and I told them to do it for you."

"Did they get you in the shower?"

"I'm still a fast runner," Robyn said, grinning.

"Max, can I tell Robyn about your bet? Okay, Max doesn't want you to know, but he backed the Panthers...won a grand," Eddie said with a hearty laugh.

"I knew he wouldn't dare bet against us! You can tell him I won five," Robyn replied.

"Five what?"

"Five grand."

"What? How much did you lay out?"

"A hundred bucks. I got good odds."

"Jeez, Robyn, a hundred dollars! Where did you get that sort of money to spend on gambling?"

"That's my business."

"Is it illegal?"

"No, Dad. Listen, I'd better go, I'll come and see you tomorrow," Robyn said.

"Okay, well, you can bring Cole if you like; I want to hear about the goal from the guy who scored it," Eddie said.

"Sure. Now, listen, eat all your dinner and no staying up too late watching boxing. Tell Max the same."

"You're sounding old, Buttercup. Max, no boxing," Eddie called to his bedmate.

She could hear Max grumbling in between coughs and she ended the call.

190

Brad came over to her and handed her a glass of beer.

"Was that Eddie?" he questioned.

"Yeah, he's excited over the win, but he wishes he could have seen it," Robyn said with a sigh, taking a swig of the drink.

"When's his operation?"

"Wednesday, if all goes as planned. If he keeps his blood pressure down, if his sugar levels are stable, if there are no other more urgent cases, if the wind's blowing in the right direction, you know, that sort of thing."

"And when does the roadhouse reopen?"

"Friday! Don't remind me about that, it's going to be a disaster. I haven't got a band and Nancy thinks all the kids will be freaked out by the clowns I've booked to do balloon animals and plate spinning. The chef needs some special sort of cheese I've never heard of to make the new roadhouse signature dish, and I'm so stressed I'm eating my way through the dill pickles I bought for the stock room and having to replenish them almost every day," Robyn exclaimed.

"Hey, if they're the only things you have to worry about, it sounds like you got it covered," Brad replied, touching her arm.

"Yeah, well, then there's Jason."

"He hasn't been near you again?" Brad asked, immediately stiffening.

"No. but he's dragging it all back up again. He's hired a lawyer to get the case reopened. If the police do reopen the case, they'll want to talk to everyone again, talk to me again, make me relive it all over again. I can't do that," Robyn said.

"It's never going to happen. It was an open and shut case. There's no way they'll reopen anything without good cause, like new evidence or something," Brad reassured her.

"Well, what if he has some or he gets some?"

"Did he say he had some?"

"Well, no but..." Robyn began.

"Then stop worrying. I'm telling you, nothing's gonna come of it. Anyway, you think my daddy's going to let him reopen the case? He worked hard on that case; he made sure justice was done for you, Robyn," Brad reminded her.

"I know, but you said he was retiring."

"Not yet. And definitely not if Jason's back in town," Brad assured her.

"I'm sorry, I shouldn't even be bringing any of this up now, I mean, Hell! We have a victory to celebrate!" Robyn said, leading the way back to the group.

He smiled as he watched her mount a chair with Mickey and sway in time to "We Are the Champions." He'd seen the way she looked at him when she'd caught him in the shower. And her seeing him had affected him, too. His groin had reacted, and he'd had to clamp down on that feeling before it had gotten out of control.

Last night, after he'd proposed and they'd lain in bed together, he couldn't go back to sleep. He'd feigned fatigue, closed his eyes and waited for her to drop off just so he could have a moment looking at her. He loved her. It was four days since he'd met her, and he loved her. That's why he'd asked her to marry him. That depth of feeling couldn't be ignored, but he knew she wasn't ready for anything physical. He was okay with that. It seemed secondary somehow. This was different from anything else he'd had before—so different. He still couldn't quite believe it. How did something like that just happen?

Chapter Twenty-six

"When is pig ready? I need pig, I have much hungry," Henrik stated, swigging from a bottle of beer.

"Pig's been cooking all day, just about to reach optimum succulence, apparently. Have some chips," Robyn said, offering him the plate she was carrying.

There were over twenty people in Cole's garden the following day. They had trained in the morning, despite most of the team being hungover from the victory celebrations that had lasted late into the night. Now they were drinking, chatting, and dancing to the music coming from the outside surround sound while eating chips, dips, and steaks from the barbecue Bob was happily tending to. Everyone was enjoying the Michigan heat and the previous night's game was still being relived.

Mickey let out a loud werewolf howl and Sarah slapped his arm.

"Stop doing that! No one thinks it's funny and you sound ridiculous," she told him, taking a sip of her white wine.

"Oh, lighten up Sar, it's a party! You know…fun," Mickey snapped, downing his bottle of beer.

"Yes, I vaguely remember fun. It's what we used to have before you were out with the boys all the time," Sarah told him.

"Hey, come on you two, Robyn's gone to a lot of effort here, let's enjoy it," Brad ordered them, handing Sarah another glass of wine.

"Oh, thank you, Brad. I didn't really need another one but…" Sarah spoke, blushing slightly.

"This house is amazing, have you seen the size of the TV?" Mickey asked Brad.

"Yeah, and the Jacuzzi's almost as big as a pool, Henrik's dying to get in it," Brad said.

"What's stopping him?" Cole asked as he joined the group.

"Can we use it?" Mickey asked, his eyes wide with excitement.

"Sure. You got trunks, right? Robyn told you to bring trunks."

"Henrik isn't going to care about trunks," Brad said with a laugh.

"No, you know what those Danes are like," Mickey replied, taking another beer from the cooler filled with bottles and ice.

"Danes? I thought he was Icelandic," Cole remarked.

"I thought he was German," Sarah admitted.

"He's Swedish," Robyn insisted as she joined the group, holding a plate of chips out to everyone.

"I thought the twins were supposed to be waitressing," Sarah said, taking a chip from Robyn's plate.

"They are. Pam's getting them into outfits," Robyn said with a snicker.

"No way! They're going to hate that!" Sarah exclaimed.

"Yeah, I know. There's no telling her though, is there? Cole, lend the guys some trunks if they haven't got any. Sarah, come up with me, I'll show you the house and you can borrow a bikini,"

Robyn said, taking one of the glasses of wine from her friend and grabbing her hand.

"Hey, Robyn! How many pairs of trunks d'you think I have?" Cole called after her.

"He has at least three pairs, I found them when I was rifling through his drawers checking out his t-shirt collection," Robyn whispered to Sarah.

"Has everyone had some pig? Sienna and Sierra, the ones in the French maid outfits, have some plated up if anyone wants any more!" Robyn called from the Jacuzzi. She shared the water with Sarah, Mickey, Henrik, Brad, and Cole.

"Pig was good," Henrik said with a nod, drinking from a shot glass and grimacing as the burn hit his throat.

"Yeah, the pig was great, Robyn," Brad told her.

"Thanks, I'm hoping we can have a hog roast at the roadhouse on opening night and fireworks. Oh, and I must organize a band. Are Special Guest still around? They used to rock," Robyn said, stretching an arm out behind Cole.

"I'm not sure. I haven't seen them advertised anywhere lately," Sarah remarked.

"Who is Special Guest?" Henrik asked.

"They're an awesome band, Henrik. They did all the classics…you know, ZZ Top, The Rolling Stones, a bit of country…" Robyn explained.

"Robyn sung with them once," Sarah informed them.

"I did not!"

"She did. She was fifteen and drunk, and she grabbed the mic and belted out a Bon Jovi number. It was truly terrible," Sarah told the group.

"Don't even think about denying it, Robyn. Bob and I were there," Pam announced, coming over to the Jacuzzi and collecting empty bottles.

"God! Who needs family?" Robyn remarked.

"You did when I was cleaning up your puke the next day," Pam added.

"Oh man, this is so embarrassing!"

"So…the party's good and all, but what we need in the town is a proper celebration, like an engagement or something," Brad blurted out, looking straight at Robyn.

She bristled immediately and pulled her ponytail forward. Why on Earth had he said that?

"Can't see that happening. Too many singletons on the team," Wade called from the sun lounger he was laying on.

"How about you and Sarah, Mick? Isn't it time you made an honest woman out of her? I mean, you've been dating like forever," Robyn continued, hurriedly swigging back some beer.

"Robyn, don't," Sarah begged, her eyes welling up with tears she was trying to blink back.

"Yeah, sure, one day we'll do it, won't we?" Mickey said, patting Sarah affectionately on the leg like she was a pet dog.

"Will we?" Sarah asked harshly, turning to look at him.

"Yeah, I mean, you drag me past the jewelers so often, I'm bound to give in one day, aren't I?" Mickey continued.

"Give in," Sarah remarked.

"I don't think Mickey meant it like it sounded," Cole said.

"Oh, don't you? Well, how did you mean it, Mickey? Because 'giving in' sounds like relenting to pressure. Is that how you see our relationship? A pressure? Something you put up with to keep me quiet?" Sarah questioned, standing up and looking down at her boyfriend.

"Shit, this is my fault. Forget I said anything," Brad said rapidly.

"Sorry, Robyn, I'm going to go. I don't want to spend another minute with him right now," Sarah said, hoisting herself over the side of the Jacuzzi.

"Sarah, don't go. Mickey, come on, don't let her go," Brad encouraged him.

"I don't know what I've done wrong. Is it that time of the month?" Mickey asked, reaching across for another beer.

"Man, you are an idiot," Brad remarked, and he leapt out of the tub and hurried after Sarah.

"I'm with Brad, you're a tool," Robyn said, scowling at him.

"Cole, the doorbell rang and there are more guests. I invited them in," Pam announced, smiling at him.

Cole looked up to greet the guests and immediately his expression darkened. A woman with long, dark hair stared over at him, tears in her eyes, one hand held protectively on her stomach. Robyn knew instinctively who this woman was and her chest tightened. The woman was perfectly presented, her hair coiled neatly onto her shoulders, and she was wearing make-up and a pink blouse. She looked so girly, so not like Robyn.

"Cole," the woman said weakly.

"What are you doing here?" he questioned, standing up and getting out of the tub.

"You won't return my calls or my messages."

"I told you and I told Bryn I never wanted to see either of you again. How much clearer do you need me to be?"

"Is this Veronica?" Robyn checked, getting out of the Jacuzzi to join him.

"Yeah, Robyn. This is Veronica." He flung his hand in Veronica's direction.

It was at that moment that a middle-aged man, wearing an expensive-looking business suit, stepped out of the veranda doors and onto the decking.

Robyn's heart rose up into her mouth and she bit down on her tongue as their eyes met.

"Hello, Robyn," he greeted with a warm smile.

"Hi, Clive," she replied.

Chapter Twenty-seven

"You didn't call, I was worried," Clive said.

With Cole's robe wrapped over her bikini, Robyn busied herself making a pot of coffee. She'd had five or more beers and she couldn't be speaking to him drunk. She wanted to say the right things and she wanted to remember saying them.

"I've been busy," she answered stiffly.

"Too busy for a phone conversation? Come on, Robyn, I was worried. I was imagining all sorts of things."

"Like what? No planes have come down, no skinny British girls have been murdered that I know of. I can look after myself. What are you doing here?" she asked, turning to face him.

"I wanted to see you. How's your father?"

"I wish you hadn't said that."

"What?"

"He's doing okay. He's having the bypass soon, as long as he steers clear of Dunkin' Donuts," Robyn informed him.

"Good, I'm glad," he replied.

"So what are you doing here and how did you find me?"

"I went to the roadhouse. A woman there told me where you were staying. This isn't your aunt's house, is it? I mean, this isn't a ranch house, this must be worth..." Clive began.

"A million at least, probably more. What are you doing here?" Robyn repeated as the coffee pot began to sputter to life.

Clive took a deep breath and held it in until his chest had expanded to full capacity. He looked older and more tired than she remembered. There seemed to be more lines around his eyes, but perhaps they had been there before and she just hadn't noticed. He looked jaded and weary, but maybe that was just the jetlag.

"Carolyn's pregnant," he announced, the breath leaving his chest in one quick rush, the words following.

"Wow," Robyn replied.

She didn't know what else to say. What was protocol for finding out your married lover's wife was pregnant?

"Obviously, it was completely unplanned. I mean, you know what it's like. I have to keep up appearances in that department but..." Clive started, shifting on the kitchen bar stool Robyn had sat him on.

"You want to end things," Robyn guessed.

"No! No, Robyn—not that. I just...well...things will be difficult for a while. She'll expect me to be there more, at the start at least, so..."

"I'm not coming back to England," Robyn announced.

She didn't know where the statement had come from but it was out and passed her lips before she knew it.

"What do you mean?" Clive asked, a puzzled look on his face.

"Dad needs me here. Even after the operation, he's not going to be able to run the roadhouse or manage the ice hockey team," she continued.

She picked up the coffee pot and rapidly filled two mugs.

"But what about your aunt? Surely she can help. I mean, how long are you planning on staying? We said a month maybe. How long do you need?" Clive wanted to know.

"I need forever," Robyn responded, passing him a mug and watching his expression.

"Cole, look at me," Veronica urged him.

They sat in the living room while the party carried on outside. Cole was still in his trunks and water was dripping onto the cream carpet. He didn't care. That was the very least of his worries.

"I can't," he responded, not raising his head.

"We need to talk about this. Bryn and I are worried about your mom," Veronica continued.

"Did he send you here? He made you fly in that condition?" Cole asked, lifting his head and gesturing to her pregnant swell.

"It was my idea to come. I know you, Cole. I know how hurt you are and I know what we did was unforgiveable, but we need to do something to straighten it out for your mom's sake," Veronica told him.

"You don't know me," Cole stated brutally.

"I know you care about your mom. And so does Bryn, and she's not doing so good right now."

"I only left a few days ago. She's fine."

"She wouldn't want you to worry. She knows you need to focus on your new job," Veronica said.

"What do you want me to say, Veronica? What do you expect me to do?" Cole asked her.

"She wants the family together for Thanksgiving."

"I hope you're kidding me," he said, standing up.

"She would never tell you herself, but that's what she wants. She wants you, Bryn, me, and your Uncle Derek around the table together as a family," Veronica continued.

"Yeah? Well, that's not happening."

"Bryn said you would be like this but I didn't believe him. I know you have a soft soul, Cole. The way you used to talk about your father, how you cried for him…he wouldn't want this division in the family. You know that," Veronica said

"That's enough," Cole warned.

"Don't shut Bryn out Cole. You're brothers."

"We were."

"You can't help who you fall in love with."

"Believe me, I know that."

"Then find it in your heart to forgive him, even if you can't forgive me. After all, he saved you once," Veronica said, tears pricking her eyes.

"What?"

"He told me what you did after your dad died. He loves you Cole, and he wants you to be part of this baby's life. We both want that," Veronica insisted.

"You need to leave," Cole told her.

"You're doing what? Getting married! You've been here less than a week!" Clive exclaimed, sloshing some of his coffee onto his trousers.

"Shh! Keep your voice down," Robyn begged, waving her arms to try and quiet him.

"What do you think you're doing, Robyn? This is madness! You've been gone a few days and suddenly you want to leave everything behind, start living in America, and marry some country bumpkin you've no doubt picked up at some ice hockey match. It's ludicrous," Clive announced.

"I don't expect you to understand, I'd just like you to accept it," Robyn answered calmly.

"Well, I don't! I don't accept it!" His voice boomed as he slammed his cup down on the counter.

"Clive, I really appreciate everything you've done for me. You helped me out when I was in a really dark place, and I'll always be grateful, but things have changed," Robyn attempted to explain.

"In a few days?"

"Yes. I know how that sounds, but yes."

"You're making it sound like you're cancelling an unwanted car warranty," Clive told her.

"This is your chance to try again with Carolyn. A new baby, a new start for the both of you," Robyn said.

"I'm not so sure about that."

"I can't be what you want me to be," Robyn stated, meeting his gaze.

"And exactly what do you think I want you to be, Robyn?"

"Clive, we eat expensive Thai takeout in the flat and talk about places we're never going to go together," Robyn said with a sigh.

"I'm always suggesting restaurants and weekends away, you always say no."

"I know I do. Because I don't want to go," Robyn admitted.

"We've been together over eight years," Clive reminded her.

"And I've never really been there," Robyn said sadly.

"I'm getting married," Cole told her.

"What?"

"Yeah."

"But…"

"What, did you think I'd never get over you?"

"No, of course not, but…so soon? I mean you can't have…"

"I've known her five days," Cole admitted.

"Five days."

"Yeah, and I feel like I've loved her a lifetime already," he said.

"I don't know what to say."

"I'm saying I don't need the family any more. Moving here was the best thing I've ever done. I met Robyn and I have a great team behind me at Gen-All. I know what's important now and it isn't the past," Cole said as he ran his hand through his wet hair.

"Then forget the past and forgive Bryn," Veronica suggested.

"It doesn't quite work like that."

"Does your mom know you're planning on getting married?"

"Not yet."

"Have you really thought this through?"

"No, I haven't, and ya know what? That's why it's right."

"I'll pay you back everything. All the gifts, all the money you gave me. I spent some of it on the roadhouse but when we make a profit I can…" Robyn began.

"I don't want anything back, Robyn," Clive replied soberly.

"I didn't expect this to happen. I didn't come here thinking I wouldn't go back," she assured him.

"Are you sure? Really sure staying here is what you want? Are you certain it isn't just being back here evoking fond memories?" Clive asked.

"I'm sure," Robyn answered with a nod.

Clive nodded in reply and ran his finger around the rim of his coffee cup.

"I care about you, Robyn."

The words were loaded with emotion, more than she'd probably given him credit for.

"I know you do and that used to be enough…but it isn't any more."

Chapter Twenty-eight

"Hey," Robyn greeted, entering the den.

Clive had left and Henrik and the rest of the team had taken the party into town. Only Bob, Pam, and the twins remained, clearing up the garden.

"Hey," Cole replied.

"The pregnant ex gone?"

"Yeah. How about the married guy?"

"Driving back to the airport as we speak," Robyn replied, sitting down next to him.

"Some party, huh?"

"Yeah."

"Listen Robyn…"

"You don't have to say anything. It's okay if you still feel something for Veronica. I mean…"

"I don't. I don't feel anything for her."

Robyn nodded and chewed on her thumbnail, looking at him and waiting for whatever was coming next. There was something, she could tell. He looked anxious and agitated.

"There's something I need to tell you," he began.

"You want to call off the wedding," Robyn stated.

"No, nothing like that," he said, holding her hands in his.

"Then tell me, whatever it is, just tell me," she begged.

He took a long breath and then let it drift out slowly as if he was composing himself for an important speech.

"When my dad died, I didn't decide to choose medicine and try to make a difference, not right away. I lost it, Robyn, I lost it big time. My dad was my rock and we were close, I mean, real close. We did everything together. Bryn, he was older, he spent more time with his friends. But me, I liked spending time with Dad. We went to hockey together, we went to football together, we fished, we played golf. We did everything together, and when I lost him, I didn't know what to do. My whole world had been taken away and I couldn't focus. My center had gone, my familiarity, my balance…nothing was there any more," Cole began.

She could see the pain of losing his father etched on his face and those dark eyes were moist with tears.

"Robyn, I was stupid, so freaking stupid. I didn't know what I was doing and I didn't care about anything," he said, looking up at her.

"What is it? You can tell me."

"I was in a bad, dark place and I just wanted him back," he said, the tears finally escaping.

"What did you do?"

"I completely lost my mind. From the moment he passed away, I went on some grief-fuelled rollercoaster ride," Cole admitted.

"You got in trouble?" Robyn guessed.

"I drank myself into a stupor every single day. I beat up my best friend, I dropped out of school, I told my mom I hated her, and I almost killed somebody when I drove through a stop sign. I spent thirty days in jail."

He looked over to Robyn, waiting for her reaction, wondering what the admission was going to do to her. It had to do something. She thought he was strong, she thought he was this ambitious, dedicated person who was going to cure the world of its ills, but the truth was, he was as weak as the next person. Weaker probably. She looked like she was thinking so hard, he could almost see the wheels in motion. He needed to be honest with her and he needed to be honest with himself. She had to know who he really was and who he was wasn't all good.

"I once took a monkey wrench to a customer when he pinched my ass," Robyn stated, her voice wobbling slightly.

"Robyn, I was a mess! I was this disgusting individual who didn't care about anybody or anything. I was filled up with rage against the whole damn world as if it was everyone else's fault that my dad had died. I hated everyone and I hated myself. I was on some road to self-destruction and that's what happened next," Cole carried on.

"What?" Robyn asked, squeezing his hands.

"Bryn found me unconscious. I'd taken God knows how many pills and drank three bottles of vodka. He got me to the emergency room. If he hadn't found me…"

"What happened then?" Robyn asked with a swallow.

"I came to in hospital, feeling rougher than you can imagine. By the side of my bed was my dad's ice hockey shirt. Mom had brought it in and she'd put it by my pillow. It still smelt of him, you know, and that smell, it just filled me up. I didn't want to die. Dad had given me all these fantastic times, and I realized those memories should have been shaping my future. I wanted to make him proud and I needed to be a better person," Cole explained.

Robyn threw her arms around him and held him close, pulling him tight to her.

"I left Chicago because I could feel those destructive feelings coming back after what Bryn and Veronica did. It didn't have anything to do with Dad, it had to do with me. I'm not good enough, Robyn, but I really want to be," Cole told her fiercely.

"What d'you mean, you're not good enough?" she asked.

"People leave me because I'm nothing. I thought the work I do would make a difference, but I can't find the answers. What if I never find them? What then? Who am I without that? Where's my focus?"

"Now you listen to me. I don't know anything about your work but I know about you. You, Cole Ryan, are far from nothing. For a start, you're my fiancé! And that makes you pretty damn special in my world."

"I don't want to let you down."

"The only way you're going to let me down is if you don't kiss me right now," Robyn ordered him.

Cole looked at her, his big eyes full of tears and regret.

"Why aren't you doing it?" Robyn asked him.

Cole tenderly took her face in his hands and brought her lips to his, parting them slowly and delivering a warm, soft touch to her mouth.

"You must never do anything like that ever again. If you've got a problem, you tell me about it. Do you hear me?" she asked.

"Loud and clear."

"I'm hiding all the Advil and the alcohol unless you promise me," she said, pulling back so she could look into his eyes.

"I promise you."

"Swear it. Swear it on your Chicago Wolves limited edition hooded sweater," Robyn said, squeezing his hands.

"I swear it on my limited edition Chicago Wolves hooded sweater and the matching track pants," Cole answered, his tone serious.

Robyn gazed at him, studying his expression, before finally nodding. She laid a kiss on his injured knuckles and let go of his hand.

"I want you to meet my mom," he stated.

"Oh."

"I want you to. It's important to me."

"Yeah, but she might test me on vacuuming techniques and I don't even know where it's kept," Robyn replied, wiping at her eyes.

"Knowing that I'm moving on—even though I'm not ready to bury the hatchet with Bryn and Veronica—it might make her worry less about things. She worries a lot about things since Dad died," Cole said.

"Will I have to wear a dress and fancy shoes and bake brownies?" Robyn asked him.

"Of course."

"Are we going to tell her we're getting married?"

"Are you okay with that?"

"I'm not sure. I mean, it isn't like we've set a date or anything."

"Do you want to set a date?"

"Do you?"

"I asked first."

"October twenty-second, I've always liked the number twenty-two," Robyn replied.

"That's in two weeks."

"Then you have a lot of planning to do. I want a cake, three tiers, all chocolate. And I want to get married here, by the lake, on the sand, and I want to arrive in Bob's boat. I want Special Guest to perform at the reception and I want that slow Eric Clapton song playing in the background when we sign the license. And I want everyone barefoot. And we don't tell anyone until the day before," Robyn reeled out.

"I'm happy with all that," Cole told her.

"Well, obviously you need to think about what you want too. I mean, Special Guest are quite versatile; we don't have to have Eric Clapton. Just as long as you don't get them playing Bruce Springsteen, never been a fan," Robyn said.

"How about REO Speedwagon?"

"Are you serious?"

Chapter Twenty-nine

"Nancy! What are these?" Robyn asked, holding up a very ancient looking plastic packet that had started to turn brown. It was Monday.

"Dunno, honey, rubbers?" Nancy responded with a hearty cackle, nudging Milo and getting him to look.

"Should have known I wouldn't get a proper answer. They resemble balloons, but they look about twenty years old," Robyn remarked, stretching one out and trying to blow into it with little success.

"I found them out back, thought we could use them to decorate for opening night," Nancy said.

"You are kidding me. They're going to go down in five seconds flat. I've ordered helium ones, two hundred of them, with the roadhouse motif on them. We can decorate the restaurant and give some away to the kids," Robyn told her.

"Waste of money if you ask me," Nancy muttered.

"Now you're even sounding like my dad. Milo, has Chef tracked down that cheese yet?" Robyn asked, looking at her checklist.

"He was on the internet earlier looking at delivery prices to have it shipped from France," Milo informed her.

"Right, let me put a stop to that. He'll have to make do with Portage's finest. I'm not having my budget blown on imported cheese," Robyn told them.

"Just balloons," Nancy remarked to Milo.

"I heard that," Robyn called back.

"Morning," Brad greeted as he entered the roadhouse dressed in full police uniform.

"Hey, mister, where did you get to yesterday? You totally missed Cole's ex turning up and Henrik almost drowning in the lake," Robyn said, smiling at him.

"Er, well, Sarah was a little upset. I walked her home," Brad responded.

Robyn scrutinized him. His cheek was twitching and he was shuffling awkwardly from one foot to the other.

"I stayed with her, you know, for a bit, and then I headed home," he continued stiffly.

Robyn carried on looking at him, her hands on her hips, unconvinced by what he was saying.

"Her and Mickey aren't too good at the moment," Brad stated.

"I gathered. So…" Robyn started.

The door of the roadhouse swung open and Sarah entered. As soon as she saw Brad, she became completely flustered and tried to hide her face behind her hair.

"I'd better be going," Brad said, nervously straightening his hat.

"Well, hang on, what did you want? You must have come here for a reason," Robyn said, following him as he rushed out the door.

"I was just…going to ask…if you were free for dinner tonight," Brad said, avoiding Sarah's gaze as she raised her head out of her hair.

"Tonight? Er, no, not tonight. I'm doing something tonight. How about tomorrow night?" Robyn suggested hurriedly.

"We've got training," Brad reminded her.

"Oh, yeah, of course we have. Well, how about after? We could get Chinese or something."

"That sounds good," Brad agreed with a smile.

"Great, well, I'll see you tomorrow," Robyn told him.

"See you," Brad said, waving his hand and heading to his squad car.

Robyn turned back to Sarah and grabbed her by the arm. She led her back into the roadhouse and pushed her down into one of the booths.

"Ow! You're hurting me! What are you doing?" Sarah exclaimed, bumping down onto the seat.

"What's going on with you and Brad? What happened last night?" Robyn demanded to know as Nancy and Milo looked on intrigued.

"Nothing happened last night. Nothing's going on," Sarah said, playing with a tendril of her hair.

"Don't lie to me! It's written all over your face and it's written all over Brad's face. Tell me!" Robyn ordered.

"We kissed. Kind of," Sarah blurted out.

"Nancy! I need a Jack and Coke!" Robyn bellowed, putting her hand to her chest.

"You want ice?" Nancy called back.

"Just bring it!"

"Look, it was something of nothing. He walked me home, I made him coffee. I bawled my eyes out and he was nice to me. He listened to me, he said he understood, and then we kind of looked at each other and the next thing…" Sarah attempted to explain.

"Jack and Coke. You want one, too, sugar? Something for the guilt?" Nancy offered, handing Robyn her glass.

"Listen, what goes on in Eddie's Roadhouse, stays in Eddie's Roadhouse. That was always Dad's rule and I'm not changing it now. You keep it zipped," Robyn told Nancy seriously.

"If you want my opinion, I wouldn't let the grass grow where the officer's concerned. Nice guy and biceps like grapefruits," Nancy spoke, chewing gum loudly.

"Thank you, Nancy, that will be all," Robyn said, dismissing her.

"I don't know what to do," Sarah admitted, her eyes filling with tears.

"What d'you mean? What happened after you kissed? I mean, who pulled away first? Did you? Did he? What did he say? What did you say? Did he go? Did you make a joke of it and share another coffee?" Robyn questioned frantically.

"He pulled away first."

"No! Sarah! What would you have done if he hadn't pulled away? Would you have gone further? Grappled with the biceps like grapefruits? Grappled with something else?" Robyn wanted to know, looking at her friend like she was insane.

"I don't know. He stood up and said he was sorry. He said he was taking advantage of the situation and it was a mistake. In fact, he apologized over and over until we got to the door."

"What happened at the door? Do I want to know?"

"He told me he's in love with you. Always has been, always will be," Sarah informed her.

Robyn gripped her glass harder.

"You knew that, though, didn't you? I mean, he lights up when you're around, becomes the Brad he used to be before Michelle left him for Randy. I knew that too, really, but I guess I was hoping…" Sarah began, still toying with her hair.

"Hoping? You were hoping something would happen with Brad? What about Mickey! You've devoted your life to Mickey," Robyn reminded her.

"I don't know what I was hoping for, really, just for a bit of attention, I guess. The knowledge that someone still finds me attractive. Even if it's a second best to you attractive. It's better than a not even on the same scale as a Dodge attractive."

"I wish you'd told me this before I accepted dinner with him tomorrow night. I thought we could be friends, I thought I'd made it clear I didn't want any more than that," Robyn said.

"He thinks you'll learn to love him, like you used to," Sarah commented.

"I never loved him! We dated in high school; we snogged at the drive-in a couple of times, that's all," Robyn announced seriously.

"Snogged?"

"Made out."

"It was more than that for him."

"Well, I need to spell it out to him tomorrow night. Now what are you going to do?" Robyn wanted to know.

"I'm going to tell Mickey it's over," Sarah said in a determined tone.

He'd tried to call his mom twice that morning. He couldn't do it. What Veronica had said about her wanting the family together for Thanksgiving had hit him hard. Why didn't he have it inside him to forgive Bryn? What he'd done was low, but did it matter now? He'd had his revenge when he'd put him in hospital and trashed his apartment. What was he hanging on to? He had Robyn, and now she knew everything about him and still wanted him. They'd been so close last night. She'd held him, she'd kissed him, and, for a moment, she had looked at him like she wanted there to be more. But he'd hesitated and she'd made a wisecrack about something from the Portage Panthers' Hall of Fame. She still wasn't ready.

Chapter Thirty

She was nervous and she didn't know what to wear. It wasn't that she thought she needed to put on an act for Cole, it was just she hadn't been on a date since high school and she wanted this one to go right. Should she stick to jeans and a t-shirt or should she wear something else? Did she actually bring anything else? Actually, she was pretty sure she'd packed a navy blue wool sweater that came to mid-thigh. It was still her, but it was a little different. Yesterday's good weather hadn't lasted and it was back to feeling like autumn again. She'd need her boots too. She searched for the items in the case she had yet to unpack. This felt so odd. She was going on a date with the man she'd said she'd marry.

He looked at his reflection in the bathroom mirror and tweaked at his hair. This date was so important. He wanted it to be perfect. He wanted to give Robyn a night she deserved. He'd wanted to get her something, but flowers or chocolates weren't going to cut it. She'd probably want to see what the flowers tasted like and make a display of the chocolates. She wasn't like any girl he'd met before, but he knew she was the right girl.

He slipped his hand into the pocket of his jeans and felt the box inside.

"I've got a confession to make," Cole said as he pulled Leonora into the parking lot of the Old Country Buffet later that evening.

"You've hired Angela Lansbury to play your mother — that's who's coming tomorrow. And your real mother really has been as stiff as a board in her cellar since well before we met," Robyn replied.

"You got me," he said with a grin.

"I like Angela Lansbury."

"I couldn't get tickets for the monster trucks," Cole admitted.

"You're kidding me! What sort of date is this? Please tell me you haven't booked a couple's manicure or tickets to see Legally Blonde or anything with Meg Ryan," Robyn said.

"No, we're going to this great country bar to shoot pool and turkeys," Cole informed her.

"What?!"

"Remember when you went out for coffee at the hospital? Your dad told me you're some sort of ace with a twelve gauge. At first that knowledge scared me, but then Gerry from maintenance told me about the bar," Cole continued.

"You've entered us in a turkey shoot?"

"This is going to be your best date ever," he told her with a smile.

She smiled back at him. He couldn't have picked anything more appropriate.

"We might have to empty out the fridge. I am a great shot. Come on, I'm starving!" Robyn announced as she ran toward the restaurant.

Cole locked the car and hurried after her.

"Two adults please, with drinks. Oh, you are going to love this place. Look at all the food! Are there burritos on the buffet today?" Robyn asked the cashier as Cole prepared to pay.

"Yes, ma'am."

"Cole, you are going to die when you taste their chili beef," Robyn said excitedly.

"Robyn, maybe we should go eat at the bar," Cole suddenly suggested as he looked out over the counters of food, taking hold of her arm.

"Are you crazy? This is the best place for great food and it's cheap. I know you have a million dollar house on the lake and a great job, but I don't, and I ditched the sugar daddy, remember," Robyn informed him, jogging off to find a table.

"Robyn, Grant and Jason are just over there," Cole explained, taking her arm again and stopping her in her tracks.

Robyn looked up and saw the two men choosing fries and fried chicken from the counter just to her right. They were chatting together and laughing. They both looked as if they didn't have a care in the world.

"Do you want to go?" Cole asked her.

"No," Robyn said, vigorously shaking her head.

"What d'you want to do? I'd quite like to punch him again, if I'm honest."

"No, I'm going to take charge," Robyn said and she set off toward them, grabbing a plate from the stack.

Cole was quick to grab a plate himself and followed right behind her.

"Grant," Robyn greeted, standing beside him.

Grant looked up and paled at the sight of her, his embarrassment clear for all to see.

"Listen, you're here and I'm here, and I love this food and I'm not leaving. And I don't think you should leave, either. But I want you to sit far away from that table just there, because that's where Cole and I are going to be sitting," Robyn said, pointing to her favorite table by the window.

She couldn't look directly at Jason but she could see him out of the corner of her eye. He was looking at her, his red hair flopping into his eyes, his plate piled high with chicken and fries.

"Robyn..." Jason began.

"Don't talk to her," Cole ordered, stepping forward.

"No, Cole, don't...please. This is our night, don't let him spoil it," Robyn begged, turning to face him, a pleading expression on her face.

"We're going to sit down over there," Grant ordered his son.

"Dad, she has to know," Jason began, nudging his father's arm.

"She has to know what?" Cole inquired, glaring at Jason.

"Jason, I'm warning you. Just go sit down and eat," Grant said gruffly.

"What do I need to know?" Robyn asked, swallowing.

"The District Attorney has decided to reopen the case; I'm going to clear my name," Jason said.

"That's enough. You've told her, now let's just go and eat," Grant ordered, taking his son by the arm.

"But why would they do that without new evidence?" Robyn asked, her tone thick with shock.

"They have new evidence. I found a witness who saw me in our backyard right around the time you were..." Jason started.

"That's enough. We're going to sit down. Now!" Grant said, shooing Jason across the restaurant.

Robyn took a deep breath and looked at Cole.

"You okay?" Cole asked her.

"If he has a witness then…" Robyn started.

How did you analyze information like that? If someone had seen Jason in his yard, then he couldn't have been the one to attack her. But then again, they had interviewed everyone at the time, why suddenly had someone come forward? Could he or she be believed? Thoughts spun around in her head and she couldn't take them in.

"Listen, let's not think about anything until you hear officially. You must have had some sort of caseworker when it was all going on. If what he says is true, they'll be contacting you," Cole reassured, putting his arm around her.

"Yeah, her name was Trudy and she kept suggesting I cry. I don't know whether it was because she thought it would help or whether she just liked seeing people cry."

"Hey, come on, nothing's changed; we're on our first date. You've brought me to this great place and you're making me hold off from the food! Man, look at it all!" Cole said, indicating the platters all lined up under the heat lamps.

"Why did he have to be here? Tonight was supposed to be special," Robyn said with a frustrated sigh.

"Hey, look at me. It is going to be special. Starting with soup, right?" Cole told her.

"Don't be fooled into having the soup. It's nice but it's stuffed full of dumplings to make you so full you can't manage anything else. I start with burritos and work my way through until I get to apple pie," Robyn explained.

"You're going to have to show me the way; it sounds like I'm a complete eating novice," Cole replied, putting his arm around her shoulders.

Chapter Thirty-one

"Now you hold the gun like this," Robyn said later at the turkey shoot at Logan's Country Bar.

"Like this?"

"Oh God, put it down! Cole! You can't be waving it around like that! Have you never shot before?" Robyn asked, grabbing the weapon from him.

"Robyn, I know Chicago has developed a bit of a reputation, but we weren't all tooled up on my street," Cole answered.

"Some weeks, when I was small, this is what you had to do for a decent dinner. Here, like this," she said, taking his gun and positioning him around it.

She held his hips as he looked down the barrel and lined up with the mid-distance target. Bringing her here had taken a lot of thought. He knew what she'd like. He accepted she wasn't a girly girl. She could feel the muscles at the bottom of his back and she felt her stomach contract.

"Where are the turkeys?" Cole asked, still looking down the gun.

"Are you kidding me?"

"What?"

"We don't really shoot turkeys, Cole. That's what they did in bygone days, now we're aiming at targets. Like there! And there!" Robyn pointed out.

She picked up her gun and released a pellet at each target.

Cole dropped his gun to the floor and hurried to cover his ears with his hands.

"Whoa! I'd forgotten how good that felt," Robyn said with a laugh of excitement.

"Really?"

"Really. Come on, it's your turn," Robyn urged him.

"I think I'm going to be lucky if I manage to hit a tree. What's the prize?" Cole asked her.

"Turkey!" Robyn announced.

"I don't even really like turkey," Cole admitted, lining up his gun.

"We'll pluck it and strip it and chuck it in with some pasta…or we could always barbecue. Shoot God damn it!" Robyn urged.

Cole fired the gun and, after the sound of his shot had echoed away, there was a loud squawk. Something large and dark gray fell out of the tree in front of them.

"Jeez, Cole, you just shot a turkey at a turkey shoot!" Robyn exclaimed, staring at him with a mixture of horror and awe in her expression.

"Does that mean we win?"

He had to drive home, but he could really have done with a beer. He was nervous and the box in his pocket was weighing heavier as the night went on. Robyn had won fifty dollars and a frozen turkey for being the best shot of the night, and the turkey he had mistakenly killed was being packaged up for them to take home.

Now Robyn was chatting to two cowboys about the Panthers and suggesting they come to watch the next match. Despite his apprehension about what he wanted to do, this was the best night he'd ever had.

"So, you don't shoot, you're not so keen on turkey, you like a loose milk carton lid...please tell me you dance," Robyn said to him, downing the contents of her beer bottle.

"Come on, Robyn, I'm a guy. Guys don't dance," Cole reminded her.

"Cole Ryan, you are sexist! You lied to me on that plane ride! How can I believe anything you say ever again?" Robyn asked, her hand on her chest.

The jukebox kicked into Brooks and Dunn and people began hurrying to the dance floor.

"Do you think Gerry from maintenance came here with Leonora?" Robyn asked him, taking hold of his hand.

"I know they did," he replied, smiling at her.

"Well, we're driving the car, we'd better not let her memory down. Come on," Robyn said.

She pulled Cole down off the bar stool and led him into the middle of the dance floor.

"Robyn, I don't dance. What are they all doing?" Cole exclaimed, looking at the people around them.

"Line dancing. Come on, try it. Just copy everyone else," Robyn urged as she put her thumbs into the pockets of her jeans and mimicked the other dancers.

"You tell any of the team about this, I mean any of them, you're on cooking duty for a month and that doesn't include barbecue," Cole said as he tried to step in time.

"You think they don't dance? You wait until the roadhouse reopens, you need to practice," Robyn shouted over the music to him.

"In Chicago we call this freestyle," Cole replied, taking her hand and spinning her around.

"Wait, don't get out yet," Cole said as he turned off Leonora's engine.

They'd arrived home, fifty dollars and two turkeys better off and high on the excitement of the night.

"You want me to sing another Reba McEntire number?"

"I really don't."

"You know, I know you weren't keen on the dancing but at the end there, you really had something going on," Robyn said, smiling at him.

"I bought you something," Cole said, getting the box out of his jeans.

He held it out to her and she took it.

"I saw it. The jeweler said there isn't another one like it. I had to get it," Cole told her nervously.

Robyn opened the box to reveal a white gold and diamond ring. The front of it was shaped into a leaping panther, encrusted in diamonds. It was the most unusual and beautiful ring she had ever seen.

"Cole," Robyn said, tears pricking her eyes as she took the ring out of its box and held it in her hand.

"I know how much the team means to you. I know how much you love this town, and I also know how much courage it must have taken you to get on that plane and come back. But I'm so glad you did or we would never have met," Cole told her.

"It's so beautiful," Robyn said, running her fingers over the panther's jewels.

"I know you don't want to tell anyone yet, but let me put it on, just for now," Cole said, taking the ring and holding her hand.

He slid it onto the ring finger of Robyn's left hand and held it in his.

"Is it too tight? The guy in the store said we could get it sized," Cole said.

"It's perfect Cole. Come on, get out," Robyn ordered, squeezing his hand and then pulling the handle of the car door.

"I was going to put her in the garage," Cole said, unmoving.

"Get out, Ryan, get up here with me," Robyn called, approaching Leonora's hood.

Cole watched as Robyn stepped up onto the hood and hauled herself up onto the roof of the vehicle.

"Hey! Are you crazy?" he yelled, hurrying out from behind the wheel.

She laid along the length of the roof, her arms folded behind her head, looking up at the sky. She took a deep breath and held it in, soaking up the still of the night.

"What are you doing?" Cole asked when he got out of the car.

"Are you coming or are you going to make me pull your ass up here?"

He heaved himself up onto the hood and followed her path up to the roof of the Mustang, sliding himself alongside her and maneuvering until he was lying on his back.

"What are we looking at?" he asked in barely more than a whisper.

"I had a pony once. She was named Mitzy. She had an aversion to anything that was good for her and barely moved above a trot. But when we rode out, I was Reba McEntire in my jeans and my Stetson, singing at the top of my voice and not caring who heard or how bad it was. I loved that horse, she gave me somewhere to escape to when Mom and Dad's fighting got to be too much," Robyn said.

Her eyes were still on the sky and the memory from long ago was jabbing at her. She felt Cole take a deep breath beside her and she let the words come out.

"She died. Got colic and it was too bad to do anything," Robyn stated.

Cole found her hand and squeezed it in his as she continued.

"I cried for a week, all day and all night. Nothing anyone said could make it better. Until Old Man Harrison came round. He bought a new halter, a whole bag of Hershey's Kisses, and he told me to get my lazy ass out of bed. He got me riding his new pony, said he needed someone to break her in, and then we ate the chocolate. By the time we'd eaten all the chocolate and named the pony, it was dark and he'd looked up at the sky and told me to pick out the brightest one. I can tell you, for an eight year old kid, that took a long time, but I finally settled on it. He said, *That's Mitzy and she'll be there, every time you look up*. He was a crazy old man," Robyn said, swallowing a lump in her throat.

"So, where is she? Show me," Cole said, looking skywards again.

"She's right there, and that one, to the left, that's the star I picked for Old Man Harrison the night Sarah told me he'd died," Robyn admitted, pointing to a bright star.

Cole gave her hand another reassuring squeeze, teasing the engagement ring against her little finger.

"I thought we could choose one for your dad," Robyn stated, looking to Cole.

She saw the tears form in his eyes and he looked away from her, up to the inky blanket above, filled with twinkling stars that all looked as bright as each other.

"My dad loved horses. Do you think we can put him next to Mitzy?" Cole asked.

"Sure. Look, she's nuzzling his hand right now."

Chapter Thirty-two

"Sarah, this is the fourth voicemail I've left for you. Where are you? What's going on? Please call me," Robyn shouted into her phone.

Today she was meeting Cole's mother and she'd been panicking about it all morning. On top of that, Sarah was being completely unresponsive to her calls and Nancy and Milo were fighting. She knew it was because Nancy was anxious about Eddie's operation, and Robyn had given her the task of making lunch for Mrs. Ryan to keep her mind off of it. Leaving them unattended at the roadhouse would go one of two ways. She'd either go back to find them bonding over the pool table or Milo would be locked up in the cellar. At the moment, it was the least of her concerns.

She carefully took the chicken stew out of Leonora and hurried up the path to the front door. Immediately she noticed someone sitting on the doorstep. It was Mickey. He was dressed in overalls and he looked disheveled, like he hadn't slept or showered. He had a bottle of lager in his hand.

"Mickey. What are you doing here?" Robyn asked, stopping in front of him.

"Is Sarah here? I rang the bell, I knocked on the door, and I went round back, but there was no sign. I tried to call you, but it kept going to voicemail," Mickey stuttered, standing up.

"She isn't here. I've been trying to call her. What's happened? You look terrible," Robyn remarked.

"She left me," Mickey stated, tears welling up in his eyes.

"What? But, I thought Cole told you what to do. You were supposed to propose to her," Robyn exclaimed, putting her key in the door and pushing it open.

"I was going to, but when I got home, she was packing her stuff."

"Well, why didn't you stop her? You should have taken her clothes back out of the case, put them back in the closet, and got down on one knee," Robyn said, entering the alarm code to stop the beeping.

"She wouldn't even talk to me. She was crying, and I asked her what was wrong and she just said nothing. Not one word," Mickey explained as tears spilled from his eyes.

"And she just left? Didn't she even tell you where she was going? When did this happen?" Robyn wanted to know.

She took the container of soup out of the bag and placed it on the side.

"Last night."

"Last night! And she isn't at work? Have you called everyone we know?"

"I called her work. I called Diane from her work. I called Brad and Henrik this morning. I didn't call anyone last night because I thought she'd be here with you, and I wanted to give her some space," Mickey tried to explain.

"Okay, right, well, we're just going to have to wait until she surfaces," Robyn said, looking out of the window and noticing Cole's car pull into the drive.

"But where is she? Do you think she's left town?" Mickey asked.

228

"No, she won't have done that," Robyn said, distracted.

She watched as Cole got out of the car and went to open the passenger door.

"I just want a chance to say the right thing. I love her, Robyn, and yeah, maybe I am scared of getting married. But if I'd known how much she really wanted to do it then…" Mickey began, wiping his nose with the sleeve of his overalls.

"Look, Mickey, I'll call Pam. I'll call everyone else I can think of, and if I find her, I will let you know. You have to go now. Cole's brought home an important client and I have to prepare soup," Robyn said quickly, watching as a small, dark-haired lady got out of the car.

"You promise you'll call me?" Mickey asked, clutching his beer bottle to his chest like it was a life preserver.

"Yes, I promise. Now give me that and get back to work. If you're going to give Sarah this wedding, you're going to need every penny you can get," Robyn said, snatching the bottle from him and dropping it into the recycling bin.

"You don't think it's too late? You think she'll give me another chance?" Mickey asked as Robyn hastily shooed him to the door.

"Let's hope so," Robyn said, smiling at Cole as he approached with his mother.

"Hey, Cole. Afternoon, ma'am," Mickey greeted in a lackluster voice as he walked past them.

"Mom, this is Mickey. Is everything okay, man?" Cole asked.

"Yeah, great. Sarah's left me and now she's missing. I'd better go…Brad said he'd check the local hotels," Mickey said, waving a hand as he headed back up the drive.

Robyn smiled at Cole's mother as they approached the door. She was petite and pretty with an almost Asian look to her features. She had olive-colored skin and was wearing a turquoise blue dress that skirted her ankles.

"Mom, this is Robyn. Robyn, this is Martha, my mom," Cole introduced.

"It's so nice to meet you. Cole talks about you all the time. How was your flight? Did they give you the Bombay mix or the pretzels? I prefer the pretzels, they don't stick in your teeth or repeat on you so much," Robyn babbled as she smiled at Martha.

"Unfortunately, we had the Bombay mix, but I didn't actually eat any," Martha informed her with a smile of amusement.

"Robyn eats more than me, Mom," Cole informed her as he led the way into the house.

"He's exaggerating. We went out for dinner last night and Cole didn't manage to finish his dessert. He's sore about that," Robyn told her.

"I stopped before I felt sick, the way I've been raised. And it was the right thing to do."

"Martha, would you like coffee or something cold? We've got apple juice," Robyn offered.

"Have we?" Cole asked.

"Yes, we have…in the healthy section of the refrigerator."

"Do we have a healthy section?"

"We do now."

"A coffee would be good," Martha accepted, her attention darting between them.

"Great! Well, I'll make some coffee and Cole can show you around the house. Excuse the mess, I only managed to vacuum once this morning. Usually, when I'm not managing my roadhouse, I do it twice a day, every day," Robyn informed happily.

Cole let out a snort of laughter.

"Cole, could you take up the freshly laundered sheets and pop them in the closet," Robyn said, and she swung round, a pile of linen in her hands.

"I think I've walked into the wrong house," Cole remarked.

"He's making a joke. Usually wash day is tomorrow, but my father's having an operation and I want to be at the hospital," Robyn said quickly.

"I see," Martha replied, smiling at Robyn kindly.

"She's trying to make a good impression," Cole whispered to his mom.

"I can see that," Martha replied.

"So, how is work going here?" Martha asked Cole.

He had given her the grand tour of the house and now they were sitting at the dining table enjoying Nancy's homemade chicken stew and cornbread.

"Good. It's a good team. They're very dedicated and enthusiastic," Cole said.

"More enthusiastic than your team in Chicago?" Martha asked.

"I don't know, things are different here, slower paced. It's the Michigan way, isn't that right, Robyn?" Cole said, grinning at her.

"That's right," Robyn answered brightly.

"Have you made any more progress with your theory?" Martha asked him.

"I thought we were going to have a breakthrough the other day. Things looked good, the science said it should work, but it didn't," Cole told her.

"Why not?" Martha asked.

"I haven't figured that one out yet. But I will," Cole assured her.

"I don't really know what he does all day, but it sounds very important," Robyn said, taking some more bread.

"Doesn't she know?" Martha asked, looking at Cole in horror.

"Mom, it isn't important," Cole said dismissively.

"Cole! How can you say that?" Martha exclaimed.

"Because my life here isn't just about the job, that's why. There is more to me than work, Mom."

"Robyn, Cole is the closest anyone's been to creating a revolutionary cancer drug. He's a formula away—a formula," Martha said firmly.

"It's more than a formula, Mom. It's a long process and there are a number of factors to take into consideration," Cole told her.

"I didn't realize. I should have realized," Robyn said, swallowing a feeling of stupidity. Why didn't she know that? She should have known that.

"No, you shouldn't have realized," Cole insisted.

"What he's going to achieve is nothing short of miraculous," Martha continued.

"Mom, don't do this. You always do this and it's embarrassing," Cole said, laying his napkin down on the table and toying with his water glass.

"You should be proud of what you do."

"I am proud of what I do, but it isn't everything."

"Did you know Cole's my best player on the ice hockey team?" Robyn asked.

"I hardly think ice hockey's as relevant to the world as finding a cure for cancer," Martha mocked.

"Here in Portage, we take ice hockey very seriously. My Uncle Bob always says hockey isn't life and death—it's far more important than that. I've never really known whether he's serious or not," she replied with a smile

"What a ridiculous statement to make. I can't believe you don't discuss your work with your girlfriend. Is she your girlfriend? Because you haven't really said," Martha said, wiping her mouth with the napkin and looking at Cole.

"Why don't I get dessert," Robyn offered, standing up.

"Mom, Robyn and I are getting married," Cole told her bluntly.

Robyn sat back down and stared at her half-eaten bowl of chicken stew. Her ring was in the pocket of her jeans and she slipped her fingers inside to touch it.

"Getting married," Martha repeated, pursing her lips and putting down her soup spoon.

"Yes, next week. The twenty-second. Can you come?" Cole asked her.

"Cole, is this some sort of joke?"

"No. I know we haven't known each other very long, but we know it's what we want. When we met, we just gelled and..." Cole started.

"Gelled," Martha said as if the very word was too ugly for her mouth.

"We connected...like you and Dad did when you first met. Remember when you first met each other, under the cherry blossom, both holding a copy of To Kill a Mocking Bird. You've told me that story so many times. You said you knew right then that there would be no one else. He was your Mr. Right and you were right for him. That's how I feel about Robyn," Cole said.

"Cole, I know how scarred you feel from what Bryn and Veronica did to you, but this isn't the way to make things better. We've been there with you making inappropriate decisions before," Martha reminded him.

"This has nothing to do with Bryn and Veronica — or Dad. It has nothing to do with any of them. It has to do with me and Robyn and how we feel about each other," Cole insisted.

"I know they hurt you, more than you will ever let on, but jumping feet first into a relationship won't lessen the pain. It's something that will ease with time, moving on too quickly will only make things worse," Martha said.

"Mom, you're not listening to me. I didn't love Veronica. When she did what she did with Bryn, I wasn't hurt because she was the love of my life, I was hurt because neither of them could tell me how they felt. They went behind my back instead of being honest with me. It was the lies and the deceit, not the depth of my feelings. Robyn and I, we tell each other everything, good and bad. The way I feel about her...it's much more than anything I've ever felt before," Cole tried to explain.

Robyn blinked back tears as he spoke. The truth hit her full force. He loved her. He really loved her, just how she was. Flawed, crazy, and a little bit damaged.

"I don't want you to do something now that you might regret a little while down the line," Martha said.

"Is that what your mom said to you when you told her about Dad?" Cole asked.

"Yes," Martha said with a laugh as she wiped at her eyes with her fingers.

"Please, come to the wedding, Mom. You can stay here, we're getting married by the lake. It's going to be a special day," Cole said, taking her hand.

Martha looked at Robyn. Robyn couldn't stop the tears from rolling down her face as she watched Cole with his mom.

"Well, how can I refuse an invitation to my son's wedding? My! I'll need to buy a new dress and a hat!" Martha said, dabbing at her eyes with her napkin.

"But no shoes," Robyn said, stirring from her trance.

"What?" Martha asked.

"It's a barefoot wedding, Mom, no shoes allowed," Cole informed her.

"Does that have something to do with religion?" Martha inquired, a puzzled look on her face.

"No, it has to do with algae from the lake. Get that on your shoes and they'll never be the same again," Robyn said with a smile.

"Have you got a dress yet?" Martha asked her.

"Er, no. I haven't really had time, what, with my dad and the roadhouse and the hockey team and..." Robyn began, looking awkwardly at Cole.

"Then you must let me take you shopping. One day next week, yes?" Martha offered.

Cole looked at Robyn encouragingly.

"Yes. That would be nice," Robyn agreed with a smile.

She'd promised not to sing but she did it every time she dried the dishes. And today his mom had joined in! Some old track by George Strait or Alan Jackson, Hell, he didn't know. Telling his mom about the wedding had been the right thing to do, despite Veronica's reservations. She had a sparkle in her eyes now as she commented on Robyn's floral blouse and scrubbed at the pot. He still couldn't contemplate Thanksgiving yet, but his mom was smiling again, properly. He hadn't seen her smile quite like that in a long time.

Chapter Thirty-three

"You should have called me last night. Has she been out at all?" Robyn asked Pam when she let her into the house later.

"No, and she hasn't eaten anything either. I made beef stew and it hasn't been touched," Pam said, leading the way to the spare room.

"Hi, Robyn."

"Hi, Robyn."

Sienna and Sierra bounded out of their bedroom wearing ice hockey pads, shirts, and helmets, all of which were far too big for them.

"Hey, look at you! Where did you get the uniforms?" Robyn exclaimed, admiring her nieces.

"Daddy got them for us. They're secondhand, but there's hardly any wear," Sierra announced excitedly.

"Mine has a number seventeen on the back," Sienna said, twirling around.

"Cool! So you all ready for tomorrow night? You're in charge of the water, that's the most important job, you know. You have to get it right," Robyn told them seriously.

"We've been practicing at school," Sienna replied confidently.

"Great," Robyn said, giving them a thumbs up.

"Sarah! Robyn's here, she's coming in," Pam called, tapping on the door.

There was no reply, so Robyn opened the door and entered.

Her friend was sitting up on the bed wearing jogging pants and a baggy t-shirt, staring vacantly at the television and channel hopping. She didn't acknowledge Robyn's entrance and flicked from the weather channel to a re-run of American Idol.

"You're a hard woman to track down. You lost your phone?" Robyn asked, sitting on the bed next to her.

Sarah didn't reply, but Robyn saw that her cell was right next to her.

"Okay, so what are you doing here when you have a perfectly good home a few streets away?"

"I told you I was leaving Mickey and that's what I've done. I didn't know where to go. I didn't want to be a third-wheel to you and Cole. Brad isn't an option given the current circumstances, so Pam was the only person I could think of that would take me in for a while and not give me a lecture," Sarah finally said.

"You wouldn't have been a third-wheel. Cole and I aren't dating," Robyn announced quickly.

"Whatever."

"Mickey loves you, he's been crying on my doorstep. He's worried about you; he wants you to go home," Robyn told her.

"He doesn't love me. He's probably just wondering why his dinner isn't magically cooking on its own or why the laundry hasn't been done," Sarah snapped.

"That isn't true. He's devastated. He's drinking, he's taken time off work, he's not himself, and he doesn't know what to do," Robyn explained.

"Robyn, you've just described an adolescent. Need I say more?"

"Listen, this is madness. Okay, he's a bit slow at coming forward, but last night, before he saw the suitcase and everything, he was going to ask you to marry him," Robyn told her.

"Why? Because you told him to?"

"No, because he loves you."

"I don't believe you. I haven't left him to prove a point, you know."

"No? Well, why have you left him?"

"Because I can't see us growing old together. He's never going to grow up. We want different things, we're two different people who got together too young and settled for what we had because we didn't know any better," Sarah tried to explain.

"That isn't true."

"Yes it is. You haven't been around for years, you don't know how it's been. You've been in England living an exciting life with new people, experiencing different things. All I've had is Portage, Michigan," Sarah complained.

"This is a midlife crisis come early. You've flipped. This isn't the Sarah Gorski I know."

"Maybe it isn't. Maybe the Sarah Gorski you knew doesn't exist anymore, and maybe the new Sarah Gorski wants more from her life than a town obsessed with ice hockey and monster trucks and a boyfriend who still acts like he's fourteen," Sarah blurted out.

"Then what do you want? You want to go to England? Go! Live my so called exciting life. I worked on cars, I worked in an office, and I slept with my fifty-five year old boss. I've decided it's not for me, but try it—it might be just what you're looking for," Robyn yelled.

"It might! At least it isn't here. At least I wouldn't be trapped with the same people and the same shit, day in and day out. Everything's just routine, drudgery, and discount coupons."

"You ungrateful bitch!" Robyn said, gritting her teeth as she looked at her friend.

"What?"

"You heard me. You're an ungrateful bitch. You know why I left town. It wasn't because I wasn't satisfied with what I had here. I love this place. I love the people and the places and all the so-called routine and drudgery. I would have given anything to have had that back. You've got a guy who's loved you for as long as anyone can remember. So, he's got his faults. He drinks too much, he likes hockey too much, he smells a bit after work, but he's real. You had a real life, doing things that real couples do. I would have given anything to have had a piece of that. Excitement and adventure aren't real, they're temporary feelings that don't last, and if you want to give up something genuine for that, you're a fool," Robyn blasted.

"You don't get it," Sarah said, tossing the remote control on the bed.

"No, I don't. And I'm giving up trying to get it. My dad's having a heart bypass tomorrow, so excuse me, but I'm going to visit him. I'm completely done here," Robyn said, getting off the bed and heading for the door.

She stormed out of the room and went marching up the hallway toward the front door.

"Is everything okay?" Pam asked as Robyn prepared to leave.

"No, it isn't, she's gone nuts. She's having some sort of menopausal meltdown. I've got to go, Nancy and I are going to see Dad," Robyn informed her, opening the front door.

"Oh, honey, give him these magazines. I keep forgetting to take them every time I go," Pam said, collecting some ice hockey magazines and handing them to Robyn.

"Sure," Robyn agreed.

"Oh, and someone called for you earlier, someone named Trudy? She left a number."

"Max! Oh, Max! Wakey, wakey old timer! Nancy's brought you your favorite chocolate muffins," Nancy said, waving a paper bag in front of his face.

"Chocolate muffins? You never told me you had those! What are you trying to do to them?" Robyn exclaimed, snatching the bag from Nancy's grasp.

"Shh, they're not really chocolate. They're oatmeal and raisin, but he won't eat raisins anymore, so I say it's chocolate. Zip it!" Nancy hissed quietly to Robyn as she snatched back the bag.

"What did you say? Stop whispering. What you got?" Max asked, snapping his eyes open and surveying the goodies.

"Chocolate muffins, Max. Hey, Dad," Robyn greeted, moving over to her father's bed and sitting down on the chair.

"Hey, yourself. What time d'you call this? I thought you were coming earlier, it's after six," Eddie grumbled, checking his watch.

"Yeah, I know. Sorry about that. It's been a busy day. The new tables and chairs arrived, then Cole's mom came for lunch, and Sarah left Mickey and…" Robyn began.

"Sarah left him in the end, did she? We weren't sure how that one was going to go after what Brad was saying. My money was on Mickey popping the question," Max said, chewing on a muffin and spitting bits all over his covers.

"You can't force someone to marry, though, can you? It has to be for love," Nancy said, putting her arm around Eddie's shoulders and kissing him on top of his head.

"Why aren't you at the arena? Isn't it training tonight?" Eddie asked Robyn gruffly.

"Yes, but I wanted to see you. Grant's there, I'm going to go later."

"You should be there now, you don't want to let things slide after the great result. Important game tomorrow, Grand Rapids is climbing the table," Eddie informed her.

"I know that, Dad, but you have your operation tomorrow. I wanted to see you and wish you luck," Robyn said, her voice weakening.

"Wish me luck? I'm not a racehorse about to enter the Kentucky Derby, it's a bypass operation. If I need luck, then there's no hope for any of us in here," Eddie growled.

"Robyn didn't mean luck. She just wants to see her grumpy old pop and wish him well. And to let him know that when he comes round tomorrow, we're both going to be here to nag him about eating right and doing some exercise," Nancy said.

"Yeah, that was it," Robyn agreed.

"He's made of stern stuff is Eddie. It'll take more than a few doctors poking around his beater to do him in," Max remarked, stuffing another muffin in his mouth.

"So how are things going with the roadhouse?" Eddie asked.

"Great. Robyn's doing a good job; we're all set for opening on Friday night," Nancy told him.

"What she means is we still have a hundred jobs to do before we're going to be ready for opening night but we will be ready—even if we all have to work twenty four seven," Robyn explained.

"She's a taskmaster. A chip off the old block," Nancy said, smiling at him.

"And you're getting along?" Eddie asked them both.

"Of course! Why wouldn't we be? It's like having my own daughter. We even cooked together," Nancy said.

"Sounds touching, Eddie," Max remarked.

"Sounds over the top to me. What are you hiding? You had a fight you're trying to cover up?" Eddie asked suspiciously.

"No, Dad," Robyn replied.

"I may be stuck in this bed, but it hasn't affected my mind," Eddie assured them both.

"Everything's running like clockwork, Eddie. When you come home the Panthers will be top of the league and the roadhouse will be the most talked about eatery in Michigan," Nancy assured.

"And what do you have to say about that?" Eddie asked Robyn.

"Maybe not top of the league, but I agree with the rest of it," Robyn said.

"You've got something on your mind. Out with it," Eddie ordered.

Robyn shook her head.

"Listen, Buttercup, you may as well tell your dad now, because I'm going to find out one way or another," Eddie told her.

"It's nothing."

"Nancy, she's hiding something from me," Eddie stated.

"I don't want to worry you, Dad, not now. I'll tell you tomorrow," Robyn explained.

"Is it Cole? Has he gone back to the Wolves?" Max guessed.

"Tell me," Eddie ordered.

"Trudy Franklin called. They're reopening my case. Jason's found a witness who saw him at home the night it happened. They're re-examining the evidence," Robyn informed him.

Eddie took in a sharp breath and gripped Nancy's hand.

"I have to go through my statement again," Robyn told him.

"Statement? Case? What case? What's this all about? I don't know anything about this," Max exclaimed.

"I've spent all these years believing it was him, knowing it was him. What if it wasn't him?"

"It was him," Eddie assured her.

"But the witness says he wasn't there."

"Paid to say that, I imagine. I don't believe a real witness pops up now after all this time. Anyway, you can't argue with DNA evidence, Robyn, it was him," Eddie stated, getting agitated.

"Would one of you kindly let me know what all this is about?" Max interrupted.

"You go through your statement and you tell Trudy exactly what happened, just like you did before. Nothing's changed," Eddie reassured her.

"I keep trying to remember if I remember anything else. I mean, I didn't see him, I didn't see who it was. I didn't see what they were wearing, I didn't see anything," Robyn babbled.

"I know, Buttercup, it was raining and it was pitch black that night," Eddie said, taking hold of her hand.

"But if I could remember something else, something concrete about who it was, all this would finally be over. If it wasn't Jason, you could be proper friends with Grant again, like you used to be. I know things haven't been the same between you since it happened," Robyn said.

"Don't you worry about me, I'm just fine."

"Do you want me to come with you and see this Trudy girl?" Nancy offered.

"No. No, it's okay, but thanks. I'd better get to training. Grant doesn't push them hard enough in the drills," Robyn said, standing up and looking down at her dad.

"You don't let them off the ice until they're falling apart," Eddie ordered.

"Yes, sir," she replied with a smile.

"I'll see you tomorrow," Eddie said.

All of a sudden she was overwhelmed by the poignancy of the moment. She threw herself at her dad and clung to him like a small child, breathing in the scent of him, relishing the firmness of his chest, the roughness of his beard against her cheek.

"I'm going to be fine, Buttercup," Eddie assured her, resting his hand on top of her head.

"I know that! Just checking you're all monitored up. There, you're good," Robyn said, adjusting one of Eddie's wires.

"Can no one hear me above all the emotion? I want to know about this cop case. I'm feeling left out over here!" Max shouted.

Chapter Thirty-four

"Someone might come in," Cole said as Robyn kissed him hard on the mouth.

"I don't care."

"Yes you do."

"I don't care right now."

"I'm burning up in this uniform, I need a shower," Cole said, kissing her back.

"I'm not stopping you," Robyn replied, pulling at his top.

"This isn't fair, we're supposed to be going slow."

"That was yesterday's plan."

"And today's?"

The dressing room door burst open and the other team members all trooped in, tearing their uniforms off and discarding them as they went.

"Man, I'm done for," Wes announced, tugging his shirt over his head.

"Me too! You were fierce tonight, Robyn!" Wade called to her.

"That was special orders from Eddie," Robyn said, moving away from Cole.

"How's he doing? We've all chipped in for a coach jacket and cap. It's beautiful, he's gonna love it," Wes informed her.

"I'm sure he will. He's doing okay; we'll just have to see how the operation goes. You okay?" Robyn asked, going over to where Mickey was taking off his kit.

"She still won't take my calls. D'you think I ought to go over to Pam and Bob's?" Mickey asked her, his eyes sorrowful.

"D'you know what? I think you deserve Chinese. Hey, Brad, you don't mind if Mickey and Cole come with us, do you? Mickey's not feeling the best and I know Cole hasn't eaten properly because I caught him eating my chips and dip earlier," Robyn called across the locker room.

"Well, I thought it was just going to be..." Brad began, looking less than pleased.

"Great! That's settled, I'll meet you out front," Robyn said before she hurried to excuse herself from the locker room.

"So, isn't this nice? I haven't been here since forever. I'm so glad they still do the sweet and sour chicken balls," Robyn said excitedly as Cole, Brad, Mickey, and she sat at a table in the local Chinese restaurant.

The atmosphere was stiff. No one had spoken on the drive to the restaurant and it had been all Robyn could do to get their drink orders out of them. Something had happened between the guys, she was sure of it. That damn locker room held a thousand secrets behind its door. There was only so much legitimate time she could spend in there without the team thinking she was present to get off on their nudity. She needed a spy — maybe she could convince Mickey to do just that. It might take his mind off Sarah for five minutes.

"Chicken balls are Sarah's favorite, too," Mickey stated with a sad sigh.

"And mine," Brad added.

"Mine too," Cole replied, glaring at him.

"Man, I never knew we all had such similar tastes. I'm going to have seaweed as a starter, I think," Robyn said, looking at the menu.

"Me too," Brad stated.

"Count me in," Cole said.

"I don't think I've ever had it before. What's it like?" Mickey asked.

"And then I'm going to have the deep fried bull's balls with intestine stew," Robyn suggested.

"I'll go for that, too."

"Yeah and me."

Robyn looked at Cole and Brad and shook her head in disapproval.

"What's going on?" Robyn asked, fixing them both with a hard stare.

"Nothing," Brad said immediately.

"Cole?" Robyn asked.

"Nothing," he replied.

"Mickey? Am I going to get any sense out of you?" Robyn asked.

"Brad wants to date you; Cole said you weren't in to him," Mickey told her.

"Jeez, man!" Brad said, throwing a napkin down on the table.

"I'm starving, can we order?" Mickey asked, taking a prawn cracker from the bowl on the table.

"What have you said?" Robyn asked, looking at Cole with wide eyes.

"Nothing. He said you have a bond. He said you're going to change your mind about the way you feel about him. I said I was pretty sure you wouldn't," Cole told her.

"Is this true?" Robyn asked Brad.

"He's in to you. Did you know that?" Brad said, slanting an accusing eye at Cole.

"Brad, I don't feel that way about you. We're friends, we'll always just be friends," Robyn began.

"Yes, we're ready to order. Can I have the crispy duck and the sweet and sour chicken balls with special fried rice and…shall we share some noodles?" Mickey offered as he gave his order to the waitress who had appeared at their table and gingerly stepped forward in a bid to be noticed.

"I don't want to talk about this in front of them. We were supposed to be having dinner on our own, so we could talk," Brad said, looking at Robyn.

"About what? Anything I need to say, I can say in front of Cole and Mickey. What is it you can't say?" Robyn asked.

"Noodles guys?" Mickey asked.

"Just get the noodles," Cole told him, watching Robyn and Brad.

"Can we just have a minute?" Brad asked Robyn.

"A minute for what?"

"Please, Robyn," Brad said, looking uncomfortable.

Robyn stood up with a sigh and walked over to the tank where they kept the lobsters. They looked surprisingly cheerful seeing as most of them would end up in a pot of boiling water before the week was out. They all looked decidedly more cheerful than Brad.

Brad followed her, removed his baseball cap, and toyed with it in his hands.

"Can't we just have Chinese like we used to? Remember that time we ate so much we were actually sick?" Robyn said.

"Yeah, I remember. I carried you from the car and put you to bed," Brad spoke.

"I was ill for a week," Robyn said with a smile.

"That's what I miss. We were so close," Brad told her.

"We still are close, you, Sarah, and Mickey, well, when they're talking…you're my oldest friends," Robyn reminded him.

"We were more than friends."

"We dated loosely for a while, it was hardly Romeo and Juliet, was it?" Robyn said.

"Wasn't it?"

"No, Brad, it wasn't—not for me, anyways," Robyn stated firmly.

Brad let out a heavy sigh and ran his hands through his hair, trembling.

"Listen, I know things have been difficult for you since Michelle left, but…" Robyn began.

"But what? I mean, what are you going to do, Robyn? Pat me on the arm and say everything's going to be all right? I don't have anything in my life apart from teaching stranger danger and ticketing speeders."

"Come on, you have the hockey. We're doing really well and that's because of you, you're the Panthers' captain. We need you," Robyn said.

"Don't patronize me, Robyn. I've tried to move on, focus on something else, throw myself into the service, but now that you're back, it's harder than ever. Robyn, Michelle didn't leave because she fell in love with Randy, she left because she knew she could never be you," Brad stated.

Robyn shook her head.

"It's true. I have never felt for anyone the way I feel about you. That's just the way it is. Michelle realized that and that's why she fell for Randy's surgically enhanced charms," Brad continued.

"Well, I'm sorry, but I don't feel the same, and I won't. There's someone else," Robyn told him firmly.

"I know there was someone in England, Sarah told me, but…" Brad started, taking hold of Robyn's hand.

"It isn't him. He was nothing, just a way of coping. This is different," Robyn said, swallowing the knot that had appeared in her throat.

"It's someone here? Well, who?" Brad demanded to know, his face reddening, the vein in his neck twitching.

"I didn't plan it to happen, it just did. I couldn't stop it and I didn't want to stop it. He makes me feel normal again," Robyn said, looking over at the table and smiling at Cole.

"Ryan," Brad said, the word only just making it past his pursed lips.

"Yeah," Robyn admitted, looking back at Brad.

"So, he wasn't hitting on you when he bought you the car and invited you to live with him and started being by your side twenty four seven? Man!" Brad accused angrily.

"No, he wasn't, not then. He was just being nice, that's all he's ever been. But then it was more than that. Like I said, it just happened," Robyn attempted to explain.

"I don't trust him. You don't know him, he doesn't know you. How can you be dating someone you don't know?" Brad yelled at her.

"I know enough and frankly, Brad, I know we're friends, but something like this is none of your business," Robyn snapped.

"I care about you, Robyn, you can't stop me from caring."

"I don't want you to care like that, it's suffocating!" Robyn blasted.

That was it. He couldn't let her stand with him any longer. Mickey had started to take him through a blow-by-blow account of every date he had been on with Sarah and he couldn't hear what was being said. He was uncomfortable being so far away, with Brad standing so close to Robyn. He needed to do something.

"Is everything okay here?" Cole asked, joining them.

"Oh yeah, everything's great, you freaking lowlife! She's just told me you're dating! You knew we had history, you knew how I felt about her...everyone knows how I feel about her," Brad screamed at him.

"You told him," Cole said, looking at Robyn intently.

"That we're dating," Robyn emphasized.

If she had told him about the impending wedding he probably would have collapsed or trashed the restaurant.

"You made out you were a good guy, down with the team, everybody's buddy, and really you were..." Brad continued as he began to perspire.

"Really he was what?" Robyn cut in.

"I didn't think you were like that," Brad continued, shifting uncomfortably from one foot to the other as he turned his attention to Robyn.

"You didn't think I was like what?" Robyn asked, staring at Brad and biting her lip.

"Let's go," Cole urged, taking hold of Robyn's hand.

"You should be with me, Robyn, not him. We were always meant to be together," Brad said.

"Robyn, let's just go. We can get take out," Cole offered, trying to get her to focus on him and deflect the intensity of Brad's rant.

"No, not yet. I think I might want to punch him first," Robyn replied.

"Robyn, we were good together, you know that. You said that yourself, the Chinese, the summers by the lake, the movies, at school, athletics club together, we..."

"They're memories, just old memories that have nothing to do with the here and now. I'm dating Cole. I'm together with Cole," Robyn told him.

"And how much do you really know about him?" Brad questioned, his eyes locking with Cole's.

"I know everything," Robyn responded.

"Yeah? Really? So you'll know he was charged with criminal damage, assault, and DUI," Brad carried on, a smug, satisfied smile crossing his face.

"You ran Cole's name through the police computer?" Robyn asked, looking at her friend open-mouthed.

"So, now you know he isn't Mr. Whiter than White. What have you got to say to that?" Brad demanded to know.

Robyn swung her arm back and punched Brad hard on the jaw, sending him reeling back into an empty table. Plates smashed on the floor, the Chinese waitress screamed and went running toward the kitchen, her face in her hands, and Mickey stopped eating the prawn crackers to turn toward the scene. He stood up and meandered over to them.

"You going to come and finish ordering?"

"No, we're done here," Robyn said, taking Cole's hand.

"Robyn, you need to think about what you're doing. You don't belong with him," Brad called, picking himself up and touching his face.

"Do you think if I called Sarah now and told her we had sweet and sour balls by the dozen she would come down? I mean she does love chicken balls. Actually maybe you should call her," Mickey suggested to Robyn.

"We're leaving," Robyn said, pulling Cole toward the door.

"Look, Sarah's dumped you. She doesn't want you, get over it," Brad hissed, his lips set in an angry scowl.

"Get over it? What like you? Pining after Robyn for years? Turning down the cell number of that dancer at Taboo? Doesn't sound like you've gotten over anything yourself," Mickey replied.

"Fuck you Mickey...and fuck you," Brad snarled, glaring at Cole.

He put his cap back on his head, roughly pushed passed Cole and belted out the door.

Chapter Thirty-five

"I want to kill him," Robyn blasted as she burst through the front door of the house.

"You don't want to kill him."

"Why don't you want to kill him?"

"Because I kind of know how he feels and it's not good," Cole told her.

"I've done nothing to make him think I feel anything for him, you know, that way," Robyn assured him.

"You don't have to explain anything to me."

"There isn't anything to explain, Cole, honestly, nothing," Robyn said, stopping in her tracks and looking up at him.

"I know that."

"Do you?"

"Yes, because I know you," Cole told her.

He reached out, took a strand of her hair in his fingers, and tucked it back behind her ear. She caught his hand in hers and brought it to her mouth, kissing his knuckles.

"I'm scared, Cole," Robyn whispered, putting another kiss on his hand.

"Scared of what?"

"Of how I feel about you...and what I should do about it," Robyn said, swallowing.

"We should eat something. We haven't eaten and I'm starving," Cole said, looking away from her.

He was trying to buy time, for what he didn't really know. He was scared too, but he didn't want her to know that. After his comment about food, she was now looking at him like he was the most insensitive jerk she had ever met. At the moment, he agreed with her. If they could just get the monster trucks on the TV and rip open a bag of chips this could all be saved for another day. Another day when he might feel able to cope with it, because he couldn't deal with it now. He was only one step away from wanting to take her clothes off, but if he did that it would ruin everything. He knew she couldn't handle that yet. He could be patient, he could wait, but it was hard—really hard.

"I love you, okay? There, I've said it," Robyn blurted out, putting her thumb to her mouth and chewing on her nail. Her eyes were fixed on his face, waiting for his reaction, whatever it was going to be. She saw him swallow, the lump at his throat bobbing down and then slowly rising up again.

"I should have told Brad the whole truth tonight. I should have told him I'm in love with you and I should have told him we're getting married," Robyn carried on, determination in her tone.

Cole shook his head.

"Look at me," Robyn ordered, her hand lifting his head up to meet her eyes.

"Don't Robyn, please," he begged.

"Don't Robyn, please? What's that supposed to mean? I tell you that I love you and you don't want me to? We're meant to be getting married!"

"We are getting married," he assured her.

"Then what's the problem?" Robyn questioned, looking at him with confusion in her expression.

"Listen, it's late, I'm tired, maybe we should just turn in," Cole suggested, glancing at his watch.

"Oh my God. I just tell you that I love you and all you want to do is eat or sleep! What's going on here?"

She kicked her shoe against the baseboard and looked at him for some sort of explanation.

He took a deep breath and finally met her eyes with his. In one quick move, he took her face in his hands and brought it to his, kissing her hard, shocking the air from her and moving his body close. Robyn wrapped her arms around his neck and drew him toward her, kissing him back, wanting more and more of him.

She slipped one hand up under his t-shirt, touching his abdomen and then tracing a line down to the waistband of his jeans. He ended the kiss and stepped back like he'd been poked by a cattle prod.

"Did I do something wrong? Is it still that bruise Brad gave you? Because if it is then you maybe ought to see the doctor," Robyn said, watching him as he ran his hands through his hair.

He grabbed hold of her hands and took them in his, softly massaging her fingers.

"I love you, Robyn. I've loved you since before I asked you to marry me," he admitted.

"It feels scary to say it, doesn't it?" Robyn asked, smiling at him.

"It isn't that. I'm not scared by that, at all," Cole said, shaking his head.

"Then what is it?"

"I want you, Robyn, you know...I want you...and that's wrong after all you've been through, and I shouldn't be thinking like that yet, I know that. We're waiting and that's cool, it really is but...well I said it and there it is," Cole told her, folding his arms across his chest.

"Right," Robyn said with a matter of fact nod.

"I'm sorry," Cole told her.

"Yeah, me too, because that wasn't who I thought you were," Robyn said.

"I don't know what to say," Cole said with a shrug.

"I don't want you to say anything. I want you to take me upstairs and we'll figure this whole thing out together. Because that's what people who are getting married should do," Robyn told him.

"I shouldn't have said anything,"

"Do you actually know how hot you look without your shirt on? Do you know how many times I've miscounted jars of pickles in the stockroom because I'm thinking about you with no shirt on? Believe me, you don't have enough fingers to count it. I don't know if I'm ready or not, but I'm not going to shatter into a million pieces if you touch me," Robyn said.

"I'm not that guy, Robyn, I don't want to do anything you're not ready for, but I love you so much and..." Cole began.

"Shh...just stop talking," she said, taking the first step up the stairs.

She took her t-shirt off and threw it on the floor. She pulled off her socks, hopping on one foot as she made her way over to the bed. She'd run up the stairs and she'd heard him follow her. Another second and he'd be in the room. How did that make her feel? Soon she'd find out.

He paused outside the door and took a breath. Was this really what she wanted? Or was she reacting to what he'd said? Maybe she hadn't really meant it. Perhaps she was waiting to see if he would do the right thing. What was the right thing in this situation? He put his hand on the doorknob.

"I own about ten sets of matching lingerie, all bought by Clive, but I didn't bring any of them. So, this is it...this is me," Robyn said as Cole stepped into the bedroom.

She was shaking and she didn't know what to do with herself. How did you make yourself look alluring in a white non-wired bra that had seen better days and plain cotton panties? She wanted to look alluring but she didn't know where to start. She looked up at him, trying to figure out what he was thinking as he gazed back at her.

She watched him remove his t-shirt and she swallowed, taking in his toned physique. He was so hot. There wasn't a better word for it, he was just hot, hot as Hell.

He sat down next to her on the bed and she took hold of his hand. She placed it onto the strap of her bra and took her hand away.

Cole put his thumb underneath the strap and slowly lowered it down toward her elbow. She took a breath in and closed her eyes as his thumb traced a line over the top of her breast, before moving over to the other strap. He eased it down her arm and teased the fabric over and off her breasts. She felt him unclasp the hook at her back and then he discarded the bra on the floor.

She opened her eyes to look at him and he caught her mouth with his and pushed her down onto the bed.

"Just hold me and touch me and tell me you love me," Robyn begged him as she ran her hands over his shoulders and down his arms.

"I love you Robyn...I love you," Cole said and his lips crashed against hers again.

Chapter Thirty-six

Robyn let the water run over her face as she showered. Last night had been so different from everything she'd got used to in her life. Cole had touched her and held her like no other man had and although they hadn't gone the whole way, what they'd done together had been perfect.

She ran a hand through her hair and it was then she remembered the other events of the night before. The knuckles on her right hand were bruised and sore, and her shoulder ached from the jarring when her hand had connected with Brad's jaw. She hadn't known what else to do. Nothing she said to him seemed to sink in. She didn't want to lose his friendship, but the way things were going, she wasn't sure how long it would last.

The shower door opened and Robyn swung round. And there he was, her fiancé, absolutely naked and gorgeous. She bit her lip and looked at him, all the way down as he did the same to her.

He stepped into the shower and kissed her on the mouth, pulling her toward him.

"You smell so good," he said, running his hand down her back.

"Exfoliation, you know, the one you're always borrowing," Robyn replied with a smile as he kissed her neck.

"You should have woken me up," Cole said, stepping under the showerhead and circling his arms around her.

"You were asleep and I needed to find the Advil."

"How's your hand?"

"Hurting. Listen, I'm going to the roadhouse this morning and then to the hospital. Dad was going down at seven, he won't be done until at least two," Robyn informed him.

"D'you want me to meet you there? I could get out of work," Cole offered.

"No, you need to work. Your mom would kill me if she thought I was making you skip work. And if you're planning to keep me in gherkins and beer and treat me to nights at the Old Country Buffet, we need to keep the dollars rolling in," Robyn reminded him.

The phone rang.

"We should get it, it might be the hospital. I'll go," Robyn said, opening the shower door.

"Hello," Robyn answered, wrapping a towel around her and holding the phone against her ear with her shoulder.

"Oh, Robyn, it's me," Pam said soberly.

"Pam? What's happened? Is it Dad? Oh God, it's Dad, isn't it? I gave the hospital my number, why didn't they call me?" Robyn exclaimed, panicking.

"It isn't the hospital, honey, it's Brad. He turned up here drunk last night and…" Pam started.

"And you're calling me why?" Robyn asked.

"Because he wouldn't stop talking about you. We made him about two gallons of coffee, but it didn't help. In the end, Bob took him down in the basement to sweat it out playing hockey," Pam continued.

"I still don't know why you're calling me. Didn't he tell you I hit him?"

"What?"

"He's being an ass."

"Robyn, he's upset. He's behaving like he behaved when Michelle left him for Randy Dennis. Could you talk to him?"

"No."

"Robyn, you didn't see him after Michelle left, he was a wreck. He almost lost his place on the force and he was out of control. I don't want that to happen again."

"You aren't his mother, Pam, and he's a grown man. Besides, I said all I had to say to him last night, and he didn't want to listen because nothing I said was what he wanted to hear."

"He said you and Cole are dating."

"Yes."

"I thought you were just friends, you told me you were just friends."

"And now we're more than that. Why is that so hard for people to get? I can't run his life for him, I'm struggling to keep mine together right now. I don't know what to suggest. Call his dad, maybe let him take responsibility for once," Robyn said as she watched Cole come into the bedroom, toweling himself dry.

"Robyn, are you sure about Cole? I mean, we've all known Brad a long time and he thinks the world of you and..." Pam started.

"Oh my God! I can't believe I'm hearing this! I'm going to put the phone down now."

"Robyn..."

"Goodbye," Robyn said, ending the call.

She tossed the phone down on the bed and began furiously rubbing at her hair with the towel.

"You okay?" Cole asked, watching her.

"I'd be better if people kept their noses out of my business."

"That's what it's like when you live in a close knit community — that's what you love about it," Cole reminded her.

"I like giving my opinion on other people's lives; I don't like it so much when they're giving me their opinions on mine."

"Who was it?"

"It doesn't matter. It isn't important. I need to get going. Old Mrs. Dill is popping in this morning with the new cushion covers. She's almost ninety, she smokes roll ups, and the last time she came around, she drank half a bottle of gin," Robyn said, getting dressed.

Cole laughed and opened the closet door to get out a shirt.

"Have you done any planning for the wedding?" Robyn asked him.

He turned to face her.

"What's that look for?" Robyn asked.

"Do you really want me to tell you or do you want a surprise?"

"You've arranged something?"

"Maybe," Cole said with a smile.

"Do you have a preacher?"

"Maybe."

"Can we write our own vows?"

"Is that what you want?"

"Don't you think it would be cool? It'd be better than all that for better or for worse stuff that I don't really get. We could say something that actually wasn't written circa the beginning of time — something more relevant," Robyn suggested.

"I'd like that," Cole agreed.

"Have you booked Special Guest yet?" Robyn asked excitedly.

"I'm not telling you any more. Go and make coffee," Cole ordered, throwing a t-shirt at her.

"Is there any more of that gin going?" Ada Dill questioned later at the roadhouse.

"I'll get you some," Milo said, taking her glass and heading to the bar to refill it.

"Better make this your last one, Ada, or you'll be asleep before lunchtime," Robyn said, smiling at the old lady as she folded menus.

"I hear that Sarah girl from the estate agents and that mechanic have split up," Ada said, snatching the glass from Milo's hand and slurping the gin down.

"Who told you that?" Robyn inquired.

"I never reveal my sources," Ada said with another raspy laugh.

"Well, I wouldn't listen to gossip, Ada, not all of it's true," Robyn told her.

"So they haven't split up?" Ada asked, leaning forward, intrigued.

"They're working through some stuff at the moment, that's all," Robyn said.

"That means they've split up," Ada said with a sniff.

"Okay, what else have you heard?" Robyn asked her.

"Heard they were reopening your case. What that boy did to you, well, castration would be too good for the likes of him," Ada said.

"How do you know all this? I only found out yesterday," Robyn stated.

"When you've lived as long as me, you get to know a lot of people," Ada replied.

"So it seems," Robyn answered.

"You got to see the police again?"

"Tomorrow."

"Fancy making you go over it all again after all this time...it isn't right," Ada said, shaking her head.

The telephone rang and Milo hurried to answer it.

"Eddie's Roadhouse. Oh hi…yeah, she is…Robyn, it's Nancy," Milo said, holding out the phone to her.

Robyn took the phone and put it to her ear.

"Hello."

"Robyn, you need to get yourself to the hospital, honey," Nancy said in a rush of words.

"Is it Dad?" Robyn asked as her knees went weak, her heart flying up to her throat.

"He's not good."

"I'm on my way."

He had a list of things to organize, and he was trying to sort through them while keeping an eye on what was going on in his Petri dish. Special Guest was booked, the preacher was booked, and he was being measured for a suit later in the week. What else needed to be done for a wedding no one knew about? Flowers? He didn't think Robyn did flowers. Leonora. He could decorate Leonora and maybe get some equipment for a turkey shoot for the reception. Hell, maybe they could eat turkey at the reception. They needed to move the carcass out of the freezer soon because it was taking up a third of the ice cream drawer.

"Do you need any help with anything, Cole?" Maggie asked, appearing at his shoulder and looking down at the list in his hands.

"Maggie, hi. No, not right now, I'm good," he answered, putting the list face down on the worktop.

"Are you organizing some sort of party?" she asked.

"Yeah, kind of."

"Well, if you need any help, my brother works at the party store in town. He could give you a good discount on streamers and balloons and stuff," she offered.

"I'm good, thanks."

She nodded and headed toward her workstation.

"Hey, Maggie, hold up," Cole called.

She turned around.

"So, it isn't a party. It's a wedding. It's my wedding, actually. Have you any idea where I can get a great cake from around here?"

Chapter Thirty-seven

"Eddie? Can you hear me, sugar? It's me, it's Nancy."

"Do you think he can hear us?" Robyn asked, peering at his face as if hoping to find the answer.

"They say so, don't they, when people are in comas and stuff," Nancy answered, holding tightly to Eddie's hand.

"Shall I sing?" Robyn suggested.

"H...hell...no," Eddie croaked and he blinked opened his eyes.

"He spoke. Did you hear that? He spoke! Eddie, honey, Robyn and me are here," Nancy said, squeezing his hand tighter.

"Yeah, I heard. He told me not to sing," Robyn said happily, looking at her dad.

"How d'you feel? Do you want some water?" Nancy fussed.

"No, you know I hate the stuff. What time is it?" Eddie asked, coughing and trying to get his voice back.

"Just after six. Do you feel any better? You gave us a bit of a scare earlier, Nancy almost asked me to be her bridesmaid," Robyn joked.

"Just after six? What you doing here, Buttercup?" Eddie questioned, trying to sit up but just managing to flail.

"Making sure you're not going to try and get another slot in the operating room."

"But you have a game, against Grand Rapids," Eddie stated, trying to adjust one of the monitors on his chest.

"The team do, I'm staying right here. I've given Cole my instructions," Robyn informed him.

"Are you insane? You're the manager! You need to be there, ice side. You need to make sure they capitalize on that victory last weekend. Get out of here! Nancy, tell her!" Eddie said, raising his voice and looking uncomfortable.

"Eddie, stop wriggling about. You've just had a long and difficult operation," Nancy ordered him.

"She shouldn't be here fawning over me—she should be with the team. I don't want you here," Eddie yelled at her.

"Eddie, will you lower your voice. Robyn, he doesn't mean it," Nancy assured her.

"Yes, he does," Robyn said.

"Yes, I do, so get out of here! Get down to the arena and sort out the team. I've got one woman who isn't going to leave my side, I don't need two—particularly when one should be filling my shoes at the rink," Eddie blasted.

"I'm going," Robyn said, standing up.

"I'll call you, sugar, let you know how he's doing," Nancy promised.

"I'll be back after the game," Robyn said, opening the door to leave.

"You will not, you'll celebrate the victory, like we always do. Get going!" Eddie barked and then he started to cough.

She did the drive in under ten minutes. The arena car lot was filling up, but she managed to get her usual spot. Looking at her watch, she saw it was a little more than thirty minutes until the face off.

Reaching the locker rooms, she could hear raised voices from her team.

"What the Hell's going on?" she demanded to know as she flung open the door and entered.

No one said a word.

"I said what's going on? Man, what's that smell? Have you been drinking in here? It smells like someone fell into a vat of Jack Daniels," Robyn announced, trying to sniff out the offending area of the room.

"It's Brad," Cole informed her.

"I had you down as someone who couldn't be trusted from day one, didn't I? Didn't I! Did you know they're dating? Him and Robyn! Yeah, all this platonic bullshit was just that—bullshit," Brad yelled to the room.

"You're drunk," Robyn stated, looking at him with disappointment in her eyes.

"Oh so what? You're not my freaking mother! I don't have to answer to you," Brad retorted like a child.

"You do when it's team business. You can't play out there like that. You'd be useless to us and a danger to yourself. Take the pads off," Robyn ordered.

"Listen, I'm just fine. I've been skating since I was two, I could probably play blindfolded. Besides, you need me, you only have six," Brad told her with a laugh as he banged into Wes' locker and hit his elbow.

"Is that true?" Robyn asked, looking to Cole for confirmation.

"Yeah."

"You're kidding me! Where are the others?"

Nobody answered.

"I don't need this right now," she said with a sigh.

Why was nothing straightforward? Her dad was recovering from a major operation and she had to manage five players and a drunk, angry ex-boyfriend.

"Get your pads off now," Robyn ordered Brad.

"You can't play this game without me," Brad said, a grin forming on his reddened, drunk face.

"Is that right? So, you're pissed with me and Cole and you're going to hold the Panthers to ransom, are you? Mess up any chance we have of not being relegated this season," Robyn said, narrowing her eyes at him.

"I'm the captain," Brad reminded her.

"Not tonight. Now, I'm going to ask you one last time — take off the pads!" Robyn ordered angrily.

"Make me," Brad spat back.

"Fine. Cole, Mickey, Wes, Henrik, take his pads off," Robyn ordered her team.

"Robyn, I don't think…" Cole started.

"I no like…how you say…fight with team friend," Henrik agreed.

"Fine! Forget his pads, I'll get some more. Have you submitted the team list yet?" Robyn barked at Cole.

"No."

"Good, cross Brad's name out, put yourself as captain, and put down Art," Robyn said as she prepared to look for more kit.

"But Art isn't here," Cole reminded her.

"No, but he's the closest build and coloring to me," Robyn replied.

"Are you crazy? You can't play," Cole told her as Robyn began to strap the pads to her body.

"I don't have any choice. You know we can't play if we can't field a full team, and we'll get points deducted and a fine, we can't afford that. And we have over three thousand people out there expecting a game of hockey," Robyn reminded him.

News of the Panthers' victory against top of the league Reading had spread, and there were new faces in the crowd, people who hadn't shown an interest in the game before. She didn't want to lose new spectators.

"But if we get caught fielding an illegible player then..." Cole started.

"We aren't going to get caught. As far as everyone's concerned, I'm Art. I'm wearing his shirt, his helmet, a mouth guard. As long as I don't speak, who's going to know except us?" Robyn asked him, pulling up the trousers and looking for something to use as a belt.

"You think you can stop talking for a whole match?" Cole asked her.

"I'll put on my gruff voice."

"I'm not comfortable with it. It's physical, Robyn, it's brutal out there...you know that," Cole said.

"And I'm quick, you know that. I can outsprint any of you on the ice. As long as I don't get caught, I'll be fine," she insisted.

"And if you do get caught? If their enforcer puts you in the boards?" Cole questioned, looking at her with concern.

"It's probably best not to think about that. I might do a really girlie scream and blow our cover," Robyn answered, putting Art's shirt over her pads.

"I'm not going to let you do this," Cole told her seriously.

"You can't stop me," Robyn told him with a laugh.

"I don't want you going out there," he repeated.

"I don't have a choice, not now that Brad's gone all psycho on us. I can't have him out there making an idiot of himself and the team," Robyn insisted.

"This is crazy. I'm going to find Bob," Cole said, heading for the door.

"Don't you do that! Don't you dare do that!" Robyn warned him.

"Then stop this."

"No." Robyn sat down on the bench and began lacing up her skates.

"Robyn, I don't want you getting hurt," Cole told her.

"You're getting sentimental on me and you're trying to look after me. I don't need looking after, remember," Robyn said, frantically lacing up her skates.

"I'm not so sure about that when you do crazy things like this," he answered.

"You won't change me, Cole. I hope you know that."

"I don't want to change you."

"Then live with the fact that I'm going out there. How can I not? I love the Panthers, you know I love the Panthers. I can't let them down because I'm scared I might get mashed by their gigantic number twenty-two," Robyn told him.

"I won't let you get mashed," Cole promised.

"I know. And that's what I'm counting on," Robyn said, looking at him and smiling.

Chapter Thirty-eight

He had never been so nervous about a game before. What Robyn was doing was insane and it was dangerous. He'd seen strong men really hurt on the ice and he didn't want that to happen to Robyn. This was a nightmare. He wasn't going to be able to concentrate on the game, his eyes would be on her and anyone who came near her. Brad was an asshole, and if his attitude cost Robyn, he'd kill him.

"Now listen to me, the game plan's the same as we played against Reading. Henrik, you're our main man up front. I'm going to sit just off of you and feed you everything I get. Mickey and Wes, I want you going in and going in hard the second they're in the danger zone. Cole, I want you working in the middle, going forward when you can, tracking back when you need to," Robyn instructed her team as they grouped together in a huddle.

"Let's do this," Mickey said encouragingly.

"Go Panthers," Henrik yelled, punching his fist into the middle of the group.

"Okay, let's go," Robyn said, encouraging them to get into position.

"Hey, listen. You might need to cover me a little," Cole said to Wes and Mickey.

"You carrying a knock?" Mickey questioned.

"No, I'm going to be covering her," Cole said, indicating Robyn.

"Hey man, this is Robyn we're talking about. You've never seen her play, have you?" Mickey said with a laugh.

Cole shook his head.

"The only thing we're going to have to worry about is how long it is before she's sent off," Mickey told him.

Robyn was absolutely terrified. She hadn't played a competitive game since her teens, and as well as hoping none of the rules had changed too much, she hoped she was going to be able to keep pace with the other players. Ice hockey was a complete physical work out and the Panthers were already down in numbers.

She warmed up her blades and turned just past the middle of the rink. She looked into the crowd and there was her family. Bob, Pam, Sierra and Sienna in full uniform and Sarah too, sat next to Brad. He had a hot dog in one hand and a bottle of beer in the other.

She could hear Pam raising her voice at Bob and him trying desperately to quiet her. Then Sierra and Sienna pointed at her and waved their pompoms in the air. They knew she was playing. No wonder Pam was going nuts. The sooner the game started and finished the better.

"You good?" Cole asked, skating up to her.

"Yeah, sure, let's go," Robyn replied, pushing her mouth guard in and pushing off toward the center.

Robyn had to admit the Grand Rapids team was good. They had plenty of players to swap in and out and they were quick. She had been out of breath from the five minute mark and as play went on she feared for her lungs.

"Are you okay?" Cole asked Robyn. Play had stopped for one of the Grand Rapids team members to reclaim their stick.

"I might need a bath and some painkillers when we get home, that number twenty-two caught me," Robyn admitted, still trying to catch her breath.

"I'm on him, don't worry," Cole responded.

"Yeah, man, cool, let's go, go Panthers!" Robyn said in a gruff, manly voice as one of her opponents approached them.

Play restarted, and within seconds, Grand Rapids had out run the tired Mickey and slotted a neat goal past Scott. Robyn ached with disappointment as the opposing team began to celebrate and hug their squad on the bench. The Panthers had played so well, but a stupid error because of fatigue had cost them.

"It's just one, we can get that back," Cole called to her. She knew he could sense her frustration.

Robyn nodded, picked up her stick, and prepared to recommence play.

It was still one to zero Grand Rapids at the end of the first period, but given the small number in the Panthers' team and how exhausted they all were, it was amazing they were only one goal down.

"Listen, I really appreciate your hard work out there guys, you're doing an amazing job. One nil is okay. If we can keep it like that, I'll be okay with it. If we can sneak an equalizer, I'll be more than okay with it," Robyn said as they skated up the tunnel and back onto the ice.

"You need to keep away from number twenty-two. He either hates the fact you're beating him to everything or he knows you're a girl," Cole told her seriously.

"Yeah, he's caught me a couple of times, but it won't happen again. I've got the measure of him," Robyn assured him.

"Look, we've only got the last period to go, just don't do anything crazy," Cole said.

"And I thought I was the manager," Robyn said, skating away from him to take up her position.

Play continued, Robyn out turned her opponent and came away with the puck. She looked up, saw Henrik trying to get away from his marker, and she sped off toward goal, number twenty-two in hot pursuit.

Henrik couldn't find any space, Cole was trying to shake off another player at his side, and Robyn was left with no options.

She shuffled the puck from side-to-side against her stick and hit it toward goal with every ounce of strength she had left. It flew across the ice, the keeper dropped to his knees, but the puck was quicker and it hit the back of the net before he could get down to the ground.

The light lit up, the crowd went crazy, and the celebratory music filled the air as Robyn was bundled by her team mates.

Mickey howled as he hugged Robyn and the team celebrated their equalizing goal.

"Goal was…how you say? Incredability!" Henrik said, slapping Robyn on the back.

"Way to go, Boss," Wade said, giving Robyn a high five.

"We need to get back into position, last five," Robyn said, urging them back into the middle section of the rink and dismissing their congratulations.

She was wired and elated, but there was a game to see out and the nature of hockey was that things changed in seconds.

"That was something else," Cole told her as he skated back.

"We'll relive it later, at least fifty times, and I'll talk you through it, but we need to keep focused. A draw would be a great result given the whole no player scenario," Robyn growled in a low tone as a Grand Rapids player got near.

"Hey! Henrik! Look sharp, yeah?" Cole called as he watched Henrik dip his head and seem to lose concentration briefly.

The game restarted and the Portage team was immediately under attack as Grand Rapids desperately tried to regain their lead.

Mickey pushed the puck forward and Robyn sped toward it, shielding it with her stick. She was about to turn around and look to pass it off to Cole, when suddenly she was hit by what felt like a truck.

Number twenty-two hammered into Robyn, his whole body weight crushing her into the boards. Robyn crashed against the hoardings, fell backwards, and landed face-down on the ice with a dull thud. Blackness filled her up.

His heart dropped out of his chest like someone had just dumped a concrete block on it. She was motionless, completely lifeless and still, laid out on the rink like a rag doll. He yanked the gloves from his hands and tore off his helmet as he sprinted across the ice to reach her. He felt sick, he couldn't focus, why was she so far away? Why hadn't he been right in that zone with her? He fell down onto his knees as he got to her and flipped up the visor on her helmet.

"Robyn, can you hear me?" Cole asked, looking down at her. His mouth could barely form the words.

There was no response.

"Get the mouth guard out! Check for her tongue." Bob, who had rushed down onto the ice from the stands, yelled at Cole.

Cole swiftly opened her mouth, removed the mouth guard, and made sure her tongue hadn't slipped down the back of her throat.

"Is he breathing?" the medic asked as he arrived at the scene.

"I'm not sure, I think so. We took the mouth guard out, the tongue hasn't slipped," Bob answered.

"Okay, let's get his helmet off," the medic instructed.

"No!" Robyn exclaimed in a deep, throaty roar, her eyes flickering open.

"We have breathing. Gurney over here!" the medic called.

"I'm okay," Robyn said.

Bob was taking her pulse, Cole held her other hand, and the medic began to strap a head brace around her. Henrik had removed his helmet and was waving his gloved hands up and down in a bid to see if her eyes were working, and Mickey had the number twenty-two for Grand Rapids in a headlock at the side of the ice where a referee was trying to part them.

"You're going to the ER," Cole informed her.

"I'm okay," Robyn said, still trying hard with her male voice.

"No arguments, young man, we need to get you checked out," the medic informed her.

"There's only a minute left. I can last a minute," Robyn said, trying to sit up but flailing back down.

"Do as you're told for once. Pam would kill me if I let you play out the game. She's going nuts over there," Bob said to her.

"We drew," Robyn said, a smile of satisfaction crossing her face.

"Yes, we did. That Matthers determination did it again," Bob agreed, smiling back at her.

"I think I want to pass out again now," Robyn said, her eyes flickering closed.

"Bruce! Get some oxygen over here!" the medic called.

"I'm not leaving you, Robyn, you hear me?" Cole said, squeezing her hand.

Chapter Thirty-nine

"Hey! You in the bed! Wake up! We've got raisins! Apparently, they're the nearest thing on God's Earth to sweets and much better for you!"

Robyn groaned. Her whole body hurt like Hell. It felt like someone had pounded her over and over with a boulder. She opened her eyes and saw a paper bag being jiggled up and down near her face. Shaking the bag was a wrinkled arm poking out from a navy blue gown.

"Max. What are you doing here?" Robyn asked, attempting to move herself into sitting position.

"Keeping an eye on you for your pop. He nearly burst his stitches trying to get out of bed when your uncle told him you were in here. Took four people to hold him down," Max announced, putting the bag of raisins in her lap.

"So how did you get down here? Don't tell me they let you wheel yourself? You can't have a license for that thing," Robyn said, looking at the wheelchair.

"Nancy..." Max began.

"Morning! How you doing, honey? I got you coffee, real stuff from the diner across the street, not that shit we had yesterday from the machine. That stuff gave me gas," Nancy announced as she burst into the room with three cups.

"It's morning? Where did the night go?" Robyn asked.

"You spent that tossing and turning and muttering under your breath," Nancy informed her, putting a cup on Robyn's table and passing a cup to Max.

"And Cole says you grind your teeth," Max added, opening up the bag of raisins and helping himself.

"He was here all night. I sent him home a couple of hours ago to get some rest," Nancy said as she threw open the curtains, letting the Michigan sunlight flood the room.

Robyn screwed up her eyes and reached over for her coffee.

"You're one crazy lady thinking you can play hockey with the guys," Max told her, shaking his head.

"I did play hockey with the guys; I have the bruises to prove it. When can I get out of here?" Robyn asked, shifting herself up the bed.

"Not until the doctor's checked you over. He's waiting for test results," Nancy said, fluffing up the pillows behind Robyn's head.

"What are you doing?" Robyn asked as Nancy helped her to lie back against them.

"Looking after you, like I look after your equally stubborn father," Nancy said, tucking Robyn back into her sheets.

"I have an appointment today, to go through my statement," Robyn said.

"I'm going to call whoever and I'm going to cancel. You're not up to that right now," Nancy said firmly.

"You shouldn't have to go through all that again, it's criminal," Max told her, his eyes watery.

"Dad told you," Robyn said, looking at the old man.

"Broke down in tears, he did. Said he wished he'd killed this Jason back in the day. I don't blame him. If I ever see him..." Max began, getting upset.

"Now you listen to me, I don't want anyone wallowing in upset over this anymore. And I don't want you to cancel, Nancy. I'm going to give my statement and then it's going to be over, no matter what. I've wasted too much time reliving it; I don't want to waste a second more," Robyn said determinedly.

There was a knock on the door and Sarah cautiously opened it and looked in. She smiled at Robyn.

"Hi. I hope I'm not disturbing anything. I just wanted to see..." she began, stepping into the room.

"She's fine; blow to the head did her the world of good as far as I'm concerned," Nancy answered smartly, taking hold of Max's wheelchair.

"We'd better check on your dad. Keep eating the good stuff, girl," Max said, gesturing to the half-eaten packet of raisins.

"We need to talk about the roadhouse!" Robyn called as Nancy and Max made for the door.

"Later, honey, Milo's got it covered," Nancy said dismissively.

"Nancy!" Robyn yelled.

"Rest! Or the doc will keep you here longer. I'll be back in an hour to check on you," she replied, and she closed the door behind her.

Robyn let out an irritated sigh and then focused on her friend who was still standing rather awkwardly too far away from the bed.

"We're fighting, aren't we," Robyn said, as if not completely sure.

"Yes. But I don't want to," Sarah answered.

"Yeah, well, me neither. I haven't got the energy," Robyn admitted.

"I've been an idiot. Just, so stupid," Sarah continued.

"Me too."

"I'm pregnant, Robyn," Sarah admitted with a wide smile.

"Oh my God! You're kidding, right?"

Sarah shook her head, still beaming.

"Oh my God," Robyn repeated.

"Be happy for me," Sarah begged, taking hold of Robyn's hands.

"I am. I mean, I am if you are and you seem like you are. So I'm happy. God, that's really like — wow — full on," Robyn said with a loud expiration.

"I know, but it's just the best thing that's ever happened to me. I can't tell you how I feel. It's just like everything's clicked into place. I've got a purpose now, I know what I'm doing, and I know where I'm going...it's just incredible," Sarah announced, her eyes shining with expectant anticipation.

"Have you told Mickey?"

"Not yet."

"Why not? I mean, if this news doesn't prompt a proposal then nothing will."

"I don't want that."

"What?"

"I don't want a proposal. Not now. I would love for us to get back together and be together as a family, but I don't want us to get back together because of the baby. Every couple that does that ends up hating each other and resenting each other, and I don't want that for me and I don't want that for Mickey, either."

"Jeez, did you get all grown up and sensible while I was being flattened by the big guy from Grand Rapids?" Robyn asked, sipping her coffee.

"I just want to do right by this little person," Sarah said, rubbing her stomach protectively.

"Man, don't rub your guts like that, not yet. It's not natural until you're at least six months gone and you have a backache as an excuse."

"Anyway, how are you doing? When can you come home?" Sarah asked.

"Who knows? When they've decided whether my body's still in one piece, I guess. I think it is. I'm just not sure how long some bits are going to stay hanging on for," Robyn answered.

He knocked a glass slide with his elbow and it smashed on the floor. The sound jerked him awake and Maggie dutifully came running to his side.

"You should go home," she said, bending down and sweeping up the shards.

"I can't sleep," Cole admitted.

"Then you should go to the hospital," she suggested.

"Robyn needs rest, I don't want to stop her resting. If I'm there, she'll have us watching monster trucks and you haven't seen her when she's watching monster trucks. It isn't relaxing," Cole remarked with a smile.

"Shall I make us some more coffee?" Maggie suggested.

"Sure, that would be great," he answered.

"Hi, honey! Oh, look at you! You look so pale. She looks pale, Bob. Doesn't she look pale?" Pam fussed as she, Bob, Sienna, and Sierra entered Robyn's room.

"She looks a lot better now than she did on that gurney last night," Bob said, smiling at his niece.

"We bought you a program. Daddy says you like to read the programs and there's a cool picture of you from the game against Reading," Sierra announced, holding the brochure out to her.

"Yeah, you're screaming at Brad. It was right when he gave the puck away and they almost scored," Sienna added.

"Am I drooling?"

"Almost," Bob answered.

"What you did last night, Robyn, was really stupid and dangerous and..." Pam started as she sat in the chair next to Robyn's bed.

"We thought it was amazing. Daddy's going to put flyers up at school and try and get a girls' team together," Sienna interrupted excitedly.

"You are?" Robyn asked.

"Sure, and if there's enough interest, I don't mind taking them for practice sessions," Bob said.

"But that could be a long way off, you know, if nobody's interested. I mean, when I was your age girls, I liked Barbie and dress up and..." Pam started.

"Jeez woman, they like hockey, get over it. It's good they have an interest at last," Bob butted in.

"We can play Barbies too, Mommy," Sierra suggested.

"Yeah, ice hockey Barbie. We can get her an outfit and pads and she can mash up Ken," Sienna said a glint in her eye.

"Ssh, not so loud girls. Robyn's meant to be resting. So, when can you come home, honey? Bob's redecorated the guest room; I can look after you, and..." Pam started.

"I'm waiting for my meds and then Cole's coming to pick me up. I'm going home, you know, Woodhams Avenue...with Cole," Robyn told her.

"But, honey, you need to rest and I can take some time off work and..." Pam continued.

"I don't do resting," Robyn said firmly.

"No, but you do have broken ribs and that means you need to slow down," Bob joined in.

"But it doesn't mean I have to stop living with Cole. That's what this is about, isn't it? Why don't you want me living with Cole?" Robyn asked, narrowing her eyes.

"We like Cole," Sienna announced.

"He's hot," Sierra agreed.

"This has nothing to do with me," Bob insisted, wanting to avoid confrontation.

"We like Cole, of course we do, but living together? In a relationship? Isn't it a bit quick, honey?" Pam asked her.

"It's my business," Robyn said.

"I know, honey, but we're your family and..." Pam began.

"I'm twenty-five. Back in England, I've been a mistress to a middle-aged car salesman. Do you want to give me your opinion on that too?"

"Cole's a lot younger and he has really nice hair," Sienna said.

"And rock hard abs," Sierra added.

"Girls!" Bob exclaimed.

"I know what I'm doing," Robyn insisted.

"We just want to look after you, don't we, Bob?" Pam continued.

"This has nothing to do with me," Bob said.

"I can look after myself," Robyn said with a sigh.

"The jury's still out on that one," Pam said, folding her arms across her chest.

"Well, if you really want to help me, you could stop by the roadhouse and see how Milo's doing. I was expecting a delivery of the jumping castle and the fake plants. He's no good at decor. Could you give it the once over? Spruce it up a bit? I'm not going to be able to get over there until the morning, and Nancy's tied up with Dad," Robyn said.

"Of course! We can do that, can't we girls? We can get it looking really nice for Robyn," Pam agreed.

"Do we get soda?" Sierra questioned.

Chapter Forty

"Hello Robyn."

Trudy Franklin was now well into her forties, but Robyn was almost certain she was wearing the same suit she had worn all those years ago when she had interviewed her following the rape. Her brown hair was graying at the temples and she was wearing silver framed glasses. Standing on the doorstep with her was a fresh-faced female police officer dressed in traditional uniform. She smiled at Robyn, but she looked almost uncomfortable.

"Hi, come in. This is Cole, by the way, he's my…well, we live together," Robyn said quickly, grimacing as she led the way into the living room.

Her ribs were on fire, breathing was difficult — walking and breathing was even worse.

"Pleased to meet you. And Robyn, this is Officer Doyle. She's here to take your statement and make sure I do everything right," Trudy said, sitting down on the sofa.

"It's Lisa," the officer informed her, smiling.

"Shall I make some coffee?" Cole offered.

"Yeah, and chips and dip," Robyn suggested.

"Not for me, thank you, I just had lunch," Trudy said.

"Yeah, me too, but you know, dessert can be savory right?" Robyn responded.

She was trying to keep things light-hearted. The last time she had to recount the night of the rape, she'd been in the police station, dressed in clothes that weren't hers while what she had been wearing was forensically examined.

Trudy smiled at her and then reached forward and took hold of Robyn's hands.

"It's okay to cry, you know. You don't have to be brave with us. I know how hard this all must be," Trudy said, looking at Robyn intently.

"I don't want to cry, thanks, but I might if you keep making me lean forward. I had a disagreement with a mountain of an ice hockey player and I've got broken ribs," Robyn informed her, trying to quell the pain.

"Oh, I'm so sorry, I had no idea. Are you sure you're up to this right now? I mean, we can..." Trudy began, dropping Robyn's hands and quickly putting a cushion behind her back.

"I don't want to postpone. I just want to get it over with and get it sorted out. I mean, if Jason didn't do it, then whoever did is still out there, right? And he could do it again. He might have already done it again," Robyn said.

"We're looking into it already. We're looking into all the unsolved rapes in the state," Lisa Doyle informed her, getting out her notepad and setting up the voice recorder.

"Right, so, let's do it—ask your questions," Robyn said, swallowing the knot of anxiety down as best as she could.

"When were you aware that someone was behind you?" Trudy asked.

Robyn cradled her cup of coffee and Cole sat next to her. The interviewing had barely started and already she was no longer in the room. She was back on the road, that night, the rain splattering her face, the wind buffeting her along, her stomach full of hot dogs, miserable because the Panthers had lost. She was rushing home because she was already well past her mother's curfew. Eddie had driven her to the game but he'd stayed behind to give the team the talking to of their lives after the poor performance. She had school the next day and unfinished homework. Nothing about that evening had been good.

"There wasn't anyone behind me. I mean, I didn't feel anyone behind me and I looked back whenever I heard a car. The rain was in my eyes and the wind was, well, you know what the wind's like around here," Robyn said, her eyes glazing over.

"So the first moment you were aware that someone was behind you was when..." Trudy started.

"The bag went over my head. The bag went over my head and he was pulling me backwards, holding onto the bag so I couldn't get it off. His fists were by my jaw, he was pulling me off the road, down the bank, toward the woods," Robyn carried on.

"What was the bag made of Robyn?"

"Something like hessian, you know, burlap, I think...it was rough. I had my eyes open, but everything was dark and distorted, I couldn't see," she said, tears welling up in her eyes.

"And what happened next?" Trudy asked as Officer Doyle continued to jot things down.

"I was trying to fight him off, but he was strong. He was holding the bag over my head and still managing to push me where he wanted me to go."

"Can you give me a body type? Tall? Slim? Broad? Anything you can remember."

"I don't know, tall, I think, but I'm not sure. He was so strong, I mean, I couldn't get away. I really tried and I tried to scream. I was screaming the whole time, but the bag and the wind were just taking it away."

"So how far did he pull you?"

"I don't know, not far, I guess…a couple of yards, just into the trees…I think, I don't know. Everything was just happening and I couldn't stop it."

"And what happened then? You said in your previous statement he pushed you down on the ground."

"He did. But he didn't ever let go of the bag. He pushed me and he kind of came down with me," Robyn said, staring into the room but only seeing the scene playing in her mind.

"And did he say anything?"

"No. He never spoke. After the initial screaming, I tried to be calm and tried to reason with him. I said if he just let me go, that would be the end of it and I would never tell anyone what he'd tried to do. I wouldn't go to the police, it would just be forgotten. But he didn't say anything, and the more I talked, the angrier he seemed to get. Then I was crying and I was screaming again and I was pleading with him to let me go," Robyn said as the emotion overwhelmed her and she let out a sob.

"Do you really need to do all this? I mean…" Cole started, reaching for Robyn's hand.

"Please, we don't want to break Robyn's concentration," Trudy told him.

"I know, but…" Cole began.

"You don't have to stay, Cole. I'll be okay," Robyn assured him, wiping her eyes with the back of her hand.

"I'm not sure I want to hear what he did to you. I don't want to even think about what he did to you," Cole whispered to her.

"I know," Robyn replied, squeezing his hand.

"Shall we take a break?" Trudy offered.

"No, I'm fine. You don't have to listen, Cole, honestly," Robyn insisted, looking up at him.

"I don't want to let you down."

"You're not letting me down."

"When I think about what he did to you, it makes me feel sick," Cole told her.

"It makes us all feel sick, Cole. In fact, I was sick, all those years ago, right after I interviewed Robyn for the first time. And I thought we had our man...to find out that we haven't is hard for me, too," Trudy assured him.

"Go make some more coffee," Robyn suggested to him.

"No, I want to support you."

"Then if you want to support me, you're going to have to hear what he did. Because like it or not, what he did to me is part of me...an unsavory part, but a part all the same."

"I know that."

"Good."

"Okay."

"But we're black-bagging the old parts as of today because I'm ready to make new parts now and I want to make them with you," Robyn said, holding his hand.

"Then I'm staying and we're going to finish this together," Cole said, squeezing her hand reassuringly.

"Take your time, Robyn," Trudy said when Robyn's breathing quickened.

It hurt her to remember. Her heart rate sped up, her mind ached with the weight of the memory, and the pain she had felt on that night she could still feel now. It was like she was being raped all over again.

"I could barely breathe, the sack was getting tighter and tighter, and my throat was hurting. I tried kicking, but nothing worked and the pain just got worse. So I stopped lashing out and I thought if I just let him do whatever he wants to do, he might not kill me," Robyn tried to explain.

"I'm sorry, Robyn; we need to know exactly what he did," Trudy reminded her.

Robyn took a deep breath and squeezed Cole's hand.

"He pulled down my jeans and my underwear and he started touching me," Robyn said robotically.

She had bitten the inside of the bag as hard as she could while he touched her, wishing for it to be over. The wind had howled and she had tried to focus on the storm rather than what was happening to her. Despite the ugliness of the event, his touch hadn't been brutal.

"He wasn't trying to hurt me," Robyn said suddenly, as if waking up.

"What?" Cole asked.

"He touched me, it was disgusting, because I didn't want it...but it wasn't rough. Not physically rough. He didn't want to hurt me," Robyn repeated.

"You didn't say this before," Trudy said, making sure Officer Doyle was noting it down.

"Because I didn't realize it before. He touched me, then he raped me, and then he left me, but don't you see? In his mind he wasn't raping me. He didn't want it to be violent; he wanted to think it was real," Robyn said.

"Putting a bag over someone's head and forcing them to have sex with you isn't my idea of real," Cole replied.

"No, but maybe that was the only way I would have sex with him. It has to be Jason. He knew me, he had a crush on me, he liked me, but he knew I would never date him. This is the only way he would ever get to sleep with me and he didn't want to hurt me. Don't you see?" Robyn asked them.

"Robyn, not all rapes are savage in the sense of physically maiming someone, even when the attacker doesn't know his victim. A lot of rapes are committed because the attacker can't forge a relationship and can't have sexual contact in the usual way," Trudy reminded her.

"I never thought of it before, I was just too caught up in the fact that it had happened rather than exactly what happened and how it happened," Robyn continued.

"I have to tell you that Jason's witness has provided a full statement and it can be corroborated. He was on his phone to his girlfriend at the time, we've checked telephone records," Trudy said.

"Why didn't he come forward at the time?" Cole asked.

"He's spent the last nine years in South America. He only returned home three months ago and Jason's lawyer did another sweep of the neighborhood."

"It has to be him," Robyn said, shaking her head.

"How long do you think you were in the woods before you made it back to the side of the road and Brad Willis found you?" Trudy inquired, looking at her file.

"I don't know...twenty minutes? Maybe longer? I couldn't move for a while, because I was shaking and I was wet and I didn't know what to do. And then I realized that if I didn't move I would probably die from the cold, so I got dressed and I went back to the road," Robyn explained.

"Are we done now?" Cole asked, wiping at his eyes.

"Just one more thing. We checked your medical records in England, just procedure, and..." Trudy started.

"Why did you check my medical records?" Robyn asked, the color draining from her face.

"It's just procedure, Robyn. We wanted to see how the counseling went, whether you have any ongoing physiological issues, whether you..."

"You could have just asked me and I would have told you. You didn't need to go snooping into my medical records," Robyn said angrily.

"Would you like Cole to wait outside?" Trudy suggested kindly.

"Sure, I can go," Cole said, standing up.

"No. I don't want you to go," Robyn said, taking hold of his hand.

"We need to ask some questions about…" Trudy began.

"I know what you want to ask about," Robyn interrupted, looking up at Cole, tears spilling from her eyes.

"Robyn?" Cole asked. She could see the immediate worry in his eyes.

"They want to ask me about the baby," Robyn blurted out.

Chapter Forty-one

He felt emotionally wrung out and now he was listening to Lonestar. He wanted to kill Jason. He wanted to get hold of his scrawny neck and squeeze the life right out of him. He wanted to make him suffer the same way Robyn had suffered. The red mist had descended when he'd found out about Bryn and Veronica, but this feeling was on a completely different level than that. That bastard hadn't just violated her, he'd left her with his baby. How did you ever get over that?

He looked at the beer bottle in his hand, gripping it tightly until his knuckles turned white. Then he threw it, as hard as he could, and watched it smash on the floor.

Robyn sat in the bath surrounded by bubbles and almost scalding hot water, but she still felt cold. She always felt cold whenever she had to speak or think about the rape. She didn't know whether it was a reflection of the time of year it happened or a reflection of how she felt inside, probably a bit of both. She had spent a lot of time feeling lukewarm inside and now, just when she had started to think a thaw was really beginning, the past wouldn't let her truly defrost.

Cole knocked on the door.

"Can I come in? I've got beer and pickles."

She didn't answer.

Cole opened the door and stepped in, holding the drinks and a plate of gherkins.

"Hey," he greeted.

Robyn's head was just poking out from underneath the foam.

"You put pickles on a plate? Don't you take in anything I tell you? They should only be eaten from the jar with a fork," Robyn snapped, looking at the food as if it were contaminated.

"I'm sorry. I'll go right back down and get the jar and a fork," Cole said, about to leave the bathroom.

"And you've been listening to Lonestar. Listening to Lonestar will make you suicidal," she continued.

"Yeah, and I smashed a beer bottle too. I've cleaned up, but no going barefoot in the kitchen for a while," Cole replied with a sigh.

Robyn took a pickle from the plate and put it all in her mouth in one go.

"Do you want to talk about it?" he asked.

"Do you?"

"Not if it's going to upset you."

"I'm sorry I didn't tell you. I should have told you when I told you about Jason in the first place," Robyn began, picking another pickle off the plate.

"I had trouble imagining how you must have felt after the attack; I can't begin to think how you must have felt to be pregnant."

"Terrified, angry, stupid. I didn't tell anyone. I started putting on weight and feeling sick, and I thought it was maybe the change of food or climate or me eating for comfort because I missed home. But no, the doctor does a test and I'm three months gone," Robyn said, swigging from the beer bottle.

"What did your mom say?"

"I didn't tell anyone, Cole. I told the doctor there and then that I wanted an abortion and if he didn't get me one I would find someone who would," Robyn explained.

"And what did he say?"

"He said he wanted me to speak to my parents, that he would like them to come in and see him, and that was all I heard. I knew he wouldn't agree to help me without involving my mom, so I had to sort things out myself," Robyn continued.

Cole offered her the plate of pickles.

"I had to do it and I had to do it real quick because if I didn't do it...maybe I wouldn't be able to do it and what would happen then? I wouldn't have known what to do and so I figured if I didn't have the baby I could forget the rape. Didn't work though, did it? I never got rid of the rape and I aborted a child," Robyn spoke.

"What you did on your own was so brave. That's one Hell of a decision for a sixteen year old," Cole told her, reaching into the bubbles and taking hold of her hand.

"I'm not certain I made the right one."

"I'm certain you made the right one for you at the time," Cole assured her.

"I'm sorry I didn't tell you. I should have told you, right away, when you told me about Veronica and Bryn..." Robyn said.

"I didn't tell you what I did after my dad died right away."

"I'm ashamed of it and I don't want anyone to know. Not Dad or Pam, and especially not Sarah, not now," Robyn said.

"Not now?"

"She's pregnant but she hasn't told Mickey yet, so keep it zipped. I'm hoping for a full reconciliation and, despite her reservations, if he doesn't do the decent thing and propose, I'm going to book a priest and a venue myself," Robyn told him.

"Wow."

"Yeah, wow."

"I understand you don't want people to know. It's hard for you — it's in the past and we're moving on, but what if I said there's a possibility I could obtain DNA that would determine who the father of your baby was?" Cole asked seriously.

"What?"

"Listen, it's a long shot, but over here at least, some clinics keep samples to determine DNA and prove paternity."

"But it was nine years ago," Robyn said, her voice shaking.

"I know, and I know the DNA they say they found on you was Jason's, but if the tissue was tested, we would know, maybe not who it was right away, but definitely who it wasn't," Cole explained.

"Can they really do that these days?" Robyn asked.

"They can, if they took samples and if they still have the information," Cole told her.

Robyn swallowed. Memories of the day she entered the clinic swollen and left bereft filled her head. It hadn't been the baby's fault, but it wasn't her time to be a mother. She had nothing and nobody, and he had been a product of an awful assault she couldn't forget.

"Do it. I'll get you the address," Robyn agreed determinedly.

"Hey, Dad. Are you awake?"

Eddie had more color in his cheeks than Robyn had seen since she'd arrived back in Michigan. He screwed up his eyes and then opened them wide, looking straight at her, a familiar scowl on his face.

"What are you doing here? You've got broken ribs, haven't you? You should be resting, not poking your nose into what I'm doing. Let your dad have a bit of peace," Eddie said.

"You sound so much better. Nancy says you even ate some food today. Pot pie, no less," Robyn said, smiling.

"God damn, it was awful! Whatever the meat was made from, it wasn't a creature on this Earth. What animal does tofu come from? Now, listen, never mind about what I'm eating, what's going on with Brad? He was here earlier, drunk out of his mind, crying and wailing like a baby; Nancy had to take him home," Eddie told her.

"Oh, Dad he's sore because I'm dating Cole. I tried to tell him that we were never going to be more than friends, but he wouldn't take no for an answer. I had to make it clear and he didn't like it," Robyn explained.

"He's had a hard ride in life, Robyn. He's not the big man he makes himself out to be. His pop's tough on him, his mom died, that Michelle left him. I tried to pick him back up, making him the captain of the Panthers, but I don't think it's enough," Eddie told her.

"Dad, I don't care for him that way. We're friends, that's it," Robyn insisted.

"Your aunt's worried about you living with someone you barely know," Eddie continued.

"I can't believe she's been in here telling you this. You're recovering from a very serious operation, you need to rest and concentrate on getting better," Robyn said crossly.

"Buttercup, I'm bored out of my mind laying here. I feel better, I want to get up and get moving. I want out of here, I want to wear this fancy new coach jacket the team bought me," Eddie told her.

"Getting up and at 'em is weeks away. The best thing is to let things heal and take your time. If you do things too quickly, it could all go wrong," Robyn said.

"I think that's what Pam thinks about you," Eddie replied.

"Well, she's wrong. Trudy came today, I told her everything all over again and I'm really healing this time," Robyn said firmly.

"And you're in love with Cole? You know that after a week?" Eddie asked.

"You want to talk about feelings?"

"It seems I have to lately."

"Yes, I'm sure about Cole. I'm so sure, I'm going to marry him," Robyn announced, and she held her hand out to her dad so he could look at her ring.

"You're what! Are you freaking insane? You can't marry someone you've known a week! What are you trying to do? Kill me?" Eddie blasted, his face reddening as he clutched at his chest.

"No, Dad, I'm trying to make you realize that I'm all grown up now and I can make my own decisions—even if you and Aunty Pam don't think much of them."

"This is the craziest thing you've ever done! This is even crazier than calling yourself Art and playing against Grand Rapids! This is off the scale!"

"Nancy told me you were high school sweethearts. She said you were the best guy she ever knew and that she knew even back then you were her Mr. Right," Robyn told him.

"She reads too many romance novels," Eddie replied with a sniff.

"I believe her. I believe she loves you unconditionally and she knew that all those years ago, just like that," Robyn carried on.

"Has she been lending you books? Because I don't remember you ever having a liking for books. You read car manuals—never books," Eddie commented.

"I feel the same way about Cole. I can't explain it, I certainly don't want to try and explain it to you because that would be really weird, but I'm certain of him. One hundred percent certain of him," Robyn said.

"Knock knock! Hey, old goat, you awake? Where's the chips?" Max questioned as Cole opened the door and pushed the old man into Eddie's room.

"Can't a man get any privacy around here? First she comes and wakes me up and now you? Don't any of you have anything better to do?" Eddie barked at his friend.

"What do you think in this place? It's wall to wall bedpans and that's the highlight," Max announced.

"I just told Dad we're getting married," Robyn told Cole.

"What? Getting married! We've only just met the guy!" Max exclaimed in shock.

"That's exactly what I said," Eddie grumbled.

"Sir, I wanted to ask you for permission, but Robyn said it was too soon, with the operation and everything, and..." Cole began nervously, appearing to be searching for the right words to say.

"What are your prospects? Can you provide for her? I'm not talking playing for a two bit hockey team here, I'm talking long term career plans," Max said, turning around and looking seriously at him.

"I'll ask the questions, Max," Eddie ordered.

"Have you got her a ring? And I don't mean something from the pawn shop, I mean a proper ring—diamonds and lots of 'em," Max carried on.

"Will this do?" Robyn asked, holding her hand out to show Max.

"Jeez! Will you look at that, Eddie! She could have someone's eye out with that. Are they real diamonds?" Max inquired, screwing his eyes up to focus.

"D'you know, I don't know and I don't care," Robyn replied, smiling at Cole.

"So, what are your career prospects?" Eddie muttered, looking at Cole out of the corner of his eye.

"Dad! He works for Gen-All, you know that," Robyn exclaimed.

"I know, but we don't know what he does, how much he earns...he could be the janitor for all we know," Eddie responded.

"I'm not the janitor," Cole replied with a smile.

"No? So what do you do, son?"

"I develop and formulate preventative vaccines," Cole answered.

"What does that mean?" Max asked, waiting for someone to translate.

"It means he's clever," Robyn helped out.

"And I earned three hundred thousand dollars last year," Cole added.

Max let out a high pitched whistle.

"Sir, I love your daughter. I know we didn't meet that long ago, but we're sure of how we feel, and even if I didn't have a good, secure job, I would give her everything I had — everything," Cole said sincerely.

"Right, well, you need to know that she loves the Panthers, nearly more than life itself. She never eats vegetables unless they're in soup or deep fried, and when she lived at home, the only way I could get her out from under the hood of a car was to tell her there were monster trucks on the TV," Eddie informed him, looking at his daughter.

"Obviously years have gone by and I'm totally changed," Robyn insisted.

"So, when's this wedding then? Have you set a date?" Eddie asked.

"Yes. Next week," Robyn said bluntly.

"Next week? Are you kidding me! What happened to long engagements? You cannot be serious!"

Chapter Forty-two

She'd been feeling completely sick with nerves all day. The clowns were late, Bob had to make an emergency repair to his tractor, and it had taken hours to fill the helium balloons. But Cole had managed to book Special Guest and, an hour after the doors reopened on Eddie's Roadhouse, the place was buzzing. There were local families, the local football team, teachers and students from Portage High School, plus most of the neighborhood. All the tables were full and Robyn, Nancy, and the agency waitresses had their work cut out. The children were enjoying the clowns and Bob's tractor rides and the adults were being entertained well by the band.

"Rare rib eye, mixed grill, two children's chicken platters, extra fries, rings, and a green salad," Robyn announced as she balanced a tray on her arm and put the food down on the table.

"This looks delicious," the woman in the party remarked.

"I hope you enjoy it, if you need anything else just holler," Robyn replied with a smile.

She turned around to go back to the kitchen when she spotted Sarah and Mickey entering, their hands clasped tightly together.

"Hey guys, do you want a table? I probably have one for two right now," Robyn said, scanning the restaurant.

"Actually we'll be wanting a table for three," Mickey announced and a proud grin spread all over his face.

"Stop saying that, we shouldn't tempt fate," Sarah replied with a giggle.

"Is there something I should know?" Robyn asked diplomatically.

"We're having a baby!" Mickey exclaimed, and he let out a loud wolf howl that made some of the other diners look around in surprise.

"Mickey stop it! People are trying to eat!" Sarah exclaimed in horror.

"Having a baby, holding hands...does this mean you two are back together the way nature intended?" Robyn asked.

"Yes. And we're getting married," Sarah announced with a blush and she extended her hand to Robyn.

"Oh, Sarah, it's beautiful. Hey mister, about time, too, huh? And who knew you had such excellent taste? It's gorgeous," Robyn said, admiring the delicate emerald and diamond ring.

"I know I said I didn't think I wanted to, but he turned up with the ring, got down on one knee, and cried and everything, and that was before I told him about the baby," Sarah explained.

"I'm really pleased for you," Robyn said, smiling at her friend.

"So, look at this place! It's amazing, Robyn. It looks fantastic and it's packed," Sarah exclaimed, looking around at the buzzing roadhouse.

"I know, we don't have any mustard, but apart from that, everything came together. I just hope we don't run out of food, or beer...beer would be worse," Robyn admitted.

"Where's Cole?" Mickey asked.

"Behind the bar—where a good employee should be. Although he seems to have got himself a female fan club. There are three women who haven't moved from the end bar stools since we opened. I'm not going to say anything just yet, though, because he's got them drinking double Jack and Cokes every round," Robyn replied.

"Robyn! We got orders backing up out there!" Nancy called as she came out onto the floor with two trays in her hands.

"Okay, I'm on it. Guys, table twelve over there. Give me two seconds and I'll come and take your drink orders," Robyn told them as she skipped off, one hand to her injured ribs.

He watched Robyn as she collected some more empty plates and glasses on a tray. She was struggling with her injury but she was never going to stop for a break when they were so busy.

"So Cole, when do you get off?" a woman with thick, dark hair and heavy make-up asked him.

She was toying with the straw in her drink and staring at him appreciatively. He'd seen plenty of women like her in the bar he worked in Chicago.

"Yeah, when do you finish so we can go and have some real fun?" her blonde-haired friend wanted to know.

"Oh, I'm here 'til late," Cole answered, serving a group of guys next to the women.

"You have to go to bed, though, right?" the dark-haired woman said in an attempt at seduction.

"Sure. With my girlfriend," Cole said with a smile. It felt nice to say that.

"Well, I don't see her and what you can't see isn't important in my book," she continued.

"Well, I'm afraid it is in mine. And she's over there," Cole replied, pointing out Robyn who was adjusting her Eddie's Roadhouse cap and taking orders from another table.

"Man! Really! She's not even wearing lipstick," the blonde replied in horror.

It was all he could do not to laugh at her comment. Robyn didn't even own a lipstick. She used gloss that smelt like mint and vanilla and tasted like an ice cream sundae. He glanced over at her as she came back out onto the floor with another tray of food.

"I'll have a Bud," Brad growled, squeezing himself between the women and putting his hands on the bar.

"Hey there, sexy. Do you come here often?" the dark-haired woman asked, turning her attentions toward Brad.

"It could be arranged," Brad replied, smiling at her and taking his cap from his head.

"That's two dollars and fifty cents," Cole said, putting the bottle down in front of him.

"And drinks for the ladies," Brad said, getting out his wallet.

"Why thank you!" the blonde said, giggling like a teenager.

"And while you're at it we'll have a pitcher of Bud..." Eddie's voice spoke.

"That's Bud Light and just the one. You've got an hour," Pam spoke seriously.

She stood behind his wheelchair and Sierra and Sienna were behind her.

"Hey, Eddie, it's great to see you," Cole called.

"Boss, I can't believe they let you out. How you doing?" Brad asked, turning around and looking down at his manager.

"A lot better than you. Look at the state of you. You haven't shaved. Have you even showered?" Eddie questioned.

"Is this your father?" the dark-haired girl asked, looking at Brad.

"One bottle of Bud Light. Robyn's over there," Cole directed.

"Pam! Bring the drink; I want to see my daughter," Eddie said, trying to move the wheelchair himself.

"Here, let me take you," Brad offered, putting his bottle down and taking hold of the arms of the wheelchair.

"Need something to help you keep balance?" Eddie snapped at him.

"No," Brad replied hastily.

"We went through this before, Brad, when Michelle left you. I don't want to go through it again. Whatever's wrong with you, snap out of it. The Panthers captain needs to be someone I can trust and rely on. If you don't want the job, I'll give it to Mickey," Eddie told him firmly.

"Holy crap! What are you doing here?" Wes exclaimed as Brad wheeled Eddie over toward the table of Panthers.

"Checking up on you boys. How are you?" Eddie asked, smiling broadly at all of them.

"We're good. Climbing the table, Boss!" Wade told him.

"We winning big Boss, but Robyn, she is, how you say? Hard pleasing," Henrik informed him.

"Oh, yeah, she's always been that. So I guess you'll be happy to see me back ice side," Eddie said with a grin.

"Are you back tomorrow game?" Henrik asked.

"No, he's not. He's not meant to be here tonight. It will be a few weeks yet," Pam insisted quickly.

"Where's Grant?" Eddie asked, noticing his assistant coach wasn't at the table.

"He...er...well..." Wes started.

"He didn't think it was appropriate to come. He has Jason at home at the moment and..." Wade filled in.

"Oh my God! Dad? What are you doing here? Why aren't you at home resting?" Robyn exclaimed, her mouth wide open.

"He's got an hour," Pam said.

"And we have a defibrillator in the car," Sienna added with a grin.

"Hello, Buttercup. Look at this place! You've taken over," Eddie said, looking around at the decor, the scores of happy customers, the great band, and the clowns.

"Dad, what are you doing here? I can't believe you're here to see this. I must get Nancy," Robyn said, looking around for her soon-to-be stepmother.

"No you won't. She knows I'm coming, she and Pam arranged it for you. You've worked so hard building this place back up in such a short time. Your dad couldn't miss opening night," Eddie told her, his eyes welling up with tears.

"Jeez, don't you weep on me, Dad, you'll kill my ribs," Robyn answered quickly, sucking in the urge to cry.

"I ain't gonna cry yet Buttercup but I might if I don't get any fries or rings," Eddie told her.

"Griddled with no oil and no salt," Pam ordered.

"I'll get you a table," Robyn said with a smile.

"Hey, Robyn. Listen, I just wanted to say..." Brad started, taking hold of Robyn's arm before she moved away.

"Not tonight, Brad. Tonight's about Robyn, not you. Look at the place...it's never been this busy, not even back in the day. Now come and sit with us and talk me through the last game. I know it was a draw, but we want a win on Saturday against Cincinnati," Eddie said.

"Are you okay? You must have served close to a hundred tables," Cole said as he passed Robyn on the way to the stock room.

"I'm fine. In fact, I'm great. Look at the roadhouse, look how the town turned out for me. When I got here, when I took on this challenge, I never believed it would be like this. I always hoped it would, but well, you know, I wasn't sure," Robyn admitted.

"You've done so well," Cole agreed, smiling at her.

"And you're a part of that. A big part," Robyn told him and she slipped her hand into the pocket of her jeans.

She took out her engagement ring and she slipped it back onto her left hand.

"It's time it stayed on — for good," Robyn said, looking up at him.

Cole took hold of her hand and smiled at her.

"In fact, it's time everyone knew," Robyn announced suddenly.

"What? Well, I thought you wanted to wait. You said the day before," Cole reminded her.

"I know and I've changed my mind. Come on," Robyn said, pulling him toward the stage as Special Guest belted out a number by Bryan Adams.

The song came to an end and Robyn took charge of the microphone.

"Hi everyone, I'm Robyn. Don't worry, I'm not going to sing," she began tentatively.

The diners all whooped their appreciation, but the loudest was the hockey team who started banging on the table. Mickey let out a wolf howl before Sarah slapped his arm and made him stop.

"I just want to thank you all for coming tonight and supporting Eddie's Roadhouse. My dad's here, just over there, eating as many of the free nuts as he can get his hands on, thinking I can't see! I see you, Dad! Anyway, I just want to take this opportunity to say thank you to the people who helped me get the roadhouse ready for tonight. Nancy, my almost step-mom...you've worked so hard, you're still carrying plates and stuff now...and I know besides all the hard work you've put into this place, you've also had to put up with my bad attitude, so thank you. I know we got off on the wrong foot, but well, it's forgotten. And then there's Milo, he's my head bartender over there — the cute one with the curly hair and the dimples. Milo, you've been fantastic, you've been here constantly when I couldn't, and you even found ice cream when I demanded it was produced immediately. And the lack of mustard was an oversight on my part and you did remind me, and I said I would handle it and I didn't. So, sorry folks about the whole lack of mustard thing, tomorrow we will have mustard!" Robyn announced.

A cheer went up and people laughed.

"And this by the way...this is Cole," Robyn said, looking at him and smiling as his cheeks flushed and people turned their attention to him.

"I met Cole just over a week ago at the airport and since then...well, he's upturned my life," Robyn informed her audience.

"Woo hoo!" Henrik hollered in appreciation.

"Not only did he buy me a car, he gave me a place to stay, and he's been steering my Panthers to victory ever since. To be honest, I can't imagine my life without him," Robyn said, turning to look only at Cole.

Mickey let out another howl and this time Sarah let him carry on.

"So, tonight I want to tell all of you that—Cole and I are getting married—next week—and you're all invited!" Robyn announced loudly.

There were shouts of excitement, and the whole room erupted into a frenzy of shock, surprise, and delight. Special Guest began a rendition of Billy Idol's "White Wedding" as Cole put his arms around Robyn and kissed her.

"This has got to be a joke," Brad stated through gritted teeth.

"I can't believe it! Getting married next week!" Wade said with a smile.

"Is anyone listening to me? I've never heard anything so messed up in my life. She's known him a week!" Brad exclaimed.

"Hey! Robyn knows what she wants, always has. You keep your opinion on it to yourself," Eddie warned, looking sternly at Brad.

"You knew! How long have you known? You should have told me," Brad blasted angrily, his face reddening.

"She told me this afternoon and I reacted the same way you just did for the same reason. We only just got her back and you don't want to lose her. The difference is Brad she was never yours in the first place," Eddie reminded him.

"Come on man; be happy for them. Look at them, they're so in to each other," Wes remarked as he watched Robyn and Cole being congratulated by well-wishers.

"It sucks! The whole thing sucks!" Brad yelled angrily.

"Hey, what about that announcement then! Sarah didn't even know! A Portage wedding next week and another one in the spring," Mickey announced as he and Sarah joined the hockey table.

"Two weddings?" Henrik queried, puzzled.

"Two?" Pam questioned.

"I asked Sarah to marry me and she said yes—oh and we're having a baby," Mickey told them all.

"Are you sure it's yours?" Brad snapped, drinking greedily from his glass of beer.

"Bradley that's a horrible thing to say," Pam said.

"Just asking. I mean it was only last week she was trying it on with me," Brad informed the table.

"Mickey, it wasn't anything. It was after we had that fight at the barbecue and…" Sarah began tears forming in her eyes.

"Well I think wedding is good—wedding means party," Henrik told everyone as he downed the remainder of his drink in one gulp.

"You Dutch know how to party Henrik don't ya?" Wes spoke.

"He's not Dutch, he's Swedish," Wade replied.

"I think you need to go," Eddie told Brad.

"Yeah? Well I'll go when I'm good and ready. I want a few words with the bride before I go anywhere," Brad snarled as Robyn and Cole made their way over to the table.

"You knew about this? Aren't you going to put a stop to it? I mean I wasn't happy with her moving in with him so fast—but marriage!" Pam remarked to her brother.

"She's twenty-five Pam, what do you want me to do? Ground her? Give her a slap?"

"Well, no, but…" Pam started.

"Look at her. I've never seen her look so happy and if that's his doing then we should be welcoming him into the family, not wondering whether he's an escapee from Death Row," Eddie replied.

"Congratulations, my girl, it's wonderful news. Will there be a reception?" Ada asked, enveloping Robyn in a hug, the gin fumes almost making her cough.

"Yes, Ada, at West Lake, I think. We haven't really finalized everything yet," Robyn said, looking at Cole anxiously.

"Straight after the ceremony, we have one of those huge, open party tents and Eddie's Roadhouse is providing all the food," Cole answered.

"You've organized it," Robyn said, smiling at him.

"I told Nancy it was a surprise party for your birthday just so I had something booked," Cole admitted.

"Can I speak to you?" Brad said, stepping in front of Ada and addressing Robyn, a furious look on his face.

"Are you going to offer your congratulations?" she asked.

"You are kidding me. This whole marriage thing is the most ridiculous thing I've ever heard about," Brad raged.

"No one cares what you think about it," Cole said.

"You're totally out of your mind. If you feel insecure because Jason's dragging everything back up again, I can help you. I can get a restraining order so he can't come near you, I can get my dad to…" Brad started.

"A restraining order? I don't want a restraining order. I don't want anything like that," Robyn said, her mind being forced back to the past again.

"Brad, I think you'd better go," Cole warned.

"If it's security you need, I can give you that."

"I don't want security and I don't want you. How many times do I have to say this, Brad? I don't want you; I never have wanted you, not like that," Robyn stated loud and clear.

"We were together once," Brad told her.

"We were high school kids. I'm not getting into this, not again. I've got people to serve and washing up to do and — just go if you've got nothing good to say," Robyn said, heading back toward the kitchen.

"If you really feel anything for her you'll leave her alone, you're upsetting her," Cole told him.

"What's upsetting her are people dragging up the past. Eddie said she gave her statement again yesterday," Brad said, watching Robyn as she took some plates from Nancy and helped serve them.

"She's fine and it'll all be over soon. They're obtaining new DNA evidence, so we'll know one way or another whether it was Jason who attacked her — no matter what his witness says," Cole informed him.

"What new evidence?" Brad questioned.

"Concrete evidence. Listen, unless you want a bruise on the other side of your jaw, you need to leave," Cole ordered him.

Chapter Forty-three

"It was awesome, wasn't it? The whole night was awesome!" Robyn shrieked happily as Cole drove Leonora back toward home.

It was almost three in the morning. The roadhouse had been a complete mess and had taken two hours to get half straight again. Pam, Bob, and the twins had stayed on to help, but there was still more cleaning up required before they opened for lunch the following day.

"It was totally awesome," Cole agreed.

"And the band was just as amazing as I remembered."

"Well, I have news for you. I booked them for our wedding," Cole told her.

"No! That's the best news!" Robyn screamed and then laughed out loud.

She was so happy. Everything in her life was finally coming together. Her dad was getting better, the Panthers were holding their own in the league, the roadhouse launch had gone better than anyone could have imagined, and she had Cole. Wonderful, gorgeous Cole.

"Stop the car," Robyn ordered him.

"What?"

"Stop the car. Pull in there, right by the lake," Robyn instructed him.

He followed her directions, stopped the car, and turned off the engine.

"So, here we are, just like you asked. What now?" Cole asked, looking at her.

Robyn just looked at him, drinking him in.

"You're trembling," Cole said, holding onto her fingers.

"I'm scared," Robyn admitted with a swallow.

"What of?"

"How I feel about you and how fast it's happened."

"Me too," Cole said, looking into her eyes.

Robyn edged closer to him until their faces almost met. Her heart was racing as she gazed at him and realized the intensity of what she felt for him.

"I want you to kiss me. Then I want you to take my clothes off and I don't want you to stop," Robyn said with conviction. She was ready.

"You mean? Like now? Here? In Leonora?" Cole asked, looking out of the windscreen at the blackness hanging over the rippling lake.

"I've never done it in a Mustang before," Robyn admitted with a swallow.

"Me neither...but...just wait there," Cole said, releasing his seatbelt and opening the door.

"Where are you going?" Robyn asked him.

"Just wait there," Cole repeated, shutting the door behind him.

She shivered as the cold air from outside blew into the car. She rubbed her hands together and caught sight of her engagement ring. Tonight she'd told the whole town she was getting married. With Ada knowing, it would be all over the state by the morning and might even make CNN. That thought didn't even concern her like it might have done. She'd hollered the announcement out in Eddie's Roadhouse because she'd wanted the world to hear.

Her door opened and Cole appeared.

"Okay, come on out," he said, taking hold of her hand.

"You're kidding right? You do know how cold it is out there? And I'm wearing a t-shirt," Robyn reminded.

"Come on, the more you think about it the colder it'll feel," Cole said, pulling her out of her seat and waving a torch around with his other hand.

She stepped out of the car, swinging the door shut behind her and followed him off over the side of the road and down onto the sand that edged the lake.

"I'm getting algae on my shoes," Robyn called to him as he paced ahead.

"Take them off!" Cole yelled back.

"Where are we going?" Robyn shouted in response.

"Keep up. I've got the torch remember!"

The night was black and Cole's image was disappearing in front of her. She pulled off her tennis shoes and hurried across the sand to catch up to him.

She rounded a small dune and then stopped as she discovered him in front of her, sitting on a blanket on the ground.

An emergency flare and a warning triangle were glowing a few yards away from the blanket, bathing the area with light. She put her hand to her mouth in surprise and smiled at the scene.

"No candles in the trunk, maybe we need to get some, you know, for moments like this," Cole spoke as she moved closer to him.

"Moments like...?" Robyn asked as she sat down on the blanket and looked at him.

"Like this," Cole said.

He kissed her lips, softly at first and then harder, with more intent. She rose up on her knees and pulled at his t-shirt. With his help, she brought it over his head.

"Robyn, I want you to be sure. We don't have to do this...hey you're shaking," Cole said, taking her hand in his again.

"I want to do it. More than anything," Robyn said, pulling at the buttons on his jeans.

"I don't want to hurt you," Cole whispered, lightly kissing her neck.

"You won't," she replied, taking his hand. She eased her jeans down over her hips, taking her underwear with them.

He'd been right. If you didn't think about the cold you didn't feel it. All she could feel was her heart beating hard in her chest as she looked at Cole looking at her.

"You are so beautiful," he whispered, helping her take off her t-shirt.

He took a deep breath as he watched her unclasp her bra and discard it on the sand.

"What's wrong?" Robyn asked, suddenly feeling vulnerable.

"Nothing," Cole said with a swallow.

"Tell me."

"Being with you, it means so much...you mean so much," Cole said, his hand tracing the line of her left breast.

His fingers, his touch was setting light to something deep inside her that had been hidden away for so long, never daring to surface.

He put his mouth on hers and kissed her so slowly she thought she was going to die from arousal. The inside of his mouth tasted so sweet, his tongue was so smooth, his lips were so softly swelled she almost couldn't bear for them to leave hers. But they did leave and he moved his mouth to her neck, her chest, her breasts. She arched her back in pleasure, coming alive in the moment, forgetting everything else.

She held his shoulders and pulled him closer to her, wanting to feel the hardness of him. He hesitated, looking at her with his dark sincere eyes. She knew he didn't want to do anything she wasn't ready for.

She touched him, drawing him into her, slowly, tentatively. Then desperately, needful.

He closed his eyes and gathered her into his arms, slowly rocking her toward him. She held onto him, matching his rhythm, almost burning with the sensuality. It felt like nothing she had ever experienced before.

He slowed, opened his eyes, and looked at her. The passion, the depth of his feelings for her were all there, set in his expression. She wanted to share everything with him, forever. He leaned her back until she was laid on the blanket, her hair in the sand and then he moved further into her. With every motion, she felt freer. She gripped his back, wanting to feel him inside her more and more, never wanting him to stop. And then suddenly, without any warning, she was freefalling. It was like her whole body had been dusted with popping candy, inside and out. She couldn't stop it; it was like being wrapped up in the warmest blanket waiting to be thrown off the top of a waterfall. And that's when the first wave hit her. She shook. It was almost too much. She screamed his name and she held him tighter, her nails digging into his back.

"Cole!"

"I know, Robyn...I know," Cole replied, holding on to her as she trembled and waited for the next wave.

"I can't stop it," Robyn said as she drifted between sweet agony and ecstasy.

"I know," Cole exclaimed, and he drew her into him as he shuddered, his breath quick, his body wet, his emotions spent.

"Your heart's still hammering," Robyn remarked, putting her hand onto his chest.

"I know," Cole replied, almost breathless.

"I think I'm lying on a rock," Robyn said, shifting slightly under him.

"I've got cramp in my leg."

"Why didn't you say? I can move."

"No. Don't move. Stay right where you are," Cole spoke, kissing her mouth again.

"Ow! My ribs! Mind where you put your elbow."

"Sorry."

Robyn laughed and kissed him. They'd just made love under the stars, in almost subzero temperatures on a blanket that felt like it had seen better days. She wouldn't have wanted it any other way.

"Do you think we'll always be this happy?" she asked him as he moved in tight beside her.

"I'd like to think so."

"Do you think when we're ninety we'll still be driving down to the lake in Leonora and making out on the sand?"

"We might not be driving Leonora. She probably doesn't have that many years left in her," Cole said.

"We should definitely get a monster truck."

"What is it with you and monster trucks?"

"What is it with you and wiping your mouth with your ice hockey shirt?"

"Tightening the lid of the milk?"

"Eating pasta for almost every meal?"

"Dill pickles and ice cream?"

"That isn't unusual!"

He held her close to him and listened to her breathing. His heart was still racing, his body aching from the intensity of the moment. He'd just made love to his future wife for the first time and he'd never felt anything even halfway close to it before.

Meeting Robyn had changed things for him. Work was no longer his priority, she was. His focus had shifted and he was okay. He mattered to her and she mattered to him, and that was more important than anything else.

"I'll teach you to shoot," Robyn remarked suddenly, breaking his thoughts.

"What?"

"I'll teach you to shoot, so you don't embarrass yourself at the town turkey shoot in the spring. And can you ride a horse?"

"I did a bucking bronco ride once. Lasted all of four seconds," he remarked.

"I'll teach you that, too."

Chapter Forty-four

It was match night and Robyn felt rough. She'd worked the roadhouse again and Advil was doing nothing to ease her rib pain. That, coupled with the fact that the Panthers were even more depleted, made her want to just go home and watch re-runs of last year's Stanley Cup and devour a pantry's worth of chips. But there were Sierra and Sienna dressed up again and Pam and Bob. She fixed a smile on her face and hurried toward them.

"Hey! Girls, water bottles aren't ready, go get them," she ordered as she came to join the men on the team bench.

"Made Cole the captain," Bob remarked as Robyn sat down.

"I didn't have a choice, did I? Brad's practically bathed himself in coffee so he can play, but he's been drinking again and I need a captain I can trust. Cole's the right person for the job. Only Brad has a problem with it," she answered.

"I was just telling everyone I've seen this beautiful wedding dress on sale, it's ivory with..." Pam started.

"Pam, it's hockey. When hockey's on, we don't talk about anything but hockey," Bob reminded her.

"I'm sure it's great," Robyn responded kindly.

"It's not, it's gross," Sienna informed her.

"It's worse than gross," Sierra added.

"Guys, we need to get forward a little more, a little quicker," Cole said to his team.

"Are you kidding me? It's all we can do to stop them netting a goal. We're just not getting the run of the puck," Mickey responded.

"We're not playing like we played against Grand Rapids," Cole answered.

"Newsflash for you. Brad wasn't playing against Grand Rapids and we had Robyn," Wade replied.

"He's losing out to everyone," Mickey said, looking across at Brad who was catching his breath by the sidelines.

"We've got no one to swap him out with," Cole reminded them.

"There's always, Robyn, she could play under Jon's name," Wade suggested.

"Newsflash for you. She has two broken ribs, she can barely walk without it hurting," Cole responded.

"Stuck with it then. What d'you want to do? Go for the win or see if we can hang on for a draw?" Mickey asked.

"Go for the win, because if they score, we're under pressure already," Cole replied, replacing his mouth guard.

"Henrik, man, you're getting everything," Mickey said, slapping him on the back.

"Come on Panthers, let's go!" Wade said, skating over to Brad and encouraging him to become more involved.

Play recommenced and the puck went straight to a Cincinnati Cyclones player who turned, neatly passed Brad, and slotted it under the goaltender's pads.

"Shit!" Robyn exclaimed, putting her head in her hands.

"It was always going to happen," Grant said.

The players' heads had dropped. Mickey was beating his stick against the ice and Brad was on his ass on the rink. Cole was calling them to regroup but their morale had just hit rock bottom.

"With Brad the way he is, yes it was always going to happen and we only have half a squad. Maybe I could play under Jon's name," Robyn mused as the referee recommenced play.

"Absolutely not. You've got broken ribs... you go out there, you're a liability to everyone," Bob told her.

"Jason could play under Jon's name," Grant proposed.

"You've got to be kidding, Grant," Bob said, looking at him with wide eyes.

"He's here, he's sitting just over there. He's a good player. Obviously he's been a little short on practice but..." Grant continued.

"I don't know how you could suggest such a thing. He shouldn't even be here," Pam said, putting her hands to her mouth in shock.

"Listen, I know what you all think of him, but he's my son, and what happened to innocent until proven guilty?" Grant asked them.

"He was proven guilty, Grant," Bob reminded him.

"And that DNA evidence was tampered with, I'm telling you. He wouldn't lie to me, not about something like that," Grant insisted.

"Get him kitted up," Robyn stated, staring out onto the ice as Cincinnati threatened again.

"What? Robyn, honey, no," Pam answered immediately.

"I said get a uniform on him. As soon as he's ready, Brad's coming off," Robyn informed determinedly.

"I think you're making a mistake, Robyn, the team feeling is..." Bob began.

"In a few days, I'm going to know for sure whether Jason was responsible or not, okay? You won't let me play, Brad's playing like crap, and Jason's good. It's a decision," Robyn told them.

"Should I go and get him?" Grant asked eagerly.

"Yes, Grant, go and get him. Tell him to get all over their number twenty-five. Cole! Watch the space there. You're giving them too much!" Robyn screamed.

"We're swapping out? You want Brad off?" Cole asked, skating up to Robyn.

"Yeah, get him off. Jon is coming on," Robyn replied.

"Who is it?"

"Don't get mad."

"What?"

"It's Jason," Robyn informed him.

"Are you kidding me?" Cole exclaimed in horror.

"Listen, you know I would do anything for the Panthers, right? Well, I'm doing this. Brad's shocking, he can't hold onto the puck to save his life, and if he keeps it up, we're going to lose big time. Jason's a good player and..." Robyn began.

"Robyn, I want to kill the guy. You let him on here, I'll put him in the boards myself," Cole stated.

"I don't think he did it," Robyn said with a swallow.

"We don't know anything yet," Cole told her.

"Look, I'm playing Jason. Call it a gut instinct. Just make sure you call him Jon and tell Brad to come off," Robyn ordered him.

"Okay, I guess," Cole reluctantly agreed.

He skated back to the center of the ice as the referee prepared to restart the game.

"What's going on? Who's kitted up?" Brad wanted to know.

"Jon. You're going off for a while," Cole informed him.

"That isn't Jon," Brad remarked.

"Look, get over there and swap out or we're going to get trashed," Cole warned as Mickey picked up the puck and prepared to pass it off.

"Robyn, thanks for giving me a chance. I can't tell you how much it means," Jason said, preparing to take to the ice.

"Good. I don't want to hear how much it means. Just go out there and play hard for the Panthers. I don't want anything else, you got that?" Robyn said, unable to meet his eye.

"I got it," Jason responded as Brad came over to the side of the ice.

"Jason! You're replacing me with Jason? What the Hell is going on around here?" Brad blasted angrily as Jason headed for the center of the rink.

"Get off the ice, Brad, go and take a shower. You're not going back on," Robyn told him.

"This is bullshit! You're taking me off for him? Him, Robyn!"

"Shut up! You sound like a five year old who isn't getting his own way. I'm taking you off because you're playing like you've never held a stick in your life. I'm putting on Jason because I don't have anyone else!" Robyn screeched, holding her ribs as she yelled.

"Everything okay?" Grant asked, stepping forward in a bid to be peacemaker.

"Oh yeah! Everything's great! Just peachy!" Brad blasted.

He vaulted the side of the rink and began stomping back toward the locker rooms.

"What are we going to do about him?" Grant asked.

"I've no idea," Robyn admitted.

"Come on Panthers! There's just over three minutes to go, a one nil loss would be something of a miracle," Grant said.

"Go Panthers! Go Panthers!" Sierra and Sienna chanted, waving their pompoms about keenly.

"Cole looks done in," Robyn remarked as Cole attempted to keep pace with the fresh legs of a new Cincinnati player.

"They all do. We need some new players in the squad. Come on Mickey! Stay with him!" Grant said.

"Pass it forward!" Robyn screamed, seeing that Jason was unmarked.

Mickey slotted the puck to Jason, Jason turned, laid it off to Henrik, who looked up and hit home, rifling the puck into the top of the net. The light went on, the horns were let off, and the home crowd expressed their delight with the goal.

"Yes! Yes!" Robyn exclaimed delightedly.

"Way to go Jason!" Grant yelled proudly.

"Yay Panthers!" Sienna and Sierra screamed ecstatically.

The team bundled onto Henrik excitedly and Jason looked over at the bench, a smile from ear to ear.

"He did well," Robyn said, seeing the delight on Grant's face.

"Thank you Robyn, for..." Grant started.

"Don't thank me. Come on Panthers! See it out!" Robyn shouted.

"What happen here? It look like storm come through," Henrik remarked as the team arrived in the locker room after the match.

Clothes were strewn about the floor, all the showers were running, and the door of Cole's locker had been ripped from its hinges.

"Shit, this is Brad," Mickey said immediately.

"What the Hell? Where's my stuff man?" Wade wanted to know.

"I'm gonna find him," Cole said, looking at his wrecked locker and his stuff lying on the wet floor.

"Oh, no you don't. I don't think you half killing him is the right way to sort this out," Mickey said, grabbing hold of Cole's arm.

"I'm just going to talk to him. He's making things difficult for Robyn. She doesn't need that," Cole said, hating that Robyn had to deal with both the Jason situation and Brad.

"Maybe I could talk to him," Jason suggested quietly.

"Are you kidding me? He hates you! We all hate you, actually. Get showered, get dressed, and get out of here," Mickey ordered him.

"I was just trying to…" Jason started.

"Here is my shower gel, you can use," Henrik said, throwing Jason the bottle.

The door opened and Robyn and Grant entered the room.

"Guys! You were amazing tonight! I… what's happened in here?" Robyn asked, seeing the changing area in complete disarray.

"Brad's happened. He's half flooded the place and he's pulled the door off of Cole's locker and he's thrown our clothes everywhere…" Wade began.

Robyn bit her lip, looking at the mess, sensing his anger as if it were still hanging around the room.

"We'll clean it up," Mickey suggested.

"No, leave it," Robyn said and she bolted from the room.

When Robyn arrived in the main bar, she could see Brad was already on the scotch. Ely, one of the stewards, was chatting to him, and there were a small group of high school girls sitting alongside him, autograph books on the bar.

"Put the glass down, you're coming with me," Robyn stated angrily, coming up behind him.

"Oh, here she is girls, the manager of the Panthers. If you want to say anything about her choice of substitution tonight, now would be a good time," Brad said, turning to face Robyn and smiling at his admirers.

"Get off the stool Brad and come and clean up your mess," Robyn spoke warningly.

"My mess? Oh no, Robyn, I think you've got that all wrong! You're the one in a mess; in fact, totally freaking messed up," Brad snarled.

"I'm not going to ask you again," Robyn stated, her temper rising.

"Good! Because to be honest, I'm sick of hearing anything you have to say!" Brad snapped.

"You either go back to that locker room and clear up the mess, or you're off the team – permanently," Robyn said.

"You can't do that. Eddie'll be back in a few weeks and, as soon as he is, I'll be reinstated as captain."

"You think he's going to have you back as captain in this state? You could barely skate out there tonight," Robyn yelled at him.

"You don't have enough players to drop me," Brad reminded her smugly.

"Grant's preparing signing on papers for Jason," Robyn snapped back.

"You have got to be kidding! You'd have him on the team over me?" Brad exclaimed, swaying unsteadily on his feet.

"Yes," Robyn answered.

"Why are you doing this to me?" Brad asked.

The tone of his voice had changed. Suddenly, he looked hopeless, the anger gone, his whole body language showing deflation.

"I'm not doing anything to you," Robyn said with a swallow.

She hated seeing him like this. He was a friend, she had known him forever. But this part of him she didn't recognize. She had never seen him act this way. She didn't know the anger or the vulnerability. Was this what he'd been like when Michelle left him and he went off the rails?

"Yes, you are, just like you used to. Always wanting to be in charge, always thinking you're right, telling me what to do, not doing what you should have been doing," Brad continued, his eyes glazing over.

It was as if he wasn't really there. The body looked like Brad, but it was as if it was just an empty shell and the real him was absent from the room.

"I don't know what you're talking about. I think you should go home and sober up," Robyn said, turning her back on him.

"You and Cole, you won't last," Brad called out to her.

"Yeah? Why's that?" Robyn asked, spinning back to face him.

"Because he isn't me and you belong with me. When you've gotten over this temporary infatuation, you'll realize that," Brad said with a determined nod.

Robyn gritted her teeth tight together and approached him. Any pity she felt was fast evaporating.

"I wouldn't be with you even if you had season tickets at the Red Wings and pit passes at the monster trucks. Do you understand that?" Robyn said.

"I don't believe you," Brad said almost defiantly.

"I want you out. I want you off of this team and I want you out of my life," Robyn yelled as Cole, Grant, Bob, Pam, and the twins hurried into the bar.

"Is everything alright here?" Grant asked, stepping up to Robyn's side ahead of anyone else.

"Is everything alright here? Are you crazy? Your son's been given my place on the team!" Brad exclaimed, staring at Grant with wild eyes.

"Listen, Brad, I know things aren't going so well for you right now, but we need you on the team, of course we do. We can talk about things and…" Grant started.

"No, we can't talk about things. I've made my decision…I want him gone, now. I want him out of the bar and out of the arena — gone," Robyn interrupted savagely.

"Robyn!" Pam remarked, shocked at the bitterness in Robyn's voice.

"D'you know, Cole? D'you know this marriage stuff has nothing to do with you? You could be anyone. This is the way Robyn deals with things. She gets scared by something, something that happens, maybe a feeling, and then she throws herself headlong into something else, anything else, any project she can. Like the hockey team. Like the roadhouse. Like Eddie. Like you. She knows how she feels about me and it frightens her. It frightens her enough to make out with someone else," Brad announced to the room.

"You need to leave. You need to go drink some coffee," Cole said.

"Truth hurt?" Brad said with a sneer.

"Right, we're done here. Ely, some assistance please," Bob called to the steward as he took hold of one of Brad's arms.

"All right! I'm going. But it doesn't change things and you'll see that, Robyn! You'll see that!" Brad told her, looking straight at her.

"Come on, let's get you a beer," Cole said, putting his arm around Robyn and shielding her away from Brad.

"She doesn't love you!" Brad called as he was led away. "She doesn't know how to!"

Chapter Forty-five

She hadn't spoken the whole drive and they were nearing home. After Brad had been escorted from the arena, she had drank only four bottles of Bud Light with the team and had turned down Henrik's offer of shots. It wasn't like her to turn down the offer of alcohol, and if she didn't break out the chips and dip when they got home, he was going to be really concerned.

"What he said back there isn't true, you know," she said as if reading his mind.

"I know."

"I do distract myself with projects, I do like to be busy, but that has nothing to do with how I feel about you. You know that, right?" Robyn continued, turning to look over at him.

"Sure."

"I didn't recognize him tonight. He looked at me like he loved me and hated me all at the same time. I didn't see Brad, I didn't know who that was," she continued.

"If we hadn't of met, do you think you would have…" Cole started.

"No. No, Cole. I don't feel that way about him. When we were together before, it was just friends making out every now and then, it wasn't anything even close to serious—not for me, anyways," Robyn explained.

"D'you think maybe we should postpone the wedding?" Cole asked.

He looked across the car at her.

"You mean cancel, don't you? You mean call it off," Robyn said with an exasperated sigh.

"No, I don't mean that, I mean postpone it, put it off for a while, until this business with your police case is over at least."

"You think Brad's right, you think if I have time, I'll change my mind or move on to another project," Robyn said, tears forming at the rim of her eyes.

"Robyn, I don't think that."

"Then what?!"

"Look, the clinic in England did keep the information from the abortion. They're emailing me on Monday," Cole informed her.

She saw him look for her reaction and she gave it to him. She stiffened and balled her fingers into fists then, stretched her fingers out and balled them up again. Turning her head she looked out of the window.

"Whoever did that to me took away everything I had. They took away my whole life, all my good memories, and they made me leave everything I loved behind. If that was Jason, has he paid enough? If it wasn't Jason, what do I do then? I've spent the whole time in England thinking I knew who it was, detesting his image, reliving what happened in my dreams. What if I've been hating the wrong man?" Robyn asked him.

"That's why we're going to find out," Cole reassured her.

"Maybe I leaned on Brad too much after it happened. Maybe I gave him the wrong impression about my feelings for him. It seems like I've ruined his whole life as well. I've been in England sleeping with Clive to try and rid myself of the ugly memory of it all, and Brad's been pining over something I didn't think we ever had. What if that's what I'm going to do to you—to us. Maybe I was right all along and I can't have a real relationship—ever," Robyn blurted out.

"No, because we're having a real relationship, right here, right now," Cole told her.

"Are we? Or are we both freefalling toward each other because we don't know what else to do?"

She looked over at Cole, checking to see if his expression showed his feelings.

He pulled the car into the drive of his home and turned off the engine.

"Get out," he said, opening the door of the Mustang and stepping out of it.

She unfastened her seat belt and followed him out of the car.

He leapt up onto the hood and pulled himself up onto the roof, where he lay down facing the sky.

When Robyn lay down beside him, he pointed up to the stars.

"One day, whether we like it or not, you and me are going to be up there, just like Mitzy, Old Man Harrison, and Don Mitchell Ryan—my dad," he said, drawing a loop between the stars with his finger.

"You think people are going to be climbing up on the roofs of cars choosing stars for us in fifty odd years' time?" she asked.

"Our grandkids, maybe?" he suggested, turning to her.

"What are you saying to me?"

"Robyn, life's too short to worry about everything, you know…what people say, what people do, what people think is right or wrong. Some people in life just aren't going to like what you do. Some people are going to be with you your whole life long and others are going to fall by the wayside for one reason or another. I want to be there your whole life long," Cole told her.

"But how do you know that already?" she asked him, her voice wavering with emotion.

"Because somehow someone wrote it up there...and I believe them," Cole said, indicating the dark blanket above them.

Robyn let out an audible cry and burrowed her head into his shoulder. He turned slightly and pulled her into him, protectively stroking her hair away from her face.

"I do need looking after and I eat far too many pickles. I'm going to end up with an ulcer if I don't get help," Robyn blubbered, raising her head to look at him.

"I know that, you need me."

Robyn shook her head and wiped her eyes with the sleeve of her sweatshirt.

"No, I don't need you, Cole, I want you," she said with conviction.

"I've spent so long trying to honor my dad and please my mom and find a cure for everything, I lost sight of who I was and what I wanted. You've helped me get that back. Yes, what I do is important, but it isn't everything," he said.

"There's ice hockey and turkey shoots and the Old Country Buffet," Robyn reminded him.

"And there's Robyn Matthers," he said, kissing her.

When they'd made love that night, she'd cried and clung to him and begged him to never let her go. She trusted him enough to show him her vulnerability and that meant so much. She was sharing everything with him, her past, her fears, and her insecurities behind the tough exterior she'd built up. This relationship that had sprung itself on them was a new beginning for them both in such different ways. But they were embarking on it together, full of hope, full of love, and full of anticipation for whatever was to come.

Chapter Forty-six

Monday arrived before she knew it. Most of Sunday had been spent at the roadhouse. Mickey, Sarah, Wes, Wade, Henrik, and Jon had come in for lunch and no one had seen or heard from Brad. Mickey had called him a "prize wiener," Sarah had sheepishly said nothing, and Henrik had suggested a night out after the next game. Jason and Grant had also come in for dinner. They had hung around the entrance awkwardly wondering whether they should be there or not until Robyn had greeted them with menus and a rundown of the day's specials. She had made Nancy serve them.

Now Robyn waited outside the mall in the rain for Sarah, Nancy, and Cole's mother, Martha. Cole had gone to pick her up from Battle Creek International and was due at the mall any second.

When Robyn saw Sarah, she waved at her frantically.

"Now listen! You've spent years walking round these wedding dress shops, have you seen anything good? Because I've been having nightmares about pearls and lace and frills and butterflies and giant marshmallows. If Pam gets her way, I'm going to be trussed up in some massive dress and everyone's going to think I'm a hot air balloon!" Robyn shrieked.

"Where is Pam?" Sarah asked.

"Oh, she's started already. You can hardly see her arms. She's loaded them up with frocks like some sort of freaking human clothes horse."

"Hey, sugar. Sorry I'm late, your dad had to give me a blow by blow account of last night's Red Wings game. I swear he makes some of it up. I mean, there can't really be a fight a minute, can there?" Nancy remarked as she joined them.

"Oh, there was last night—it was pure filth," Robyn replied.

"Is Cole's mom coming?" Sarah asked.

"Yeah, she should be here any minute," Robyn said, looking at her watch.

"What's she like? I mean, am I going to have to speak proper?" Nancy asked.

"Properly," Robyn corrected.

"Whatever."

"She's nice. I mean, how could she not be nice? She's Cole's mom."

"Yeah, but ain't she also the mom of the brother that did the dirty with his girlfriend?" Nancy asked, chomping on her gum.

"We don't talk about that. Not today, not ever," Robyn warned her.

"The brother coming to the wedding?" Nancy wanted to know.

"Shh, there's Cole's car. She's coming. Oh, and by the way, she has a vacuuming obsession," Robyn said, waving her hands in a bid to silence Nancy.

"Stand up straight, shoulders back," Nancy whispered to Sarah.

"Was she in the Army?" Sarah asked.

"Hi, Martha. How was your flight?" Robyn asked as she greeted her.

"Bombay mix. Cole's given me a bottle of water," Martha said, showing it to her.

"Martha, this is my best friend, Sarah, she's getting married, too. My Aunty Pam is already in the store neck deep in dresses, and this is my almost step-mom, Nancy," Robyn introduced with a swallow of nerves.

Martha was wearing a floral shift dress and matching jacket; Nancy was wearing jeans with open zips across the knees and a hoodie with the word "Cougar" written across it.

"Pleased to meet you," Nancy said first, moving the gum to the side of her mouth.

"And you," Martha said, smiling at both Nancy and Sarah.

"Nancy helps me at Eddie's Roadhouse. Eddie's my dad, I told you about him. He's had his operation, everything went well. Nancy's so particular, you know, about cleanliness, particularly vacuuming," Robyn stated.

"I have a Dyson, too. It's second-hand, but it still sucks real well," Sarah chipped in.

"Goodness! People sure vacuum a great deal around here," Martha said.

"Don't we all?" Robyn asked, rolling her eyes.

"Well, if you have the time, I guess. I try and avoid it as much as possible now that the boys have left home," Martha told them.

Sarah stifled a laugh.

"Shall we go in?" Robyn suggested hastily.

"Sure, honey. I have your daddy's credit card — this dress is on him," Nancy announced.

"Oh no, he doesn't need to do that. I have money," Robyn said.

"He wants to, honey, almost made me have the PIN tattooed on my butt before I came here," Nancy said with a cackle.

"Okay, well, let's go," Robyn said, leading the way into the mall.

His mom had looked a little tired today. She said she was sleeping, but he wasn't sure she was telling him the truth. And she hadn't even mentioned Bryn. Perhaps she had resigned herself to the fact that a reconciliation wasn't going to happen. The idea of that would be killing her.

Cole picked up the phone and forced himself to press a sequence of numbers. He took a deep breath and looked out of the window at the park. Two boys were chasing each other with small branches from a tree, using them like fencing swords.

"Bryn, it's Cole. Listen, don't hang up, I haven't called to fight. This is stupid. I want to move on."

"Pam is carrying like ten dresses. Is she expecting me to try them all on?" Robyn asked Sarah.

"I think that's exactly why she's holding them," Sarah said, browsing the racks.

"Can you try some of them on? I mean, they might be perfect for you."

"They might be perfect for you."

"I can barely see her under them! There are more pearls in there than in a whole colony of oysters."

"You can't see them properly over her arms like that."

"I can see enough."

"Well, what style are you looking for?" Sarah asked, looking up at a crystal embroidered bodice.

"I don't know, I've never looked at wedding dresses before."

"But you must have some idea."

"Must I? Oh jeez, Nancy's in the spangly section and Martha's looking at stoles. What am I going to do?" Robyn asked.

"Suck it up."

"Like your second-hand Dyson?"

"Robyn, honey! I've picked some beautiful gowns for you to try on," Pam called, waving her arms underneath a blanket of tulle.

"Great!" Robyn said, faking excitement.

"Sugar, there's some real pretty gold ones over here," Nancy called.

"Have you thought about a stole or a wrap? It's bound to be windy by the lake," Martha added.

"This was such a bad idea," Robyn murmured to Sarah.

"Well, I'm going to try this one on," Sarah said, taking a dress down from the rack.

"Just one? The crazy women over there are expecting me to make a whole day of it!"

"Come on, I don't see the problem. You're looking for something beautiful to wear when you marry Cole. Cole, the gorgeous guy you met on a plane, the one who swept you off your feet, the guy who adores you," Sarah reminded her.

"I know. That's why it's got to be right," Robyn said with a frustrated sigh.

"It's nerves," Sarah decided.

"It isn't nerves, I'm not nervous. I have nothing to be nervous about, right?"

"Then look excited about it! You're getting married! On Friday!" Sarah reminded her enthusiastically.

"I know!" Robyn said, this time with a happy smile.

She was excited. She was so excited she could almost burst. Cole was amazing.

"Then let's get an assistant to help us try on everything in the whole damn store," Sarah suggested.

"We'll need snacks," Robyn said.

"I'm not totally sure about the feathers," Robyn said.

The dress, Pam's choice, had a figure-hugging boned bodice with ostrich feathers sewn in and a full skirt. She wasn't sure whether to hold her arms out straight or bend them at the elbows and cluck like a chicken.

"You look like a Thanksgiving turkey before the plucking," Nancy stated.

"I'm not sure it's you," Martha agreed.

"Oh, I think it's beautiful. It really complements your hair, honey," Pam said.

"My hair looks like feathers?" Robyn exclaimed in horror.

"That wasn't what I meant," Pam began.

"Na. I hate it," Robyn declared for about the twentieth time.

"Try on the gold," Nancy suggested.

"Try on the ivory bodice, full skirt, and the fur wrap," Martha piped up.

"How about this one? The beads are so delicate," Pam said, holding up another intricately designed gown.

"I think I'm going to try this one," Robyn said, picking a dress off the rack of gowns the assistant had chosen.

"Oh no, not that one. There's nothing to it, it's so plain, honey," Pam exclaimed, putting her hands to her face in horror.

"You are definitely going to need a shawl with that," Martha remarked.

"Yeah, sugar, a sequined one at the very least," Nancy added, putting a handful of pretzels into her mouth.

"I like it," Sarah said, nodding at Robyn encouragingly.

The dress was cream, had a scalloped neckline, and spaghetti straps.

"Try it on," Sarah said.

"With this," Nancy added, passing over a sequined bolero.

"Or perhaps this?" Martha said, finding a fur shrug.

Robyn took both items offered and the dress and disappeared into the changing rooms, anxious to rid herself of the feathered frock she had on.

She closed the door and tugged at the zipper. None of the dresses had felt right yet.

"It isn't going to be that cold by the lake," she heard Nancy remarked to Martha.

"It isn't Vegas either," Martha commented back.

"I thought she would like something that makes more of a statement. I mean it is the most important day of her life," Pam added.

Robyn unfastened the door and opened it a crack to listen. She peeked out and saw Pam picking up a gown that wouldn't have looked out of place on a limited edition Disney Princess.

"It's all a rush though isn't it? I mean she hasn't had time to plan anything, let alone consider the importance," Martha said, folding up a fluffy cape.

"What you mean by that?" Nancy snapped immediately.

Robyn smiled at her almost step-mom's defensive attitude.

"Well, I can't be the only one here who thinks this marriage decision is far too hasty," Martha stated frankly.

"I agree," Pam admitted.

"Well I don't. When you know, you know — end of story," Nancy replied.

Robyn nodded her head and felt something inside her warm even more to the woman she'd thought was such a bad influence on her dad.

"I agree with Nancy. I mean I know me and Mickey have had our ups and downs just lately but..." Sarah started.

Wow! Now her best friend was wading in with support. She needed to make more time for her. Now the roadhouse was up and running she should really set aside some time for Sarah.

"They've known each other just over a week," Martha said.

"I know and I think all this stuff with Jason being raked up again is affecting her judgment," Pam carried on.

"Who's Jason?" she heard Martha ask.

Robyn closed the door again and hurriedly removed the dress. She looked at the one hanging on the peg on the door and she put it over her head. It slipped down over her shoulders, fell lightly over her breasts and dropped to the floor. She looked at her appearance in the mirror, turning to the side and back again. She picked up the sequined bolero and put her arms into it. It would have been perfect on Nancy but made her look like a chorus girl. She took it off and swapped it for the fur shrug Martha had given her. It made her look like Bugs Bunny. She discarded it on the floor and looked at herself in the mirror. The simplicity of the gown made it beautiful. It made her look beautiful.

She pushed open the door.

"Jason's a guy that was convicted of raping me. What do you think?" Robyn announced as she stepped out of the changing booth.

"Oh my!" Nancy said as she looked at Robyn.

"You look amazing!" Sarah told her, tears pricking her over-emotional eyes.

"Like a princess," Pam added.

"It's perfect," Martha agreed.

"You think? I tried the bolero on and the shrug, but it just didn't feel right," Robyn told them.

"Nah, too jazzy for the dress and as I keep saying, you don't need thermal wear for the lake in autumn," Nancy said, making her point and looking at Martha.

"How much is it?" Sarah wanted to know.

"Hey, I told you that don't matter. We have Eddie's plastic," Nancy said, and she started to ferret in her leopard print bag for her purse.

"It's two hundred dollars," Robyn announced proudly.

"Jeez! Are you kidding me? I was hoping to pay a lot more than that. I mean, if you get a dress for two hundred dollars, Eddie's going to expect me to find one for that sort of price and I have bigger plans. Much bigger plans," Nancy informed her.

"Why didn't you tell me about this Jason?" Martha asked seriously.

"It isn't the sort of thing you bring up over lunch when you first meet your future mother-in-law. And by the way, it has nothing to do with why I'm marrying Cole. Is that clear for everyone?" Robyn asked, her eyes meeting all of theirs.

"I told them, honey. I said when you know, you know," Nancy said.

"And if anyone isn't fully on board with this wedding, and I mean one hundred percent, then you don't have to come. We only need two witnesses, and I don't care if that's the drummer and the bassist from Special Guest," Robyn told them firmly.

"We just have reservations because it's happening so quickly, that's all," Pam said.

"Well, speak for yourself, because I don't have reservations — not one," Nancy said supportively.

"Me neither," Sarah agreed.

"Martha?" Robyn asked.

"I know Cole knows his own mind and I trust his judgment," Martha spoke sincerely.

"Good! Then can we please pay for this dress and get out of here?" Robyn asked.

"Hey, what about me? I've tried stuff on but I haven't found anything I like yet," Sarah said, passing Robyn the bowl of pretzels.

"Oh God, I'm so sorry. Here I am carrying on and…" Robyn began, feeling bad.

"I'm only kidding! I only came to get an idea. I mean, I don't even know what size I'm going to end up yet, do I?" Sarah stated with a laugh.

"You planning a long engagement, honey?" Nancy asked her.

"Yes, we think so. What, with the baby and everything, it will give us a chance to save up," Sarah said.

"Long engagements aren't my thing. Too much time for the guy to change his mind," Nancy remarked.

"Dad hasn't changed his mind," Robyn reminded her.

"That's because he knows if he did, I'd chop off his..."

"His beard! He loves his beard, does my dad, but Nancy's not really into facial hair...not that she'd tell him," Robyn interrupted.

"For a second there I thought she was going to say she'd chop off his balls," Martha stated with a deadpan face.

Sarah let out an audible gasp, Pam's eyes widened, and Robyn whitened.

"I think Cole's given you a very straight laced image of me. So, just for the record, I go to the gym just to look at the weightlifters, I did a bungee jump last year and I'm still too scared to tell my family about it, and I'm buying so much brandy lately the cashier looks at me like I'm halfway to alcoholism already. Which I'm not, by the way, I just like brandy and I make a lot of cakes. What do you make Robyn?" Martha asked.

"I usually make calls—to the takeaway," Robyn admitted boldly.

"Oh I'm with you on that one. I may bake, but nothing quite hits the spot like Mr. Chan's sweet and sour pork," Martha said with a smile.

Chapter Forty-seven

"Roadhouse was busy for a Monday, huh?" Cole remarked as he drove them toward the hospital.

They had both worked a shift that night while Nancy spent some time with Eddie. Now they were going back to the hospital to visit Max.

"People are still making use of those coupons," Robyn said.

"I'm glad it went good with Mom," Cole said.

"Was she okay getting the plane back? I said she could stay."

"I know, she told me, in between hiccupping and swigging back water. What were you feeding her?" Cole asked suspiciously.

"It had nothing to do with food," Robyn answered with a grin.

"She told me you found a dress," Cole stated.

"I might have."

"So?"

"Not telling. There's a space right there, pull in that one," Robyn said, pointing to a good spot outside the entrance.

Cole stopped the car and turned off the engine.

"Got the muffins?" Robyn asked.

"Yeah. Listen, before we go on in...I got the information from the clinic today," Cole informed her.

"What did it say?" Robyn asked, her breath almost catching in her throat.

"Jason wasn't the baby's father," Cole said bluntly.

Her bottom lip began to tremble, and she tried desperately to maintain control over the torrent of emotion welling up inside her.

"You okay?" Cole asked, taking hold of her hand in his.

"What have I done to him? All these years. All the time he spent in prison, all the things that everyone said, and Grant, I've treated him really badly," Robyn blurted out all at once.

"How were you to know? And you didn't convict him, a jury did," Cole reminded her.

"I did convict him, the whole town convicted him. It's horrible! How could this happen? I mean, the whole point of DNA evidence is so it's accurate," Robyn said, wiping at her eyes.

"I've emailed everything over to Trudy, and what I'd expect them to do is run the profile through the police database. If the person who did this is in the system, they'll know."

"But what if they aren't in the system? We might never know," Robyn said, running her hand through her hair.

"Hey, this is a good thing. We know conclusively that it wasn't Jason."

"There's no doubt?"

"None."

"So how long? Until the police know, well, you know, if the guy is on their database," Robyn asked.

"I don't know. Trudy wasn't there today, she's back tomorrow. It could be tomorrow," Cole told her.

Robyn nodded.

"You okay?"

"What am I going to say to Jason? Sorry isn't really going to cut it, is it? How do you give someone their life back?" Robyn asked, looking up at Cole.

"It wasn't your fault. None of it was your fault," Cole told her.

"It doesn't feel like that," Robyn said with a sigh.

"Pummel him! Hook him with the right! God damn!" Max exclaimed as he weakly punched his arms out, copying the boxers on the television.

"He's had it. He needs putting out of his misery now," Eddie remarked, shifting in his seat.

"My money's on the guy in the red shorts...Dad! What are you doing here?" Robyn asked as she and Cole entered the room.

"What you doing here, Buttercup?" Eddie asked, greeting them.

"I asked first."

"Nancy dropped me here on the way to the roadhouse, house is quiet," Eddie remarked.

"He misses me, gal...what can I say?" Max said with a wheeze.

"Well we were going to drop by the house after, but seeing as you're here...low sugar brownies and pecan pie," Robyn informed Eddie, passing a bag to him and putting a bag on Max's bed.

"Okay, what are you going to tell me? If you're giving me sugar, low or not, then something's up."

"I don't care what you've got to say, I'll have it anyway," Max said greedily.

"You two broken up already?" Eddie asked, eyeing Cole with suspicion.

"No! Of course not!"

"Then what?"

"Jason didn't rape me," Robyn said bluntly.

"Buttercup, we've been through this. Just because some guy says he saw him doesn't mean…" Eddie started.

"Cole got new DNA evidence. He didn't do it, Dad," Robyn said seriously.

"Jeez," Max remarked, his mouth half full of pie.

"I don't understand," Eddie said quietly, as if finding the information difficult to process.

"I was pregnant, Dad, after the rape. I didn't keep it, but the clinic kept information, DNA profiling. Cole got the DNA profile of the father," Robyn attempted to explain.

"There's no doubt. The profile doesn't match Jason," Cole informed him.

"Just hold on one second. You're not only telling me that Jason didn't attack you, but you're also telling me you were pregnant? And this is the first I hear about it?" Eddie exclaimed, his face reddening, his eyes bulging.

"I didn't tell anyone, Dad, I had an abortion."

"What about your mother?"

"What about my mother?"

"Well, why didn't she call me? She was supposed to be looking after you," Eddie continued.

"I didn't tell her, either. You know what she was like after the rape, making me shower three times a day and making me wear jumpers. She was ashamed of me, telling her about being pregnant would have made things worse. I just had to deal with it on my own. Anyway, that doesn't matter now. What matters is that Jason didn't do it," Robyn said.

"Then if Jason didn't do it, who did?" Max wanted to know.

"The police are going to try and find that out," Cole said.

"Dad?" Robyn said, desperate for him to say something.

"I don't know what to say, Buttercup," he said, his voice faltering.

"In a few days, we can finally put all this behind us. It can be a new start for everyone. You with your new body parts and me with a husband," Robyn said happily.

"Be good to put it all to bed before the wedding. Extra cause for celebrating," Max said, chewing up the pie and spitting crumbs everywhere.

"Dad, this is a good thing. Focus on the fact that it wasn't Jason and he's going to play for the Panthers," Robyn begged.

"Something doesn't feel right," Eddie said with a shake of his head.

"Everything's fine, properly fine, for the first time in a long time," Robyn assured him.

"Got any beer?" Max asked hopefully.

"You okay?" Cole called into the darkness.

Robyn was dressed in his robe, looking out of the window at the lake. Everything was still and calm. The water was lapping softly against the sand, and there was hardly a breeze to move the rust colored leaves on the trees.

She didn't respond to him. She was too engrossed in looking at the West Lake scene. He got out of bed and joined her at the window.

"Hey," he said, putting a hand through her hair.

"Oh, hey. Sorry. Did I wake you up? Should I close the curtains?" Robyn suggested.

"No, leave them. I like it," Cole told her, putting his arms around her waist and holding her body to his.

"Even though I don't know who did it, I know who didn't, and it's like this weight's been lifted off me," Robyn said.

"I can't imagine how it must feel," Cole said, holding her tight.

"I'm going to see Jason tomorrow. I have no idea what I'm going to say, but I have to see him. Do you think he knows?" Robyn asked.

"He's always known, Robyn."

"Yeah, of course. He told everyone time and time again and we didn't listen."

"It wasn't your fault."

"I should have known it wasn't him. I mean, he's Jason! Yeah, he was a bit dorky and weird at school and we didn't hang out, but we spoke in passing about hockey. I knew he liked me, you know, had a crush, I guess. But I should have known he wouldn't do anything to hurt me. He was always sweet to me," Robyn said.

"You were told it was him."

"I know. I just want to make things right, somehow. But how can I give him all those years back?" Robyn asked.

"You can't. But you can make things better. Start by giving him that place on the team," Cole suggested.

"And a lifetime's free meals at Eddie's, at the very least," Robyn continued.

"It might take time. He's spent half his life being shunned by everyone; he'll need to learn to trust people again," Cole said.

"I wouldn't blame him if he told the whole town to go to Hell…that's no more than we deserve."

"I don't think he'll do that."

"No, because he's Jason. Plain, slightly freaky Jason, who collected bottle tops and wore tank tops," Robyn said, smiling at the memory.

Cole smiled back at her.

"You okay?" she asked.

"Yeah."

"What is it?"

"I called Bryn earlier," Cole said quietly.

"Oh, Cole, why didn't you say? What happened?" Robyn asked, turning to face him.

"We talked, for almost an hour, about pretty much everything," he told her.

"And? Have you sorted things out? Did you invite him to the wedding?"

"Yeah. He's coming, him and Veronica," Cole said slightly hesitantly.

"Are you okay with that?" Robyn asked.

"Are you okay with that?"

"Of course. He's your brother and she's...your brother's girlfriend," Robyn said diplomatically.

"Well put."

"I'm meeting Brad tomorrow, at the arena. I don't know what I'm going to say to him, but I can't be responsible for him going off the rails, I have to try," Robyn told him.

"You can't have a wedding day without one of your oldest friends there and things can't be left how they are," Cole said, kissing her.

"Have I told you you're really hot when you're being understanding?" Robyn asked, her fingers circling his chest.

"Is that so?"

Chapter Forty-eight

The next day Robyn called into the roadhouse to see how the breakfast session was working out. She'd ended up serving coffee and breakfasts for two hours before relieving Nancy at the house to sit with her dad and then fitting in an hour with Max at the hospital. His coughing had worsened again and he looked pale, despite being as incorrigible as ever. She worried about him and, before she'd left, she'd asked the nurse to keep an extra eye on him.

By the time she got to the arena and onto the rink, Brad was already on the ice powering around it to the strains of the eighties band Heart. The cleaning team had a selection of soft rock classics they liked to sweep up to.

"Hey," Robyn greeted, crosschecking him and stealing the puck.

"Hey! Come back with that!" Brad ordered, chasing after her.

"You look like shit," Robyn said, weaving away from him.

"It was a late night," Brad remarked.

"At Taboo?"

"No, I was working."

"In a vat of beer?"

"If you just want to kick a guy when he's down, why don't I just lie on the ice and let you get on with it?" Brad suggested loudly.

"Tempting," she answered back.

"Look, why are we here? I know I've been playing like crap lately, I know I went a little crazy and I trashed the locker room, I know I can't stomach the fact you're marrying someone like him, so what's the point of all this? You want to give me a training session? Make me sweat out the way I feel about you? Think that will help?"

"I don't know. Will it?"

"I doubt it."

"Listen, things can't go on how they are right now. The Panthers are a player away from falling apart, you know that. We need you here, on the team. The Brad Willis I know can out maneuver anyone else in this league. I'm sorry if you thought you and I had a future together. If I said or did anything to make you think that, then I apologize," Robyn said.

"It isn't too late," Brad said.

"Brad, don't! You're making this impossible. I don't want to not have you in my life and on the team, but Cole and I are the real thing. You have to accept that. We're crazy about each other, I can't imagine spending a day without him. I would do anything for him. I love him," Robyn stated firmly.

"I don't want to lose you, you only just came back," Brad spoke softly.

"You've always been one of my closest friends, someone I could trust. I don't want to lose that, but you're making it so difficult," Robyn said, kicking the ice in frustration.

"I'm sorry," Brad apologized.

"Tell me how to make this right? Because I've got Pam begging me to talk to you, I've got Dad worrying about you when he should be worrying about getting better, I've got Sarah freaking out because she's scared you'll tell Mickey you almost ended up in bed together, and I've got Cole, yes Cole, who would gladly punch you out, telling me that I shouldn't lose such a good friend," Robyn said.

"I don't know what to say."

"Say we can put how you feel to one side and be friends, for the sake of the team, for the sake of our friends, and for the sake of the arena locker rooms," Robyn suggested to him.

"I guess we can try, if you're really set on marrying the guy," Brad answered with a heavy sigh.

"I am really set on marrying him. Really set," Robyn said confidently.

"I don't think I can come, though. It would be too much," Brad said sadly.

"I would love for you to be there, the whole town's coming. It's going to be the biggest town party there's ever been. I'm even hoping Jason's going to come, but it might be too soon," Robyn said.

"Why would you want him at your wedding?" Brad exclaimed.

"Because he didn't rape me. We just found out. It definitely wasn't him," Robyn said.

"I don't believe it. How? What about the DNA evidence?" Brad said a look of shock on his face.

"It wasn't accurate. Don't ask me about these sorts of things, Cole's the scientist. Another sample was tested and the DNA didn't match," Robyn explained.

"What other sample? What d'you mean, another sample?" Brad demanded to know.

He was agitated and his face was flaming. He stopped skating.

"It doesn't matter. But there's no doubt," Robyn said with a swallow, stopping opposite him.

"What d'you mean, it doesn't matter? Of course it matters! There were no other samples! There was one sample, my dad dealt with it, and it was Jason's DNA!" Brad yelled at the top of his voice.

"Well, there must have been contamination or something, because Jason wasn't the father of my baby!" Robyn screamed back at him.

Robyn watched the color drain away from Brad's face and his hockey stick dropped from his gloves and fell to the ice with a clatter. He put his hand to his mouth, his eyes wide, unsteady on his skates.

And all at once she knew.

His reaction spoke a thousand words. Robyn felt the bile rise in her throat as she looked at him. He bent in half, fell to the floor, and doubled over on the ice, sobbing onto the frozen ground.

"It was you," she said, her limbs paralyzed, her skates stuck to the spot.

Brad just howled like someone who had been cut in two. He didn't lift his head, maybe couldn't lift his head.

"You raped me," Robyn stated as calmly as her trembling voice would allow.

"No!" Brad howled, finally looking up, his face pained, his eyes spilling tears.

"It was you," Robyn said again, furrowing her brow and staring at him, confused.

"You had a baby?" Brad questioned, looking at her for confirmation.

"Tell me the truth! When the police check this DNA profile on their computer, is it going to match yours?" Robyn yelled at the top of her voice.

"Robyn..."

"Is it going to match yours?" Robyn screamed hysterically.

She felt like the arena seats were moving in on her, shrinking the rink. There was no air, she wasn't even sure she was breathing, it was almost like time was standing still.

"Yes," Brad said and then put his gloved hand over his mouth and let out another sob of despair.

Her insides contracted, her heart thumped in her chest, and her head felt like it was ballooning. She looked at him, slumped on the floor, wailing like a baby, and she was overwhelmed by a feeling of disgust.

She gripped her stick tightly with both hands and she hit him across the back of the head with it.

He clutched at his head and tried to crawl away from her, but Robyn hit him again.

"You bastard! How could you do that to me? How? You put a sack over my head and you violated me in the worst possible way! You were my boyfriend, Brad! My boyfriend!" Robyn screamed, continuing to hit him with all her strength.

"I loved you, Robyn. I really loved you," Brad told her, grabbing the stick before it could hit him again.

"You loved me? You loved me so you raped me? Are you insane?" Robyn cried, tears falling down her face as she wrestled him for control of her stick.

"I wanted you to be serious about me, but you never seemed to think that way. You didn't treat me like a proper boyfriend. Yeah, we went to the movies and we hung out with Mickey and Sarah but…" Brad started, keeping a firm hold on the stick.

"I wouldn't sleep with you," Robyn stated, horrified.

"I loved you. I still love you," Brad repeated.

"I wouldn't sleep with you, so you followed me home from the arena, you put a bag over my head, and you made me have sex with you? You make me sick!" Robyn exclaimed, clutching at her stomach and struggling to stay on her skates.

"I just wanted to be with you, Robyn, be close to you…like we should have been," Brad said, reaching for her hand as he stood up.

"Don't you touch me! I'm calling the police," Robyn said, backing away from him.

"Look, I know some of what I did was wrong. You were scared and I didn't want you to be scared, that's why I came back," Brad said.

"You raped me, then you left me, then you came back and pretended to find me," Robyn said, her mind returning to the dark, wet night.

"It was so cold that night, and I remember your mom's coat was soaked right through. I watched you put your clothes back on, and when you made it back to the road, I went back to my car and made sure I was the first one to find you. I wanted to look after you and take you home," Brad continued.

"You put your arms around me and held me when I told you what someone had done to me. It was you," Robyn stated, unable to truly believe it.

"Where's our baby?" Brad questioned bluntly.

"Our baby," Robyn said, the words almost hurting her mouth.

"You said you had our baby."

"I had an abortion," Robyn stated.

Brad looked visibly shaken. Tears sprung out of his eyes and he let go of her hockey stick.

"Then I really don't have anything left," he yelled out, his voice echoing around the arena.

"Do you expect me to feel sorry for you? You've ruined half my life...you've ruined half of Jason's life," Robyn said, staring at him.

"Jason didn't have a life. I did him a favor. What was he going to do around here? He's a better person now, he's read a lot and taken classes he would never have done on the outside," Brad continued.

"I can't believe you're justifying what you did. And what your dad did covering it up? You framed an innocent man and sent him to jail!" Robyn screamed.

"I wanted you to realize what we had was special," Brad continued, reaching out and taking hold of Robyn's hand.

"Get off me!" she shrieked, trying to pull back her hand.

"You call it rape, but it wasn't really like that, was it? I didn't really hurt you, I loved you that night, just like I've been loving you ever since," Brad said, keeping a firm grip on her hand.

He'd driven flat out all the way to the arena. He only hoped he wasn't too late. Sweat was beading on his forehead and his heart was thumping in his chest as he ran up the corridor toward the rink. A friend of a friend had run the DNA profile through the police database, and he now knew the identity of the rapist. When he got to him, he was going to make him pay, and if he'd done anything else to hurt Robyn, he was going to kill him.

He burst out of the tunnel and saw Brad holding onto her. Leaping over the barrier, he skidded across the ice toward them.

"Give me your stick, Robyn," Cole ordered, appearing on the ice, out of breath and shaking with rage.

"Let me go!" Robyn begged, tears seeping from her eyes as she tried to release her fingers from Brad's grip.

Cole picked up Robyn's ice hockey stick and caught Brad around the head with it, knocking him off his skates and onto the ground.

He hit him across the face and raised it again for another strike.

"Police! Put the weapon down!"

Robyn looked toward the tunnel at the team of officers making their way into the stadium, and she hurried over to Cole and took the stick from him.

"I know what you want to do, but give me this one. Let me see them put the cuffs on him," Robyn begged.

"Bradley Willis, you are under arrest on suspicion of the rape of Robyn Matthers. You have the right to remain silent. Anything you say can and will be used against you in a court of law. You have the right to speak to an attorney. If you cannot afford an attorney, one will be appointed to you. Do you understand these rights as they have been read to you?" the officer asked as he cuffed Brad's hands.

"Yes," Brad replied, bloodied and battered, but still looking at Robyn.

"Let's go," the officer said, pushing Brad forward.

Robyn watched them disappear out of view and then she fell to the ice in a heap, the emotion finally catching up with her.

"Hey, it's okay, come here," Cole said, joining her on the floor and putting his arms around her.

"How could he do that to me? And lie about it, all these years?" Robyn wanted to know.

"I don't know," Cole admitted.

"I've been an idiot. How could I not have seen it? There must have been signs I should have picked up on. There must have been something."

"He was the first person you saw after it happened. His DNA was all over you, anyway. The only DNA he couldn't control and should have thought about controlling was what made the baby. His dad took care of that sample and changed the records...put Jason in the firing line," Cole explained.

"I feel sick," Robyn said, wrapping her arms around herself.

"We'll go home," Cole said, hugging her to him.

"No. I don't want to, not yet. Can we just sit here for a bit?" Robyn asked, looking up at the scoreboard advertising the Panthers' next match.

"Sure," Cole said.

"I've always liked Aerosmith, you know," Robyn said as a new tune began over the PA system.

"Yeah, me too. But don't tell anyone," Cole replied, taking hold of her hand.

"I want lilies for the wedding, you know the pink ones with the gooey orange stuff in the middle that cats are allergic to, and we still need to compile a set list for Special Guest, you know, ZZ Top, Bryan Adams...do you like Train? I love Train. And I'm not sure one party tent is going to be enough, we might need two, with proper sides and everything because Max isn't too well at the moment and I don't want him or Dad getting a chill. And we need plenty of gin for Ada, she's hand embroidered napkins with our initials on them. It wasn't my idea, she insisted, but I like it. And although I'm coming on Uncle Bob's boat, I want Leonora decorated, you know, something classy, like shaving foam and balloons. The twins are wearing their hockey outfits by the way."

Chapter Forty-nine

Now that they were home, she wouldn't cry. She had rearranged the talking fridge, polished Leonora within an inch of her life, and now she was outside scrubbing the decking. He could only imagine how she was feeling.

"We've brought chicken and rice and stuff for the barbecue. We didn't know what was best," Pam said when Cole opened the front door.

Standing on the doorstep were Pam, Bob, Sienna, Sierra, Nancy, Sarah, Mickey, Henrik, Wade, Wes, and Jason.

"We hear news about Brad, what he did. To shoot would be too good," Henrik said, handing Cole a bottle of tequila.

"Thanks for coming. Come on in," Cole invited, letting them all through.

"How is she?" Sarah asked, her eyes brimming with tears.

"Not too good," Cole admitted sadly.

"If I ever set eyes on that boy again, I'll…" Bob began passionately.

"We'd all like to do that, Bob," Mickey said, patting him on the back.

"Shall I warm the food?" Pam asked.

"She isn't eating, but sure, I'm guessing everyone here is hungry," Cole said as they all moved into the lounge.

"Where is she?" Sierra asked.

"We've made a card," Sienna added.

"She's outside. Cleaning the hot tub," Cole informed them.

"What?" Pam exclaimed.

"She's been at it for over two hours, says it isn't clean yet," Cole replied with a shrug.

"Leave this to me," Nancy said firmly and she marched toward the patio doors.

"She says she doesn't want to talk about it any more. She's been writing lists and lists of stuff to do with the wedding and now she's cleaning the hot tub," Cole informed everyone.

"I go in hot tub?" Henrik asked, producing trunks from the pocket of his jeans.

"No, Henrik. God, you Danes are obsessive over your hot tubs, aren't you?" Sarah spoke

"What?" Henrik asked.

"Right now is in-appro-priate," she sounded out.

Outside Robyn was scrubbing the side of the Jacuzzi with a nail brush. Her hands were red and sore from the chemicals, but she couldn't stop. If she stopped for just a second, she would have to think about what had happened that day.

"Jeez, sugar! You wanna clean something, you could have a go at the kitchen at Eddie's. Chef's great, but not exactly splatter free," Nancy remarked, standing next to her.

"I'll do it tomorrow, if you like," Robyn answered.

"Put the brush down, honey," Nancy ordered.

"It needs finishing, in time for the wedding. You know, people will want to use it and…" Robyn started.

"You can't hide behind things," Nancy said seriously.

"Why not?"

"Because sooner or later, you're going to have to come out," Nancy continued.

Robyn let out a heavy sigh and threw the brush into the hot tub.

"If we make it sooner, then we can get on with finalizing these wedding plans," Nancy told her.

"I feel dirty all over again. Do you want to talk about that?" Robyn snapped.

"This isn't your fault."

"Cole keeps saying that, over and over again. It is my fault! I mean, if I'd just slept with him when we were dating, he wouldn't have done what he did."

"You don't know that."

"Yes, I do. He told me."

"Honey, you weren't ready to do that with him. If you were, you would have done it. You were fifteen," Nancy reminded her.

"I trusted him," Robyn said with a shake of her head.

"We all trusted him," Pam added as she and Sarah joined them outside.

"He betrayed us all," Sarah said, dabbing at her eyes with a tissue.

"How could he do that to me?" Robyn asked them, tears threatening to spill.

"He lied to all of us, all these years. And as for his father…he's as guilty as Brad, changing evidence, ruining Jason's reputation," Pam continued.

"I can't even speak to Jason. I don't know what to say to him. I'm scared he's never going to forgive me and that's no more than I deserve," Robyn said.

"Hey, none of this is your fault Robyn. I'm just glad you know the truth now," Jason replied as he and the rest of the team came out of the house to see her.

"Jason. I am so sorry. If I could turn back the clock, if I could do anything different to change things I would," Robyn said, looking at him shamefully.

"It wasn't you, Robyn. I understand that you only ever told the truth, the rest of it was out of your hands," Jason said, taking hold of her hand and squeezing it in his.

"I condemned you, though, everyone did. We should have remembered who you were. A kind, sweet boy who liked Marvel comics," Robyn said, wiping her eyes with her sleeve.

"Shh, don't tell the Panthers. They'll never let me live it down," Jason replied with a smile.

"We heard!" Mickey yelled out.

"I want you back on the team and meals for life at Eddie's," Robyn stated.

"Whoa, now hang on a minute," Nancy said.

"I'll take the place on the team, but not the food. Your dad needs to be making all the profit he can right now. But maybe a team dinner after our next win?" Jason suggested.

"Sweet," Wade agreed.

"And Dad says he's been meaning to ask you since about 2003 about his Chevy, she's not running right. I thought now that things were back to normal, you might want to take a look some time," Jason added.

"Hey! I'm the mechanic around here! Why hasn't he asked me?" Mickey wanted to know.

"Because Grant knows I could strip the engine of his Chevy blindfolded," Robyn answered with a smile.

"We have drinks and refrigerator say low on beer. It is amazing, I want," Henrik said as he, Bob, Cole, and the twins came out onto the deck.

"Robyn, we made you a card," Sierra said, bounding up to her with it.

"Mom said Brad's going to jail," Sienna added.

"I didn't tell them the whole thing, you know..." Pam started.

"What did he do to you?" Sienna wanted to know.

"Well, he told a lot of people a lot of lies, and if you don't tell the truth, you get in trouble," Robyn said, looking at the card.

It had a picture of a girl on ice skates wearing a Portage Panthers shirt.

"Logan Hamilton at school tells lies; he says his mom has a girlfriend. Mom's don't have girlfriends!" Sierra exclaimed with a roll of her eyes.

"Will he go to jail?" Sienna asked.

"No," Robyn answered.

"Beer and pickles?" Cole offered as he held out the jar and a fork and Bob held out a bottle of Bud Light.

"You remembered to forget the plate," Robyn said, smiling at him.

"Yes, I did," Cole replied.

Chapter Fifty

October in Michigan is usually a mixed bag. One day it could have a month's worth of rainfall in two hours, the next it could snow. Throw in a tornado and showers of leaves and you've pretty much got it covered. But the twenty-second of October broke like a summer morning, and the blue, cloudless sky looked set to last all day.

As Robyn sat in Bob's boat and slowly sailed across West Lake, she smiled. Here she was, back where she belonged, with all the people she loved, on her way to get married to a man who knew everything about her and still adored her.

"Daddy, shouldn't Robyn be wearing a life jacket?" Sienna called out, lifting the shield of her helmet.

"Yepper," Bob replied, steering the boat.

"Then why isn't she?" Sierra questioned.

"I don't want to crease my beautiful dress," Robyn answered them.

"But what about safety first?" Sienna shouted over the boat's engine.

"No safety for me today, just fun," Robyn replied with a grin.

"Relax man, stop looking at your watch, she'll be here. Well, that's if Bob's boat doesn't break down or anything. One time he took me fishing and..." Mickey began.

"Not helping," Cole replied with a nervous sigh.

"Listen, are you sure you want me as your best man? I mean, your brother's just over there and you know, things are cool with you two now, right?" Mickey asked.

"I guess."

"And he'd have to be a pretty fast worker to like steal Robyn between now and the altar," Mickey added.

"Mickey!" Sarah hissed from behind him.

"Sorry," Mickey said.

"Have you got the rings?" Cole asked as Bob's boat came into view on the horizon.

"Actually, I gave them to Bryn," Mickey admitted with a swallow.

Bryn stood up from his seat and made his way up the shore to where Cole and Mickey were standing with the wedding party.

"Hey," Bryn greeted.

"Hey."

"Look, I'll just sit down here with my pregnant fiancée. If you need any help, just holler. Oh, and when it gets to the speeches, we can have five minutes each," Mickey bargained before being pulled down onto a chair by Sarah.

"So, you're getting married," Bryn said, patting his brother on the back.

"Yes, I am."

"I'm so happy for you," Bryn said sincerely.

"Yeah, I'm happy for you, too," Cole replied, looking over at Veronica.

"She come! She come!" Henrik announced as Bob began to steer toward the jetty.

Cole watched as Bob moored the boat and helped Robyn and the twins alight.

She stopped for a second, saw him waiting for her, and her stomach turned over. He was going to be her husband in a few minutes. Her whole life was starting over.

And there in front of her was her dad and Max, sat in wheelchairs. Both were dressed in matching suits, a white orchid in their lapels, waiting for her on the shoreline.

"Buttercup," Eddie choked as his daughter came down onto the sand to join him.

"How do I look?" Robyn asked, holding out her dress and doing a twirl.

"Have I ever seen you out of pants?" Eddie questioned.

"You look a million dollars, gal," Max responded, a tear in his eye.

"A princess," Eddie said, wiping at his eyes.

"Pull yourself together, man, this is a wedding not a funeral. Let's get this gal to her Prince Charming," Max said, trying to push on his wheels.

"I didn't know that when I offered to help a girl with a broken bag I was going to end up marrying her. I don't know whether to thank American Airlines for putting us on the same flight or thank the bag manufacturer for producing poor goods. Robyn, I don't know what to say. I hope you know how I feel about you. I'm going to love you my whole life, and I'll honor you every single second of every single day," Cole said.

Tears fell from his eyes as he held both her hands and made his vows.

"Cole...well, I had it all prepared...what to say...but it wasn't right. Your dad is up there with Old Man Harrison and Mitzy, and I don't want to let them down by saying something stupid. You're everything to me, Cole, and you're the only person who's ever been everything to me. You're special and I'm very lucky. Cole, I marry you today because you met the real Robyn Matthers at Chicago O'Hare. You brought her home and...you put me back together again," Robyn said as she looked up at Cole's face.

There was a collective sound of appreciation as Cole drew her into him and held her protectively against his chest.

"Cole and Robyn have exchanged their vows and given rings as a symbol of their marriage. It is now my absolute pleasure to pronounce them husband and wife. And let's hear some applause!" the minister ordered as Special Guest's drummer kicked the band into action.

"So, how does it feel to finally have a connection with Meg Ryan?" Cole asked Robyn as he handed her a bottle of beer.

"What?"

"Robyn, you share a last name with her now," Cole reminded her.

"Ah, well, we never actually discussed which name to take, did we? I've been trying Cole Matthers out over the loudspeaker at the arena and you can get a really good, long rah sound at the end. I like it," Robyn replied with a grin, running off toward the party tent.

"No way, absolutely, no way," Cole said, chasing her.

"And now we party, yes? Julha!" Henrik exclaimed, punching his hands in the air excitedly.

"Joola? What does that mean?" Mickey asked.

"Is Finnish for party. We have party, yes?" Henrik said, slapping Mickey on the back.

"He's Finnish," Mickey said.

"What?" Sarah queried, confused.

"He's freaking Finnish! Hey! Robyn! Henrik's Finnish!"

12458794R00221

Made in the USA
Charleston, SC
06 May 2012